About the Authors

Farrah Rochon hails from New Orleans. She has garnered much acclaim for her New York Sabers football series. Farrah has been nominated for the prestigious *RITA®* Award from Romance Writers of America and the *RT* Reviewer's Choice Award. She can usually be found on Twitter or at a Broadway show.

USA Today bestselling author **Jules Bennett** has penned more than fifty novels during her short career. She's married to her high school sweetheart, has two active girls, and is a former salon owner. Jules can be found on Twitter, Facebook (Fan Page), and her website julesbennett.com. She holds competitions via these three outlets with each release and loves to hear from readers!

In a testosterone filled home (a husband, five boys between ages fourteen and eighteen, and one squeaky boy guinea pig), it's hard to imagine not going insane. The trick is to escape. So in her charming Southern world filled with politics, football, and after school snacks, **Carolyn Hector** utilises her knack for spinning every plausible situation into a romance story. Find out what she is up to on Twitter @WriteOnCarolyn or find her on Facebook.

Tempted Under the Mistletoe

FARRAH ROCHON

JULES BENNETT

CAROLYN HECTOR

MILLS & BOON

First Published in Great Britain 2023
By Mills & Boon, an imprint of HarperCollins*Publishers* Ltd,
1 London Bridge Street, London, SE1 9GF

www.harpercollins.co.uk

HarperCollins*Publishers*
Macken House, 39/40 Mayor Street Upper,
Dublin 1, D01 C9W8, Ireland

Tempted Under the Mistletoe © 2023 Harlequin Enterprises ULC.

A Mistletoe Affair © 2014 Harlequin Enterprises ULC.
Best Man Under the Mistletoe © 2017 Harlequin Enterprises ULC.
Her Mistletoe Bachelor © 2018 Carolyn Hall

Special thanks and acknowledgement are given to Farrah Rochon for her contribution to the *Wintersage Weddings* series.

Special thanks and acknowledgement are given to Jules Bennett for her contribution to the *Texas Cattleman's Club: Blackmail* series.

ISBN: 978-0-263-32041-1

This book is produced from independently certified FSC™ paper to ensure responsible forest management.

For more information visit: www.harpercollins.co.uk/green

Printed and Bound in the UK using 100% Renewable Electricity at CPI Group (UK) Ltd, Croydon, CR0 4YY

A MISTLETOE AFFAIR

FARRAH ROCHON

For my aunt, Gail Becnel.

She looks well to the ways of her household
and does not eat the bread of idleness.
— Proverbs 31:27

Chapter 1

Stealing a brief moment to decompress after a hectic morning of back-to-back-to-back customers, Vicki Ahlfors closed her eyes and inhaled a healthy lungful of rich, pine-scented air.

God, she loved this time of year.

The delicate perfume of tea roses in spring was lovely, but it couldn't compare to the crisp freshness of balsam fir. The fragrant scent filling Petals, her floral-design shop, was a telltale sign that her favorite time of the year was finally upon her.

She snipped a wayward thatch of pine needles from the thick spray, then draped the nine-foot garland across her custom-made chest-high worktable. She gathered sprigs of deep red hypericum berries and, using floral wire, attached them to the garland in perfectly measured six-inch increments. She knew how precise Mr. Wallace liked his floral arrangements, and she would not give that old curmudgeon a single opportunity to complain about the treatments she'd designed for his front door this year.

"Oh, my goodness! It smells amazing down here."

Vicki lifted her head to find Sandra Woolcott-Jacobs, one of her partners in crime in the Silk Sisters event agency, rounding the newel post at the base of the winding staircase. She walked over to Vicki's workstation, leaned over the garland and pulled in a deep breath.

"I love this time of year," Sandra said with a satisfied sigh. "Laurel Collins was hanging Christmas lights around the window of her gift shop when I walked past there this morning. I nearly broke out into 'Jingle Bell Rock.'"

Vicki arched a brow in knowing amusement. "That may be the case, but for some reason I don't think it's *just* the time of year that has you singing these days."

Sandra dipped her head, a coy grin lifting the corners of her mouth. "There may be another reason," she admitted.

Vicki burst out laughing. "Sandra Woolcott-Jacobs, is that an actual blush forming on your cheeks?"

"Oh, stop it," Sandra said, the blush deepening.

If that wasn't a sign that Sandra had undergone a radical change since reconnecting with the love of her life, Vicki didn't know what was. Isaiah Jacobs had swooped back into town and swept her girlfriend right off her feet.

"You've got that special newlywed glow," Vicki said. "It looks really good on you."

She denied the slight twinge of envy that pinched her chest, refused to even acknowledge its existence for fear that it would show on her face. She was thrilled for her friends. Truly, she was. Both Sandra and Janelle

Howerton-Dubois, the third member of their trio, had found love in the past few months, and Vicki could not be happier for her two best friends.

But happiness and envy weren't mutually exclusive. She was a multitasker; she could feel both.

"I can already tell that my first Christmas with Isaiah will be magical," Sandra said with a look that could only be described as dreamy. "If you're not booked solid already, I may have you put together a wreath for our front door."

"You know I'll make time for you," Vicki said. "What about a tree?"

Another of those soft, faraway smiles graced Sandra's lips. "I think we're going to decorate that ourselves. It'll be our first tree as a family."

Vicki could barely contain her own wistful sigh. In the epic battle between happiness and envy, envy was winning by a landslide right now. There was no doubt about it, decorating her tree at home, once again by her lonesome self, would suck even more this year.

"I will, however, have you order our tree from the supplier you usually use," Sandra said, finally coming out of her it's-a-wonderful-life-with-Isaiah-induced daze. "Have you ordered the tree for the Victorian yet?"

Vicki nodded. "It's being delivered later today. I was able to find the most gorgeous twelve-footer for the front parlor. It should fit perfectly in the curve of the staircase."

Petals inhabited the majority of the first floor of the three-story Victorian she, Sandra and Janelle owned in their New England hometown of Wintersage. Dubbed the Silk Sisters since their high school days at Wintersage Academy, the three had gone into business together soon after college graduation. Swoon Couture,

Sandra's dress boutique, was on the second floor, and Janelle's event-planning business, Alluring Affairs, occupied the third.

"The place looks great so far," Sandra said, gesturing to the gathering room, which served as the lobby for all three businesses. The room's focal point, a pillared, carved wooden mantelpiece, was festooned with silver ribbon, ice-blue glass ornaments and glitter-dusted seashells to bring in the essence of their seaside town.

"If you need help decking the halls, just give me a ring," Sandra said.

Vicki waved off her offer. "You've got enough on your plate with getting Swoon Couture Home off the ground."

Sandra and her new husband were starting a new venture, marrying her design business with Isaiah's family's furniture business.

"Only if you're sure," Sandra said.

"I'm sure. Besides, I get a bit territorial when it comes to holiday decorating."

"Don't I know it," Sandra said with a snort. "One piece of tinsel out of place and the girl goes crazy."

Vicki pointed her pruning shears at her. "If you even *think* about bringing a string of tinsel in here..."

"No tinsel! I promise." She laughed, raising her hands in mock surrender. "I'll leave the decorating to you. I can't wait to see the finished product." Sandra started up the stairs, but stopped on the second step and called, "The Quarterdeck at seven?"

"I'll be there," Vicki returned.

Even though the Victorian served as their home base, it was rare for the three of them to be in one place at one time. Even when they were all here, they were so busy with their respective businesses that there was never much time for idle chitchat. Years ago they made a pact to meet on Monday nights for dinner, drinks and girl talk at the Quarterdeck, a landmark eatery on Wintersage's waterfront.

They were in for some serious chatting tonight. These past couple of months had been a whirlwind of activity, with life-altering events happening for Sandra and Janelle.

After witnessing the transformation in both her friends' lives, Vicki had decided it was time she undergo a few changes herself, on both the professional and personal fronts. She had sensed for quite some time that she was in a rut, but as far as ruts went, hers had been comfortable.

Honestly, what did she have to complain about? At twenty-eight years old she owned her own business, her own home, and had family and friends who loved her. She was blessed.

But she wasn't happy. At least, not as happy as she wanted to be. As she *deserved* to be. Witnessing both her friends enter into that much-sought-after world of wedded bliss had brought what was missing in Vicki's own life into stark relief.

So she'd taken matters into her own hands, undergoing a radical makeover. Okay, not entirely radical; it wasn't as if she'd dyed her hair purple and gotten a nose ring or anything.

But for quiet, reserved Vicki Ahlfors, a chin-length pixie haircut and a closet of new cleavage-revealing blouses and dresses were pretty darn drastic. By the slew of new male clients Petals had garnered over the past week, the results of her transformation could not be denied.

She was Wintersage's hot new item.

"Whatever," Vicki said with a snort.

She had definitely caught the eye of several men around town, but instead of being flattered, Vicki found herself just a tad pissed off. She'd lived here her entire life. Why in the heck had it taken a makeover for all of them to finally notice her?

Despite the umbrage she'd taken over her admirers' obvious shallowness, Vicki wasn't entirely blind to the romantic opportunities that her newfound popularity had created.

There was just one problem: not a single one of the men who had come calling in the past week held an ounce of appeal. She found their overaggressiveness off-putting, and for the few who'd strolled into her flower shop as if they were God's gift to the female population, Vicki had taken great pleasure in knocking the wind out of their overinflated egos.

Talk about egos! What about her own? After all her bellyaching over being single, she now had the nerve to play hard to get.

"Damn right," Vicki said.

Not only did she refuse to settle for the first guy who walked into her flower shop and offered to buy her a dozen roses, but she planned to make sure that any man she dated was worthy of her precious free time. Life was much too short to waste it on a relationship that was going nowhere. She wanted to find what Sandra and Janelle had both found.

So why are you still dragging your feet?

Setting down the shears, Vicki walked over to her laptop and flipped it open. Inhaling a fortifying breath, she logged on to the online-dating profile she'd created after she'd got home from Sandra's wedding this past weekend. The message sitting in her inbox seemed to pulse with a life of its own. She'd read over it at least a dozen times since it had arrived, had attempted to hit Reply more than once. Yet there it sat, staring at her, goading her into donning the new, confident, vivacious mantle she was determined to wear.

The new Vicki.

Was she *really* going to take this step? As popular as online dating had become, Vicki could never bring herself to try it. She'd held steadfast to the romantic notion of meeting her Prince Charming the old-fashioned way. They were supposed to spot each other across a crowded room, fall madly in love, start a family and live happily ever after.

Blah. Blah. Blah.

The old-fashioned way hadn't worked for her. The old-fashioned way had her still single, while her two best friends were now both married and living their happily ever afters. She was done waiting for things to happen the old-fashioned way.

Especially after accepting the harsh reality that the one man she'd been waiting on—the one whom she'd carried a torch for so much longer than she would ever admit to anyone but her own foolish heart—would apparently never see her in that way.

A dull ache settled in her chest, but Vicki quickly tamped down the gloominess before it could take hold.

She was done pining for what would never be. It was time to move on.

Ignoring what felt like a million butterflies flittering around in her stomach, Vicki replied to the date request from a handsome E.R. doctor who, according to his profile, was an attending physician at Tufts Medical Center in Boston. The moment she hit Send, a weight seemed to lift from her shoulders.

There. That hadn't been so bad. And it was yet another step on her journey to finding the new Vicki.

Maybe she should give her new journey a name—something along the lines of The Reinvention of Vicki?

She rolled her eyes as she closed the laptop.

That was something the *old* Vicki would do. The new Vicki would not be so lame.

The rumbling of a truck engine had her dashing toward the front door. All morning she'd been anticipating the arrival of the Christmas tree she'd ordered. It was the final piece required to transform the bottom floor of the Victorian into the picture-perfect New England seaside Christmas escape.

Vicki stepped out onto the gabled front porch and stopped dead in her tracks.

"What is this?" She pointed to the truck bed. "I ordered a twelve-foot Fraser fir. This tree isn't even eight feet."

"This is what they gave me, lady," the deliveryman replied in a thick Boston accent. He rounded the truck and pulled the tree out by its thin trunk.

Vicki shut her eyes against the thumping that instantly started up at her temples. With a full slate of projects lined up, hassling over the tree farm's obvious mistake was exactly what she did *not* need today.

But she'd had her heart set on that Fraser fir. She'd purchased the most amazing hand-painted ornaments from a gift shop on Main Street, along with a crystal tree topper that would bring the entire ensemble together.

Dammit, she'd *paid* for that Fraser fir, not this scraggly little pine that looked as if it was a reject from *A Charlie Brown Christmas* school play.

The old Vicki would just accept the tree and move on. The new Vicki wasn't standing for it.

She stomped down the porch steps and blocked the deliveryman's path. "Sir, would you please bring this… this thing," she said, pointing to the tree, "back to the lot and return with the tree I ordered?"

"Come on, lady. A tree is a tree."

Vicki folded her arms over her chest. "I want the tree I ordered," she annunciated in a clipped tone.

The man let out a grunt. He shoved the tree back onto the truck bed and mumbled something unintelligible under his breath.

"Thank you," Vicki said with a curt nod. She marched up the steps and walked inside, closing the door behind her. She fell back against it, covering her hand with her chest.

"Holy crap," she breathed. A grin curled up the corners of her lips. "I think I'm going to like the new Vicki."

Vicki buried her chin deeper into her scarf as she braced herself against the brisk wind coming off the water. She could have taken her car, but with the Quarterdeck so close to Silk Sisters, it felt unnecessary, even in the misty, frigid weather. Besides, she could not fully appreciate the holiday decorations adorning the businesses on Main Street from behind the wheel of her car. Even the shops that were closed—now that the tourist season was over—were bedecked with festive lights.

She entered the Quarterdeck and headed straight for the table she, Sandra and Janelle usually occupied.

"Sorry I'm late," Vicki said as she came upon them, planting a kiss on Janelle's cheek. She hadn't seen her at all today. "There was a mix-up with the Christmas tree. I'm convinced the driver took extralong delivering the correct one just to be difficult."

"That just means that you'll have to play catch-up with me and Sandra," Janelle said. She signaled a waiter, who was at their table in an instant.

His pen poised over his notepad, he asked, "The usual?"

"Yes," Vicki automatically answered. Then she thought better of it. "Actually, no. I'll have a vodka martini with two olives."

The waiter's brow shot up. "Okay, then. Coming right up. I'll have that fried calamari appetizer out in a minute, ladies."

Vicki looked across the table to find both Janelle and Sandra staring at her with their mouths open.

"What?" she asked.

Sandra put her hands up, her eyes wide with shock. "First the new hair and makeup, and now a vodka martini instead of a white-wine spritzer?" She slanted Janelle a questioning look. "Can you tell me what's happening with our girl over here?"

"I'm not sure, but I like it," Janelle said.

Even as she waved off their teasing, Vicki could feel a warm blush turning her cheeks red. She knew these changes were a shock to her friends. They were used to her being demure, staid.

Dull.

The fact that a simple change in her drink order could elicit that kind of reaction from them was as telling as anything.

As they snacked on crisp calamari tossed in a sweet ginger sauce, Sandra filled Vicki and Janelle in on the plans for her and Isaiah's belated honeymoon in Paris in a few months.

"It just makes sense to wait. We're both looking forward to several art exhibits, and I'll have the chance to check out Fashion Week. Besides, we can do what we're going to spend most of our honeymoon doing right here in Wintersage," she said with a wicked grin. She batted her eyes and added, "Wink. Wink."

"Subtle," Vicki said with a good-natured eye roll. She laughed, but deep down it was hard not to feel the tiniest bit jealous. Of the three of them, she was, by far, the romantic at heart. She was the one who had always believed in one true love, happily ever after, the whole nine yards. Yet she was the one who was perpetually single. Both Janelle and Sandra, cynics to the core, had found love. Where was the fairness in that?

Vicki squelched a groan. When had she turned into such a complainer? She was beginning to work on her own nerves with all this bellyaching.

The waiter came over to take their orders. Vicki bypassed her usual Caesar salad in exchange for the almond-crusted cod in a lemon *beurre blanc* sauce, garnering yet another pair of baffled looks from her friends.

Seriously? Was she *that* predictable that they could be so surprised at her ordering fish instead of a salad? It looked as if the decision to become the "new Vicki" couldn't have come fast enough.

The discussion around the table soon segued from Sandra's honeymoon plans to Vicki's plans for the float she'd entered into the Wintersage Holiday Extravaganza Day float competition. Her submission had yet to be accepted, and now Vicki was starting to regret ever telling her friends about it. If Petals wasn't chosen as one of the businesses to contribute a float to this year's extravaganza, it would leave some serious egg on her face.

"Building this float won't interfere with the decorations you're putting together for the Kwanzaa celebration, will it?" Sandra asked.

"Absolutely not," Vicki said.

The Woolcotts' Kwanzaa celebration had become an institution in Wintersage. As had been the case for the past few years, Janelle had been hired as the event coordinator and Vicki was, once again, in charge of decorating. Janelle set her fork on the edge of her plate and folded her hands. "Speaking of the Kwanzaa celebration." She paused for a moment, and then continued, "Things were a bit, well, strained at the dinner table this Thanksgiving when my dad asked if Alluring Affairs was still involved in the planning of your parents' party."

"Because of the election?" Sandra asked. "Does he expect you to give up a job you've taken on for years just because of this thing with Jordan?"

A few weeks ago, Janelle's father, Darren Howerton, had claimed victory in a statewide election against Oliver Windom, the candidate Jordan had campaigned for. The ensuing fallout had caused much tension between their families.

"Can you blame him? My dad should be celebrating his victory as the new state representative and preparing to head to the legislature. Instead, there's a huge cloud hanging over the election now that your brother has called the results into question."

"You can't put the entire blame on Jordan," Sandra retorted.

"Who else is to blame? He's the one who won't let this go."

Vicki held her hands up. "I thought this topic was off-limits? We're Switzerland, remember?"

"You're right," Janelle and Sandra murmured in unison.

"I'm sorry," Janelle continued. "We did agree not to talk about it, but I do wish Jordan would drop this."

"I know." Sandra blew out a frustrated sigh. "I don't see that happening anytime soon, though. Jordan took an extended leave of absence from the law firm. He was so confident Oliver Windom would win the election and would need Jordan to work on his transition team."

"So should I tell my dad that Jordan plans to be a pain in the ass until he returns to practicing law?" Janelle drawled.

Sandra shrugged as she tipped her wineglass to her lips.

"It sounds as if he needs something to occupy his time now that the election is over," Vicki said.

"*I* think he needs to get laid," Sandra said.

Janelle pointed the lime wheel from her cosmopolitan at her. "Bingo. Has he even been on a date since his divorce? It's been long enough."

Sandra waved her hand. "His pat response is that he's too busy to get involved with a woman, but Jordan's not fooling anyone. He could find the time to go on a simple date if he really wanted to."

"What about his wife?" Vicki asked.

"*Ex*-wife," Sandra stressed. "And let's not even go there. I don't know the last time Jordan spoke to Allison, and as far as I know, she's made no attempt to contact him, either."

"Not even about Mason?" Janelle gasped. "That's ridiculous. I don't understand how a woman could leave her baby and not even bother to see how he's doing."

"Especially a sweetie pie like Mason," Vicki agreed.

A smile broke out across Sandra's face at the mention of her nephew. "He is the most adorable child on the face of the planet, isn't he? He takes after his auntie Sandra."

"It's a good thing he doesn't have his auntie Sandra's attitude," Janelle said with a laugh, and then laughed harder when Sandra flipped her the finger.

As the two went back and forth trading good-natured barbs, Vicki's mind remained stuck on Jordan.

No surprise there.

How often had just the mention of his name prompted a long spell of daydreaming about what could have been? If only Jordan had any idea that she'd been crushing on him like a lovesick fool since the age of fifteen.

Actually, it was probably better that he *didn't* know. The only thing worse than Jordan discovering that she'd been clutching so tightly to this torch she'd carried for him all these years was for him to discover it and then pity her because he didn't feel the same way.

Oh, God. A rush of heat swept across her skin just at the thought of how mortified she would be if that ever happened.

Her chagrin quickly turned into annoyance, along with a healthy dose of self-disgust. She would not allow thoughts of Jordan Woolcott to turn her back into the starry-eyed romantic she'd been just a week ago. The new Vicki wasn't spending her days hoping that Mr. Clueless would finally notice her.

Yet despite her anger over his obliviousness, Vicki couldn't help but feel sorry for Jordan's current predicament. The madness following the state representative race had caused such turmoil. After Darren's victory over Oliver Windom, Jordan had demanded a recount, claiming that there must have been some sort of tampering.

His accusations had driven a wedge right between

the Howertons, Woolcotts and Ahlfors. It all must be weighing heavily on Jordan's peace of mind, knowing that so many people were against his dogged determination to contest the election. Vicki hated that he was at the center of the friction currently rubbing their families raw.

Of course, if she was making a list of the things she hated regarding Jordan, she had several other items she could add. Like the fact that he'd settled for such a cliché when he'd married his now ex-wife. Sure, Allison Woolcott was beautiful and vivacious, but that was *all* she was. The woman had no substance.

Another item on the list would be how much she hated that Jordan had never bothered to see her as anything other than a friend of his little sister. After all these years, Vicki still felt like nothing more than an acquaintance in his eyes.

Getting past this long-held obsession with Jordan should be at the very top of her priority list. If she was to fully embrace this new outlook, she could not continue to pine over a man who had never shown even the slightest romantic interest in her. It was time for her to move on, to concentrate on all the changes she was ready to make in her life.

New Vicki. Think new Vicki.

"I've got some news," she blurted.

Janelle and Sandra both stopped talking and looked at her expectantly.

Oh, great. Now that she'd put it out there she would actually have to share some news. She should have considered that before she opened her normally not-so-big mouth. A lesson for the new Vicki.

"So?" Sandra raised an expectant brow.

Vicki sucked her bottom lip between her teeth. "I,

uh...I signed up for an online-dating website. Just before I came here tonight, I accepted a date with a guy that contacted me a few days ago."

"What!" Janelle and Sandra both whooped, high-fiving each other.

"I told you our girl was breaking out of her shell," Sandra said. "Who is it? Have you been talking to him through email? Have you two had a phone conversation yet?"

"Slow down," Vicki said with a laugh. "His name is Declan James. *Doctor* Declan James. And yes, we've shared a couple of emails. I haven't talked to him on the phone yet. He seems nice," she finished with a casual shrug, as if it didn't feel like she had a million butterflies doing an aboriginal rain dance in her belly.

"So," Janelle prompted, circling her hands in a give-us-more motion.

"He suggested dinner," Vicki continued. "But then he said if I wanted to take it slow and start off with a coffee date he would be okay with that, too."

"I take it you two are going out for coffee?" Sandra asked.

An impish grin tilted up the edges of Vicki's lips. "Dinner. And dancing."

"Ooh," both Janelle and Sandra said.

"I'm scared of you, girl," Janelle said.

"So when's the date?"

"Tomorrow," she said. She hunched her shoulder. "I know a Tuesday night isn't your typical date night, but he's on call a lot at the E.R. Tuesday is his only night off this week."

"Who cares what night," Sandra said. "All I know is that the men of Wintersage had better watch out. Vicki Ahlfors is on the move."

Chapter 2

"Don't be an idiot," Vicki murmured around the piece of twine she'd stuck between her lips. "You know better than this."

Even though she *did* know better than to try to balance on the wobbly, backless stool, she remained standing on it. If she fell and broke her tailbone it would be sufficient punishment for forgetting to bring the stepladder she'd taken from the Victorian to hang the new artwork in her living room at home. As far as punishments went, maybe a broken tailbone was a *bit* harsh.

"But you don't have to worry about that," she said as she tied that last bit of twine around the garland, fastening it to the molding that framed the front door. She hopped off the stool and slipped back into her heels. Then she took a couple of steps back and observed her handiwork.

"Perfect," Vicki said.

"I'd say so."

Vicki whipped around, spotting Jordan Woolcott walking up the walkway. Sixteen-month-old Mason toddled alongside him on legs that still didn't quite have that whole walking thing down yet. Vicki smiled as the chubby-cheeked sweetheart fought for his independence, trying to walk ahead of his father.

She stood on the top step and waited patiently while he slowly climbed up to meet her. She scooped Mason into her arms, plopping a kiss on his too-adorable-than-it-had-a-right-to-be face.

"How're you doing today? You and your daddy coming to see your auntie Sandra?" She looked up at Jordan, who remained at the base of the porch steps, a tired smile tilting up the corners of his lips.

"Hello, Jordan," she said.

"Hey there, Vicki."

There went her idiot heart, doing that stupid fluttering thing it did whenever she saw him. Goodness, how pathetic that at twenty-eight she still had the same reaction to him that she did as a teenager. No, it was more than just pathetic, it was downright pitiful, because never once had anything in Jordan's demeanor suggested that he felt anything even remotely similar toward her.

Yet when she'd sat in that salon chair last week and told the stylist to glam her up, it was with the intent of seeing Jordan's reaction to the finished outcome.

Pathetic.

If the man hadn't caught a clue in all these years, he certainly wouldn't notice her just because she'd cut her hair.

"Is my sister up there?" he asked, gesturing to the

building's second floor with the hand that held Mason's diaper bag.

"She sure is." Vicki looked down at Mason. "You want to get out of this cold and see your auntie Sandra?"

Jordan joined them on the porch, but before Vicki could turn toward the door, he stopped her.

"What exactly did you do here?" he asked, motioning at his own head.

"You mean my haircut?"

"Yeah. The light brown color you added to the ends, too."

"They're called highlights."

He nodded. "I like it. It suits you."

"Thank you," she answered.

She was *not* going to blush at a simple compliment.

Dammit, she was *so* blushing. She could feel the heat climbing up her cheeks. Her fair skin hid nothing, so in a matter of seconds Jordan would see it, too.

With Mason in tow, Vicki quickly turned for the door, leaving him to follow her inside.

"Wow," Jordan said once they'd entered the building. "You all are really getting into the holiday spirit, huh? There are more flowers in here than at the Rose Bowl parade."

"Well, it *is* a floral-design shop," Vicki noted with a laugh.

"A busy one at that," Jordan said, pointing to various arrangements in different stages of completion. They covered every available surface.

"When it comes to flowers, the Christmas season is second only to Valentine's Day. Although, to be honest, I've been a bit busier than usual this week."

Jordan peeled Mason's puffer jacket off while the

baby was still in her arms, and then stuffed it inside the diaper bag.

He gestured to her feet. "You don't normally wear fancy shoes to make flower arrangements, do you? Is this something special you're doing for the holidays?"

Vicki's eyes narrowed. "Are you trying to be funny?"

The blank look on his face gave her his answer even before he said, "No."

"I'm wearing fancy shoes because I have a date," she said.

"Really?" Jordan's head reared back slightly. He took Mason from her arms and the baby immediately started to fuss. "A date?"

Vicki couldn't see past her irritation over Jordan's apparent surprise at the news that she had a date. It both stung *and* pissed her off.

"Is it so hard to believe that someone actually wants to go out with me?" she asked.

"No," he said with a hasty head shake. "It's just that I didn't know you were dating anyone."

Not that *that* should come as a surprise, either. When had he ever taken interest in whom she was dating?

Vicki held no illusions about where she stood as far as he was concerned. She had never been in Jordan Woolcott's league. For that matter, she had not always been in Sandra and Janelle's league, either.

Unlike her two best friends, Vicki hadn't been born into money.

She and her three brothers had spent the majority of their formative years in the public school system, not moving to Wintersage Academy until her sophomore year of high school, once her father's business had taken off.

Ahlfors Financial Management's success secured

her family's place among Wintersage's elite, but their wealth didn't reek of "old money" like that of the Howertons and Woolcotts. Although her friends never made her feel inferior, Vicki never let herself forget that one difference between them.

When it came to Jordan, there was no denying that they were different.

He had been several years ahead of her in high school, having already graduated from Wintersage Academy by the time she'd started there. Vicki had developed the most ridiculous crush on him from the very first day she'd gone over to the Woolcotts' to study with Sandra one afternoon. It had taken her years to accept the fact that, if not for her being one of Sandra's very best friends and their families knowing each other for years, Jordan wouldn't know she existed.

Well, that wasn't entirely true. Wintersage was a small town. He would know she existed—in the same way he knew Jocelyn Cornwell, who ran the realty office on Main Street, or Agnes Ripple, the owner of the corner bakery, existed.

That thought annoyed her to no end. And when she thought of how long she'd pined over Jordan, it irritated her even more.

Vicki returned to her worktable, picking up the stem cutters and attacking the stubborn stalks of the lilies that had just been delivered by one of her suppliers. But as Mason's crying intensified, she walked to where Jordan stood struggling to get the baby to calm down. The minute she lifted him out of Jordan's arms, Mason's cries quieted. Vicki bounced him softly, running her hand up and down the baby's back and whispering soothingly into his ear.

"I don't know what's going on with him today," Jordan said. "I usually don't have a problem getting him to calm down, but he's been more agitated than usual."

"Maybe he can sense that you're—" she started, but then she stopped.

"I'm what?"

Vicki bit her bottom lip, but then she stopped that, too. The old Vicki would keep her mouth shut to spare his feelings. She was no longer listening to the old Vicki.

"Uptight," she finished. "You've been rather uptight lately, and I think Mason can sense that."

He rubbed the back of his neck and grimaced. "You're probably right."

The sheer exhaustion on his face quelled the ire that had risen within her just moments ago. Vicki couldn't help but feel sorry for him.

Jordan cocked his head to the side and looked down at his son. "The problem is I can't seem to unwind because he constantly has me on the go. I get agitated, and then *he* gets agitated. It's a vicious cycle."

"You need some rest, Jordan."

"You're not telling me anything I don't already know. But I don't see rest anywhere in my immediate future, not with this little rascal who wants to get into everything these days," he said, pinching the baby's chubby leg through his cute corduroy pants.

Vicki took a moment to consider the suggestion she was about to make before she asked, "How about I watch Mason for you so you can get some rest?"

Jordan's neck stiffened with shock. "Really?"

She nodded. "Sure."

"I can't ask you to do that."

That was what his mouth said; the naked hope in

his eyes, on the other hand, said that he was dying for a little help with the baby.

"It's not as if it would be a hardship," Vicki reasoned. "How could I pass up the opportunity to spend time with this little heartbreaker?" She kissed the baby's chin. "And while I do, *you* can get some much-needed rest."

Jordan's shoulders sank with relief. "God, Vicki, that would be wonderful."

"I'm happy to do it. Just not tonight," she said.

"Yeah. You have a date," Jordan said. He lifted Mason from her arms but remained standing there, his gaze trained on her.

"What?" Vicki asked. After several moments of his staring, her self-consciousness ramped up to skin-tingling levels.

He shook his head as if to clear it. "Nothing." He gestured toward the staircase. "We'll go up to Sandra's."

"Okay." She leaned forward and gave Mason a little baby wave. "See you later."

"When?"

Vicki's head popped up at Jordan's question. "Excuse me?"

"When will you see us?" He shook his head. "Him? Mason. To babysit?"

She hadn't thought that far in advance, but it was obvious Jordan needed to rest as soon as possible. "What about tomorrow, maybe around seven?"

"Tomorrow is good. It's great, actually."

"Okay, well, I guess I'll see you both tomorrow, then."

"Good." He gave her another of those tired, grateful smiles before he started up the stairs. After he'd climbed a couple of steps, he stopped and turned. "Vicki?"

"Yes?" She felt her face heat after being caught still staring at him.

"You really do look nice," Jordan said. "I hope this guy you're going out with tonight realizes how lucky he is."

The instant warmth that traveled across her skin from his simple compliment was embarrassing to say the least.

"Thank you," Vicki said. "I'll see you tomorrow."

She fingered the wispy end of a lock of hair and grinned as she returned to her workstation. Her stylist would get a very nice tip after her next haircut. Even though she no longer cared whether or not Jordan Woolcott noticed her, apparently the pixie cut had gotten her just the result she'd initially hoped for.

"Anybody home?" Jordan called as he arrived on the second-floor landing of the huge Victorian where his sister's dress shop was located.

Sandra turned from the glittery ball gown she was adjusting on a mannequin and smiled.

"Well, look who's here." She walked over to them and reached for Mason. "Give me my nephew."

Jordan handed the baby off and plopped into an empty chair. The exhaustion of the past week had him on the verge of both mental and physical collapse.

"So what brings you two here?" Sandra asked, taking the chair opposite his and bouncing Mason on her lap.

Jordan shrugged. "Just thought we'd get out for a bit. He doesn't understand that it's too cold for the beach or the park, so I've been taking him other places. We just came from the dry cleaners."

"Such party animals," Sandra said with a snort. She snapped her fingers. "I know exactly where you should take him—the children's museum in Dover. I saw something on TV about a special exhibit they have going on for the Christmas season."

Sandra turned the huge computer monitor around to face her and grabbed the wireless keyboard from her desk. As his sister searched the web, Jordan pitched his head back and let his eyes fall shut. He tried to shake off the edginess that had his skin tingly. The weird vibe had settled over him after his exchange with Vicki, and hell if he knew what to make of it.

She had popped up in his head more than once this week, creeping into his thoughts and setting off memories of how shocked he'd been when he'd noticed her standing on the beach at Sandra's wedding. The new haircut and that curve-hugging dress had been something to behold.

Jordan couldn't remember if he had ever once noticed what Vicki wore. Of course, he'd noticed *her*—no man could deny that Vicki was gorgeous in her own right. He just had never looked at her in *that* way.

She was just...just Vicki.

She was the quiet one; the one who, if Sandra or their other best friend, Janelle, ever got into trouble, would get them out of it. She was steady. Reserved. She wasn't the type that normally produced the prickle of awareness that climbed up the back of his neck when he'd spotted her standing on the porch in sexy leopard-print heels.

"What do you think about that?" Sandra asked.

Jordan blinked. "Huh?"

His sister stabbed him with the most aggravated look. "Are you even listening to me? I just listed every special exhibit going on at the children's museum in

Dover. Or maybe there's something in Portsmouth the two of you can do."

"Maybe." Jordan shrugged. "I need to find something to keep him occupied. It can get boring sitting around the house. Makes me wonder what Laurie does over there all day," he said, speaking of his housekeeper.

Sandra started on the tirade Jordan knew was forthcoming. "Oh, let's see. She takes care of your son, keeps the house impeccable and cooks dinner."

"I meant besides all that," Jordan said, his mouth tipped up in a smile.

He saw the moment that Sandra caught on to his teasing.

"You're such an ass," she said.

"Not true. You're just an easy target," he said with a laugh. "Don't worry, I know exactly how indispensable Laurie is, especially now that she's away on this extended Christmas vacation. I haven't done the best job at keeping up the housework since, and when it comes to dinner Mason and I have tried just about every takeout place within twenty miles of Wintersage. He likes gyros. Who'd have thought?"

Sandra shook her head, a pitiable look on her face. "I'm almost tempted to tell you to hire a temporary nanny to cover for Laurie while she's away, but that won't solve your problem."

"I don't have a problem," he said.

"You most definitely *do* have a problem. You have no life. And yes, I know you've been taking care of Mason full-time since the election ended, but that's not the life you're used to living. Maybe you should just go back to work. Maybe you'd be less irritable."

Hadn't Vicki just accused him of the same thing?

"Why does everyone think I'm irritable?" Jordan

asked. "I'm just tired. Besides, I can't go back to the firm. I took an extended leave, remember? I thought I would be working on Oliver's transition team right now."

Sandra rolled her eyes. The election was a sore subject for everyone in his family, especially his sister.

When he spoke, Jordan kept his voice low. "Hey, Sandra? The fallout from the election, it hasn't caused any friction, has it? You know, between you three?"

"What do you think, Jordan? You accused my best friend's father of trying to steal an election. Do you think things would be all sunshine and roses around here? The three of us decided that when it comes to the election we're Switzerland, but things are still a bit awkward."

"Switzerland?" he asked.

"Completely neutral."

"Oh. Well, I wish I had that luxury."

"You do." Sandra reached over and clamped a hand on his forearm. "The election is over. You can accept the results and move on."

Jordan shook his head. "I can't. I know something—"

She lifted her hand and held it up, stopping him. "Switzerland. I don't want to know."

"That's too bad," Jordan said. "I'm pulling the 'sibling in need of an ear' card, because I need to talk this out with someone."

Sandra blew out an aggravated breath. "What is it?"

"I heard from the election commissioner this morning. According to Massachusetts's election laws, only the candidate can officially file for a recount, so they can't go forward unless Oliver requests it."

"Oliver has already conceded."

"I know. I told him he was making a mistake, but he

refused to listen to me. I just don't understand how he can sit back and do nothing."

"Maybe he wants to be gracious in his defeat and move on with his life," Sandra said. "Just as *you* should move on."

Jordan shut his eyes and pitched his head back again.

"I wish I could," he said. He straightened in the chair and looked at Sandra. "Something fishy happened with that election. My polling data was solid."

"Well, if the commissioner's office refuses to go forward with a recount, none of that matters, does it? You need to just put this election behind you."

Jordan pressed his palms together and tapped his fingers against his lips. "I hired my own investigators," he finally admitted.

Sandra groaned. "Okay, Jordan, I'm just going to say it. This election has driven you right off the deep end."

"I'm only doing what I think is right," he said. "If I just rolled over and played dead the way Oliver has, then it's like admitting that my polling was wrong, and I know it wasn't." He put both hands up. "If I don't find anything before Darren takes office in January, then I'll drop it. But until then, I'm going to search for the proof I know is out there."

"Can we please stop talking about this election? You're giving me a headache."

"Fine," Jordan said. He picked up what he could only assume was some kind of dressmaking thing from a nearby desk and twirled it around his finger. "Are you and Isaiah planning to hang around until after the Kwanzaa celebration?"

"Of course," Sandra answered, balancing Mason on her lap while he bounced up and down. "This is Isaiah's first Christmas in Wintersage in years. He wants to experience it all again—the big extravaganza and Christmas parade, and our family's annual Kwanzaa celebration. We'll likely spend Christmas Day shuttling between Mom and Dad's and his parents' place." She glanced over at him. "What about you guys?"

Jordan shrugged. "We'll be at Mom and Dad's."

"What about spending Christmas with *his* mom?" She nodded toward Mason. "Have you heard from Allison at all?"

"No," Jordan said. "Subject closed."

"Jordan—"

"Subject *closed*," he repeated. He ran his hand down his face. "I'm sorry. I'm just not in the mood to talk about Allison."

"After I just had to listen to all that election crap?"

"Do you really want to use your 'sibling in need of an ear' card on talk about Allison?"

"Whatever," Sandra said. "Why did you come over here in the first place if you don't want to talk about anything but that election?"

"Maybe I wanted you to spend time with your nephew, but if you don't want to we can leave." Jordan made as if he was about to get up. His sister shot him an evil look.

"Sit down," she said.

He grinned, knowing that would get under her skin. He took his seat, picked up the shiny tool again and resumed twirling it around his finger.

"Would you put down my eyelash curler?"

"Your what?"

She gestured to her eyes. "Eyelash curler. You know, to extend my lashes."

Jordan tossed the thing on the desk as though it had

suddenly caught fire. He blew out another weary breath and stretched his legs out in front of him.

Folding his hands over his stomach, he said, "I saw Vicki downstairs. She looks nice today."

"She has a date."

"Yeah, that's what she told me. She offered to baby-sit Mason so I can get some rest."

"I hope you took her up on her offer. You can use it. You look like a reject from *The Walking Dead*."

"You do know how to flatter a guy," Jordan said with a snort.

She sent him a saccharine smile. "I try."

"So," Jordan asked, picking up a pencil from Sandra's desk and tapping it against his thigh. "Do you know the guy she's going out with tonight?"

The moment the question left his mouth Jordan wanted to take it back. *Why* had he just asked that? Especially of Sandra.

His sister's eyes narrowed. "I haven't met him," she said. "Why do you ask?"

"Forget it."

Her brow arched. "No, why don't you tell me, Jordan? Why the sudden interest in Vicki's dating life?"

Just as he was about to tell Sandra to drop it, Mason threw his head back and started to wail. Not since his first moments of life in the delivery room had Jordan been so grateful to hear his baby boy cry.

"I hope your mother appreciates these," Vicki said as she handed Samson Cornwell his credit card. "It's sweet of you to buy her a dozen roses just because."

"I thought it would be nice to brighten her day," Samson said. "And you do such an amazing job, Vicki. These roses are just amazing."

"I can't really take the credit. I just arranged them. Mother Nature did the hard work."

His roaring laugh echoed against the walls. The effort it took for Vicki not to roll her eyes was downright admirable.

"Did you have this sense of humor back in high school?" Samson asked, wiping tears of mirth from his eyes. "Who knew you were so funny?"

Vicki hunched her shoulders in a "who knew?" gesture. She pushed the vase filled with blush-colored Antique Silk roses and baby's breath toward him, hoping he'd take the hint and leave. He didn't.

Sam rested an elbow on the counter and leaned in close. "When did you get interested in flowers?" he asked. "You know, I read somewhere that there are over twenty different species of roses. That's amazing, isn't it?"

"Try nearly two hundred," Vicki said.

His eyes went wide. "Really? Two hundred? That's amazing."

She wondered if he would be offended if she threw a thesaurus in with his dozen roses. That was the fifth *amazing* since he'd walked through the door.

The phone rang. Vicki decided then and there to give whoever was on the other end of the line a free centerpiece for their holiday dinner table.

"I have to get this, Samson. Thanks again for utilizing Petals for your floral needs. I hope your mother enjoys her roses."

"Oh, I know she will," he said. He winked at her.

It took everything Vicki had in her not to groan. She answered the phone. "Petals."

It was Declan. As she listened to his apology and explanations for canceling their date tonight, her spirits deflated. Well, there went her big plans. Maybe she should run outside and stop Samson before he drove away.

The door swung open and Samson rushed back in. She immediately regretted the thought she'd just had. She so was not going out with Samson Cornwell. She didn't care how *amazing* a date with him would be.

"My wallet," Samson said, retrieving it from where he'd left it on the counter.

Vicki walked him to the door, then turned and spotted Sandra, Jordan and Mason marching down the stairs.

Sandra pointed to the door as she reached the landing. "Let me guess, another new male customer who suddenly has a penchant for flowers?"

"Samson Cornwell," Vicki said. "You remember him?"

Sandra pulled a face. "That fool who nearly blew up the chemistry lab at Wintersage Academy?"

"The very one."

"Don't tell me he asked you out."

"I didn't give him the chance," Vicki said.

Jordan stood there with Mason, his gaze volleying back and forth between her to Sandra.

"The men of Wintersage have developed an amazing interest in flowers this week," Sandra explained to him.

Vicki groaned. "Please don't say the word *amazing*." Sandra's forehead dipped in question. "Don't ask," Vicki added.

"Anyway," her friend said, turning once again to Jordan, "one came in yesterday and bought a bouquet for his dentist. His *dentist*. It's ridiculous."

"Petals appreciates it," Vicki said. "Petals's owner, however, is so over it."

"Wait." Sandra frowned. "Why are you still here? Don't you have a date tonight?"

Vicki tried to keep the defeated sigh from escaping, but failed. "Declan had to cancel. He was called in to cover the E.R. Apparently they just got slammed with food poisoning from a birthday party."

"Aw, honey, I'm sorry."

"There's always a next time," she said, hunching her shoulders. She turned her attention to Jordan, who was now fighting to put Mason's jacket on him, a battle he was clearly losing. Vicki bit the inside of her cheek to stop herself from laughing. "Do you need some help?" she asked.

He held the jacket out to her and let out a relieved sigh. "Please."

Instead of taking the jacket, she took Mason. The little boy leaned his head on her shoulder and stuffed his thumb between his lips, and Vicki's heart instantly went the way of ice cream on a hot summer day.

Her heart did something all together different when she looked up again and found Jordan with his bottom lip between his teeth, concentrating hard as he threaded Mason's chubby arms through his jacket sleeves. She absolutely hated that everything he did looked so damn sexy on Jordan. And that she couldn't help but love it.

She suddenly discovered a bright spot to her canceled date.

"I'm free to babysit tonight," she said to Jordan.

His head popped up. "You sure? What if your date manages to get away from the hospital after all?"

"From the way things sounded, that doesn't seem likely. Besides, you look as if you can really use the rest."

"I told him he looks like shit," Sandra said.

Vicki covered Mason's exposed ear. "Not in front of the baby," she admonished.

"Don't waste your time," Jordan said. He hooked a thumb toward his sister. "I've already accepted that this one will teach my son every swearword there is by the time he turns three."

"That's what aunties are for," Sandra said, giving the baby a kiss on the cheek before heading back up the staircase.

"So are you really up for babysitting tonight?" Jordan asked. "Because if you are I won't turn you down. Sandra's right, I do look like shi… Crap," he finished.

"Saying *crap* isn't much better," Vicki said, unable to hide her grin. She jiggled Mason's chubby cheek. "Just wait until his grandma Nancy hears those swearwords coming out of his mouth. Then both your daddy and Auntie Sandra will have some explaining to do."

"Don't remind me," he said.

"Don't say I didn't warn you." Vicki laughed. She turned her attention back to Mason. "What do you think of me coming over, huh? We can play games, or watch a movie, or even make a snowman while your daddy gets a little rest. What do you say about that?"

The little baby teeth that peeked out as his face broke into a smile was hands down the most adorable thing she'd seen in months.

"I think he's okay with it," Jordan said with a grin of his own.

Her reaction to *that* smile was wholly uncalled-for. Maybe if she refused to acknowledge the flutter that swept through her stomach, she could pretend it didn't really happen. Because, seriously, how could a simple smile give her butterflies?

She could not wait until the day she was past this ridiculous infatuation—*if* she could ever move past it.

No. There was no *if* about it. When it came to her feelings for Jordan, the new Vicki was not going down the same road the old Vicki had traveled. She'd come to that decision after Sandra's wedding. It was the reason she'd signed up on that dating website: she was done pining for Jordan Woolcott.

Yet she'd just agreed to babysit for him tonight. What in God's name had convinced her to come up with that stellar suggestion?

She studied the look of exhaustion etched around his face and was reminded of just why she'd made the offer.

"Are you on your way home now?" Vicki asked.

"You done here?" he asked, gesturing to the refrigerated display case.

"Yep, Petals is closed for the day. I was supposed to be on a date, remember?" Vicki refused to read anything into the way his brows dipped at the reminder. "Just let me grab my purse and keys and I'll follow you to your place."

She retrieved her phone from the counter and sent Sandra a text message, letting her know she was leaving. When she went outside, Jordan was strapping Mason into his safety seat. A few minutes later, they were making their way along Seaside Drive, the stretch of highway that hugged the coastline that wrapped around Wintersage. Jordan lived on the opposite side of town, what locals called "below the bay."

Jordan's gray, single-story, shingle-style cottage, with its charming white shutters and walkway bordered by weather-beaten boulders from the shoreline, was, in Vicki's opinion, one of the most charming homes in this section of Wintersage. Though modest for someone of Jordan's means, it seemed to fit him perfectly.

He turned into his driveway and both doors of the double garage opened. Vicki pulled her car in alongside his. When she walked over to Jordan, he was holding a finger against his lips.

"He fell asleep on the drive over," Jordan whispered.

"Ah." Vicki nodded. She pointed to her car and mouthed, "Should I go?"

He hunched his shoulder. "I guess," he whispered as he unstrapped Mason. He took great care in lifting the baby from the safety seat, huddling him close to his chest.

Vicki waved goodbye and started back for her car, but her feet stopped at the sound of Mason's sudden wailing. She spun around and instantly took pity on Jordan's pathetic expression. He looked on the verge of collapse.

"I guess I'm staying after all," Vicki said, returning to Jordan's side. She lifted Mason from his arms. "It's okay, honey." She patted his back as she followed Jordan up the garage's steps and into the mudroom.

By the time they entered the house, Mason's wail was down to a soft whimper. Vicki carried him through the short hallway that led into the kitchen, but stopped short as she passed the threshold.

The place was a mess.

Plush teddy bears and plastic toys littered the floor. There were newspapers and empty coffee mugs strewn about the table in the breakfast nook. Dirty dishes and at least a half dozen sippy cups filled the sink.

"Uh, excuse the mess," Jordan said as he pushed aside an open box of animal crackers to make room on the counter for the baby bag he'd carried in from the car. He perched against the counter and folded his arms over his chest.

He looked from her to Mason and huffed out an exhausted laugh. "I don't know what you do, but I wish you'd tell me," he said. "I'm starting to believe you have some kind of magical powers when it comes to my son."

"I already gave you my theory," she said. "You're agitated, and I think Mason can sense that."

"I guess your theory makes more sense than magic. I have been wound pretty tight since the election results came in. I can't seem to relax."

"Have you tried?"

"Not really," he said with another weary chuckle. "I've never been good at it. Always seems as if my time could be better spent doing something more productive."

"Get some rest, Jordan. I'm sure some uninterrupted sleep will do you good."

He walked over to them and smoothed a hand over Mason's head. This brought him *way* too close to her for her peace of mind.

"Maybe you're right," he said.

"There's no 'maybe' about it," Vicki said, taking a step back to create some distance between them. "Put the election and everything else out of your head for a few hours and rest. This little one and I will be just fine."

He came over to them again and pressed a kiss to Mason's forehead. "Thanks again for doing this," he said to her, his grateful though exhausted smile setting off all kinds of sinfully delicious tingles in her belly.

Goodness, but she was pitiful when it came to this man.

"If you need me, just come in and wake me," he said

before walking through the arched entryway that led to the rest of the house.

Vicki remained standing there until she heard the click of a door closing.

She looked down at Mason. "The new Vicki needs to remember what she said about not acting a fool for your dad."

"Ball," Mason said, pointing to a multicolored ball on the table.

Vicki picked up the ball, along with several other toys scattered along the kitchen counter, and brought Mason into the living room. Lifting an afghan with a seaside lighthouse pattern on it from the sofa, she spread it out on the hardwood floor and set Mason on it, then she plopped down next to him and rolled a plastic ball toward him.

After several minutes of playing with the ball, Mason's mouth twisted in a frown. Seconds later, Vicki caught a whiff of something that made her stomach turn.

"Oh, you would do that *after* your daddy has gone to nap, wouldn't you?"

She scooped the baby up and went in search of diaper-changing supplies. Vicki opened several doors, including a linen closet and what had to be Jordan's home office, which was impeccable—a surprise— seeing as how the rest of the house was in shambles.

Finally, she came upon Mason's brightly colored bedroom. Unfortunately, she didn't find any diapers in there.

Vicki remembered the baby bag Jordan had brought in and returned to the kitchen where he'd left it on the counter. With the baby perched on her hip, she searched the bag but only came up with baby wipes and a small bottle of baby powder.

"Well, we'll definitely need these, but we're missing the most important thing."

She hated to wake Jordan up so soon after he'd gone in for his nap, but if this diaper didn't get changed soon the stench would probably wake him.

She went through the great room and down the hallway to the master bedroom. Tapping lightly on the door, she softly called, "Jordan?"

"Come in," came a voice that was much too robust to come from someone who should have been asleep.

Vicki pushed her way through the door and frowned.

Jordan sat up with his back against the headboard, his stocking feet crossed at the ankles. An open laptop rested on his thighs and a pair of reading glasses was perched upon his nose. Make that an astonishingly sexy pair of reading glasses.

She tried to block the sexiness from her head, otherwise her impending lecture wouldn't be nearly as effective as she needed it to be. She plopped a hand on the hip that didn't have a twenty-two-pound toddler on it and narrowed her eyes at Jordan.

"Seriously?" she said, jutting her chin toward the laptop.

"Yeah, I know." He grimaced. "I just needed to check one thing."

"You're supposed to be *resting,* Jordan, not working. Those are two very different concepts. It's easy to tell them apart."

He looked at her over the rim of his glasses and grinned. "Who knew Vicki Ahlfors was such a smart a—" He glanced at Mason. "Aleck," he finished.

No, no, no. Her cheeks would *not* heat up at his teasing.

"No changing the subject," she said, keeping her voice as firm as possible. "I didn't volunteer to watch Mason so you can work." The little boy shifted in her arms and Vicki caught another whiff of his aroma, reminding her of the reason she'd come in here in the first place. "Please tell me you have diapers," she said.

"In there." He pointed to the master bath.

Vicki cursed the deep flutter that traveled through her belly as she entered Jordan's bathroom. There was something way too intimate about this. The discarded facecloth hanging on the rim of the sink, the bottle of multivitamins, the razor—not an electric one, a classic manual razor, the kind that required control and a steady hand.

She briefly shut her eyes against the image that tried to crop up in her head. Thinking about Jordan and his steady hands was bound to get her in trouble.

At the far end of the long vanity sat a stack of disposable diapers, along with more baby wipes, lotion and powder. She grabbed a plush towel from the wooden towel rack and gently laid Mason on top of it.

She'd just pulled off his pants when she heard Jordan say, "I can do that."

Vicki's back stiffened. She'd been so busy with Mason that she hadn't heard him approach.

"I've got it," she called over her shoulder.

The tingle that raced down her spine was completely inappropriate, but wholly expected. Those tingles were par for the course when it came to being in close proximity to Jordan. The new Vicki was supposed to be done with those tingles, but apparently she hadn't gotten the memo.

Standing watch just over her shoulder as she efficiently went about changing Mason's diaper, Jordan said, "You handle that like a pro."

"Changing a diaper?" she asked.

"Yeah, especially with the way that one squirms."

As if on cue, Mason immediately started to writhe around on the vanity. Vicki caught his feet together in one hand and moved her hip to block him from rolling right off the counter.

"I see what you mean." She leaned over and nibbled Mason's chin. "But your cute little booty isn't getting away from me." She looked back at Jordan. "Goodness, is there anything more adorable than those two bottom teeth that peek out whenever he smiles?"

"Nothing I've found," he said with a laugh.

He finally backed away, making it easier for Vicki to get her breathing under control. His nearness was pure torture on her new quest to not be affected by him.

He settled in the doorway and leaned a shoulder against the jamb. "How'd you learn to change a baby's diaper?" Jordan asked. "You don't have any kids of your own."

Vicki snorted as she glanced over her shoulder. "Thanks for pointing that out."

"Damn. I'm sorry. I didn't mean for that to sound the way it did. I'm just impressed," he continued. "It took me a while to get the hang of diaper changing."

"I guess it's instinctual for some," she said. She gave the two pieces of tape a firm pat before pulling Mason's corduroys up over his fresh diaper. "There you go, sweetie," she said, tickling the baby's belly. He giggled and treated her to that wide, sweet grin that was sure to break hearts.

"So did you reschedule your date with the doctor?" Jordan asked.

Vicki's head jerked up. She met his eyes in the bathroom mirror.

"Uh...no," she stammered, caught off guard by the subject change. "He was already at the hospital when he called earlier. He didn't really have time to talk."

"Oh. Well, maybe you two can find a time that works later this week."

Hefting Mason into her arms, Vicki turned and faced him. "I doubt there will be any future dates with Declan."

"Really?" Jordan's brows rose. "So it wasn't anything serious, whatever it is you had with the doctor?"

Should she tell him the truth, that before it was canceled, her date with Declan would have been her first in well over a year? And that the last date she went on—with the cousin of a friend of a friend—was so unremarkable that she couldn't even remember the guy's name?

Vicki considered it for a moment, but decided against mentioning it. She had no desire to be pitied, especially by Jordan.

Instead, she said, "It's pretty obvious that Declan is too busy for even a casual relationship, let alone something more serious."

Still leaning against the doorjamb, he crossed his arms and cocked his head to the side. "And you're opposed to casual?"

"I wouldn't say I'm opposed to it. But it's not what I want." When it came to this particular issue, Vicki decided that being vague would do her no good. "I've done the casual-dating thing in the past. I'm ready for something more stable...something that has potential."

She fought against the self-consciousness brought on by Jordan's thoughtful, probing gaze.

Several long moments passed before he asked in a curious tone, "Does this have anything to do with Sandra and Janelle both getting married? Are you feeling left out?"

Vicki's head reared back. Had he really just asked her that?

"You do realize how insulting that is, don't you?"

He looked completely baffled. "Insulting?"

"Yes. Your question insinuates that I only want a serious relationship because my two best friends have recently found their soul mates. It's insulting."

He grimaced, bringing his hand up to massage the back of his neck. "Now that you put it that way..." When his eyes returned to hers, they were filled with contriteness. "I'm sorry if that offended you. I swear that wasn't my intention." He lifted his shoulder in a half shrug. "It's just that the three of you have always done everything together. With Sandra getting married so soon after Janelle, it just seemed natural that you would be next."

Vicki had to work hard not to release a deflated sigh. He was likely one of many who shared that same sentiment.

"It's okay, Jordan. Both Janelle and Sandra would tell you that of the three of us, I'm the one who they both suspected would be the first to marry." She gave him a wan smile. "Things don't always turn out the way we expect."

"Tell me about it," he said with a gentle smile of his own. His gaze shifted to the little boy in her arms. "But sometimes those unexpected detours in life turn out to be the best thing to ever happen to you."

The complete adoration in his eyes made her heart squeeze.

"A blessing in disguise," Vicki said.

"Ball," Mason said, pointing in the direction of the living room. "Ball, ball, ball."

She laughed. "We were playing with the ball before the diaper change became mission number one." She scooped up the towel she'd used to cushion Mason and tossed it on top of the overfilled clothes hamper before heading past Jordan on her way out of the bathroom. Her elbow brushed against his chest and a shudder went through her.

Pitiful!

"You *are* going to nap, right?" Vicki called over her shoulder. When he didn't say anything, she turned and scowled. "Jordan," she said in a warning tone.

"I will," he said, following her out of the bathroom. "I just need to finish rerunning some polling data."

"Seriously?" Vicki rolled her eyes. "You can't keep going at this pace. This election is going to drive you crazy."

"It already has." He ran a hand down his face, the exhaustion in his eyes becoming more apparent with every second that passed. The man was dead on his feet.

"Maybe I'm missing something here, but if Oliver Windom can accept the election results, why can't you? I don't understand why you're allowing this to consume you."

"Because I messed up, and I can't figure out what went wrong." He shook his head. "I've been racking my brain, but nothing makes sense. It doesn't matter how many angles I look at, I still don't see how Darren pulled it off." He pointed at the laptop. "According to my statistics, Oliver should have won."

"Polling isn't an exact science. No one really knows what happens when a person enters the ballot box except for that person."

"I know there are margins of error, and I know that this race was close, but when I look at the districts that Oliver lost, it makes me even more convinced that there was some sort of tampering. Those were the ones that he should have won by the biggest margin." He shook his head. "Maybe it's the math nerd in me, but I just don't see how I could have been so off with the data."

His pained expression was full of anguish. "I wish I could let this go, Vicki. I'm not oblivious to the rift this has caused between my family and the Howertons, and to a certain extent your family, too. I truly hope that it hasn't affected the relationship between you, Sandra and Janelle."

"We're Switzerland," she said.

"Yeah, that's what Sandra told me, but still, it can't be easy."

No, it wasn't. There had been an underlying layer of tension around the Victorian since the end of the election. Yet as much as she wished Jordan would drop this, Vicki couldn't help but be impressed by the way he'd held to his convictions, despite the enormous pressure he was obviously getting from all sides to let this go.

"I doubt anything is going to change with the numbers in the next couple of hours, so why don't you put that stuff away and get some rest?"

"You're right," he said. He lifted the laptop from the bed and set it on the tufted ottoman in the sitting room area. He turned to her and held his hands up. "I promise that I'll sleep this time."

"Good," she said with a firm nod. A blue-and-white pamphlet caught her eye as she passed the dresser on her way out of the room. "Do you work with Mass Mentors?" Vicki asked, referring to the mentorship program she'd been a supporter of for the past few years.

"Yeah," he answered. "I've been helping out there."

"It's a great program. I've brought in several of the kids to intern at Petals. They go out on deliveries and a few are even starting to learn floral design."

"I didn't realize you were involved with the program," he said. His voice softened with appreciation. "That's wonderful, Vicki."

Their gazes locked and held for several weighty moments. Jordan was the first to look away, picking up a pen from the lap desk on the bed and tossing it on the nightstand.

"Uh, we didn't discuss any kind of payment for the babysitting. How much..." His words trailed off and his mouth dipped in a frown. Probably because of the daggers she was shooting at him right now with her stare. "What?" he asked.

"Are you deliberately trying to annoy me?" Vicki asked, making sure her displeasure came through her voice. "I *volunteered* to watch Mason out of friendship. Don't you dare suggest paying me, Jordan."

"Sorry." He held his hands up in mock surrender once again. "It looks as if I've made a world championship sport out of offending you today."

"Yeah, well, you don't have to try so hard to sweep the medals," she said, wrangling a laugh from him. With Mason in tow, she headed out of the room.

"Vicki," Jordan called just as she reached the door. She looked back at him. "Thank you," he said.

She smiled. "You're welcome. Now sleep."

Chapter 3

Jordan's eyes popped open.

He sprung up in bed, but quickly relaxed when he remembered that Vicki was here, watching over Mason so he could rest.

Vicki.

Jordan shook his head, still confused as hell over what to make of her. He'd dreamed of her while he slept, his mind conjuring images that would probably make her blush. But he couldn't help it. Vicki Ahlfors had burrowed her way into his brain, and he enjoyed having her there too much to let those delicious fantasies of her vanish anytime soon.

Jordan dragged his palms down his face.

He'd mulled over these feelings that had started swirling within him the night of Sandra's wedding and had decided to ignore them, but fighting thoughts about Vicki was more than his taxed mind had the ability to deal with right now. It was easier to just go with it and let the fantasies play out.

Jordan knew her dating status shouldn't matter to him one way or another, but damn if something akin to relief hadn't hit him when Vicki had confirmed that she wouldn't be rescheduling her date with the doctor. She'd said she wasn't into casual relationships anymore; he could respect that. He'd grown weary of carefree flings that were only fun for the moment, but left him unfulfilled. Now that he had Mason, his taste for meaningless relationships had soured even more.

He wanted substance. He wanted stability. He wanted someone who could appreciate the simple pleasures of a quiet night at home, someone who would value the absolute joy he found in raising his son.

But whether or not he was even ready to explore a relationship with a woman again was still up in the air. He'd been burned so badly by the last one that just the thought of exposing himself to that kind of hurt again scared the hell out of him. And that was nothing compared to how he felt when he considered bringing another woman into Mason's life.

Protecting his son was his number one priority. He would not allow his own needs to supersede those of Mason's.

Jordan glanced at the digital clock on the nightstand and did a double take. It was nearly 10:00 p.m.

What the hell?

He'd been asleep for *four hours?*

He hopped out of bed and rushed from the room. Finding the great room empty, he took off for the kitchen.

He crossed the threshold and stuttered to a stop.

The kitchen was spotless. Vicki had washed and put

away the dishes, swept and mopped the floors. She'd piled Mason's toys into one of the wicker laundry baskets from the laundry room and tucked it into a corner.

She looked up from the table she was scrubbing and smiled. "You're up," she said.

"Yeah," he replied with a sheepish grin. He rubbed the back of his neck. "I…uh, I'm sorry I slept so long. You should have been gone a long time ago."

"I didn't mind staying," she said. "You obviously needed the rest."

"More than I thought I did," he agreed. "Is Mason asleep?"

She nodded. "He actually fell asleep less than an hour after you did."

"You should have woken me, Vicki, or at least brought him in bed with me and taken off."

"I wasn't going to just leave without you knowing, Jordan. It's okay. As you can see, I found a way to occupy my time."

"I can see that." He motioned around the impeccable kitchen. "Thanks for doing all this. I've been meaning to clean since Laurie left but haven't gotten around to it."

"Have you been interviewing new housekeepers?"

Jordan frowned. "Why would I do that?"

"I thought your housekeeper quit."

"She didn't quit. She's just on an extended vacation, visiting her family in Toronto for the holidays."

"Oh, thank goodness, because you obviously need her," she said with a good-natured laugh. A devious smile tilted up the corners of her mouth. "Maybe I should have charged you after all. This kitchen was no small task."

He reached for the wallet he'd tossed on the kitchen counter earlier.

"I'm joking, Jordan."

"I'm not."

Vicki plunked a hand on her hip. "You'd better leave that wallet right where it is," she said in a warning tone.

He dropped the wallet and held his hands up in surrender. "Okay, okay. Don't hurt me," he said. He folded his arms across his chest and perched against the counter. "If you won't take money, at least let me pay you back with dinner."

The awkward silence immediately following his suggestion was deafening.

Where had *that* come from?

"Dinner?" Vicki asked, the dubious lift to her voice echoing her confusion.

Jordan was just as stunned as she was. He hadn't asked a woman to dinner—one who wasn't his sister, mother or a member of Oliver Windom's campaign committee, that was—in nearly two years. Not since Allison.

But now that he'd asked, he couldn't very well rescind it, could he?

An unexpected rush of adrenaline raced through Jordan's gut as he realized he didn't want to rescind anything. He wanted her to say yes. Later, when he had time to process it, he would have to figure out just why, after all this time, he was suddenly excited—damn near ecstatic—at the thought of sitting across a table and sharing a good meal and even better conversation with Vicki Ahlfors.

There was time to think about that later. At the moment, his main objective was making sure he secured an opportunity to see her again in the very near future. Tomorrow, if he had anything to say about it.

"Yes, dinner," Jordan continued. He pushed away from the counter and took a couple of steps forward. "There's nothing wrong with two friends going out for a meal, is there? It's the least I can do to express my thanks for everything you've done here this evening."

She looked up at him, and for the first time he detected the faint flecks of gold in her light brown eyes. How had he never noticed those before? Why had he never paid attention?

"You really don't have to, Jordan. As you pointed out earlier, I don't get the chance to hang around babies all that much. Mason has such a sweet temperament. I was happy to babysit."

Her words doused the excitement that had begun to flow through his bloodstream, reminding him that she had been here for Mason, not him.

He halted his advance toward her and hoped like hell that his disappointment didn't show on his face.

"In that case," he said, "let me at least follow you home."

"Be real, Jordan. You're not going to wake Mason and go through the hassle of bundling him up in his coat just so you can follow me home. I'm a big girl. I'm perfectly okay getting home on my own."

She gave the table a final swipe and folded the dishcloth. She hung it over the gooseneck faucet and picked her purse up from the counter, pulling the strap over her shoulder.

She held up a finger. "There's just one thing I need to do before I leave."

Jordan followed her to Mason's room. He stood in the open doorway and watched as she tiptoed to the crib and placed a gentle kiss on Mason's forehead. An odd feeling pulled at his gut. His son's own mother had not bothered to kiss him good-night in months. Seeing Vicki show him such attention—such affection—made the emotions stirring inside him intensify to unprecedented levels.

Why had he never noticed these things about her before? He knew she was sweet and quiet and kind. But she was also generous and giving and surprisingly funny.

And sexy. Even while wiping down his kitchen table she was sexy.

He followed her back to the kitchen, through the mudroom and to the garage. Jordan opened the garage door then went over to her car. Bracing his hand on the hood, he leaned in and asked, "You sure you'll be okay?"

"Of course, Jordan. It's not as if I have to drive to Connecticut, just to the other side of Wintersage." She closed the door but lowered the window. "Promise me you won't mess up your night by diving right back into work. Why don't you pull one of those novels off the bookshelf, or pop in a DVD? Anything but work."

"I'll think about it," he said, chuckling when she rolled her eyes and let out an exasperated sigh. He reached in and put a hand on her shoulder. "Thanks again for doing this, Vicki. I didn't realize how much I needed it."

The moment he touched her, things changed. Their gazes locked and held. Jordan didn't miss the way her chest rose with the deep breath she sucked in, nor could he miss the way *his* skin tingled with something he couldn't identify.

"It was my pleasure," she finally answered in a breathless tone.

His hand remained on her shoulder a second too long to be considered just a friendly gesture, but at the moment Jordan couldn't bring himself to care. He had no desire to stop touching her.

"Jordan, I should probably get going," she said.

Funny, he thought she should get out of her car and return to the house with him. At the moment, nothing would give him greater pleasure than to have her follow him into his bedroom so he could relive some of the fantasies he'd dreamed about a short while ago.

And that was when Jordan realized he needed to let her go.

Reluctantly, he withdrew his hand and backed away from the door. As she put the car in Reverse and pulled out of the garage, Jordan followed. He stopped at the edge of the garage and gave her a silent wave as she drove away.

Jordan brought his hand behind his head and tried to rub away the tightness in his neck muscles.

He was so damn confused. Hell, he'd been puzzled over these feeling for *days* now, and it became more perplexing with every day that passed.

He'd known Vicki for years. Why was he just noticing the slightly mischievous curve to her subtle smile? Or the way her eyes lit up when she laughed? Why was he suddenly feeling this bolt of electricity when she was around?

It was probably just the lingering effects of not being with a woman since Allison had left.

"That has to be it," Jordan said.

You don't believe that.

Jordan shut out the annoying voice in his head. If he

paid attention to it, he would be up for the rest of the night dissecting these new emotions Vicki had started to stir within him. It was a combination of exhaustion and horniness; he couldn't afford for it to be anything else.

The last time he'd allowed himself to get caught up in a woman, he'd been careless and had quickly found himself with a one-way ticket to fatherhood. He couldn't bring himself to regret it, not with Mason as the outcome of those less-than-stellar decisions he'd made a couple of years ago.

But that was why he had to be even *more* careful now. He had his son to think about. After the hard lessons he'd learned during his short marriage to Allison, he had to be more careful when it came to whom he exposed his son to. He couldn't allow his own baser needs to supersede what was right for Mason.

Though it wasn't as if Vicki would ever do anything to harm his son. She had a way with him—a special touch that seemed to calm Mason when nothing else could.

Jordan's spine stiffened, his back going ramrod straight.

Was *that* what this was about?

Were these feelings simply the result of gratitude over the compassion Vicki showed his son?

But a lot of women doted on Mason. On those occasions when Jordan had brought him over to Oliver's campaign headquarters, the females working on the campaign would get so wrapped up in Mason they would hardly get any work done. Why had he never felt his breath quickening or this low and steady burn in his gut toward any of those women?

He exhaled a frustrated sigh.

He didn't have the mental energy to deal with this

right now. His focus needed to remain on the election. The investigators he'd hired would need him to go over the information they uncovered—if they uncovered any—so that they could discern if there really was ballot tampering. He couldn't allow any outside forces to steal his attention away from what was really important right now.

Jordan returned to the house, locking up behind him. Despite the four-hour nap he'd just taken, he fell asleep as soon as his head hit the pillow.

The next day, after a morning of scouring the newspaper and web for any new news on the election and coming up empty, Jordan zipped Mason into his heavy coat and headed over to his parents. His father was likely at Woolcott Industries, but at this time of the day he had a good shot of finding his mother at home.

Jordan used his key to enter through the front door. His parents had never asked for the key once he'd moved out, and he never once considered giving it back. Even with a house of his own, this place was home.

He made his way through the massive house, finding his mother in the formal dining room. She looked up from the table, where she was replacing the silver cutlery with gold-plated ones. She put the mahogany box down and raced toward them.

"Well, hello there," she said, scooping Mason from his arms. "How are the two most handsome men in the world doing today?"

Nancy Woolcott was every bit the society wife, entrenched in her role among Wintersage's elite. But to Jordan's surprise, his mother was just as passionate in her role as a grandmother. She'd made her displeasure over his relationship with Allison known from the very beginning, and at first, Jordan thought she would project those feelings onto her grandson.

He should have known better. Mason was the apple of her eye.

"Do you have kisses for Grandma?" She peppered Mason's cheeks with loud pecks that had his son squirming and giggling in her arms. Turning to Jordan, she asked, "Why didn't you call to say you were coming over? I could have had something prepared for a late lunch."

"It's no big deal. We had a lazy morning, which seems to have stretched into a lazy afternoon. I figured I'd drop in and say hello." He pointed to the array of decorations adorning the twelve-foot dining table. "Getting the house ready for the holidays?"

"It's called tablescaping. Like landscaping, but for the inside of the house. I saw it on one of those home-decorating shows and knew I had to do it for the holidays."

His mother hired people to come in and decorate throughout the year, but when it came to Christmas she always insisted on doing things herself. Jordan doubted any outsider could ever put the amount of love and care his mother put into getting the house ready for Christmas.

"Have you picked out a tree yet?" she asked him. "You need to make sure they trim a good portion of the bottom limbs so that this little one won't reach them."

"I wasn't planning on getting a tree at all," Jordan said.

His mother looked at him as if he'd just confessed to armed robbery of an orphanage.

"What?" he asked defensively. "It doesn't make sense

to go through the hassle of a tree when we'll be spending Christmas Day here anyway."

Her chastising frown was a throwback to his days in elementary school after coming home with a note from the teacher for "bucking authority," which Jordan later realized was code for speaking his mind.

"Jordan, you have a baby now. This munchkin needs a Christmas tree. And it's more than just one day, it's an entire season. Get a tree," she stated in a tone that brooked no argument.

Jordan grunted, just as he used to do when those notorious letters arrived from his teachers, but he grudgingly accepted that, in this case, his mother was probably right.

He had never bothered with decorating for the holidays when it was just him, but now that he had Mason, he had to think about the kind of childhood he wanted his son to have. Some of his fondest memories as a boy were from Christmas. His parents went out of their way to make this time of the year special for both him and Sandra. He wanted Mason to have the opportunity to make those same memories.

"Okay," Jordan said. "We'll get a tree today."

His mother gave him a firm, regal nod, as if she never doubted he wouldn't do just as she'd requested. She turned her attention back to Mason.

"Now that that's settled, why don't we go into the kitchen? Grandma has a special treat for you."

"What's new about that? You always have a special treat for him," Jordan said as he followed her to the kitchen.

"Oh, hush," she called over her shoulder. "If I have to wear the title of grandmother, then I want to enjoy all the privileges, which includes spoiling my grandson."

She retrieved a package from the pantry. "I ran across these organic fruit chews the other day. I figured any healthy snack is a good snack. Let's just hope he likes them."

Perched in his grandmother's lap at the breakfast table, Mason took the dried fruit between his stubby fingers and immediately started to devour it. The smile on his mother's face stretched to the Massachusetts state line.

"Yes!" she said. "Score one for Grandma Nancy."

"I hope you bought a case. He's at this stage where he gets fixated on a certain thing and that's all he wants. Last week it was canned peaches."

"I'll make sure Millie picks up a few more boxes when she does this week's grocery shopping," his mother said, referring to the live-in housekeeper who had been with their family for years. "But you do know that you shouldn't let him have too much of any one thing, even if it is healthy. Not that I'm trying to tell you how to raise your son," his mother quickly interjected.

"I know," Jordan said. She made a point not to butt in, as she called it. Unless it concerned Christmas trees. Apparently, all bets were off when it came to proper holiday preparations.

Jordan walked over to the fridge and grabbed a can of soda. "I try to practice moderation as much as possible, but I've been somewhat lax these past few days. Mason's been fussier than normal lately. If I find something to appease him, I'm doing it."

"What's got you fussy, huh?" his mother asked, smoothing a hand over Mason's head.

"I don't know what it is," Jordan said. "Maybe he's missing Laurie? He's used to having her around."

"How long will she be gone?"

"Until after the New Year."

Jordan groaned just thinking about it. He appreciated his housekeeper/nanny, and paid her well because of it, but he didn't realize just how much she handled until she'd left for this extended vacation.

Maybe that was why he was feeling off-kilter. With Laurie gone and him stuck at the house all day, things seemed out of whack. He needed his life to return to normal.

"I'm thinking about maybe shortening my leave of absence," Jordan said. "I'm not used to sitting around the house doing nothing."

"You are not doing 'nothing,' Jordan," his mother said. She stood and brought Mason over to him. "You are enjoying the holidays with your son. Do you even realize how lucky you are? Your father would have loved to have weeks off around the holidays to spend with you kids, but it was a luxury he couldn't afford. He was always too busy with Woolcott Industries when you and Sandra were little."

His mother cupped his jaw in her soft palm. "Enjoy this time with Mason. Take it from me when I tell you that he's going to be grown and on his own before you know it. It's Christmas, Jordan. Enjoy Christmas with your son."

He nodded. "Okay, Mom. I hear you."

"Good. No more of this 'shortening your leave of absence' nonsense again. And when you *do* go back to the firm, you need to think about cutting back on your hours. You're a single father after all. This little one needs to have at least *one* of his parents around."

Jordan didn't miss the thinly disguised dig at Mason's *other* parent.

To say his mother wasn't his ex-wife's biggest fan

was an understatement that put all other understatements to shame. She'd somehow seen through Allison's facade from the very beginning. Jordan had been too blinded by his ex-wife's stunning beauty, vivacious personality and ridiculously hot body to pay attention to anything else. He'd ignored the warnings his mother tried to send him. And he'd paid for it. Dearly.

Water under the proverbial bridge.

He couldn't go back in time and change what had happened with Allison. He wouldn't even if he could. His son was worth every bit of the heartache and strife Allison had caused him.

Millie, who had been the Woolcotts' housekeeper for decades, came into the kitchen, and when she discovered Jordan had yet to have lunch, insisted on whipping up a quick meal. After demolishing the seared tuna over arugula that was worthy of a restaurant menu, Jordan patiently followed his mother around the house so she could show off the rest of her holiday decorations.

A half hour later, she followed them out to the car and strapped Mason into his car seat.

"You *are* going to get that tree this very instant, right?"

"Yes," Jordan said with an exaggerated groan.

"Good."

"Should I expect a surprise visit from you tonight to make sure I have the tree?"

"Your father and I have plans for tonight, but I expect you to text me a picture." She kissed his cheek before closing his car door and giving him a wave.

Jordan chuckled to himself as he rounded the circular driveway and drove away from his parents' home. As he pulled up to the stop sign at the end of the street, his cell phone trilled with the special ringtone he'd set

for the investigator he had looking into the election results. Jordan pulled over to the curb.

He answered the phone. "What do you have for me,
Mike?"

Several minutes later, he flipped his blinker to turn
left, back toward his house. The news he'd just received
was the most promising he'd heard in days.

Tree shopping would have to wait.

Chapter 4

"Ouch!"

Vicki stuck her finger between her lips, sucking on the spot where the prickly holly leaf had just nicked her.

"Careful," her mother admonished. She looked up from the leather-bound organizer spread out before her on the marble kitchen island. "You don't have to do that, you know. I could hire someone to put those together."

"Very funny," Vicki said. She looked over the tall centerpiece and caught the glimpse of a smile tipping up her mother's lips. "If you want to pay me, go right ahead, but if I catch another florist within twenty yards of this house I cannot be responsible for my actions."

"I wouldn't dare." Her mother blew her a kiss. Vicki pretended to catch it and threw it back at her.

Her mother's shocked laugh echoed around the massive kitchen. "That was rude."

"That's what you get for suggesting bringing in another florist to decorate the house," she said, but then to show her mother that she knew it was all in good fun, Vicki walked over and plunked a kiss on her cheek.

Sitting with her legs crossed on the high-backed stool, Christine Ahlfors was the epitome of everything Vicki had thought she wanted to be. Physically, they were unmistakably mother and daughter, with their fair skin and naturally wavy hair. Her mother had thrown a fit when Vicki had chopped half of hers off, but when she'd arrived today to help ready the house for Christmas, Christine had remarked that the chin-length pixie cut was growing on her.

Vicki joked that she could give her the number for her stylist, but found that she was actually grateful when her mother laughed it off. Her new hairstyle was just one of the ways that she was finally starting to come into her own. She'd followed in her mother's footsteps in so many ways, being on the cheer squad in high school, majoring in the arts in college, serving on the boards of several philanthropic groups.

But as the years marched on, Vicki had begun to realize that they had different goals. Unlike her mother, she would never be satisfied filling her days with charity events and the other things that occupied her mother's time. Vicki needed more.

"I was thinking of a shopping trip in Boston this weekend. Why don't you join me?" her mother asked. "We could have lunch. I can even get us tickets to the Boston Pops' Saturday-night performance."

"I doubt I'll have time," Vicki said. "I have to drive up to a supplier in Scarborough to look at a few things for the Woolcotts' Kwanzaa celebration."

Her mother made a tsking sound. "That's going to

be one interesting party if this thing with the election isn't settled by then."

"You're still planning on going, aren't you?" Vicki asked.

Her mother looked at her as if she'd lost her mind. "I wouldn't miss it for the world. Who knows what's going to happen if Jordan is still accusing Darren of stealing the election."

"Let's hope this has all blown over by then," Vicki said.

"Speak for yourself. I'm looking forward to a little drama."

They looked at each other and burst out laughing.

As she returned her attention to the centerpiece, Vicki shot a surreptitious glance at her mother. She was trying to determine whether or not to tell her the other reason she would be too busy to frolic around Boston this weekend.

So far, Sandra and Janelle were the only people she'd told about her entry into the float competition. She had decided not to mention it to anyone else until she knew whether or not her submission was accepted. But this was her mother. She would be just as stoked over the possibility of Petals being selected as an entrant, wouldn't she?

"Mom, another reason I can't go with you to Boston this weekend is because I'm hoping that I'll be too busy working on a float for the Holiday Extravaganza Day Parade."

"Oh?" Her mother said, her attention still directed on the organizer. "Who are you decorating a float for this year?"

Vicki hesitated for the tiniest second before she answered, "Petals."

Her mother's head popped up. "For *your* business?"

She nodded. "I submitted an application for Petals to sponsor a float this year."

Genuine concern creased her mother's normally flawless skin. "That's a lot to take on by yourself, isn't it?" she asked.

"I won't be totally by myself. I have part-time employees."

"Those little kids from the high school that deliver for you?"

"They're hard workers, Mom. And they do more than just deliver. I'm also teaching them basic floral design. I haven't done so these past couple of weeks because of the holiday madness and their semester finals, but after the New Year I'm actually hiring two more students."

"But putting together an entire float? That's so much to take on, Vicki."

"You do realize that I have supplied the flowers for many of the floats that take part in the parade every year, don't you?"

Her mother stepped down from the stool she'd been perched on and rounded the kitchen island. She clamped her arms around Vicki's shoulders and gave her a gentle squeeze.

"It's not that I don't think you can do the work."

Judging by her reaction, Vicki wasn't so sure about that.

She knew exactly what her family thought when it came to her desire to be an entrepreneur. They didn't see Petals as the thriving small business that it was; they saw it as "Vicki's little flower shop." That was often how her father even referred to it, as if it was some hobby she played around with on the side, instead of a business that she'd poured her blood, sweat and tears into.

The fact that he had built Ahlfors Financial Management from the ground up should have made him even *more* proud that his daughter was following in his footsteps, but that had never been the case. And as supportive as her mother tried to be, Vicki knew deep down that Christine Ahlfors's expectations for her daughter were that she would get married and step into the role she was supposed to play—the society wife and mother. Becoming a wife and mother was one of Vicki's most cherished dreams, but it was not her *only* dream.

She was a businesswoman. She took her work seriously. It was time her family took it seriously, as well.

She turned to her mother. "If you think I can do the work, why were you so dismayed when I told you I'd entered the float competition?"

"I wasn't dismayed," her mother said. She gave Vicki a patient pat on the arm. "I just don't want you to be humiliated."

Humiliated?

The word knocked the wind right out of her.

Vicki managed to keep her expression indifferent, but on the inside her soul was breaking.

She shouldn't have expected anything different. Foolishly, she had. Which was why she only had herself to blame for being naive enough to think a new wardrobe and new haircut would change the way her family regarded her. They didn't see the *new Vicki,* they still saw polite, reserved, nonconfrontational Vicki. The Vicki who would rather keep her mouth shut in order to keep the peace, who never would have had the guts to even attempt to enter the float competition.

They still saw the Vicki she *used* to be. She would have to show them she wasn't that Vicki anymore.

She put the finishing touches on the centerpiece she'd created for the foyer, but that was all she was willing to do today. She had a float to design.

"I just remembered that the Buckleys want a second wreath for their guesthouse," she said. "I'll come back later to finish the decorations."

"That's fine, honey," her mother said, her focus once again on her calendar.

Vicki studied her for a moment, wishing she'd given Vicki the reaction she'd been hoping for when she'd told her about the float. Couldn't her mother have surprised her just this once? Couldn't she be proud, or even just excited? Why had her first reaction been to doubt that Vicki could pull this off?

She should have gone with her first instincts and kept this news quiet until she was sure her submission was accepted. If it turned out that she wouldn't have a float in the parade after all, she would have to hear "I told you so" for the next six months.

Yeah, she had no one to blame but herself.

Jordan braced his elbows on his kitchen table and ran both palms down his face. The longer he stared at this stuff, the less sense it made. For the past two days he'd pored over the data, running the numbers over and over again, trying to figure out just where the inconsistencies had come from.

When he'd gotten the call Wednesday from the investigator he'd hired, notifying him that he'd found a sharp decline in the number of voters for several counties in the western part of the state that normally had high voter turnout, Jordan thought he was on to something.

But the gap in voter turnout wasn't as wide as Jordan had anticipated, and there could have been a number of factors that accounted for it, including the weather in that part of the state on Election Day.

Dammit. Why couldn't this have been the break he'd been looking for?

He massaged the bridge of his nose. "You're driving yourself crazy," Jordan murmured.

"Crazy," came a little voice from around his feet.

Jordan looked down at Mason, who had started to climb up his leg.

"Did you just call daddy crazy?" He scooped his son up and sat his cushy bottom on the table. "What do you say we finally pick out that Christmas tree before Grandma Nancy comes over and murders Daddy, huh?" He tickled the pudgy rolls underneath Mason's chin. "You think you're up for that?"

"Crazy," Mason said.

"Great." Jordan groaned, then laughed. "Of all the words you could have picked up on, that's the one you go with?"

They went through the ten minutes of torture also known as dressing Mason for the cold. The temperature had dropped overnight, so Jordan broke out the heavier coats, along with scarves, gloves and an extra hat for Mason. When he strapped him into his safety seat, the only things visible were his eyes. The poor kid was going to bake under all those layers.

He'd put off buying the tree because it would just be an extra bother, but the more he thought about it, the more he began to look forward to bringing a little Christmas cheer into the house. It was a tradition that he wanted his son to have, memories he wanted him to cherish years from now.

Jordan tried to be mindful of spoiling Mason too much. He'd attended high school with a number of friends who were products of divorce. They had made manipulating their guilt-ridden parents an art form. Jordan never wanted to create that sense of entitlement in Mason, but giving his son the kind of Christmas he had enjoyed as a child wasn't spoiling him.

He remembered his mother's warning from a couple of days ago about trimming the low-hanging tree limbs so that Mason couldn't reach them. That brought about another concern: pine needles all over the floor. He was sure he'd read somewhere that some trees were more susceptible to losing their needles than others, and with the way Mason had of putting everything in his mouth these days, he needed to make sure he bought a tree that wouldn't have dozens of dead pine needles scattered about the floor.

What in the hell did he know about picking out the safest Christmas tree?

A slow grin lifted one corner of Jordan's mouth as a thought occurred to him.

He might not know much about trees, but he knew one person who did.

He didn't give himself time to deliberate before making a U-turn and heading toward Wintersage's main business district. As he drove toward the yellow-and-white Victorian that housed the Silk Sisters, Jordan tried to discredit the sudden quickening of his pulse. And the reason for it.

He wanted Vicki's expertise. She worked with this stuff for a living. She could give him advice on the safest tree, the one that would last the longest, maybe even the one that would look the best in his great room. That was all he wanted here—a little advice.

She's going to see right through you.

Yet he stayed on the same trajectory, because it didn't matter if she didn't buy his flimsy excuse. He hadn't been able to get her off his mind since she'd left his house Tuesday night. Scratch that, since Sandra's wedding.

Jordan still couldn't pinpoint exactly what it was that had changed about her that had him so intrigued. It couldn't be just because of her new look, could it? He wasn't *that* damn shallow, was he?

But what else could it be?

He had always viewed Vicki as just one of Sandra's friends. He definitely had never looked at her with romantic interest. But Jordan couldn't deny the current of electricity that had shot through him when he'd first seen her standing on the beach at Sandra's wedding.

A slow burn started low in his belly.

He could recall with incredible clarity the way his breath had caught in his throat. She'd stolen the air from his lungs, and turned the heads of more than a few of the single men at the reception. The fact that he had even noticed the attention that other men had paid to her that night should have been the first clue that something had changed.

He just didn't get it. Vicki Ahlfors wasn't his type. She was restrained and demure, while he tended to gravitate toward sassy and vivacious.

Jordan huffed out a sardonic laugh. His experience with Allison should have taught him something about his "type" and the trouble that it could lead to. The more he thought about it, the more he realized that he'd never had much luck with his usual type. Once the shine wore off, he found that he wasn't all that attracted to what was underneath.

Still, was Vicki the kind of woman he could see himself getting involved with?

"Hell yes," Jordan whispered to himself. If the excitement skittering across his skin just at the thought of seeing her again was any indication, hell *yes* he could see Vicki becoming much more than just a friend of his sister's.

The question was did *she* see *him* that way?

Jordan refused to believe he was the only one who'd felt the electricity that had sparked between them Tuesday night. He'd seen it in the way she'd looked at him, in the way her breath had caught. There had been interest in those beautiful brown eyes. Maybe she would be willing to see if there was anything more to the awareness that had ignited in those moments just before she'd left his house.

Jordan's chest tightened as he contemplated whether or not *he* was really ready to take that momentous step.

He sure as hell wasn't going to go the rest of his life without a woman. He loved women too much. He cherished the feeling of waking up with a soft, warm body snuggled up next to him. Relished the simple pleasures of sharing his life with another human being.

But Jordan would be the first to admit that his ex-wife had done a number on him. After the whirlwind that had been his love affair with Allison and the heartache she'd caused when she walked out on him and Mason, the thought of allowing another woman to get that close, of trusting another woman not to hurt both him and his son, was something he just didn't know if he could do.

The image of Vicki's sweet, subtle smile flashed before him, and the tightness in his chest eased ever so slightly.

Something about this felt right. Whether it was because of the way she treated Mason, or something deeper, he couldn't say yet, but Jordan had the suspicion that if he didn't explore these new feelings he would regret it.

He pulled up to the Victorian, unstrapped Mason from his car seat and started up the stairs. Even though clients were in and out of the Victorian all the time, he still knocked on the front door before walking in.

Vicki was in the front parlor, straightening a bow on the massive Christmas wreath that hung above the fireplace.

"Hi there, you two," she greeted.

If he was a betting man, Jordan would put his money on Mason being the reason her face lit up the way it did. But it felt damn good to pretend it was because she was happy to see him.

She hurried over to them and took Mason from his arms.

Yeah, that was what he'd figured.

Vicki tickled Mason's chin. He responded with that smile made to melt hearts. His son was such a flirt.

"Sandra isn't here," she said. "She had to meet with a client in Portsmouth."

"I'm not here to see Sandra. Actually, I'm here to see you."

Her pretty brown eyes widened. "Me?"

"Mason and I are going shopping for a Christmas tree. I figured I should probably get one." There was no need to mention that it was initially his mother's idea. "I was hoping you could give me some advice on the type of tree I should get. I don't want one that will shed pine needles. He loves putting things in his mouth."

"I noticed that Tuesday night," she said as she grinned

down at Mason. "When it comes to picking out a tree, it's more about how you maintain it than the particular variety. Needle retention is better in some, but honestly, as long as you keep it properly watered, any tree you get should keep its needles well past Christmas."

"Ah. Okay," Jordan said.

Her brow dipped in a curious frown. "Was that the only thing you needed?"

It suddenly occurred to him that if he'd wanted her to think he was just seeking advice, a simple phone call would have sufficed. Which made his trip here even *more* transparent.

Which begged the question, why was he being vague?

Over the past week, if his mind wasn't occupied with Mason or the election, he was thinking about Vicki. The more he thought about it, the more he realized that thoughts of Vicki had usurped the election.

What he felt for her was real. He wanted this. He wanted *her.*

And if he was going to do this—if he was really going to pursue Vicki, then he needed to *do* this. No more skirting around the issue.

"Actually," Jordan began, "I was…uh… I was thinking that maybe—if you have time, that is—that you'd like to come with us? If you have the time."

Well, that was as smooth as a porcupine's ass.

When had he become so inept at asking a pretty girl out? He wasn't even asking her *out* out just yet; he was only asking her to help him pick a Christmas tree, for crying out loud. How was he going to ask her out on a genuine date if he couldn't do something this simple?

"I know it's still pretty early." He glanced at his

watch. It was just after two in the afternoon. "I understand if you can't leave your flower shop just yet."

A delicate smile drew across Vicki's lips. Either she went for bumbling idiots, or she was laughing at him. Maybe both.

"You're inviting me to go tree shopping?" she asked.

"I'd appreciate an expert's opinion." He shook his head and blew out a frustrated breath. "That's not true," he said. "At least that's not the only reason."

He shifted from one foot to the other like a nervous schoolboy, which put the final stamp on this humiliating episode.

Dammit, enough of this!

It had been a while since he'd approached a woman, but he wasn't completely out of his element. Not to brag, but he'd won a few hearts in the past. He could do this.

"Look, Vicki. The truth is I really enjoyed hanging out with you the other night. Even though I slept most of your visit, the brief time I *was* awake it was nice to talk to someone—another adult who isn't my mom or Sandra or someone involved with the election."

He gestured to the topiary adorned in glittering gold-and-red foil ribbon.

"You're really into all this Christmas decorating and floral-design stuff, so I thought you'd enjoy tree shopping." He paused for a moment. "Now that I think about it, it was pretty presumptuous to assume that you'd just drop everything to help me pick out a Christmas tree. Maybe I'll come over another time, when you're not busy. I'll let you get back to what you were doing."

Feeling like an ass, he lifted Mason from her arms and started for the door.

"Jordan?" He looked back to find her staring at him, an amused expression edging up the corners of her lips.

"I would love to go Christmas tree shopping with the two of you."

His eyes widened. "Really?" Maybe she *did* go for bumbling idiots.

She nodded. "Yes, really. Give me a few minutes to lock up, and we can go."

Jordan tried to stop the huge smile from spreading across his face, but that wasn't going to happen. He would probably smile like this for the rest of the night.

Chapter 5

Vicki cursed the nervous energy shooting through her bloodstream and the stupid butterflies fluttering around her idiot stomach. But how in the heck was she supposed to control them when Jordan Woolcott was in the parlor—not waiting to see Sandra, but to see *her?*

"Calm down," Vicki cautioned herself. Apparently, she was in need of a little refresher history lesson.

How long had she pined for this man?

For years, Jordan had never bothered to look her way. Yet all of a sudden, he was showing interest. What made him any different than the dozen men who'd strolled into Petals this week with a newfound appreciation for fresh flowers?

Because this was Jordan.

As much as she wanted to make him work for her attention, she just couldn't play hard to get when it came to Jordan. Because he was the one she'd always wanted.

Vicki's chest tightened with anticipation at the thought of him finally wanting her in the same way she wanted him.

She'd sensed a change in the air. Something about the way he'd looked at her on Tuesday, as if he was seeing her for the first time. She'd tried to disregard it, too afraid she was looking for something that wasn't really there. But the look in his eyes as he'd so adorably fumbled his way through that invitation to go tree shopping confirmed what she thought she'd seen before leaving his house the other night.

She paused for a moment and inhaled a deep, calming breath. She didn't want to get ahead of herself. It wasn't as if she was the best at reading men; she didn't want to think how foolish she would feel if she'd misjudged his intentions.

Vicki lifted her purse and coat from the coatrack and then shut down her computer. Just as she started for the foyer, the phone rang. She almost let it go to voice mail, but remembered that she was expecting a call from a fellow florist in Durham who possibly wanted to go in on a huge decorating job in Boston.

"Petals," she answered. "This is Vicki. How may I help you?"

"Ms. Ahlfors, this is Robin Tooney with the Wintersage Holiday Extravaganza Day Parade."

Her heart instantly started to thump a million times faster against the walls of her chest.

"Yes. Hello," Vicki stammered.

"Ms. Ahlfors, the committee has made its decision on the submissions that were entered for this year's competition." Vicki's heart jumped right up into her throat. "It is my pleasure to inform you that you've been granted a float in this year's parade. Congratulations."

"Oh, my," she whispered. Her capacity to think evaporated, but she quickly pulled herself together. "I'm stunned, and thrilled, of course. Thank you so much."

"The committee was completely charmed by your idea of Christmas celebrations from around the world. I know you've had a hand in creating several floats for other participants in the past. I can't wait to see what you create for your own."

"I'm looking forward to showing you. Thank you again."

Robin Tooney instructed her on where to find the newly updated guidelines for float building on the committee's website and filled her in on the deadline information.

After ending the call, Vicki just stood there for a moment in stunned disbelief. Then she threw her fists in the air and yelped.

"*Yes!* Yes! Yes! Yes!"

"I don't mean to pry, but I'm assuming you just received some good news?"

She whipped around to find Jordan standing in the arched entryway that led to Petals's retail area. Heat instantly flooded her cheeks, but she was too excited to try hiding her embarrassment.

His brow arched. "So?"

"I got in," Vicki said with a breathless laugh. "I can't believe I got in."

"In where?"

She pointed to the phone. "That was the head of the float committee for the Wintersage Holiday Extravaganza Day Parade. I submitted an idea for a float, and it was accepted! After providing flowers for dozens of other floats over the years, for the first time Petals will have its own in the parade."

"That's wonderful, Vicki. The Christmas parade is a pretty big deal. But that's also a pretty big undertaking, isn't it?"

"It is, but I think I can do it," Vicki said. She shook her head. "No, I *know* I can do it."

Wintersage Holiday Extravaganza Day had grown into a region-wide event, reaching far beyond the boundaries of their small New England town. And the parade had become the focal point of the entire day. Businesses from several cities stretching along the coast, and as far inland as Lowell, used the opportunity to promote their brands.

As the floats had grown more elaborate over the past several years, larger floral-design shops had begun courting the businesses. A number of those larger shops had managed to steal away several of her customers. One of her previous clients, a marina that catered to Wintersage's elite, had the audacity to take the design Vicki had created for them and bring it to a competing florist to actually produce the float.

And, like the pushover she *used* to be, she'd allowed it.

Not anymore. The new Vicki was not going to quietly sit back while others took all the glory. This year she had something to prove.

When her float took to the streets of Wintersage and held its own against the stiff competition she was sure to face, her family would be forced to see her as the serious, career-minded entrepreneur that she was, and not the owner of just a "little flower shop."

A mischievous grin spread across her lips. "I'm really going to do this," she said. "I'm going to put Petals on the map. I really, *really* wanted to get in. It feels amazing."

"You need to celebrate," Jordan said.

"Yes, I do. Luckily for you, Christmas tree shopping is exactly the kind of thing a florist does to celebrate." She sent him a cheeky wink. "Let's go."

Vicki was stunned at her own audaciousness, but she didn't care. She was much too giddy over the news she'd just received to feel self-conscious.

It didn't make sense to take separate cars, so she joined Jordan in his. As she sat ensconced in the supple leather seat, she closed her eyes and pulled in a healthy whiff of his scent. There was something about the combination of sandalwood and a man's unique essence that drove her crazy.

Of course, when that man was Jordan Woolcott, the sandalwood was optional. He drove her crazy merely by existing—always had.

"Have you thought about a theme for your float?" Jordan asked.

"Christmas from Around the World. I got the idea from my favorite ornament from when I was a little girl. It has Santa Claus dressed in traditional garb from various cultures around the globe. My mom used to tell me that Santa's clothes would magically change as the reindeer flew him to different countries."

He grinned. "And you believed that, huh?"

"I was five, of course I believed it."

"Do you still have the ornament?"

She nodded. "I've kept all of my ornaments. I buy a new one every year to add to the collection."

"So what's this year's?"

"I haven't gotten one yet." She stared out the window at the myriad boats hugging the harbor's shoreline. "I always try to find an ornament that reflects something significant that happened during the previous year. Maybe I'll find something to commemorate all the changes that have happened over the past couple of months." She looked over at him. "This is turning out to be a year that I'll want to remember for a long time to come."

"I know what you mean," he said in a quiet voice. "It's been memorable in more ways than one."

There it was again, that flicker of awareness she'd felt the other night. It started with a spark that turned into a slow burn, humming in the air around them.

"Do you have any Christmas traditions from when you were a little boy that you plan to pass on to Mason?" she asked.

He shrugged the shoulder closest to her. "Just being with family. That's always been at the core of the Woolcotts' holidays. Although I do like the idea of an ornament collection," he said. "Maybe I should start one for him."

Vicki looked over her shoulder at the baby. He was engrossed in a colorful plastic centipede with antennae that rattled.

"You should," she said. "He'll cherish them for the rest of his life."

She twisted back in her seat and caught Jordan staring at her, his gaze probing, penetrating. Once again, the air pulsed with energy, a tangible force that provoked all manner of interesting ideas to blossom in her head.

"You, uh, should probably pay attention to the road," Vicki said.

"Oh," Jordan said, quickly turning his head forward.

The flutter that had previously traveled around her belly returned with a vengeance. The awareness that had been a faint suggestion just a few moments earlier now saturated the air around them, flooding the space with a potent mix of something Vicki couldn't quite describe.

She'd thought about the spark of desire that had flashed between them Tuesday night at least a million times over the past couple of days, trying to decide whether it was real or just a figment of her wishful imagination. But she had not imagined the look in Jordan's eyes just a few moments ago, when his piercing gaze had captured hers and held it. He'd looked at her as if he was seeing the real her for the first time.

There was just one problem: she had yet to decide if this really *was* the real her.

As much as she loved her new wardrobe and haircut, she was still the same Vicki Ahlfors she'd always been on the inside. Quiet, sensible, reliable Vicki. How could she be sure Jordan was interested in more than just the aesthetics?

They arrived at a parking lot jam-packed with cars as the residents of Wintersage and its surrounding towns scoped out Christmas trees. Vicki unstrapped Mason from his car seat and waited while Jordan unfolded the stroller he'd just taken out of the trunk. The minute she tried to sit him in the stroller, Mason started to wail.

"I don't know what's up with him today," Jordan said. He took the baby from her and held him over his shoulder, patting him gently on the back. "Something has him fussier than usual. Hopefully the walk will calm him down."

They started for the entrance to the tree lot. Vicki pushed the empty stroller, just in case they were able to cajole Mason into sitting in it a bit later.

"Is this the only tree lot around?" Jordan remarked. "This place is packed."

"It's definitely the biggest for several counties," she

said. "And they have the widest selection. Let's just hope people haven't picked over all the good ones."

Vicki felt a familiar excitement building as they traveled along the rows of freshly cut trees. Christmas carols floated from speakers nestled throughout the vast lot, and the scent of pine and evergreen hung in the air. It encompassed everything she loved about this time of the year.

She was having a hard time keeping her active imagination at bay. It was all too easy to let her mind wander into the cozy yet dangerous territory of this being the real thing. She, Jordan and Mason strolling through the crowd of other young families made her long for things that were not a guarantee.

After contemplating several choices, they chose a balsam fir because of the low maintenance and its tendency to retain its needles.

After Jordan paid for the tree and for home delivery, he turned to her and said, "That was relatively painless. Now I guess the next thing I need to do is get some ornaments."

"You don't have ornaments from last year?"

"I wasn't really in the spirit last year," he said.

"Oh, right," Vicki said, feeling a bit like an idiot. His ex-wife had just left him to raise their young baby on his own around Christmastime last year. That would take the holiday spirit out of anyone.

"To be honest, this will be my first time putting up a tree," Jordan said.

Vicki's mouth fell open in horrified shock.

"Hey." His palms shot up in mock surrender. "I didn't kill an elf or anything. Not everyone gets into the whole stocking-and-tree rigmarole. My mom has always done more than enough at Christmas to make up for my lack of decorating." He shrugged. "I just never found it necessary."

"Well, you do realize that's changed now, right?"

He looked down at Mason, who had finally allowed Jordan to put him into his stroller about ten minutes ago.

"Yes. Like so many other things, he's changed the way I celebrate the holidays. He's changed everything."

"For the better," Vicki said.

"Absolutely," he said, his eyes still focused on his son.

Once they were in the car again, they headed back toward Wintersage.

"The guy at the lot said they would have the tree delivered no later than six o'clock. That will give me time to bring you back to the Victorian." He looked over at her. "Unless you want to help pick out some ornaments?"

His tone, the look in his eyes, the way his voice dipped ever so slightly... It all gave her the impression that his question was more than just an invitation to go ornament shopping.

"I don't think you need help picking out ornaments," Vicki said. "But if you don't mind the company, I would love to join you."

"You're right. Your decorating expertise isn't exactly what I'm interested in." His hands tightened on the steering wheel. "This is new territory for me, Vicki."

Her heart started to pound in her chest.

"What's new territory?" she asked.

"This uncertainty, the awkwardness." He blew out a heavy breath. "I'm not used to questioning myself— questioning my feelings—and that's all I've done since Tuesday night." He paused, and then he looked over at her, his eyes full of intent. "I don't want to question it anymore."

The pounding intensified, to the point that she thought her heart would burst right out of her chest.

"I'm enjoying your company," he continued. "And you can tell me if I'm way off base here, but I get the feeling you're enjoying this, too."

She swallowed deeply, then shook her head. "You're not off base," she managed to get out.

The slow smile that drew across his lips sent a swarm of tingles skittering along Vicki's spine.

"Then what do you say we do a little ornament shopping?" Jordan said.

As they browsed the department store shelves stacked high with glittering hanging ornaments, fake fur-trimmed stockings and tree toppers, Vicki came to her most shocking realization of the night.

Jordan Woolcott was utterly charming. *And* funny.

To hear Sandra talk about her brother, one would think he was an oaf with zero personality. *He's an attorney,* Sandra would always say, as if that explained it all.

But Jordan had no problem making a fool of himself in the middle of a crowded store, especially when it came to trying to get Mason to laugh. He grabbed a Santa hat from the shelf and plopped it atop his head. He put on a plastic Rudolph the Red-Nosed Reindeer nose that blinked like a beacon, then did an awful rendition of the beloved Christmas song, mixing up the words and skipping some lines entirely.

Vicki laughed until her eyes watered, but Mason's crabbiness only grew.

Jordan's shoulders sagged with defeat. "I don't know what's wrong with him. He woke up irritable and it's just gotten worse as the day's gone on."

Frowning, Vicki took the baby out of the stroller and pressed her lips to his forehead. "He's a little warm, but I can't tell if it's a fever. You wouldn't happen to carry his thermometer in his diaper bag, would you?"

He shook his head. "It's at the house, but I can get one from the pharmacy department."

"Do it. It doesn't hurt to have a spare, especially at his age. I'm going to bring him to the car and away from all this noise."

Jordan gave her the keys before going off in search of a thermometer. Less than ten minutes later, Vicki spotted him exiting the store's sliding doors, both hands burdened by several bags. He walked up to the passenger side and handed her a bag through the window.

"Can you open this up while I put these in the trunk?"

She hadn't bothered to put Mason in his car seat, so the task of opening the ear thermometer's hard plastic packaging wasn't the easiest. By the time she got it open, Jordan had slid behind the wheel. Vicki held the squirming baby in her arms as Jordan placed the thermometer in his ear. A second later it beeped.

"Ninety-nine point one," he said, looking at the readout.

"That's not bad as far as fevers go, but apparently that's enough to make him irritable," Vicki said. "Do you have a fever reducer at home, or do you need to go back in and get one?"

"I have some at home from the summer cold he caught back in August."

"I remember when he had that cold," Vicki said, pressing a kiss to the side of Mason's head. "I think he'll be okay in a bit, once we get a little medicine in him."

Jordan got out of the car and came around to her side.

"Let me get him strapped into his car seat, then we can get out of this cold."

He drove Vicki to the Victorian so she could pick up her car, but she insisted on following him back to his place to make sure all was well with Mason. When they arrived at his house, a Christmas tree wrapped in blue netting was leaning against the front door.

The tree, along with all of the ornaments, remained exactly where they were until after Jordan had given Mason some cherry-flavored syrup. Vicki carried Mason over to the sofa in the great room and watched while Jordan carted the bags of ornaments into the house.

Cuddling Mason to her chest, she folded her legs beneath her and pulled an afghan over the both of them. A satisfied sigh escaped her lips as she relished in the feel of the baby's soft weight against her, so close to her heart. She murmured a soothing lullaby into Mason's ear as she watched Jordan bring in the stand that had also been delivered with the tree. He set it up in the corner of the great room, and then he walked over to where she sat.

"Vicki, I don't want to keep you here any longer than you need to be," he said. "I'll hold Mason until he falls asleep, then I'll finish getting the tree up."

"Jordan?"

"Yeah?"

"Get the tree," she said.

His forehead creased in a frown. "Vicki, you don't have—"

"As someone whose job calls on you to read people for a living, you should be able to tell that I am perfectly content right where I am."

"Are you sure?" he asked.

"I'm sure, Jordan." With a brazenness the old Vicki never would have even contemplated displaying, she finished, "I can't think of anywhere else I would rather be right now."

That surge of electricity, the one she'd felt before leaving here Tuesday night, pulsed between them again.

"I can't think of anyone else I would want to be here," Jordan said in a voice so soft she could barely hear it, as if the admission both surprised and thrilled him as much as it surprised and thrilled her.

His eyes slid closed and he dropped his head, releasing a weary breath. He brought a hand up to massage the back of his neck before lifting his head and looking at her.

"What's happening here?" he asked.

"You tell me, Jordan."

She knew he was questioning his feelings again. She could tell by the confusion clouding his face.

He held his hands out, as if in a plea for her to understand. "I know what I'm feeling," he said. "I just don't know what to do about it. I don't want to give you mixed signals."

"Good, because I don't want them."

"I just need…" He shook his head again. "Can I take some time to figure this out? I feel what's happening, but I need to be sure."

"This doesn't have to be complicated, Jordan."

"That's the thing. From here on out, it will always be complicated."

Now it was her turn to look confused.

Before she could question him, he continued, "I accepted months ago that the choice to bring another woman into my life will never be an easy one. I'm more cautious now than I've ever been in the past. I have to be. I have Mason to consider." He put a hand up before she could say anything. "I'm not suggesting that you would ever treat Mason unfairly in any way. The way you are with my son, the care you take with him, I can't tell you how much that means to me, Vicki."

He paused for a moment. "But it's hard for me to drop my guard where he's concerned. His own mother refuses to put him first. I have to make sure I'm with someone who will."

"What makes you think I wouldn't?" she asked.

"I know you would," Jordan said. He shook his head. "But I still can't help but feel cautious when it comes to him."

"Here's the thing, Jordan." With the hand that wasn't cradling Mason, she reached out and captured his wrist. "Whether or not you decide that you have romantic feelings for me, I would still do exactly what I've been doing as far as Mason is concerned. This little guy wormed his way into my heart from his very first visit to the Silk Sisters." She paused for a moment before continuing in a softer voice. "But it's my heart that I'm thinking about right now. I don't want to be hurt."

"I won't hurt you. But I'll be honest. This scares me, Vicki. I trusted my heart the last time, and look what happened."

"Don't make me pay for her mistakes," Vicki said. "I'm nothing like Allison."

"No, you're not. I know that. But you also said you weren't looking for casual, that you want serious. A part of me thinks I'm ready, but another part—"

"I have an idea," Vicki said, cutting him off. Nothing good could come of him continuing to overanalyze his feelings like this. "Why don't we just enjoy the time-honored tradition of putting up a Christmas tree? We can think about casual versus serious and just what all of that means later." She pressed a kiss to Mason's soft head, then looked up at Jordan. "Right now, I just want to enjoy this time with you and Mason."

He shook his head, a grateful smile spreading across his face. "You have to be the most understanding woman I know," he said. "I promise I'm going to figure this out—"

"Jordan, get the tree."

He smiled again, then nodded. "I'll get the tree."

Chapter 6

The moment Jordan left the room, Vicki exhaled the unsteady breath she'd been holding in. Not too long ago, she would have shied away from what was happening between them, too afraid to take a chance.

But things were different now. *She* was different. She was no longer willing to sit on her feelings. She was putting it all out there, and whatever happened, happened.

Vicki didn't even try to hide her amusement as Jordan struggled to get the eight-foot tree through the door. Back at the tree lot, she'd told him that he would be just fine with a small five-footer, but he had proclaimed that if he was going to get a tree, it would be a *real* tree.

He set it up in the corner of the great room and filled the stand with water, then turned to her. "This feels more significant than I thought it would," he said.

"Having a tree?"

He nodded. "It's yet another of those milestones,

you know? House, kid, Christmas tree. I'm gradually moving into this new phase of my life. At one time it scared me, but I'm beginning to realize that I've been ready for this for a long time now. I'm enjoying all of these new experiences."

She had been insanely attracted to him well before fatherhood had turned him into this insightful person who actually took the time to appreciate something as simple as decorating for the holidays. To see him embracing life's simple pleasures made him a thousand times sexier.

He clapped his hands together. "Now that I have the tree, I guess it's time to put stuff on it." He reached over and lifted Mason from her arms. "Let's see if my little man is feeling well enough to help out."

Vicki looked on as Jordan showed Mason how to hang the ornaments. Her chest swelled with emotion every time he put his hand up for a high five and Mason responded with an awkward little slap of his palm. This was all beginning to feel too domestic for her own good.

Instead of shying away from it in an attempt to shield her heart—just in case Jordan decided he really didn't feel the same way about her as she felt about him—Vicki decided to hold on tighter. She would enjoy this while she had the chance and deal with the consequences later.

"You know what this calls for?" she said, pushing up from the sofa. "Hot chocolate."

"That sounds great," he said.

"Will I find everything I need in the kitchen?"

He nodded and she turned toward the kitchen.

Vicki felt his eyes on her, following her as she walked out of the great room. Once in the kitchen, she had to brace herself on the counter and catch her breath. She was still getting used to dealing with the consequences of this new Vicki's boldness. Inviting herself into a man's kitchen to make hot chocolate was something she never would have done before.

A smile drew across her face.

She liked this new Vicki a hell of a lot more than the old one.

She searched around for the things she needed, grimacing when all she found was a box of instant hot chocolate mix. She should have known a man who had never bothered to put up a Christmas tree wouldn't have the real stuff. She was able to doctor it up with vanilla extract and cinnamon sticks; both were surprise findings in the pantry.

She carried two mugs of hot chocolate back into the great room, but stopped short when she discovered Jordan taking the ornaments off the tree. Mason sat on the floor a few yards away, playing with the packaging the glittery reindeer ornaments had come in.

"What happened?" Vicki asked.

Jordan looked over at her and gave her a chastising frown laced with humor. "I would have expected better advice from a person who does this for a living," he said.

Vicki lifted her shoulders in question, unsure what he was talking about.

His hands burdened with ornaments, he nodded toward the coffee table.

Her head flew back with a laugh when she spotted the boxes of Christmas lights. "Ah, yes. The lights go on first."

"I realized that after we'd already put about twenty ornaments on the tree."

"Well, why don't you sit and have some hot chocolate while I hang the lights? Then you and Mason can do the fun part."

Their fingers touched when she handed him the mug, setting off a torrent of tingles up and down her arms. Jordan undoubtedly felt it, too. Their eyes held over the steaming mug and Vicki's inner muscles pulled tight with need.

He set the mug on the coffee table, then lowered himself on the floor next to Mason, who remained mesmerized by the array of shiny plastic ornaments.

Vicki did her best not to feel self-conscious as she walked around the Christmas tree, stringing the lights on its full branches. She couldn't help but be hyperaware of every move she made, because Jordan's eyes remained on her the entire time.

"How did your interest in floral design come about?" he finally asked after some time had passed. "I doubt that was one of the majors offered at Nillson."

"No, it wasn't," she said with a laugh. "I majored in art history."

"So you've always had this artistic side?"

"I can't draw to save my life. Not like Sandra, for sure. But there is a certain artistry to floral design. It's all art, I just happen to create my pictures with flowers."

"According to Sandra, your 'art' has acquired a number of new admirers."

Vicki could tell by the inflection in his voice that he was fishing for information about those new admirers, but she wasn't taking the bait. Instead, she kept their conversation lighthearted.

"Don't get me started on Sandra. She and Janelle have had their share of fun at my expense this past week. However, they've been so supportive of my plans to participate in the float competition that I've pretty much forgiven them both."

The glint in his eyes told her that he saw right through her subject dodging. Thankfully, he didn't press her.

"It's unbelievable that you all have remained such great friends," Jordan said. "It must be comforting knowing you always have someone you can count on."

The envy in his voice caused a bit of sadness to tug at her heart. "You have people you can count on, Jordan."

"I know I do. But I also know that I've made a few enemies lately."

"If you're talking about the election—"

He held up a hand. "If you don't mind, I'd rather not get into all of that. Not tonight. I'm decorating my family's Christmas tree," he said, running a hand over Mason's smooth hair. "I want to enjoy this." He looked up at her. "Having you here with us is going a long way in making tonight special, Vicki. Thanks for sticking around."

"I said it before, but I guess it bears repeating. There is nowhere else I'd rather be right now, Jordan."

They shared a smile before Vicki went back to stringing the lights on the tree. As she continued to thread the multicolored lights through the branches, she wondered if she'd eventually convince Jordan to trust her, not just with Mason, but also with his heart.

She understood his hesitancy. At the height of Allison's treachery, a fair amount of the conversations over Monday-night dinner at the Quarterdeck had centered on the debacle between Jordan and his ex-wife. Sandra had kept Vicki and Janelle abreast of his ordeal and the toll it seemed to take on Jordan.

Suppressing her reaction to the demise of Jordan's marriage became harder and harder with every story

Sandra shared. She hadn't wanted to appear overly interested. Even though Sandra and Janelle were the closest things she had to sisters, Vicki had kept her feelings for Jordan hidden from her two best friends.

If even half of what Sandra had claimed Allison had put him through was true, Vicki couldn't blame Jordan for being gun-shy, but she had to think about herself, as well. She knew what she wanted out of life. As she caught glimpses of Jordan and Mason playing on the floor, she couldn't help but think of how much the scene resembled everything she'd fantasized about for herself.

If she dwelled too long on just how close it was within her grasp, yet how far, it would crush her mood. Tonight was about living in the moment and enjoying it for as long as she could.

Jordan tried to get Mason to resume their decorating duties, but the little boy was more interested in the cylindrical container the Christmas balls had come in than actually putting the balls on the tree. When it was time to place the pointy star on the very top of the tree, Jordan grabbed a two-step ladder from the utility closet and held it steady while Vicki climbed. After a brief wobble, she positioned the star in the place of honor.

"There," she said. "That looks pretty perfect to me."

"I agree," Jordan said.

She glanced over her shoulder and realized he wasn't looking at the tree.

"I was talking about the star," she said.

He lifted his eyes from her backside, a slight, sexy grin tipping up the corners of his lips. "Yeah, that, too."

As she gingerly climbed down from the stepladder, acutely aware of Jordan's eyes still on her, Vicki just knew her cheeks were flaming red.

"Where are the stocking hangers?" she asked once she was off the ladder.

That grin still on his lips, Jordan reached into one of the shopping bags and retrieved the hangers. He handed them to her, deliberately brushing his fingers over her palm.

"Do you remember what I said about needing time to figure this all out in my head?" he asked. Vicki nodded. "It's taking me a lot less time than I thought it would."

His words sent a rush of pleasure shooting through her veins, but she refused to allow herself to be over-whelmed by it. Despite how long she'd wished for this very thing, she knew she needed to be careful. Jordan was still "figuring this all out." Meanwhile, her heart was in this—had been in this for far longer than he knew.

She walked over to the fireplace and placed the brass-plated stocking hangers between framed pictures of Mason. Vicki refused to acknowledge the envy that streaked through her at the sight of Jordan's ex-wife holding an infant Mason in her arms. Allison was all smiles, yet judging by Mason's size, she had left Jordan and her new son only weeks after this photo was taken. Vicki still didn't understand how the woman could do such a thing.

But, in the most selfish way, she was happy Allison had. Because the thought of Allison here tonight, sharing in this wonderful evening with Jordan and Mason, made Vicki sick to her stomach.

"Let me see if he'll at least hang up his own stocking," Jordan said, going over to the couch where Mason now lay with his toy centipede clutched to his chest.

Jordan picked the baby up and frowned.

"Something wrong?" Vicki asked.

He touched Mason's forehead with the back of his hand and his frown deepened. "He seems warmer than he was even before I gave him the fever reducer."

Vicki quickly made her way to his side and pressed her lips to the baby's forehead. "His fever has definitely spiked," she said, gingerly lifting the baby from Jordan's arms. "Get the thermometer."

Jordan was gone before she finished the statement. He came back seconds later with the thermometer and stuck the instrument in Mason's ear.

The readout said 103.4.

Vicki's eyes shot to Jordan's. "That's a dangerous number. We need to get him to the doctor."

They quickly bundled Mason into his outerwear and were out of the house in less than three minutes. Jordan's thumbs tapped nervously on the steering wheel as he tested the speed limit of Wintersage's roadways.

Vicki reached over and covered his forearm.

"It'll be okay," she said.

He looked over at her, but he didn't respond—only nodded.

Less than ten minutes after leaving the house, they pulled into Wintersage Urgent Care. The twenty-four-hour medical clinic that had recently opened was closer than the area hospital. Their wait was brief but agonizing. Vicki could see Jordan's anxiety increasing with every second that passed. Mason, on the other hand, was quiet. Despite his high fever, his fussiness from earlier in the day had actually dissipated.

Once in the exam room, Vicki stood next to Jordan while the young doctor assessed Mason. She didn't even hesitate before taking his hand and threading her fingers through his. He looked down at their clasped hands and gave hers a squeeze. His grateful expression, mixed with the underlying worry over Mason, tugged at her heart.

"Just as I expected," the doctor said, wrapping the stethoscope around her neck. "This little one is cutting a few new teeth. He must be a late bloomer."

"He only got his first teeth a few months ago," Jordan said.

"It happens. Anywhere from six to sixteen months is normal. However, he also has an ear infection. Have you noticed him pulling on his ear or favoring his right side lately?"

"He's been doing that for the past few days," Jordan said.

Vicki nodded. She'd noticed it Tuesday night. She couldn't believe she hadn't picked up on that.

"They're prone to ear infections at this age," the doctor said. "I'm going to give you some drops. They won't be easy to administer, especially to a baby Mason's age. One of you will probably have to hold him down while the other inserts the drops, but it should all clear up in a few days."

"So that's it?" Jordan asked.

"That's it." The doctor nodded. "It looks as if those teeth will break through any day now. He'll be back to normal soon."

"Thank you," Jordan said. Vicki detected the faint catch in his voice and her heart swelled with empathy. The minute the doctor vacated the room, Jordan slumped back against the exam table, his entire body sagging with relief.

"Jordan, he's okay," she said in a soft voice.

He blew out a weary breath and ran both palms down his face.

"This is never going to get easier, is it?" Vicki saw

his throat move as he tried to swallow. "When he was eight months old he rolled off the bed and hit the back of his head on the hardwood floor. I rushed him to the E.R. Nothing came of it, just a little bump that went down in a couple of days." He looked over at her, his eyes filled with worry and pain. "I thought I was going to die when that happened. I felt the same way tonight." He shook his head. "I'm never going to not worry about the next time he bumps his head, or gets an ear infection, or any of that stuff, will I? This will never get easier."

"It won't," she said in a hushed tone. "But he's worth it."

"Yes, he is." Jordan looked down at the baby, who was now sleeping in Vicki's arms. "There is nothing in my world worth more than him."

Her heart pinched at the love in his voice. What she wouldn't give to become a part of that world, a world where Jordan and Mason were both a part of her everyday existence.

The old Vicki wouldn't dare to dream of it. As for this new version of herself that was slowly starting to emerge, the fantasy didn't seem out of reach.

Once in the car, Jordan slid into the driver's seat, but he didn't turn over the ignition. His hands gripping the steering wheel, he released another of those exhausted breaths and let his head fall forward.

"He's okay, Jordan," Vicki said.

He raised his head and aimed his eyes at the brick urgent-care building. In a voice that was terribly soft and filled with emotion, he said, "Thank you for being here with me, Vicki."

"You're welcome," she answered, her voice equally soft.

"I've never been a fan of the double standard that

says that women should be the automatic caregivers. If Allison had even bothered to ask for custody, I would have fought her on it. Being a single father isn't easy, but I know I'm the better parent." His eyes closed briefly. "But on a night like tonight, I'm grateful that I didn't have to go through this alone."

Vicki reached over and put a comforting hand on his arm. "You're an amazing father, Jordan, and despite what you may think, you didn't need me here tonight. You would have done just fine on your own."

Finally, he looked over at her, his eyes teeming with gratitude and something else, something that warmed every inch of her skin.

"I'm happy I didn't have to," he said.

Vicki didn't know how much time passed as they continued to stare into each other's eyes. It wasn't until Mason let out a loud yawn from the backseat that they snapped out of their daze.

"I guess that's our cue." Jordan chuckled as he started the car, but before backing out of the parking space, he turned to her and said, "You wouldn't let me take you out to dinner to thank you for babysitting Tuesday night, but this time I insist."

"We can't go to dinner, Jordan. You need to get Mason home and in bed."

"I know. I was thinking something more along the lines of takeout. Between the tree shopping and the trip to urgent care, I'm starving."

"I haven't eaten anything since noon," she said, making a point of looking at the time illuminated on the dash. It was after eight o'clock.

"Since noon?" Jordan put the car in Reverse. "It's no longer a question. You, Ms. Ahlfors, are joining me for dinner."

* * *

Jordan stared at the tapered candles in the kitchen drawer, debating whether or not to take them out. Who would have thought candles could be such a big damn deal?

But they were a big deal. Candles made all the difference. Candles turned a casual meal shared between two friends into a cozy dinner shared between two people who wanted to be *more* than friends.

Was he ready to become more than just Vicki's friend?

He took out the candles.

He found a couple of Waterford crystal candleholders in the closet that housed most of his and Allison's wedding gifts. They had been married long enough to keep the gifts without feeling beholden to send them back, but not long enough to unpack at least half of the stuff they'd received.

He ran across the wedding china and considered setting the table with it, but then thought better of it. He would not subject Vicki to eating on dishes meant for Allison. He would give that china to Goodwill the first chance he got.

Jordan was setting a match to the second candlewick when Vicki emerged from the back of the house where she'd just tucked Mason into his bed.

"Is he asleep?" he asked.

"He is," she said, a surprised smile slowly stretching across her face as her eyes darted from the candles to the wine chilling in the electronic wine chiller. "I checked his temperature again and his fever is already going down."

"Hopefully he'll sleep through the night," Jordan said. He snatched the baby monitor from the counter. "But just in case he wakes up…"

She walked over to the table and trailed her finger along the rim of one of the wineglasses. "This is...nice," she finished. "Very nice."

He lifted the bottle of wine from the ice. "Are you okay with Riesling? I like my wine on the sweet side."

"Sure." Her eyes followed him as he rounded the table.

"What?" Jordan asked.

She motioned to the setup. "This is just a little more... involved than I was expecting."

He paused in the middle of pouring his wine. "Look, Vicki, if it makes you uncomfortable, you can just consider this a thank-you for being there for me tonight."

There was a questioning lift to her brow. "Is there another way to consider it?"

Time stretched between them as they stared at each other across the brief expanse of the table separating them.

Jordan measured his words before speaking. "For me, this is more than just a thank-you," he said. "I've known you for years, Vicki, but I don't *know* you."

"We ran in different circles," she pointed out. "It's not all that surprising that we've never really gotten the chance to know each other."

"How do you feel about changing that?"

The words came out on a deep, husky whisper. Jordan's chest tightened as he awaited her answer. He couldn't deny the significance of it. Her answer would tell him whether or not she was willing to give this thing he felt growing between them a chance to blossom, or if it would dwindle and die.

After several long moments passed, Vicki finally said, "I'd like that."

The relief that tore through his body was strong enough to bring Jordan to his knees.

One corner of his mouth edged up slightly. "So would I," he answered.

Once seated at the table, Jordan dished up steaming noodles and chicken satay from takeout containers. Suddenly realizing how famished they both were now that the intensity of the urgent-care visit had worn off, they dived into their meal. As tasty as the Thai food was, it was the conversation, and particularly Vicki's musical laugh, that Jordan found himself enjoying the most.

In fact, they both laughed so hard that they had to remind themselves to quiet down lest they wake Mason. Vicki told him stories of some of the antics she, his sister and Janelle had pulled back in college, some so devious that Jordan teasingly threatened to tell all of their parents, even though years had passed since the pranks. He found himself wiping tears from the corner of his eyes several times.

He stopped Vicki in the middle of the story she was currently telling.

"Wait a minute." He held both hands up. "First, who came up with the idea to put pepper in the basketball team's jockstraps, and second, how in the hell did you all pull it off?"

"It was Sandra's idea, but I'm the one who got us into the locker room. My chemistry partner was a kinesiology major, so she had access to the locker room as part of her work study."

"I never would have thought you could be so Machiavellian."

Vicki mimicked his previous pose, her palms facing him. "Keep in mind that I was always roped in. They were never my ideas."

"Doesn't seem as if you regret it," he said.

A wry grin curled the edges of her sensual lips and she shook her head. "No, I don't. Those were some really good times." She took a sip of wine and asked, "How about you? Any regrets?"

Jordan laughed, but this time it didn't hold much humor. "If I had to go through the list, we'd be here until New Year's."

"It can't be that bad," she said.

"It's definitely not all good. Alienating lifelong family friends, marrying the most selfish woman in the world." He shook his head. "I have to remind myself not to say things like that. I don't want to get in the habit of talking bad about Allison, especially in front of Mason."

"Even though she deserves it?"

"She does, but I have to own up to the part I played, too," he said. Jordan moved his plate to the side and put both elbows on the table. He studied Vicki over his folded hands, contemplating whether or not he wanted to get into the morass of misery and frustration that he always fell into when he thought about his ex-wife. He decided that he didn't.

He reached across the table and took her hand. Running his thumb back and forth over her smooth skin, he said, "I don't want to spoil our dinner with talk of Allison. This is supposed to be about us, remember?"

"And exactly what are we, Jordan?" She slipped her hand away. She matched his recent pose, placing her elbows on the table and folding her hands. She rested her chin on her clasped fingers, her face serene.

"What's behind the candles and wine? What were you hoping to accomplish when you set them out?"

"What do you mean?"

"I mean I'm not interested in playing games," she

said. She gestured to the table. "The wine, the candles... What are we doing here?"

It was not as if he hadn't expected the question. It was not as if she didn't have the right to ask it. But Jordan had been dreading it all the same. Because he'd asked himself the same question, and he still didn't have an answer.

"I'll be honest with you, Vicki. I've been asking myself that same question since you left here Tuesday night." He ran a hand down his face, then held that hand out to her in a silent plea. "It's been a long time since I've been with a woman, longer than I've ever gone. I wasn't sure if that's what was fueling my attraction to you."

Her composure slipped for a moment, her eyes growing wide with outrage. "Excuse me—"

Jordan cut her off. "I know I sound like a jerk, and maybe I am."

"Maybe?"

He reached across the table and took her hand. "The more I thought about it, the more I realized that needing a woman had nothing to do with why I'm attracted to you. Shit," he cursed. "That sounds just as insulting."

Vicki nodded. "Yes, it does."

He squeezed her hand slightly. "Look, Vicki, I like you. I like you a lot. You're great with Mason—"

"So is that what's behind this? Are you wining and dining me in hopes that I'll become a convenient babysitter?"

"No!" Damn, he was blowing this. Big-time. "I don't have to tell you that Mason is the most important thing to me," he continued. "Seeing how much you care for him makes a difference, a huge difference. But when I look at you, a caregiver for Mason is not the first thing that comes to mind. I like you because you're sweet, and beautiful, and you have this dry sense of humor that comes out at the weirdest times. You're intelligent and giving and you have one of the kindest hearts I know."

Not letting go of her hand, he stood and walked over to her. Taking both of her hands in his, he lifted her from the chair and wrapped an arm around her waist, settling his hand lightly at the small of her back.

"The wine? The candles? They're here because I wanted to make tonight special. Not just to thank you for helping me pick out a Christmas tree or because you held my hand while Mason was being examined."

He looked into her eyes. "I wanted tonight to be special because for the first time in a very long time I'm sharing a nice meal and good conversation with a woman I find unbelievably attractive and funny and interesting. You deserve wine and candles and everything else that makes a first date special."

Her brow arched. "So this is our first date?"

"I'm not sure it started out that way, but that's how I would like to end it." He trailed the backs of his fingers along her cheek. "You said you didn't want casual. I wasn't sure if I was ready for anything more. But I am."

"Are you sure about that?"

He nodded. "Casual doesn't have the appeal it once did. I'm ready for something serious. Are you willing to take this to the next level, Vicki?"

It felt as if hours went by as she studied him, but it was only a few moments. Finally, she said, "So how do you usually end your first dates?"

The smile that stretched across Jordan's face was so wide it made his cheeks hurt.

"It's been a while since I had a first date," he said. "But if I remember correctly, it usually ends like this."

He dipped his head and connected his lips to hers. The minute their mouths touched, Jordan was bowled over by the sheer softness of her lips, the sweetness of her delectable kiss. It had been so damn long since he'd experienced anything even remotely close to the feelings racing through his blood that he had to slow himself down before he attacked her mouth with the passion suddenly coursing through his veins.

Jordan closed his eyes and focused on the breathtaking gentleness of her mouth as it became pliant underneath his kiss. He brought his hands up to her neck, his fingertips brushing lightly along her jawline as he held her steady. He hesitated for only a moment before he swept his tongue along the seam of her lips and had his first taste of what awaited him.

A groan tore from his throat the moment Vicki parted her lips and let him inside. She was sweet and spicy and warm and undeniably sexy. His tongue moved with determination, sweeping inside the silky depths of her hot mouth, claiming it, relishing in it. His fingers inched up to the back of her head and held her head steady while he explored every delectable crevice.

As one hand cradled her head, the other traveled down her spine, stopping in the shallow dip at the small of her back before lowering a few inches farther. Jordan smoothed his hand over the curve of her firm backside before cupping it and pulling her to him. He held her close, his body instantly hardening at the feel of her stomach against his groin.

As his tongue plunged in and out of her mouth, his thickening erection mimicked the motion.

God, how he'd missed this.

But it was so much more than just missing the feel of

a woman against him. It was *this* woman that he wanted, *this* woman that made it special.

"Damn, Vicki," Jordan whispered against her lips before swooping his hands underneath her thighs and lifting her up and onto the table. Her legs clamped his hips, and their kiss grew hungry.

Hands, lips and tongues all collided in the hottest, most intense kiss Jordan had ever experienced. His body ached with the need to tear her clothes off and take her right there on the table. The urge to bury himself inside her obliterated all thought from his brain. He couldn't think of anything else he wanted more.

And that was when he realized he needed to stop.

This was moving too fast.

Yet with every soft moan that climbed up from Vicki's throat, Jordan felt that it wasn't moving fast enough. She wanted this as badly as he did. They were two adults. They were attracted to each other. And, most of all, they both wanted it.

But he'd learned the last time that being swept away in a fit of passion carried a price.

Jordan moved back a step, his breaths coming out so harsh it hurt his chest.

"That was...um... That was way more than just a thank-you," he said.

Vicki's dazed expression, her full, just-kissed lips, had him on the verge of finishing what he'd just started.

"I agree." She nodded. "This is probably far enough for a first date."

Jordan stared into her eyes. "I'm not stopping on the second date, Vicki."

"Good," she said. "Because I won't let you."

Chapter 7

Vicki measured out the dark blue ribbon that was threaded with gold, hoping she would have enough on the spool. Just under ten feet. She was cutting it close, but this was a last-minute job, so the customer would have to take what she gave them.

They'd better be happy she'd taken on the job at all.

Vicki could hardly choke back her resentment. The accounting firm of Crawford and Daniels had been one of her best clients. She'd provided weekly fresh flower arrangements for their lobby and decorated for several holidays throughout the year. Until last year, when they'd decided to go with a bigger florist in a neighboring town.

When the accounting firm's office manager had called that morning, frantic because their new florist had dropped the ball and wouldn't have their offices decorated in time for their yearly Christmas-card photo, a tiny, evil part of Vicki had wanted to turn down the job. It would have served them right for dropping her.

But she was a professional. And despite how satisfying it would have felt to be petty—and it would have felt *damn* satisfying, she had no doubt about it—she just couldn't sink that low.

They would pay where it counted, because, even though she didn't need the money, Vicki had tacked on a 30 percent upcharge for the rush job. She felt justified. She'd never given them reason to be dissatisfied with her work.

In a way, she owed Crawford and Daniels a huge thanks. The idea to enter a float in this year's Christmas parade had been planted after they'd pulled their business. She'd decided then to show them—to show everyone—just what Petals was made of.

"Thank you for your disloyalty, Crawford and Daniels," Vicki said into the empty florist shop. "It gave me the kick in the butt I needed."

She nestled intricately painted blue-and-gold ornaments around the gigantic wreath that would hang prominently on the wall at the accounting firm. They were lucky she'd had the pine garland on hand. It was for a Christmas party she'd been hired to decorate for that weekend, which meant she would have to make a special trip to one of her suppliers so she could replace what she'd used. Maybe she should change that upcharge to 35 percent.

Vicki heard the front door open moments before Sandra and Janelle both walked in.

"Hey," she called. "What are you two doing together? I thought you both had separate meetings."

"With the same couple." Janelle laughed. "The mother of the bride hired Sandra to design the dress and the mother of the groom hired me to coordinate the wedding. We didn't realize it until we all showed up at the restaurant together."

"Well, I hope you both told them which florist would be perfect to design the floral arrangements for the wedding," Vicki said.

"Don't we always?" Sandra said.

"When you have a minute we need to go over the list of floral arrangements we'll need for the Woolcotts' Kwanzaa celebration," Janelle said. "Nancy wants to make sure the centerpieces on the buffet tables are completely different from those on the tables where guests will be eating."

"That's Mom," Sandra said with a laugh. "Makes you wonder why she even hired you if she's going to stick her nose in every little detail."

Janelle waved her off. "I go through this every year with your mother. I know what to expect."

"Speaking of my mother," Sandra said, a sage smile lifting the corners of her lips, "Isaiah and I had her and Dad over for dinner last night and she said Jordan came to see her yesterday."

Vicki cursed her stomach for the flip-flop it did just at the sound of his name.

"Oh?" she said. It was the sorriest excuse for nonchalance she'd ever engaged in.

"Mmm-hmm," Sandra murmured. "She said Jordan could not stop talking about a certain florist. She said you two went tree shopping, then you helped him with Mason's trip to urgent care."

"What happened to the baby?" Janelle asked.

"Teething and an ear infection," Vicki provided without thinking.

"So you *have* been hanging out with my brother," Sandra said with an excited lilt to her voice.

"It isn't that big of a deal," Vicki said.

Although it was. Kind of.

Okay, it was a *really* big deal.

Over the past week she'd seen Jordan every single day. He and Mason had come over to her place for dinner, and on the nights they were not at her house, she was at Jordan's.

When the float builder had delivered the base for her float yesterday, Jordan had dropped what he was doing and had come over to the storage facility she'd rented to house the float while she worked on it. They'd gone over her sketches and talked out the logistics of what she planned to do. It had felt amazing to have him there with her, to see his excitement over her project.

Other things she did with Jordan felt amazing, too.

They had yet to take that next step, but the kisses they'd shared over the past week were hot enough to melt every bit of snow in Wintersage.

Vicki turned her attention to the garland twining up the banister so her friends wouldn't see the blush that was no doubt reddening her cheeks.

"So?" Sandra prompted.

"So what?" Vicki asked.

"So what's going on with you and Jordan? How serious is it?"

"It's nothing serious, Sandra. I babysat Mason and helped Jordan decorate for the holidays." *And nearly died when his hands crept up my stomach and over my breasts when he kissed me goodbye last night.* "Honestly, it's nothing to get worked up about," Vicki reiterated, even as she stood there as "worked up" as she'd ever been.

"Are you kidding me? I think it's great," Sandra squealed. "I told you that Jordan needs to get laid."

"Who said anything about him getting laid?" Vicki asked. Her cheeks were definitely red now. "I'm just helping him out with Mason. That's it."

"Are you sure that's it?" Janelle asked.

"Yes!" *No!* She was doing so much more than just helping him out with Mason. "Goodness, would you two stop it!"

"Okay, okay, we'll leave you alone," Sandra said. "However, let the record show that I have absolutely no problem with whatever it is that's going on between you and Jordan. Allison caused him a lot of heartache. He needs someone in his life who can show him that not every woman is like his ex-wife."

"But Vicki said there's nothing going on between them," Janelle said.

With another of those knowing smiles, Sandra playfully lifted her brows before going upstairs. Janelle started to follow her, but Vicki caught her by the wrist.

She waited for Janelle to look at her before she asked, "If there was anything going on between me and Jordan—not that I'm saying there is, but if there was—would you have a problem with it?"

"Does it even matter?" Janelle asked.

"It does to me," Vicki said.

Janelle's eyes softened with understanding. "I know we all agreed that we would remain neutral as far as the election goes, but I can't say that I'm not at least a little resentful toward Jordan. He's accused my father of cheating. I can't just pretend that I'm okay with that." She hunched her shoulders. "It's difficult, Vicki. My entire family is up in arms over the fact that I'm still coordinating the Woolcotts' Kwanzaa celebration."

"I'm so sorry this is all happening."

Janelle nodded. "I'm sorry Jordan is still petitioning the election results. Every person who adds their name to that online petition is like a slap in the face to my dad."

"Have you looked at it from his perspective? He has—"

"Don't." Janelle put her hands up. "Please don't stand here and try to justify Jordan's actions to me." Janelle blew out a weary breath. "Look, Vicki. Whether or not anything is going on between the two of you, I'll be happy for you, but I don't want to hear about how you think Jordan is right or that I should look at things from his perspective. I just can't."

Vicki nodded. "I understand."

Janelle looked down at her from two steps above and caught her chin in her hand. She smiled, and said, "Your face has had a bit of a glow this past week. If Jordan is the one responsible for it, I am grateful to him for that. You deserve to be happy."

"Thanks," Vicki said.

Janelle's smile dimmed just a bit. "I just want you to think about something."

"What's that?"

"What happens when things get back to normal?"

Vicki frowned. "What do you mean?"

"Once everything with this election is finally put to bed and Jordan returns to work. When Mason's nanny returns. What happens then, Vicki?"

"I don't know why anything has to change."

"What about if Allison comes back wanting to reclaim the little family she left behind?"

Vicki's head reared back. Where had *that* come from?

"Allison hasn't been around in months," Vicki said.

"What makes you think she would return making demands?"

"Stranger things have happened," Janelle said. "And you know what Sandra used to say about her. That Allison was like catnip for Jordan." Janelle raised both palms up. "I'm not trying to influence you one way or another. I just don't want you to get hurt." She patted Vicki's hand, then turned and headed up the stairs.

Vicki remained standing there, Janelle's words playing over and over again in her head. Thinking about Allison and the influence she'd once had over Jordan caused a bunch of Vicki's old insecurities to resurface.

Even more upsetting, she couldn't help but think that Janelle had brought up Jordan's ex-wife for exactly that reason.

She hated the thought of there being a rift between her and Janelle because of her blossoming relationship with Jordan, but she also had to respect his stance, as well. Jordan understood the strain his petitioning of the election results was putting on everyone, but he believed he was right. Who was she to tell him to disregard his belief just because it made things awkward for her?

Vicki just hoped she didn't have to choose between the man she could easily see herself falling in love with and one of her best friends.

"Mr. Jackson, I don't want you to think that just because the election is still up in the air that it will affect the promises we made to Mass Mentors one way or the other. No matter what the final results turn out to be, I will make sure the program is fully funded."

Even if he had to fund it himself, Jordan thought. His emails and texts to Oliver Windom regarding the program had gone unanswered, but Jordan wasn't allowing that to deter him.

"I made a pledge to your program, and I'm going to make good on it," he told the program director before ending the call.

Releasing an aggravated sigh, Jordan tossed the phone on his desk and ran both palms down his face. It wasn't supposed to turn out this way. According to the schedule he'd laid out in his head, he and the rest of the transition team should be well into preparation for Oliver to take office. Instead, here he was, stuck at home, waiting for even the tiniest bit of evidence from one of the investigators he'd hired to look into the ballot tampering.

As for the candidate himself...

Jordan didn't know what to make of Oliver's actions since the election. For some reason, the man he'd backed and had believed in so strongly was more than willing to roll over and play dead. It frustrated Jordan to no end! Why in the hell was *he* more upset over Oliver's loss than Oliver himself?

Jordan had tried to come at this from every rational standpoint he could, but it just didn't add up. His polling data couldn't have been off by so much. Someone had to have tampered with those ballots.

But what if no one had touched the ballots? What if he *was* wrong?

"It's not as if you've never been wrong before," Jordan said with a cynical, self-deprecating snort.

He swerved his chair around and grinned at his son, who was becoming increasingly frustrated with a wooden block that would not stay where he'd stacked it on top of another block.

Scooting onto the floor, Jordan said, "Mind if Daddy

joins you?" He picked up a block with a green *A* on it, but Mason reached for it.

"Mine," his son said with a frown.

Jordan raised his hands up. "Okay, okay. Looks like we need to have the 'learn how to share' talk when you get a little older."

As if Mason understood him, he picked up a yellow *Y* in his chubby little hand and held it out to Jordan.

"There you go," Jordan said. "You know how to share."

He stared down at his son with wonder, still amazed at how much his perspective had changed in such a short amount of time. It had been a whirlwind these past couple of years. He'd met Allison and had been swept right off his feet, marrying her only six months after they'd met, after she'd gotten pregnant with Mason.

He'd known from the beginning that when it came to children, her feelings were lukewarm at best. Jordan had hoped those feelings would change once Mason was born. He'd expected her to take one look at their son and fall in love, just as he'd done.

He didn't doubt that Allison loved Mason. She was just too selfish to give up her lifestyle in order to raise a child.

"I, on the other hand, can't imagine my life without you," Jordan said, placing Mason in his lap. He kissed Mason's chubby neck, thanking God for blessing him with this unbelievable gift. It was a gift he hadn't known he wanted, a gift that had come to mean everything to him.

Jordan's breath caught in his throat just thinking about the sheer terror that had hit him last week when Mason had spiked that high fever.

It hadn't been all that long ago that the only thing

that concerned him was getting ahead. He'd been on track to rise to the top of his law firm faster than any associate had done in the past. His career had been his only focus.

None of that seemed important anymore.

He recalled his mother's recommendation after he mentioned shortening his leave of absence, and realized she was right. What would he gain by returning to his law firm earlier than necessary? He had more money set aside than he could spend in a lifetime, and he sure as hell didn't need the stress of fourteen-hour workdays.

What he needed was to relish this time with Mason. In the blink of an eye he'd gone from a helpless infant to a fast-moving toddler ready to explore the world. Blink again and Mason would be in kindergarten, then high school, and then before he knew it, Jordan would be watching him move out on his own. He didn't want to miss a minute of the precious time he had with him.

Besides, he'd grown used to working shorter hours since joining Oliver's campaign. Although things had become hectic during the past few weeks of the election, for the most part, Jordan was home by six, as opposed to eight or nine at night. He had time to play with Mason instead of only going into his room and giving him a small kiss, careful not to wake him up. How was he going to go back to that when his housekeeper returned and they all went back to their old routine?

Simple. They weren't going back to the old routine.

Working those crazy hours had been okay when he was single and trying to climb his way to the top, but his priorities had changed. He didn't need the top. He had all he needed right here.

He kissed Mason's head, a gentle smile lifting the

corner of his mouth as he thought about the future that awaited them.

His cell phone rang.

Jordan sat Mason back on the floor with his blocks and picked the phone up on the third ring. He recognized Vicki's number and couldn't help the thread of excitement that coursed through him.

"Hello," he answered.

"Hi," she said. "How is Mason doing?"

"He's just fine as long as no one touches the building blocks his grandma Nancy got for him. He's a bit territorial when it comes to his toys."

Vicki's laughter flittered through the phone line, causing another rush of excitement to skate across Jordan's skin.

"Well, I wasn't sure if you two would be up for it," she continued, "but I was wondering how you would feel about taking Mason to see Bright Nights at Forest Park in Springfield. There's a big Christmas lights display there every year."

"I've heard of it, but I've never been."

"I went a few years ago and it was incredible. I heard they've added even more displays since then. I was hoping to find some inspiration for my float and figured Mason would enjoy all the lights. It's a two-hour drive, though. I wasn't sure if you would be up for it."

Jordan didn't have to think but for a moment.

"We'd love to," he said.

He heard the smile in her voice as she said, "Wonderful. Why don't I pick the two of you up in a half hour?"

"I'll see you then."

Jordan raced to get both himself and Mason ready. He opted to give Mason a quick wipe down with a damp towel instead of a bath. His mother had drilled it into his head not to give him a bath too soon before bringing him out into the cold.

Jordan had just finished packing some toys, animal crackers and juice boxes in a bag when he heard a car pulling up. Excitement shot like a lightning rod through his veins.

Now that he'd decided to fully own this attraction that had been building between him and Vicki, he could barely contain the pleasurable exhilaration that flooded his brain whenever she was around. He'd allowed the turmoil he'd been through in his first marriage to scare him off from getting involved with anyone else, but he was not going to let that happen this time.

Honestly, this was the first time he'd even *wanted* to get involved with someone since Allison left. Who would have ever thought Vicki Ahlfors would be the person to break down the wall he'd erected around his heart? How had he allowed her to fly under his radar for all these years? He felt like a shallow, callous fool for not recognizing just how attracted he was to her.

Jordan considered himself lucky that Vicki had even bothered to give him the time of day. She could have held it against him that he hadn't noticed her until after she'd gone through a complete makeover, but she hadn't.

And *that* was what he was attracted to the most. She was so unbelievably tender and giving, and she had a heart of pure gold. She was more than he probably deserved.

No, she was *definitely* more than he deserved.

"You better not mess this up," Jordan said.

The doorbell rang. He damn near ran at the speed of light to get to it. The moment he opened the door, one thing became crystal clear: there was no way in hell he could ever deny that these feelings were real. Just the sight of her warm smile had his skin tingling and long-dormant areas of his body coming to life.

"Hey there," she greeted with a smile that could make every unpleasant thought in the world melt away.

"Hey," Jordan returned, his body humming with energy now that she was near him again. He leaned over and captured her lips in a kiss so sweet it drew a moan from her. God, she tasted good.

"Well, hello to you, too," Vicki whispered against his mouth.

"You have no idea how much I love doing that."

"Mmm…I don't know about that. I think I have an inkling." That wicked smile tilting up her lips set off way too many naughty thoughts in his brain. A glimmer of shared desire flashed in her brilliant brown eyes before she said, "The feeling is mutual. And as much as I love doing that, I want to do more."

A delicious shudder cascaded down Jordan's spine.

It was obvious what they both wanted. A barrier had been crossed, a step taken. With those few words she'd just spoken, this new relationship they'd found themselves in had just moved to the next level.

"We don't have to see the Christmas lights," Jordan said.

If he called his mother right now she would be here in ten minutes, more than happy to take Mason for the night. He and Vicki could spend the rest of the evening exploring this new step in their relationship.

"Yes, we do have to see the Christmas lights," she said, her smile widening. She reached for Mason, taking him from Jordan's arms. "This little one is going to love them."

Jordan's chin fell to his chest. *So close!* He'd been so damn close to satisfying the fantasies that had overwhelmed him over the past two weeks. Instead, he was off to see Santa.

Jordan groaned. "Just let me grab Mason's bag," he said, sounding like a sulky teenager. He felt like one, too. A sulky, horny teenager who was being denied something he knew they both wanted.

"That's a good daddy," Vicki said. The amusement tinting her voice told Jordan that she was having way too much fun at his expense. "Can you bring a blanket, as well?" she called after him. "It's going to be cold out."

Jordan grabbed a blanket from the hall closet, and then met Vicki at his car. She was already strapping Mason into his car seat.

Jordan was once again struck by how right this all felt. She'd slid into place so seamlessly, as if she'd been a part of his life forever. It felt as if she belonged here, like she was the missing peg that fit so much better than his ex-wife ever had.

Jordan waited for panic to set in just at the thought of the word *wife,* but there was no panic, only a surprising sense of peace. It was crazy. Their relationship wasn't even two weeks old. Sure, he'd known Vicki all his life, but not in *this* way. What business did he have thinking in terms of a wife? Hell, they had yet to do more than kiss. Granted, they'd shared some of the hottest, most intimate kisses he'd ever experienced, but still, that was the furthest they'd gone.

But they would go further.

Jordan's hands tightened on the steering wheel.

If he'd read the signs correctly—and he was pretty damn sure he had—they would go a lot further. And soon.

The appendage behind his zipper responded to the

decadent thoughts flooding his brain, setting him up for what was sure to be the most uncomfortable two-hour drive of his life.

Before they even broke past the Wintersage city limits Mason had already fallen asleep.

"The car really is like a sleeping pill for him, isn't it?" Vicki said with a laugh.

"It's my go-to lullaby. Whenever he's having a hard time falling asleep, I strap him in and we take a ride. I should have known it was more than just crabbiness when he didn't go out like a light when we went tree shopping."

"Did you schedule a checkup with the doctor?"

Jordan nodded. "This coming Tuesday. She wants to see if the antibiotics are clearing up the ear infection. Of course, my mom thinks I should take him to a specialist in Boston just in case it's something more serious. She was never this nervous with us kids."

"But this is her grandbaby. I'm sure my mother will be the same way. Of course, at this rate, she doesn't think she'll ever have grandkids."

"You still have plenty of time to make her a grandmother."

Vicki shrugged. "All hope isn't lost, but I'm much closer to thirty than I am to twenty."

"Vicki, you have nothing to worry about. The right man is going to come to his senses and realize you're the perfect woman to share his life with."

The air in the car grew heavy with anticipation, saturated with desire.

"You think so?" she asked in a breathy whisper.

Jordan looked over at her. "He would be a fool not to." He took her hand and brought it up to his lips, kissing the back of it.

"Can I be honest with you?" he asked.

"Always," she said. "I refuse to have it any other way."

He glanced at her again, both surprised and turned on by her direct attitude. She knew what she wanted; it was *such* a freaking turn-on.

God, he wanted her.

Jordan blew out a heavy breath. "This scares the hell out of me, Vicki," he admitted. "I've spent the past year and a half trying to convince myself that feeling this way for a woman again was more trouble than it was worth. But you're proving that to be wrong. Every minute I'm with you, you chip away at the wall I built, and it scares me."

"You have nothing to fear, Jordan. I'm not your ex-wife. I'm nothing like her."

"I know you're not." He squeezed her hand. "You're so different that it makes me question just how I could have ever been attracted to two women who are the polar opposite of each other."

"Did you come up with an answer?" she asked.

"Yes," he said. "I discovered that substance is so much sexier than style. Not saying that you don't have style," he quickly interjected. "You're gorgeous, Vicki. And it has nothing to do with your hair or makeup or any of that other stuff. What makes you gorgeous, what makes you the sexiest woman I've ever met, is that beautiful heart of yours."

She leaned over the center console and kissed his cheek.

"Thank you for saying that," she said. Entwining her arm with his, she rested her head against his shoulder and, with a touch of playfulness in her voice, said, "But you don't mind the new wardrobe, do you? I treated myself to a nightgown that I'm pretty sure you would appreciate."

Jordan groaned so loudly he was sure he'd wake up Mason. "Please tell me I'll get to see it soon."

She looked up at him and grinned. "Seeing as I bought it yesterday with the sole purpose of seeing your face when I put it on, I would say that's a yes."

"Thank God," Jordan breathed. He put a bit more pressure on the accelerator. "Let's get through these damn lights so we can get back home."

Chapter 8

Vicki spent the remainder of the drive to Springfield trying to talk herself out of telling Jordan to find the nearest U-turn so they could return to Wintersage. Now that they both knew what would happen when they got back home tonight, the desire to get there was more than she could stand.

However, all thoughts of rushing through their evening vanished the moment they arrived and Mason caught his first glance at the brilliant display of Christmas lights. The wonder in his wide brown eyes—eyes that looked so much like his father's—wrapped a ribbon of warmth around Vicki's heart. His little mouth formed a perfect O as they drove underneath the arched lit sign welcoming them to the annual Bright Nights at Forest Park holiday display.

As they pulled up to the attendant to buy tickets, they discovered that instead of driving through in their own vehicle, for a small fee they could take a horse-drawn carriage ride through a portion of the display.

"It's pretty cold out here. You want to?" Jordan asked.

"Absolutely," Vicki said. "We have a blanket, remember?"

"Is that why you told me to bring the blanket? You'd already planned this?"

"No, but I'll take credit for it anyway," she said with a cheeky wink.

After parking, she suggested that Jordan take Mason into the gift shop while she scheduled the carriage ride. She spotted them at the huge display of stuffed snowmen and reindeer.

Sidling up next to Jordan, she said, "The next carriage leaves in fifteen minutes."

"Uh-oh," Jordan said. "This one can do some damage in fifteen minutes. He already wants everything he sees."

"Me and him both," Vicki said as she browsed the shelves. She found several items for her float—a wooden train set that she could put under the tree with the American version of Santa Claus, and several angels that would look perfect with the Papa Noël from France.

"These are gorgeous," she said, picking up a set of jewel-toned wineglass charms.

"Check out the monogrammed ones." Jordan nodded to a nearby shelf.

"Oh, I have to get these for Sandra and Janelle," she said. "They're perfect stocking stuffers."

By the time she'd finished shopping, Jordan had to run back to the car to deposit their packages, which numbered too many to take on the carriage ride. Vicki had opted for a private carriage to take them through the winding tour instead of the shared one.

The horse hoofs clopped along the roadway as they passed under the arching lights of Seuss Land, which brought the stories of Dr. Seuss alive through Christmas lights. Vicki couldn't contain her laughter as Mason's eyes grew wide as saucers. He squealed with delight, reaching out and trying to touch Horton the Elephant from the beloved *Horton Hears A Who!* book.

"Please tell me you have all of Dr. Seuss's books and that you read to him every night," Vicki said to Jordan.

"I don't have them all, but you can bet I'll have the entire collection ordered by the weekend."

Mason's chubby finger remained in a pointing position as he oohed and aahed over *The Cat in the Hat* and *How the Grinch Stole Christmas!* done up in thousands of twinkling lights. The tour continued through the Garden of Peace, with its dozens of flowering blooms and angel wings. Vicki nearly gave herself whiplash looking from side to side at the gorgeous display.

She turned at the sound of Jordan's low chuckle.

"What's so funny?" she asked.

"You," he said, amusement coloring his voice. "You're as enthralled as Mason."

She felt her cheeks heat. "I can't help it," she admitted. "It's just so amazing to see what they've created with Christmas lights."

"You can create something just as beautiful with flowers," he said. "I've seen you do it before."

"So you don't think I'm wasting my time with this float?"

"Who said you're wasting your time?"

She shrugged. "My family. My father and brothers,

in particular, but even my mom to a certain extent. They think I'm going to make a fool of myself."

"Did they actually say that to you?"

"Not in so many words, but when I told my father and brothers about it over Sunday dinner this past weekend, they did everything they could to discourage me. I told my mom about it first, just to gauge her reaction, and she basically said the same thing. They think I'm going to be humiliated."

"Vicki, you have as good of a chance of winning that float competition as anyone else. No, you have an even better chance, because you want it more." He took her hand and gave it an affirming squeeze. "Forget what your family thinks. Don't allow it to cross your mind again. You're going to kick ass in that float competition."

"Thank you," she said, a gentle smile touching her lips. She held up a finger. "But don't use that language in front of Mason."

"Can I do this in front of Mason?" he asked before leaning to the side and capturing her lips in an easy kiss.

Their fingers remained entwined throughout the rest of the tour. The carriage meandered through Jurassic World, with its towering brontosaurus, triceratops and an exploding volcano. After Mason's reaction, it was obvious that a few toy dinosaurs would have to be added to the shopping list.

Once the carriage ride was over, they returned to the car and continued on the driving tour, viewing the Noah's ark display, Peter Pan and Captain Hook in Never Never Land and the charming Victorian Village.

After parking the car once again, they walked through Santa's Magical Forest to Santa's Cottage, where Mason took pictures on Jolly Ol' St. Nick's lap.

Following picture taking, they walked through the rows of trees, their twinkling lights imbuing Forest Park with a magical touch.

"Here we are. The arching reindeer," Jordan said, unfolding the blanket and laying it on the ground.

"What makes the arching reindeer special?" Vicki asked. Before he could answer, a teenager dressed in an elf costume interrupted them. The young boy carried a tray with two steaming paper cups and a basket of chocolate-chip cookies.

"What's this?" Vicki asked.

"I thought it would be nice to sit for a while underneath the stars, both the real ones and the thousands they've put here in the trees," Jordan answered.

Her heart melted at his thoughtfulness.

At the same time, her body hummed with anticipation of what was to come. The heated looks they'd shared across the carriage and Jordan's tender yet sensual little touches throughout the night had turned her body into a throbbing ball of nerves. She needed relief in the form of a release she was more than ready for Jordan to deliver.

Vicki's face heated to unheard-of levels. It felt heretical to have such erotic thoughts while surrounded by the innocent, festive Christmas lights.

The copse of oak trees provided a perfect spot for them to settle with Mason. Jordan lay on his back and held the giggling baby high above him.

"Wow, you're getting heavier every day," Jordan said with a laugh as his elbows started to buckle under Mason's weight.

"He is growing quickly, isn't he?" Vicki agreed. "You'll look at him one day and realize that your baby is gone. He'll reach those terrible twos soon, then the next thing you know it'll be time to start school."

"Don't remind me," Jordan said. "I've already missed so much time with him because of my work schedule." He paused for a moment before continuing, "I'm beginning to rethink my approach to this whole thing."

Vicki tilted her head to the side. "What thing?"

"This. Life. The future." Jordan placed Mason on the blanket between them and set several of the toys he'd bought at the general store in front of him. "A few times a year the partners bring in this consultant to talk about the work/life balance. I've always seen it as a load of crap, because even though they tell you they want all associates to have a healthy balance between work and family, everyone knows that the more time you give to the firm, the quicker you'll rise in the ranks."

His eyes found hers. "I'm not sure rising in the ranks is what I want anymore. I'm starting to learn that there are many definitions of success. Who's to say that raising a healthy, happy son doesn't make me just as successful as bringing in seven figures a year?"

"It's not as if you need the money," Vicki pointed out.

"It's never been about the money. It was always about winning. It's *still* about winning. I just think the prize has changed. I don't want the things I used to want in life. Those things aren't as important to me anymore.

"My mom said something to me the other day and it's been gnawing at my brain ever since. She said that my dad would have given anything to have more time to spend with me and Sandra when we were growing up."

"I'm sure he would have."

"If you'd asked me a few years ago—hell, a few *months* ago—if I felt neglected by my dad, I'd have called you crazy. But the more I think about it, the more

I realize that, in a way, I *did* feel as if Woolcott Industries came before me.

"Damn," he added with a low, self-deprecating chuckle. "Could I be any more of a whiner? It's not as if I have anything to complain about. My parents gave us everything we could have ever asked for."

"Look who you're talking to, Jordan. Do you know how many nights I stayed up past my bedtime, waiting for my dad to come home from the office so I could share the perfect grade I received on a test, or so he could read the remarks my teacher made on my research papers? Even though I knew he would be too tired to really pay attention to it. I started to resent AFM with a passion, yet at the same time I knew that without Ahlfors Financial Management, I wouldn't have the life my dad was working so hard to give us."

He stared at her. "You're right," he said. "I did resent it. Maybe, in a way, I even resented him." Jordan shook his head. "I don't want Mason to grow up resenting me. I don't want him to think that I'm putting anything ahead of him."

"Then don't," she said simply. She pointed to Mason. "That little boy is the center of your world. Do what you have to do to keep him there."

He smiled at her. "Good advice, Ms. Ahlfors. I think you may have missed your calling. Maybe you should have been a life coach, or whatever the heck those people are called."

Vicki laughed. "What do you know about life coaches?"

He rolled his eyes. "Not much, and I'm just fine with that. Allison thought a life coach was the answer to everyone's problems."

Vicki acknowledged the blend of emotions that rioted through her at the mention of his ex-wife. It was insane to feel even a drop of jealousy. Allison wasn't the one here with Jordan tonight. *She* was. Why would she still be jealous of his ex?

Yet even though she knew she would probably regret it, Vicki heard herself ask, "What about Allison? Do you have any contact with her at all?"

"She calls occasionally," Jordan said with a shrug. "As in maybe four times in the past six months. Her excuse is that she's dating some jet-setter and they're always traveling."

"That's no excuse. With all of the technology available these days, she can tell Mason good-night via video every night if she wanted to."

"You hit the nail on the head. She *could* do that if she *wanted* to. She doesn't. Allison's only concern is Allison."

Vicki reached out and covered his shoulder, giving it a gentle squeeze. "I'm sorry she isn't at least there for Mason."

"Allison didn't want to be a mother, I knew that. Hell, I wasn't all that sure I wanted to be a father. I hadn't really thought about it. But when Mason was born—" Jordan shook his head "—he changed everything. From the moment I first heard him cry, I wondered how I'd ever lived my life without him in it."

"You're so lucky to have him," she whispered, looking down at the baby with a wistful smile as he played with the plush toy snowman. She brought her eyes to Jordan's again. "You're lucky to have each other."

"What about you?" he asked. "Do we have you? Because that's what I want, Vicki. I want you in our lives."

That did it. Those few words, spoken in that velvety-soft voice, melted her heart.

"I want to be in your lives," she said. "There are no words to describe how much I want that."

He shook his head again, his eyes filled with wonder. "Why did it take me so long to see how amazing you are?"

"I've been asking myself that question for years," Vicki said with a wry grin. "Don't worry, I won't hold it against you. I'm just relieved you finally came to your senses."

She leaned over and they shared the kind the kiss she would love to come home to every single day for the rest of her life.

They sat underneath the tree's twinkling lights for a while longer. Jordan played catch with Mason, rolling the ball covered with fat snowmen that he'd bought from the gift shop along the blanket. After the temperature dropped to unbearable levels, they finally got into Jordan's car and headed back for Wintersage.

"Thank you for tonight," Vicki said, reaching across the console and covering his arm. "This is my favorite time of the year, and tonight you showed me just why that is."

"Thank you for inviting us to join you," Jordan said. "I haven't taken the time out to enjoy the holidays in years. I'm beginning to see just how special it is. I think this trip to Springfield will become an annual thing."

"I'll mark it in my calendar. If I'm invited, that is?"

He sent her a look that said she knew darn well that she was invited. The thought warmed Vicki from the inside out.

The snow began to fall in earnest as they drove along Interstate 291.

"I thought they said the snow wouldn't be here for

another few hours," Vicki said, pulling out her phone and checking her weather app.

"It definitely wasn't supposed to be this heavy," Jordan pointed out.

Vicki held the phone out to him. "Looks as if the forecast changed in just the past few hours."

By the time they arrived back at his house, the snow wasn't only falling, it was coming down in thick, heavy sheets and was accompanied by swirling wind that made the driving conditions treacherous.

Pulling into the garage, Jordan said, "It's a good thing you're not driving over the bay in this."

"I'm not?"

He glanced at her. "There's only one place you're going tonight. And the quicker I get you there, the more time we'll have."

Despite the excited shiver that ran through her at his words, Vicki couldn't allow him to get away with such arrogance unchecked. She waited until he rounded the car and opened her door, then asked, "So you just went ahead and made that decision all by yourself, huh? You didn't feel the need to consult me on it?"

"No," he answered without hesitation. "I already knew your answer. You've got a new nightgown you want me to see, remember?"

She crossed her arms over her chest as she waited for him to unstrap Mason from his car seat. "What if I decided on the drive back that hot chocolate under the stars is all I'm willing to give tonight? I know you're a Woolcott and all, but even Woolcotts don't get to have their cake and eat it, too."

Hefting the toddler over his shoulder, he turned to her and allowed his eyes to slowly roam the length of her body. "When it comes to what I'm planning to eat tonight, cake isn't on the menu."

Vicki nearly orgasmed then and there.

"Go put the baby to bed," she said, the words coming out in a husky rasp.

She followed Jordan into the house, her skin vibrating with every step she took. The time it took for him to tuck Mason in for the night gave her body the opportunity to cool down. She went into the kitchen and slid a bottle of wine from the rack. She heard Jordan approaching and turned, finding him standing in the entryway.

Vicki held up the bottle of wine.

"I know there's a snowstorm raging like crazy outside, but I have a feeling this wine would taste a whole lot better in front of the fire bowl on your enclosed deck."

Jordan's mouth pulled into a frown. "You want wine? Right now?"

"We both know what's going to happen tonight, but I expect to be romanced just a little before I give up my goodies." She nodded toward the glass-fronted cabinets that held the stemware. "Grab a couple of glasses, will you?"

"Really, Vicki? You want wine? Now?"

A smile curled up the edges of her lips. "Stop being so shortsighted, Jordan. Think of all the fun things we can do with the wine."

His eyes grew wide with interest, and he headed straight for the cabinet.

Ten minutes later, Vicki grinned as she eyed Jordan's surly expression from where she sat with one leg curled underneath her. The other was stretched out on the cushioned love seat glider, her toes inches from his thigh. His frown had appeared from the moment she poured the wine into the glasses instead of the more... interesting place he'd suggested.

Vicki moved her foot another few inches toward him.

He eyed her over the rim of his wineglass. "If that foot gets any closer I'm going to think you're trying to tell me something."

"I was trying to be discreet," she said. "But apparently you don't take hints very well. I guess I just have to come out and ask for a foot rub."

He set his glass next to the baby monitor on the side table and pulled her foot onto his lap.

Vicki let her head fall back as she released a soft moan. "That feels like heaven," she murmured. "Being on my feet at Petals all day is agony."

"You can't put flower arrangements together while sitting down?"

Vicki sent him a horrified look. "No," she said. "I need to walk around so I can see what I'm creating from all sides. There's no such thing as sitting for a florist. It's murder on my feet."

"On your hands, too," Jordan said. "I didn't want to mention it earlier, but when I took your hand in the car I think I nearly cut myself. Those things are brutal."

Vicki burst out laughing. "Yes, I definitely have florist's hands." She held them up in front of her, observing the many nicks and scratches.

"Be proud of them," Jordan said. "They're your own personal battle scars. You earned them." He took her hands in his and placed light kisses upon each and every mark.

A ribbon of desire curled through her belly. He was so tender, so unbelievably attuned to what her body craved.

"Vicki?" Jordan's deep, velvety voice grazed over her skin like a silky promise.

"Yes?"

"Are you done torturing me?"

She looked up at him and grinned. "I've discovered that this new Vicki has a bit of a vindictive streak. I thought I'd pay you back for taking so long to realize that I've been here waiting for you, wanting you, all these years."

Jordan's head fell forward. "So you're not done torturing me."

"But I realize that the longer I make you wait, that's the longer I have to wait, too. And I don't want to wait any longer."

His head popped up. His eyes grew intense, their smoldering depths lighting her skin on fire as he stared into her eyes.

"I'm sorry it took me so damn long to see what's been standing right in front of me," he said. "But I'm about to make up for it."

Jordan's gaze remained locked with hers as he lifted the back of her head and lowered his mouth to hers. The first touch of his soft lips sent Vicki's head on a cosmic spin. It was sweet and sexy and everything she'd expected of him.

Yet so much more.

His kiss was mesmerizing—the taste, the texture, the urgency... It all combined to drive her mad with desire she could feel down to her toes. With gentle insistence, he applied pressure to her lips, his delicious mouth urging her to join him. She did, wrapping one hand around his neck and caressing the back of his head. She licked at the seam of his lips until his mouth opened, then she thrust her tongue inside, claiming his mouth as if it had always belonged to her.

Jordan released a low groan as he turned her more fully toward him and cradled her against his body. He began a slow journey down her sides until he cradled her waist. As his mouth continued to ply her with strong yet gentle kisses, his fingers inched their way along her torso, moving gradually up her belly until they neared her breasts.

Vicki stuck her chest out, dying to feel his hands on her, but he held back, his hands stopping just short of the place where she wanted them the most.

"Is this payback?" she panted.

"I just don't want to move too fast."

"You're not moving fast enough." She caught the hem of his sweater and pulled it over his head. Then she trailed her fingers down his muscled chest, her nails leaving faint streaks.

The guttural moan that crawled from Jordan's throat was the very definition of agony.

"Do that again," he said.

"Not until you do it to me," she returned.

Her nipples hardened from mere anticipation, the achy peaks reaching for him, waiting for him to touch her. Jordan pushed her shirt over her head, taking her bra with it and flinging them both to the floor. Vicki climbed on top of him, straddling his lap. She hooked her arms around his neck and tilted her head back as his lips and tongue swept up and down her throat.

"Oh, my God, you taste good," he whispered, his warm breath heating her blood.

The rasp of his tongue against her skin set off a mass of powerful sensations along her nerve endings. He cupped her breasts, his palms squeezing them, massaging them. He rolled her nipples between his fingers, pinching the rock-hard nubs before flicking his thumb across them.

Moisture pooled between her thighs as desire surged throughout her bloodstream. Every fantasy she'd ever held, every night she'd lain in bed, wishing, dreaming, praying that this one day would become her reality... It all coalesced into this delicious, momentous moment in time. It was so beautiful, so incredibly earth-shattering, Vicki wasn't sure she could handle it.

Jordan dipped his head low and lapped at her nipple, and she decided she could handle it just fine.

A moan tore from her throat as he sucked the rigid peak into his mouth. She undulated in his lap, rubbing her swollen sex against his hardening erection.

That was when Vicki decided there were too many layers between them.

She needed him stripped bare, his naked body displayed for only her eyes to see. She tugged at his belt.

"Take this off," she said.

"Soon." He returned his mouth to her breasts. He molded one mound in his palm, cupping the underside, holding it up so that his lips and tongue could have full reign over her nipple.

"Jordan, please," she cried.

Mercifully, he finally decided to put them both out of this sweet misery. He grabbed the condom he'd tucked into his pocket before levering himself up and pulling his pants down his legs as Vicki took hers off, too. Together they quickly rolled the condom over his hard flesh, and then, taking it in his hand, Jordan guided his erection inside of her.

Vicki's entire being seemed to scream with pleasure. The delicious give as her body stretched to receive him made her wetter, hotter, more turned on than she had ever been in her life. She welcomed his hot, solid length into body, sliding slowly along his erection until she was fully impaled.

Jordan dipped his head forward and sucked her breast into his mouth, his teeth nipping and biting, his tongue swirling and lapping at her nipple, before moving over to the other one. Vicki curled her fingers around the top of the love seat and held on tight while she rode his lap. Down she moved, taking his entire length inside of her and rolling her hips before she pulled back up.

She rode him hard and fast, then easy and slow, changing the pace, driving them both wild. The groan that tore from Jordan's throat reverberated around the glass-enclosed room.

"I...I have to," Jordan said seconds before he clamped his hands against her waist and guided her up and down. He pumped his hips in rapid thrusts, pounding inside of her until Vicki exploded in a haze of hot white light.

She fell against him, her breaths coming in short pants.

She'd waited half her life for this. Never had she imagined it would surpass even her wildest fantasies. But it had. *He* had. Jordan Woolcott was everything she'd ever dreamed of and more.

As she lay against his naked chest, Vicki knew with certainty that what she felt was no longer the dreams and fantasies of a lovesick schoolgirl. What she felt was love.

Jordan looked up at the back porch's ceiling, staring blindly as the thick snowflakes continued to shuttle down the slanted glass. He ran his fingers lazily up and down Vicki's back, trailing lightly along her smooth, moist skin. He could spend the next week in this very spot, with her naked body spread out on top of his.

Yet even as he luxuriated in having her here with him, something uncomfortable pulled in Jordan's gut.

Was he moving too fast?

Vicki and Allison could not be more different, but Jordan couldn't deny that this scenario felt like déjà vu. He'd been swept away by Allison, caught up in a whirl-wind romance that had him married and expecting a baby all within a few months.

With Vicki it hadn't even been months, only a few short weeks. And the feelings he'd started to develop for the woman cradled in his arms went so far beyond anything he'd felt for Allison that it wasn't even worth comparing.

Was he setting himself up for another fall?

"No way," Jordan whispered. Vicki would never do to him what Allison had done. Forget the new, sexy hair and makeup. Strip all of that away and she was still Vicki on the inside.

And *that* Vicki was the one he found himself fall-ing in love with.

Jordan's chest tightened at the word, but how could he deny it? He'd been in love before; he understood what that intense, all-consuming feeling felt like.

He was there, neck deep in it. And he didn't want to get out anytime soon.

"You're thinking really hard," Vicki murmured against his chest.

"You're awake," he said.

"Barely," she said before yawning. She twisted so that she could look out the glass walls surrounding the deck. "It's still snowing."

"Hasn't stopped for hours," Jordan said.

She looked up at him from where she lay on his chest. "Have you checked on Mason?"

"Kind of hard to do that with a hundred pounds of satisfied woman draped over me."

"A hundred pounds?" She laughed. "You've already scored, Jordan, there's no need for flattery."

She started to rise, but Jordan clamped his palms on her naked backside and pulled her against him. He grew so hard so damn fast it hurt.

"Where do you think you're going?" he asked.

"To check on the baby."

"He's almost a year and a half, Vicki. He's been sleeping through the night for months." Jordan brought his hand around and slipped it between her legs. "You can stay right here. I'm still trying to atone for my sins, remember?"

He slipped one finger inside of her and quickly added another moving in and out; he nearly came when she began to undulate against him in rhythm to his thrust. Capturing her mouth, Jordan removed his fingers and held his erection steady so that she could glide her body on top of it. Their twin moans of pleasure echoed against the walls as he slid his hard length into her hot body.

They started slow, but Vicki soon quickened the pace, flattening her palms against his chest as she pumped her hips up and down. Her head flew back, exposing her neck and breasts to his lips. Jordan pulled a nipple into his mouth and sucked hard. He couldn't get enough of her, and he didn't want to.

After several long, deep thrusts, he felt her body shudder around him. He followed quickly on the heels of her orgasm, his body jerking with the power of his release.

"My God," Vicki breathed against his chest. "You've totally changed the way I see lawyers."

Jordan's head dropped back with his breathless laugh. "How did you see lawyers?"

"Serious and conservative. Definitely not the kind to let loose in the bedroom the way you do." The edges of her lips tipped up. "You probably felt the same way about me, didn't you?"

"You have been a surprise," he said. "A good one, but a surprise nonetheless."

"What were you thinking about...you know... before?"

"Before what?" he asked.

Her cheeks turned beet-red. It was the most adorable thing he'd ever witnessed, especially when he took into account where they were and what they'd just done. "Come on, Vicki," he encouraged. "I want you to say it."

She rolled her eyes. "Before we made love," she said. "For the second time. I want to know what you were thinking before we made love for the second time."

"I was trying to think of how I could convince you to do it a second time, and then maybe a third."

"You were not," she said with a laugh, pushing up from where she'd been draped on top of him. Jordan instantly missed her weight and warmth.

She grabbed the afghan that he kept on the deck furniture and wrapped it around herself. A tiny part of him died as she covered up her nakedness. If he could, he would keep her naked for the next week.

"Tell me," she said. "What were you thinking?"

He blew out a sigh as he realized that she wasn't about to let this go.

"I was thinking of how fast this is all moving." He paused for a moment before continuing, "And of how it all turned out the last time I allowed things to move so quickly with a woman."

In a soft, slightly accusatory voice, Vicki said, "You're still comparing me to her."

"It's hard not to make comparisons," Jordan said. "She was my last serious relationship." He moved over to her and pulled her onto his lap. He didn't miss the way she stiffened against him. "But also know that things are different with you, Vicki. Because *you're* different." Jordan pressed a kiss to her bare shoulder. "I can't help this fear. It's been a part of me since Allison walked out, but I'm determined to fight through it, because you're worth it."

"*We're* worth it," she said. "I don't care what it takes, I'm going to prove to you that I'm better than Allison."

"You don't have to prove anything to me. These issues I have over what happened with Allison are just that—they're *my* issues. I don't want you to feel that you need to compete with my ex-wife. You've already won that battle." He paused for a moment before continuing, "I'm going to admit something that I've been too ashamed to admit to anyone."

Several moments crept by before Vicki prompted him. "What is it?" she asked.

In a voice that was barely a whisper, Jordan said, "I don't think I ever really loved her. I was enamored with her, some might even say enthralled, but if Allison had not gotten pregnant with Mason, I doubt our relationship would have lasted more than a couple of months." Jordan shook his head. "When I think of my parents' long, loving marriage, I feel ashamed that I made such a mockery of the institution by marrying a woman I wasn't in love with."

"You thought you were doing the right thing. Giving Mason a two-parent home."

"And just look how that turned out. I probably scarred him for life."

Her expression softened. She cupped his jaw in her palm. "To quote the great Dr. Seuss, 'Oh, the things you can find if you don't stay behind.' The mistakes you made with Allison, the hurt she caused you, it's in your past, Jordan. Leave it all behind and look toward the future."

"I'm going to try my best to take that advice," he said. He pulled her more firmly against him. "Who would have thought Dr. Seuss would come to the rescue yet again tonight?"

"You'd better pay attention to those books when you read to Mason. Dr. Seuss was filled with those little nuggets of wisdom. Whenever things start to get overwhelming, I read it and remember that I'm continually striving to make my business the best that it can become."

Jordan trailed his finger along her temple and down her cheek. "You're amazing, you know that? You have the ability to change my entire perspective with just a few words. I don't know if I can ever find a way to thank you for everything you've done, Vicki."

A wicked smile lifted the corner of her mouth. "If you think long and hard enough—" she wiggled on his lap "—I'm sure you can come up with something."

Jordan barked out a laugh. He pressed a swift kiss to her lips. "I think I may have found it," he said as he flipped her onto her back and inched his mouth down her body. "Give me just a second. I'll show you."

Chapter 9

"You mind sharing whatever it is that put that smile on your face?"

Vicki jumped to attention at her mother's question. She knew the heat creeping up her face was turning her fair skin red, but how in the heck was she supposed to prevent that when thoughts of the night she'd spent in Jordan's arms invaded her mind every waking minute?

"I'm not sure it's something a mother would be all that comfortable hearing from her daughter," Vicki replied.

Christine Ahlfors's eyes narrowed as a smile drew across her lips. "Who is he?" her mother asked.

"Just because I'm smiling a little more than usual today, you automatically assume there's a man behind it?"

"Yes," her mother stated. "Now, tell me who he is?"

"How many centerpieces will you need for the senior citizens' Christmas luncheon?" Vicki asked.

"Don't even try changing the subject on me," her mother said.

Vicki arranged the poinsettia in the brass pot and set it in the center of the table in her mother's informal dining room.

"Vicki!" Her mother screeched.

She whipped around. "What?"

"Tell me who he is," she practically whined.

With a sigh, Vicki finally relented. "Jordan Woolcott."

She watched as her mother's mouth formed a perfect O. He eyes grew just as round. "Really," she said. "After all these years."

It was Vicki's turn to stand with her mouth agape. "Was it that obvious?"

"Honey, I'm your mother. Do you really believe I could miss those longing looks you would send Jordan's way whenever he was around? I'm just happy he finally caught a clue." Her mouth curved with a coy grin. "As far as catches go, he's a good one."

"He has some issues," she said.

"The election?"

"And the ex-wife."

"Ah, yes." Her brows arched. "She is a bit of baggage, but she hasn't really been around, though, has she?"

"No, but she left her mark on Jordan," Vicki said. She fingered the poinsettia's silky petal. "To say he's gun-shy about trusting another woman is an understatement."

"He just needs a good woman to show him the right way. At least he's finally opened his eyes to the possibilities. I'm grateful for that."

"So am I," Vicki said with a grin. She kissed her mother's cheek. "I have to go. I've got several arrangements to complete for the Williamses' holiday party and a lot of work to get done on the float. The kids have been working on it everyday, but I need to be there to make sure it's all going according to plan."

Her mother caught her by the wrist. "Vicki, you know it's not too late to pull out of this float competition, don't you?"

Vicki's heart deflated. "Really?" she asked. "Are we back to this? What is it, Mom? Are you afraid that I'm going to embarrass the family or something?"

"Of course not," her mother said. "I just don't want you to be hurt if this doesn't turn out the way you think it will."

"Oh, so you think I'm going to come in last place? Is that it?"

"Vicki, you know that's not the case." The sting of her mother's chastising tone was softened by the gentle smile on her face, but it didn't do much to assuage the disappointment Vicki felt at the realization that her mother still didn't believe in her. Would her family ever take her seriously?

"I have to go. I'll see you later," she said, giving her mother a kiss on the cheek.

Three hours later, Vicki began to wonder if there wasn't something to her mother's concerns. As she stared at the planks of particleboard littering the ground around the base of the float, Vicki had to stop herself from crying.

"Are you okay?" Jasper Saunders, one of the high school students she mentored through Mass Mentors, asked.

"No," Vicki answered. "This is not good."

"It's just a setback, Ms. Vicki. They can probably cut you more particleboard in a day."

She looked over at Jasper and smiled at his attempt to make her feel better. "What have I told you about calling me Ms. Vicki?" she asked. "It makes me feel older than I really am."

He grinned. "Sorry." He hitched a thumb at the door. "Since we can't do any more on the float today, do you mind if I go? A few of us are heading to the mall to celebrate being off for winter break."

"Sure," Vicki said. "Have fun. I'll text you when I get the new particleboards."

Once she was sure Jasper had left the building, Vicki thought long and hard about indulging in a much-needed cry. But she wasn't going to do that. This was a setback—a big one, but not insurmountable.

She unrolled the float's design plans and cursed. She acknowledged that she was the one who'd made the mistake in the calculations. The particleboards she'd had custom cut for her float were short by several inches.

"A math whiz, you are not," Vicki said.

If she had the pieces shipped to her, it would cost her another two days that she couldn't spare. She would have to drive down to the lumberyard in Cambridge where she'd ordered them and hope that they could cut her all new boards today.

"You can still do this," Vicki said. But she was not relying on her own math skills to get it done this time.

It was a good thing she was dating a self-proclaimed math nerd.

If anything could brighten her sullen mood, it was thoughts of Jordan. She took out her phone and explained her dilemma to him. Twenty minutes later, Vicki heard his car pulling up.

"Where's Mason?" she asked, immediately noticing that he didn't have the toddler in tow.

"Grandma Nancy insisted on taking him to Boston to see some ice-skating show at TD Garden arena."

"Oh, I saw the commercial for that. He's going to love it."

"He loves being spoiled by his grandmother, and she loves spoiling him. It's a win-win." He motioned to the float. "What's going on here?"

"I'm in over my head," Vicki admitted. She explained the mishap with her measurements. "I called the lumberyard while you were driving over and they said if I emailed the correct measurements they could have new boards cut by this afternoon, which makes me the luckiest girl in the world. But it still sets me back by at least a day. It's time I can't afford to lose, but there's nothing I can do about it."

Jordan covered her shoulders with his palms and pulled her toward him, placing a gentle kiss on her forehead. "You've got this," he said. "Don't worry about it. We'll make up whatever time you lost today."

There he went again, making her heart melt. Vicki found herself falling more and more in love with him every day, and this was just one of the reasons why. He always knew the exact thing to say to set her mind at ease.

Jordan pulled out a tape measure and started assessing the dimensions of the float base. Vicki typed the numbers he called out into her phone and emailed them to the lumberyard.

"See how easy that was?" he said.

"Painless," she said. "Now to get down to Cambridge before the lumberyard closes for the day."

"Do you want some company on the drive?"

"You have time to drive down to Cambridge with me?"

"I'll make the time," Jordan said, pulling her in for another kiss, this one leaving her knees weak.

They drove to Cambridge together and picked up the newly cut boards for her float, but instead of returning to Wintersage, Jordan took her on the Jordan Woolcott personal tour of the town where he'd gone to both college and law school. They visited several of his old haunts. Vicki laughed until her sides hurt as he regaled her with stories of his days as a hotheaded law student who thought he knew everything.

"I've been put in my place by quite a few professors in this town." He palmed the massive burger he'd ordered at Doyle's, a historic pub in Jamaica Plain, just south of Cambridge.

"I can totally see you as a know-it-all," she said.

"Thanks," he said with a sarcastic grunt as he bit into the burger.

Vicki reached across the table and patted his arm. "That's okay. You're reformed."

"You may be the only person who thinks so." He laughed, wiping the corners of his mouth. "I consider myself a work in progress."

"I'm sure if any of your old professors saw you now, they would be extremely proud."

With a grin, he threw the words she'd used the other night back at her. "You've already scored, Ms. Ahlfors, no need for such flattery."

By the time they arrived back in Wintersage, Nancy and Mason had returned from their outing. Vicki couldn't help but feel a bit self-conscious as she entered the house she'd spent untold hours in as a teen, when she and Janelle would come over for sleepovers. It felt different being here as a guest of Jordan's instead of Sandra's.

The moment she entered the house, Nancy's face lit up.

"Well, hello," she said, taking Vicki by the hands. "You look fabulous, honey. I meant to tell you at Sandra's wedding just how much I love the new haircut. It accentuates those cheekbones that I've always been so jealous of."

"Thank you," Vicki said. She'd always adored Nancy.

Jordan's mother's brows arched as she looked from Vicki to Jordan. "So," she said, leaving the word hanging.

"Very subtle," Jordan said.

"I was trying to be," Nancy said. "Did I succeed?"

"No." He kissed her on the cheek. "How did Mason enjoy the ice-skating show?"

"He loved it." She pointed a finger between Jordan and Vicki. "Someone needs to tell me right now how long this has been going on. And, if I may be so bold, tell me exactly *what* is going on."

Jordan barked out a laugh. "Aren't you just dying to know?"

"Jordan!"

"Thanks for taking Mason on his outing today," he said. "We'll see you later."

Nancy followed them to the door. "Vicki, you're reasonable. I just want to know how serious things are between you two."

"We're leaving, Mom," Jordan called as he carried Mason outside.

Vicki turned to her. "I'll explain everything when we meet to discuss the final plans for the Kwanzaa celebration," Vicki said.

Nancy grabbed both of her hands and squeezed them, letting out an excited squeal. "I don't know who finally knocked some sense into his head, but it's about time it happened. I'm so happy for the two of you."

Vicki stood there with her mouth agape. For years she'd thought she'd done a good job of hiding her feelings, only to find out that both her mother and Nancy had seen it all along.

It was starting to look like the only person who *had* been clueless all this time was Jordan.

"Vicki? Vicki!"

Vicki's head shot up. She looked across the table to find her brother Terrance staring at her, his expression a mixture of annoyance and concern. Of her three brothers, she had been closest to Terrance, but probably because he was the closest to her in age. Vicki never quite knew if it was by design or not, but their parents managed to space their four children out equally, having them all two years apart.

Spence, the eldest at thirty-four, was two years older than Jacob, who was two years older than Terrance. Being the only girl and the baby had not been easy for Vicki. She was convinced her intimidating older brothers were the reason she hadn't been asked out on more dates in high school.

"What is it, Terrance?" she asked, breaking off a small piece of the grilled salmon her mother had served for Sunday dinner. Even though all four of the Ahlfors children were no longer living in the family home, they all came together for dinner at least twice a month.

As usual, talk about Ahlfors Financial Management had dominated much of the conversation. Her father's company had recently scored a big client; it was as if Christmas had come early for the men at the table. Vicki had allowed her mind to drift as her father and brothers strategized how best to capitalize on this boon to the business. Apparently she'd tuned them out to the point that she hadn't heard Terrance calling her name.

"I asked how things were coming along with the toy drive?" her brother said. "We'll have to start distributing the toys soon, won't we?"

Her spine went rigid. "Terrance, I told you weeks ago that I wouldn't be able to work on the toy drive this year."

His eyes widened with shock. "You haven't done anything?"

"I told you I couldn't," Vicki stressed. "I've taken on several new clients at Petals and they all had big projects for the holidays."

"Oh, come *on,* Vicki. You've got to be kidding me. All this time I thought you were handling things."

"So there's no toy drive this year?" her father asked. "Isn't the local paper coming to do a story on it?"

Everyone around the table looked to her. Vicki put her hands up. "Don't blame me," she said. "I specifically told you all that I wouldn't be able to take on as many projects this year."

"But the toy drive is your thing," Terrance said.

"No, it's not. It's *your* thing," Vicki countered.

Her brother had first come up with the idea for AFM to sponsor an annual toy drive, but that was where his input ended. For years Vicki had planned and organized the drive, collecting the toys and coordinating with local charities and children's hospitals to see that they were distributed. The only time Terrance made an appearance was when it came time for the local media to do a human-interest story.

And was her name ever mentioned? Of course it wasn't!

It had never been about praise and acclaim for her. The driving force behind why she'd happily coordinated the event in the past was because she loved seeing the kids' faces when the wrapped gifts were placed in their hands. It broke her heart knowing that, for some, it was probably the only gift they would receive for the holidays.

And now some of those kids wouldn't even get *that* gift.

"I can't believe you dropped the ball like this, Vicki," Terrance said.

"*I* dropped the ball?"

"Yes! How will it look when the paper comes and we have to tell them there's no toy drive? You should have—"

"Everybody calm down," Spence interrupted in his calm voice. "This is easily solvable." He pulled his wallet from his pocket and tossed a credit card on her placemat. "Go to the toy store tomorrow and just buy a bunch of toys. See, problem solved."

"It isn't that simple," Vicki said, tossing the credit card back at him. "I don't have time to go toy shopping."

"What else do you have to do with your time?" Jacob said with a snort.

Vicki slammed her fork down. "Kiss my ass, Jacob."

"Vicki!" her mother yelped.

"I'm tired of the way everyone in this family thinks that they have the right to decide how I'm going to spend *my* time."

"I understand that you're upset," her mother said, "but can you please watch your language at the dinner table?"

Vicki huffed out a humorless laugh. "Seriously? With all that's been said in the past ten minutes, my saying *ass* is what bothers you?"

"There's no need for the sarcasm," her father said.

"I agree with Vicki," Terrance said. "If Mom's going to point out something, she should point out her daughter's selfishness."

"Selfishness!" Vicki saw red. She stared her brother down. "For the past five years you've strutted around this town accepting praise for that toy drive when you know damn well you don't lift a finger to put it on. If this toy drive really mattered to you, you would have started looking for an alternative from the moment I told you I couldn't do it."

"I'm busy."

"And I'm not?"

Terrance rolled his eyes. "Here we go again with the hardworking florist. Remind me again how much time it takes to shave thorns off rose stems."

Vicki put her hands up. "I'm done. I don't need this." She pushed away from the table and tossed her cloth napkin over her barely touched food.

"Vicki, please sit down," her mother begged.

"So I can be subjected to this? I don't think so. Besides, I have work to do," she said. "Unlike *some* people, as a small-business owner I don't have the luxury of taking the weekends off."

The last thing Vicki observed as she stormed out of the dining room was how much all the men in her family resembled each other when all their mouths were left hanging wide-open.

Without much thought to where she was going, she got behind the wheel of her car and headed below the bay, driving straight to Jordan's. She didn't even think to call to see if he was at home. It didn't matter at this point. If he was not there, she would wait in his driveway until he arrived. She needed to see him. She craved his steadiness right now. She needed someone who was willing to take care of *her* for a change.

Jordan was in his front yard when she pulled up to the house. A trio of wired lit reindeers now decorated the lawn.

A huge smile broke out over his face the moment he saw her, and just like that, everything in Vicki's world seemed right again. She got out of the car and ran right into his arms, leaning her head against his chest and wrapping her arms around him.

"Hey," he said, smoothing a hand down her back. "What's going on?"

"I just need you to hold me." She wiped her eyes on his soft lamb's-wool jacket. They stood there for several moments, quietly holding on to each other.

"You have new holiday decorations," Vicki remarked.

"I wanted to surprise Mason. He enjoyed the ones at Bright Lights at Forest Park so much."

Vicki looked up at him. "You're such a wonderful father."

He grinned. "I'm trying."

"Where is he?"

"Sandra agreed to watch him. I wanted to get some work done."

"I'm sorry," Vicki said. "I knew I should have called before just coming over."

He reached down and took her chin in his fingers.

"Never feel sorry for coming here. You're always more than welcome to stop by whenever your pretty little heart desires."

He sure knew exactly what to say to make her pretty little heart beat faster.

"Work can wait," Jordan continued. "What do you say we go inside and pop open a bottle of wine, and you can tell me what prompted this particular visit. I can tell that whatever it is, it has you upset."

She nodded and followed him into the house. Ten minutes later, ensconced in the steadiness of his arms as she sat with her back against his chest on the sofa in the great room, Vicki told him about the argument she and her brothers had had over Sunday dinner.

"I'm just fed up with them never taking me seriously, and always taking me for granted. It's at the point where they barely ask anymore. It's just automatically assumed that Vicki will take care of everything."

"You probably don't want to hear this, but it's not entirely their fault," Jordan said. "You share some of the blame here."

She looked up at him over her shoulder. "Excuse me?"

"Besides now, of all those times they demanded you take care of something, how many of those times did you tell them no?" he asked. "Especially when you knew you didn't have the time?"

"That's not fair. I've always gone out of my way to *make* the time."

"That's my point," Jordan said. "Face it, Vicki. You've made it too easy for your family. The reason they automatically assume you're going to handle everything is because you always do. They don't have to worry that something won't get done because you go out of your way to make sure that everyone else is taken care of."

"You say that as if there's something wrong with being helpful."

"That's not what I'm saying at all." He turned her around and wrapped his arms around her, settling his hands at the small of her back. "What I'm saying is that you need to stop being everything for everybody. I've had to learn that the hard way," he said.

"So you're a pushover, too?" she asked.

He chuckled. "Not exactly."

He motioned for her to scoot to the other side of the sofa. Vicki knew what was coming next. She moved to the other end and placed her feet in his lap. Jordan took her right foot between his hands and began massaging her sole with the pad of his thumbs. She damn near melted all over his sofa.

Vicki was still amazed whenever she took the time to consider how easily they had fallen into this comfortable place. In her previous relationships—not that there had been many—it had taken months to find the same level of familiarity and contentment that had taken her and Jordan only weeks to discover.

"What did you mean when you said you've had to learn your lesson the hard way?" Vicki asked, retrieving the glass of wine from the coffee table.

"My problem is that I have a hard time delegating responsibility," Jordan said. "You know the saying 'if you want something done right, do it yourself'? Well, that's been my motto for way too long. Take the election, for example. I started out as a volunteer on Oliver's team, and then when his campaign manager had to resign, I stepped into that role. I didn't like his pollster's methods, so pretty soon I was doing that job, too."

"The man who wears many hats," she remarked.

"Too many hats," he said. "If it's something I really believe in, I tend to take ownership over it. And when things don't work out to my expectations, I'm extra-hard on myself."

She tilted her head to the side and studied him. "That's why you won't let this election go, isn't it?"

"Probably." He shook his head. "I still don't understand how Oliver could let it go so quickly, though."

"What I don't understand is what it is about Oliver Windom that attracted you to his campaign. Don't get me wrong, he seems like a good guy—at least what I know about him from his campaign appearances during the election—but what made him a better candidate than Darren Howerton in your eyes?"

Jordan's fingers stilled for just a moment before he continued massaging her foot. Thank goodness he hadn't stopped. Vicki would be just fine having him pay such attention to her aching soles for the next hour.

"Oliver seemed different," Jordan began. "He's not the same old politician. He has fresh ideas. He would bring something new to the legislature."

"And you don't think Darren is capable of doing the same?"

"I have nothing against Darren. Our families have known each other for ages. Hell, Darren Jr. and I went through Wintersage Academy together. But Darren Sr. is of the same ilk as the previous state representative."

"So you decided to back Oliver because he was different."

"Actually, one of the driving forces behind why I chose to back Oliver is because he agreed to support Mass Mentors."

"Well, I can't argue with that reasoning. It's such a

special program," Vicki said. "It's been a blessing not only to the kids who are a part of it, but to the businesses that support the program, as well."

"I didn't even know about Mass Mentors until last year when an old college friend asked me to do a job-shadowing thing for a day. He's one of the cofounders."

"Really?" she asked, her brows arching in surprise.

Jordan nodded. "Instead of continuing on to law school, he started Mass Mentors to expose underprivileged youth to opportunities beyond what they would find in their neighborhoods. How could I not get behind something like that?" He put a hand to his chest. "I know my family has been blessed. It was never a question of whether or not I would go to college, or how it would be paid for when I got there. Some of these kids have the brightest minds I've ever seen, Vicki. They just have never had anyone to show them their full potential."

"You don't have to convince me of the merits of Mass Mentors. I've seen how it has changed lives. And, unlike yours, my family wasn't always in this position, Jordan. Remember, I didn't move to Wintersage Academy until my sophomore year, after AFM finally took off. If my father had not busted his butt to build that company, I could have been one of those kids in the Mass Mentors program."

"You do understand," he said, sliding his hand up her pants leg and caressing her calf.

"Yes. It's an important part of the community. Just think of how great it would be if it were in more places in Massachusetts."

"That's just it. One of the items on Oliver's agenda once he got to the state legislature was to work for funding for the program so that it could be launched statewide. *That's* the reason I worked so hard to get him elected."

Vicki reached over and stilled his hand. She waited until Jordan looked up at her. "What makes you think Darren wouldn't work just as hard to get the program funded?"

His forehead creased in a frown, as if the thought had never occurred to him.

"God, I'm stupid," Jordan said. He exhaled an anguished sigh. "I became so hung up on finding the discrepancy to prove that my polling was right that I forgot what was really important. The goal should be to make sure Mass Mentors gets funded, no matter who is in the state representative seat."

"That can still be your goal," Vicki said.

"Except that I've pissed everybody off because I let my own damn ego get in the way."

"Go to the Howertons, Jordan. Talk to Darren about Mass Mentors. Explain what the program is about, and how it played into your decision to support Oliver's candidacy. Darren is a reasonable man."

"Reasonable enough to back a program I support, even though I still have investigators looking into whether or not he stole this election? And what if he did steal it, Vicki? That question hasn't been answered yet."

"Do you really believe that?" she asked softly.

"My gut tells me that I've got those investigators on a fool's errand," he said. "But I still believe in my polling data."

"Then you have to go with what you believe," she said, "or you'll question it forever."

Vicki set her wineglass down and scooted over to him, resting her head on his chest. She could hear his steady heartbeat beneath her ear. As the seconds flowed into minutes, the heartbeats began to thump at a faster pace. His fingers trailed lightly along her cheek, the faint caress seductive in its gentle promise.

"When is Sandra bringing Mason home?" Vicki asked.

Jordan lifted his wrist to check his watch. "Not for another hour."

"Hmm," she murmured. "I know you mentioned that you had work to do, but can you think of anything else you'd like to do with that hour?"

The soft rumble of his laugh reverberated along her skin. He lowered his head and whispered in her ear.

A cluster of wickedly erotic sensations traveled up her spine.

"I think that's the best idea I've heard in a long time," she said as she wrapped her arms around his neck and lost herself in his kiss.

Chapter 10

Jordan picked up a package of baby spinach and tossed it into the shopping cart. The "homemade" dinner he was planning to prepare tonight for Vicki consisted of prepackaged salad, canned vegetables and a frozen lasagna. He gave himself a fifty/fifty shot at not messing it up.

He never claimed to be a cook. The closest he usually came to cooking was warming up whatever leftover takeout was in his fridge. If his housekeeper, Laurie, were to see him in an actual grocery store, she would probably fall away in a dead faint. But he wanted to do something special for Vicki, even if his brand of "special" came already prepared. He decided to stop in at the bakery section to pick up an extrarich chocolate cake to make up for the lackluster meal.

"It's a good thing Vicki likes us for more than Daddy's cooking, huh, buddy?" he said to Mason, who was devouring the animal crackers Jordan had yet to pay for.

After adding a tomato, red onion and cucumber to his basket, he left the produce section in search of salad dressing. He had no idea if there was any at the house. The take-out restaurants always included more than enough with his order.

As he rounded the endcap stacked high with the canned artichoke hearts that had won the privilege of being this week's special hot-item buy, Jordan nearly ran his cart right into Darren Howerton, Jr.

The tension that stretched between them as they stared at each other in the middle of the grocery store was palpable.

"Jordan," Darren Jr. said, his voice stoic.

"How's it going, Darren?" Jordan replied, trying to infuse a bit of lightness into his reply. It wasn't all that long ago that he and the man standing before him had been friends. Jordan didn't want to lose that friendship over this election.

"How do you think it's going, Jordan?"

"I know things are a little awkward—"

"A *little* awkward?" Darren Jr. asked. "You accused my dad of cheating. I'd say things are more than just a *little* awkward."

"I never explicitly said it was Darren Sr. who cheated," Jordan said in his defense. "I said it was the campaign."

"Ah, yes. The campaign. My *father's* campaign. You can play whatever semantics game you want to, Jordan, but actions speak louder than words, and the minute you started up that petition you made your thoughts about my father's integrity loud and clear."

"Explain how he managed to win," Jordan challenged. "Oliver was leading in the polls up until election day. Explain to me how your father pulled off that defeat."

"I don't have to explain anything," Darren Jr. said, his mouth twisting with derision. "The election results speak for themselves."

Jordan released a weary breath. He was suddenly very tired.

"Look, Darren, despite what you may think, I didn't start that petition without giving it some serious thought. But something was not right with those election results. I would never have petitioned the outcome if I didn't think there was some credibility to my theory."

"You want to know what I think, Jordan? I think you're full of crap."

With that Darren Jr. turned and walked away, leaving his cart of groceries in the middle of the aisle.

Jordan's head fell forward. It suddenly felt as if the weight of the entire world had climbed onto his shoulders and sat there, weighing him down.

He was no longer convinced that this fight was worth it.

Hell, Oliver refused to take it up, and it was his seat in the state legislature that was on the line. If it wasn't worth it to Oliver to fight, why in the hell was he alienating lifelong friends over this? What did he expect to gain? Was it worth it just to prove that his polling data wasn't faulty? Did any of that even matter anymore?

It was as if Jordan was running on autopilot as he went through the checkout line and drove home. He put the lasagna to bake and the wine to chill, but his mind was occupied with thoughts of his run-in with Darren Jr.

The only bright spot in his gloomy afternoon was Mason's bath time. His son enjoyed himself so much in the tub that Jordan couldn't help but delight in it. But when Vicki arrived not long after he'd dressed Mason in his pajamas, Jordan still hadn't shaken off his moroseness.

"Hey there," Vicki greeted as she entered the house. She lifted Mason from his arms and planted a kiss on his cheek. "How are you two handsome guys doing?" She turned her attention to Jordan and frowned. "Okay, really, how are you doing? You look like someone rolled over your dog, or, in your case, your favorite attaché case."

"Good one," he answered with a wry smile. She always managed to get a laugh out of him.

Motioning her to follow him into the kitchen, he shared his earlier encounter with Darren Jr. in the condiments aisle at the grocery store. While Vicki strapped Mason into his high chair, Jordan retrieved the lasagna from the oven and served them both healthy portions, all with salad and sweet corn. He waited for Vicki to take her seat before pouring them both a glass of wine.

As he mashed up a bit of lasagna noodles on Mason's Thomas the Tank Engine plate, Jordan brought his story to a close with Darren Jr.'s dramatic grocery store exit.

Vicki paused with the fork halfway to her mouth. "He left the shopping cart in the middle of the aisle?"

"Yeah. I was nice enough to return the ice cream to the freezer."

"Wow." She put the fork down and picked up the wine instead. She took a sip, then brought her elbows onto the table and rested her chin on her folded hands. "Now that I think about it, I'm not all that surprised by his reaction, Jordan. You knew you would alienate people when you started that petition."

"Maybe I should just call the whole thing off."

"And you think *that* will help?"

"I can't piss anybody off any more than I already have."

"Really? So you think calling a stop to it now, before bringing the investigation to a conclusion, is going to endear you to anyone?"

"No," he said with a frown.

Vicki reached over and covered his hand with her own. "You demanded a recount because you believed there was an issue with the election. Do you still feel that way?"

"I do," he said. "But the longer this drags on, the worse it's going to get, Vicki."

"The damage is already done, Jordan. Calling a halt to the investigation will only leave you with a bunch of unanswered questions. Whether or not the answer is the one you're expecting, you won't be satisfied until you see this through to the end." She squeezed his hand. "See it to the end."

Jordan tugged her hand to his mouth and placed a gentle kiss in the center of her palm. "You are the personification of the voice of reason, Vicki Ahlfors."

"In the past that trait has led to some unflattering comments, usually by your sister when I've talked her out of doing something outrageous. Today, I take it that my voice of reason is a good thing."

"It's a very good thing," he said.

As he smiled into her eyes, Jordan couldn't help feeling that this was exactly what he wanted his life to be like for the next fifty years. Sitting at the dinner table with Mason and Vicki every night, sharing their day, planning out their future; at the moment, he couldn't think of a single thing he wanted more. Never had a woman fit more perfectly in his world. He wanted her to stay here. Permanently.

He'd always been a man of action. He needed to figure out just what he had to do to make that happen.

"Oooooh. I recognize that glow," Sandra said in a singsongy voice as she leaned against the counter where Vicki was working on the centerpieces for the Woolcotts' Kwanzaa celebration. Sandra rested her chin on her fist, and said, "It's the 'I just got laid' glow."

"Really, Sandra? Must you be so crass?"

"How is that crass? You're the one who's wearing the glow." She picked up a red-and-black Peruvian lily and pointed it at Vicki. "Let the record show that I said weeks ago that this was a good thing. Lord knows Jordan needed it."

Vicki was pretty sure her face was the color of a fire hydrant. If anyone knew how to embarrass her, it was her friend here.

Sandra's cell phone rang, halting her commentary on the positive effects a healthy sex life would bring to both Vicki's and Jordan's lives. When her face immediately beamed, Vicki automatically knew who was on the other end of the line.

Her own cell phone dinged with the arrival of a text message. She snatched the phone from the counter, hoping to see Jordan's name. Instead, it was a message from Angela Darrow, a fellow florist who had a thriving design studio and nursery in North Andover, a town just west of Wintersage. She and Angela were far away enough that they didn't compete for business, but close enough that, if necessary, they could help each other out.

Angela had a huge project—a decorating job for a

wedding with a winter-wonderland theme—and had asked to borrow Vicki's snow machine. In exchange for the machine Vicki had purchased last year when she'd decorated for the homecoming dance at Winter-sage Academy, Angela was going to loan her the five-foot-high cornucopia she had in storage. She had no idea why her friend had a cornucopia that was almost as tall as she was, but it would be the perfect focal point for the Woolcotts' Kwanzaa celebration.

As she headed west to North Andover, Vicki decided to stop in at Jordan's to check in on Mason, who had developed a cold over the past couple of days. When she'd left Jordan's last night, the baby had been so congested she could hear the rattle in his chest with every breath he took.

As she turned into the cul-de-sac where Jordan lived, Vicki spotted an unfamiliar black BMW in the driveway. She slowed her car, but continued toward the house. Vicki's stomach dropped at the sight of the woman standing on the porch with Jordan.

Allison Woolcott.

She slammed on her brakes, not even thinking to look to see if there was a car behind her. Vicki just sat there for several long moments, paralyzed by the scene in front of her. Allison stood mere inches from Jordan, one hand resting on his shoulder. She wore stylish dark blue jeans tucked into calf-length boots, and a shapely white coat that showed off her drop-dead-gorgeous figure.

Every inadequacy Vicki had ever harbored came roaring back. There wasn't a haircut or eye shadow palette in the world that could ever make her measure up to the woman standing on the porch with her hand on Jordan. Some women were born with that amazing beauty and the personality to match. Allison was one of them; Vicki was not.

Janelle's earlier warning came back to haunt her.

What if Allison decides to come back?

Jordan's ex had not been around in months. Vicki was certain that she was out of Jordan's and Mason's lives forever. Yet, here she was, looking as if she fit perfectly with Jordan.

Just as she was putting her car into Reverse, Jordan looked her way. Their eyes caught and held through the windshield, but Vicki didn't dare to stay another minute. She didn't want to see guilt or pity or sorrow in his eyes. She didn't want to witness Allison gloating.

Vicki backed into his neighbor's driveway and drove away. She didn't even consider confronting them like some jealous girlfriend, and she damn sure wasn't going to shed a tear over this.

She and Jordan had made no promises to each other. What they had was too new; she wasn't even sure if it could even be classified as a real relationship.

"It sure felt like one," Vicki whispered.

Still, it paled in comparison to what Jordan had with Allison. The two of them had a history—a rocky one, but nevertheless significant. They had been married; they had a *child* together, for goodness' sake.

How could she ever compete with that?

It was simple: she couldn't. She wouldn't even try.

Holding her head up, Vicki didn't bother to so much as glance in her rearview mirror. She continued driving, proud at how she was able to hold her emotions in check.

She stayed in North Andover longer than necessary, helping Angela decorate the reception hall and then treating herself to a nice dinner at a local steak house.

That was right, she could dine alone and be just fine with it.

It was after nine o'clock by the time she drove through the gates of her subdivision. When Vicki pulled up to her house, she spotted Jordan's car in the driveway. Maybe she should drive right past it.

What in the heck was she thinking? This was *her* house.

She pulled up next to his car and took her sweet time gathering her things before opening the door and sliding from behind the steering wheel.

"Let me explain about Allison," Jordan said the moment she got out of the car.

"You don't owe me an explanation, Jordan."

"Apparently, I do, especially since you wouldn't answer my calls or text messages."

Vicki hoisted her purse higher on her shoulder, folded her arms across her chest and leaned back on the driver's-side door.

"Okay," she said. "If you feel you have something to explain, go right ahead."

"I called Allison," he started.

His words slammed into her like a fist to the gut. *He'd* called his ex-wife?

"And she came running back? Just like that?" Vicki asked, proud that she could maintain the air of nonchalance she certainly wasn't feeling at the moment.

"No, she took two weeks before she even responded. I called her because I wanted to talk to her about her family's medical history."

Her spine stiffened. She had not expected to hear that. "Medical history?"

"Yes," Jordan said. "I called her the day after we brought Mason to urgent care. I had to fill out that patient information form and it had all these questions about both our medical histories. I realized then that I didn't know anything about her family's medical history."

He held his hands out, pleading with her to understand.

"Allison and I were together for such a short period of time. We never discussed whether diabetes runs in her family, or if there's a history of high blood pressure, or any of that. I need to know those things for Mason's sake."

"Of course you do," Vicki said. She suddenly felt like the biggest idiot in the world.

"I can only imagine what you thought when you came over and saw us together this afternoon," he continued. "I tried to call and explain, but you wouldn't answer your phone."

"I was an idiot. I'm sorry."

"I think the idiot title belongs to me. I should have told you that I'd called her."

"You don't owe me anything, Jordan. We haven't made any kind of declaration to each other. I'm sorry I made you feel as if you had to give me an explanation. Whether or not you see Allison shouldn't matter one way or the other."

He stared at her for some time before he shook his head and reached over to take her hands in his. "You don't get it, do you?" he asked, rubbing his thumb along the backs of her fingers. "I *want* it to matter, Vicki. I'm making my declaration right now. I want this to mean more."

He took a step forward and brought one hand up, cradling her jaw.

"I'm falling for you so much faster and harder than

I've ever fallen for anyone before. You need to know how much you've come to mean to me."

She tried to speak, but her heart was lodged in her throat.

"I'm in this, Vicki. You've told me what you want, and I'm telling you that I'm *in* this. Are you with me?"

Her head bobbed with her vigorous nod. "Yes," she managed to choke out. "I'm in this with you."

His eyes slid closed as he lowered his forehead to hers. "Thank you," he whispered. "These past few hours of not knowing whether or not I'd completely messed things up with you have been some of the most tortuous of my life." He opened his eyes and peered into hers. "I meant what I said, Vicki. You never have to worry about another woman, especially Allison. I'm with *you*. You're all I need."

His words washed over her like a soothing balm, restoring her confidence after the beating it had taken earlier today.

"I'm sorry I doubted you," she said. "If you follow me inside, I'd like to make it up to you."

His mouth tipped up in a smile. "With pleasure."

Chapter 11

Vicki could feel the excitement building in her veins as she opened the final box of carnations. The mixture of exhilaration and accomplishment swirling in her belly grew more wonderfully turbulent with each stem she stuck into place. She was so overwhelmed by the time she pinned the final flower to the float that she had to stop herself from bursting into tears.

She'd done it. She'd actually done it.

Petals wasn't a huge floral shop with corporate sponsors and a dozen employees working around the clock, just a one-woman shop with a handful of dedicated teens who believed in the work they were all doing.

At this point she didn't even care if Petals placed in the competition. Just the fact that her float would travel the streets of Wintersage on Saturday was enough for her.

"You lie through your teeth," she whispered to herself, a grin curling up the corners of her mouth.

She wanted to *win*. She'd come this far. Now she wanted it all.

A high-pitched whistle had her spinning around. A huge smile broke across her face when she spotted Jordan standing in the doorway. He started toward her.

"If this float doesn't come in first place this weekend I may just have to launch another investigation into voter fraud."

"I think one investigation is enough," she said, wrapping her arms around his neck and pulling him in close. She gave him a loud smack on the lips, then went in for a deeper kiss. God, she loved kissing him.

"This looks amazing," Jordan said. "You are going to shock your brothers speechless on Saturday."

"If they even bother coming," she said. "I haven't spoken to them since the Sunday dinner when I told them off."

"They'll be there," Jordan said.

"I hope they are," she said. "I can't wait to see their faces when they see my float. And if I win? My gloating will be so obnoxious they won't want to be around me."

His head flew back with his laugh. "There is not an obnoxious bone in your body."

"Just let this float take first place on Saturday. You'll see."

He shook his head, his mouth still twitching with mirth. "So now that the float is finished, is the Woolcotts' Kwanzaa celebration the only thing left on your plate?"

"Yep. I've completed all of the centerpieces. I don't have anything else to do for your parents' party until the morning when we set up."

"So you're free?"

"Until the parade on Saturday," she said, suddenly suspicious of the wicked gleam in his eyes. "Why?"

"Because I just filled your calendar for the next thirty-six hours. We're going to Vermont."

"Vermont? Jordan, I can't go to Vermont."

"You just said you were free until Saturday."

She opened her mouth to speak, but then closed it. He had her there.

"*You* can't go to Vermont," she countered. "You have Mason."

"He's already being spoiled to pieces by Grandma Nancy and Grandpa Stu."

A slow smile spread across Vicki's face. "We're really going to Vermont."

He nodded. "There is a suite at the Equinox Resort in Manchester with our name on it. We leave right now and return to Wintersage tomorrow evening. You'll be back in plenty of time to get a good night's sleep before the parade on Saturday." He leaned in and nipped at the skin just beneath her ear. "And you're going to need it, because you won't be getting any sleep while we're in Vermont."

The spot between her thighs instantly grew damp.

"You are so bad." She cupped his jaw and placed a tender kiss on his lips. "But you're also incredibly sweet."

"I haven't always been this sweet. You're a good influence." He kissed her neck. "Now let's go and get you packed up so we can hit the road."

They quickly made it to her house and in less than an hour were heading northwest on 495. Light snow flurries peppered the windshield as they climbed into the higher elevations of southern Vermont's Green Mountains.

When they pulled up to the luxury resort's grand entrance, Vicki couldn't hold in her gasp. The towering white columns stretching to the stately structure's second floor added such elegance, while the rocking chairs on the promenade that wrapped around the massive exterior created a cozy feel.

A bellman retrieved their bags from the car, and Jordan checked them in while she toured the spacious lobby with its simple yet refined furnishings. Moments later, Jordan claimed her by the hand and guided her to the Green Mountain Suite on the resort's top floor.

He held up his index finger. "One minute," he said, before inserting the key and opening the door just wide enough to peek inside. When he turned to face her, a secretive grin had made its way to his lips.

"After you," he said.

Eyeing him suspiciously, Vicki entered the suite and, once again, was so blown away that she let out a sharp gasp.

Never mind the sheer luxuriousness of the massive space. What truly stole her breath were the dozens of roses and multitude of candles decorating the downstairs room.

"I hope you don't mind that I had to use another florist," Jordan said. "It would have ruined the surprise if I'd ordered the flowers from you."

"I don't mind," she said with a laugh. She turned to him and wrapped her arms around him. "I don't know what to say, Jordan. This is just... It's amazing."

"*You're* amazing," he said before leaning forward and gracing her lips with the sweetest, most decadent kiss. "I want you to forget about everything tonight. The float competition, your family, the business. All of it. I want you to just concentrate on what we have here.

"You've come to mean so much to me, Vicki. I don't know why I've been so blind, but I thank God every day that my eyes have been opened."

Her heart swelled to the point that Vicki thought it would burst clear out of her chest. Wrapping her arms around his neck, she tugged his head toward her and kissed him with all the love filling her soul.

They stumbled into the great room, leaving a trail of clothes in their wake. Within minutes they were both naked and sprawled out on the rug in front of the fireplace.

The blaze turned Jordan's chest a brilliant shade of bronze. As he hovered over her, Vicki relished in the beauty of his fit body. He worked a white-collar job; how he maintained such a fabulous physique was beyond her.

He pulled a condom from the wallet he'd tossed on the sofa. His intense gaze burning with passion, he rolled the latex over his erection, then hooked his arms beneath her knees and pulled her to him. Vicki reached down between them and fisted his erection, rubbing her palm up and down the solid length before guiding him into her body.

Her eyes fell shut and her back bowed off the floor as he filled her. She would never, ever get enough of this feeling, the moment when his welcoming thickness first entered her. Nothing she'd ever experienced in life could match the pleasure she felt when his erection stretched her body to its limits.

As he pumped his hips, Vicki surged with him, the ebb and flow of their bodies creating a beautiful, sensual dance. She settled her palms against his chest, caressing them up and down his glorious skin. The cadence of his heartbeat matched her own, nearly bringing tears to her eyes as she realized the depth of their connection. They were linked together on so many levels, body and soul.

Jordan dipped his head to her neck and glided his tongue down the gentle slope, trailing it along her skin to the shallow valley between her breasts. He traced the underside of each breast before pressing delicate kisses to the tips.

The light teasing was too much for Vicki to withstand. Thrusting her chest out, she cradled his head in her hands and held him to her, pleading with him to relieve the ache his wicked tongue had created.

"Suck them," she breathed. "Please, Jordan."

His deep chuckle reverberated against her skin, but seconds later he put her out of her misery, closing his lips over her left breast. He massaged her right nipple, pinching and plucking it before bringing his mouth over and laving the tip with several long, wet licks. Then he sucked. Hard.

At the same time his hips thrust. Harder.

The sensations collided in her brain, shooting sparks from all of her pleasure centers and turning her entire body into a numbing mass of ecstasy.

Jordan continued his outrageously satisfying assault on her senses. His hips and mouth worked in tandem. The harder he sucked, the deeper his rigid hardness plunged inside her. Vicki didn't know which to focus on, the magic his mouth was creating or the erotic pleasure that hummed throughout her body with every delicious slide of his solid erection.

Just as she felt the climax building in her belly, Jordan quickened his pace, plunging in and out, driving his hips against hers in rapid succession until her entire being seemed to explode into a million pieces.

And still Jordan continued to thrust, his hardness driving deeper and faster until his body stiffened above her and a groan tore from his throat.

He collapsed on top of her, the feel of his delicious weight something to be cherished. Vicki wanted nothing more than to remain in this very spot for the next twenty-four hours.

"Damn, you're good at that," Jordan said between shallow breaths.

"You're not too shabby yourself," she said with a laugh.

He braced his hands on either side of her head and started to push himself up, but Vicki stopped him, clamping her hands on his shoulders and her legs around his waist, holding him to her.

"Where are you going?" she asked.

"I want to salvage the plans I had in place. Believe it or not, my intent was to wine and dine you before we got to this part of the evening."

"I'll bet you're happy I'm easy."

His grin matched hers. "That means that I can expect more of this *after* I properly wine and dine you, right?"

"You can count on that."

It soon became apparent just how much trouble Jordan had gone to in order to wine and dine her. Dressed in plush bathrobes provided by the resort, they settled in for a candlelit dinner at a table overlooking the impeccable gardens and, just beyond them, the majestic mountain range.

After feasting on a superb meal of Maine lobster and mouthwatering filet mignon, they shared a decadent chocolate lava cake from one of her favorite bakeries in Boston. The fact that he'd both remembered her mentioning the cake from a silly conversation they'd had during one of their earlier dates, and gone to the trouble of having it brought from Boston, touched something deep inside of Vicki.

Following dinner, Jordan insisted she sit by the fire and enjoy her second glass of wine while he took care of "something special" upstairs. Several minutes later, he guided her up to the suite's impressive bathroom, with windows overlooking the mountain landscape.

Vicki was wholly overwhelmed by the fantasy he'd created. Dozens of thick pillar candles blazed brilliantly around the bathroom. There were even more roses scattered around, including dozens of petals floating on the surface of the steaming water in the huge sunken tub. Another bottle of wine stood chilling in a wine bucket.

Her hand to her throat, she turned to him and said in a soft voice, "I can't believe this, Jordan. No one has ever done something this remarkable just for me."

He trailed a single finger along her cheek. "I wanted you to feel as special as you really are," he said. "It is nothing less than you deserve."

Vicki's chest tightened with the sweetest ache, and emotion clogged her throat.

God, she loved this man.

It had happened much quicker than she ever thought possible, but in that moment it was impossible to deny it.

She loved him. And she wanted him to know it.

Cradling his jaw in one hand, she rested her forehead against his and stared into his eyes.

"I'm in love with you, Jordan Woolcott. I don't know if that was in your plans. I don't even care if you don't feel the same way yet. But I need you to know that I am in love with you."

"Vicki, how could you ever think that I don't feel

the same way?" he asked. "What do you think this is all about? Just saying the words wasn't enough for me. I wanted to show you how much I love you."

Everything inside of her melted at his achingly sweet words. He drew his lips over hers in a kiss that left her breathless, then stripped her out of her robe and helped her into the perfumed bathwater. Discarding his robe, he climbed in and settled against the rim of the tub. Vicki molded her back to his chest, savoring how good it felt to feel his smooth skin against hers.

Jordan traced dewy circles along her arm, listening as she went through the schedule of events for Saturday.

"Are you nervous about the parade?" he asked.

"A part of me is more than ready for it, but there's still a part that is so afraid that I'm going to make a fool of myself."

"Don't," Jordan said, pressing a kiss to her damp shoulder. "No matter where you place in the competition, you need to remember that you've done something that very few people have the courage to do, Vicki. You put yourself out there."

"You're right," she said. "Just a few months ago, I never would have contemplated doing something like this. I guess it's all a part of the process."

"For growing your business?"

She shook her head. "For finding myself."

She turned and looked up at him. "I've been hiding the real me for so long, Jordan. I've always been so cautious, afraid of what people would say if I stepped out of those tight boundaries that I've always been pressured to remain in. I was too afraid of how my parents and brothers would view me, of what Sandra and Janelle and everyone else who's become accustomed to sweet, sensible Vicki would think if I ventured too far away from this role I've been confined to my entire life."

"So what do you think about the person you've found?"

A small smile tipped up the corner of her lips. "I like her."

"I like her, too," he said. "She's so much stronger than she realizes."

"I'm starting to realize it," she said. "It took me a while, but I now see that winning this float competition was never my real goal. The most important thing in all of this is finally proving to myself that I'm strong enough and capable enough to do whatever I set out to do."

"You amaze me," Jordan said, the reverence in his voice making her skin tingle. "You have nothing to prove, Vicki. You're amazing. That's all there is to it."

She lifted herself slightly so that she could reach his lips, then she settled back against his chest and asked, "What about you?"

"What about me?"

"Are you done proving whatever you set out to prove when you started that petition? Are you ready to accept the results of the election, even if it comes out that you were wrong?"

Jordan exhaled a deep breath. "I don't have much choice, do I?"

"Yes, you do," she said. "You can continue on the way you have for the past month. You can allow it to fester and drive yourself crazy." She looked at him over her shoulder. "Or you can accept it and move on."

Bracing her hands on the edge of the tub, Vicki lifted herself up and turned to face him, straddling his thighs. She cupped his jaw in both hands.

"You said that the most important thing about Oliver Windom's campaign is that he agreed to help Mass Mentors. If you explain to Darren exactly why you supported Oliver and why you are so passionate about the program, he will listen to you."

"You don't think I've burned that bridge?"

"Not only is Darren a sensible man, but he's a *good* man, Jordan. I know you believe that Oliver is a breath of fresh air because he's younger and cut from a different cloth than the older generation, but don't sell Darren short."

"I probably won't do anything until I hear from the investigators that I hired, but you've given me something to think about."

"Good," Vicki said. She settled onto his lap and dipped her head, running her tongue along his moistened neck. "Now let me give you something else to think about."

Vicki hugged her arms across her chest as she tried her hardest to appear cool and collected on the outside. On the inside, she was a ball of chaotic nerves.

When she'd driven up to the staging ground for the parade, stunned was the only way she could describe how she felt as she stared at the elaborate floats. Stunned and overwhelmed. The participants had stepped their games up to a new level this year.

There was a float dedicated to significant milestones in New England's revolutionary history, including the Boston Tea Party and a musket made out of black lilies to signify the famous "shot heard around the world." Another float showcased the eight U.S. presidents born in the New England area. There were several seaside-themed floats, staples in the parade every year.

One of the most elaborate was dedicated to the region's professional football team. For a minute, Vicki feared the team's star quarterback was on the float. Thank goodness that wasn't the case. It would have been the automatic winner by sheer popularity.

Her Christmas from Around the World float wasn't as large as some of the others, and it didn't have the animatronics and other mechanical marvels, but for a one-woman shop, Vicki couldn't help but be proud. As she looked at the excited faces of the kids from Mass Mentors who had put such hard work into the float and who would be riding on it during the parade, she knew that no matter the outcome, every sacrifice she'd made for this competition had been worth it.

"I think you've got this," came a voice from behind her.

She turned to find Jordan and Mason a few feet away.

"Hey there, you two," she said.

The toddler looked as adorable as ever, dressed in black corduroy pants, a white button-down shirt, a red sweater vest and a Santa hat on his head. His father looked downright edible, showing off his casual side in fashionable dark blue jeans, a black cashmere sweater and a black leather jacket.

"You think I have a shot, huh?" Vicki asked, leaning over for a kiss as she took Mason from his arms. "Maybe if this little one here was the grand marshal."

"I can't deny that he would help, but I think you've got this even without this charmer riding shotgun." Jordan trailed a finger along her cheek before capturing her chin in his hand and tipping her head up. "I'm so proud of you. You did an incredible job."

"I had a lot of help from my team."

"But it was your vision, and it is spectacular."

Her heart swelled with gratitude. "Thank you," she said.

The parade coordinator blew a whistle and directed the tractor drivers to line up the floats according to the numbers that had been assigned to them. The parade would start at 2:00 p.m., which meant they had just under an hour to enjoy some of the other festivities of the annual extravaganza.

Vicki and Jordan brought Mason to Santa's Workshop, which was held in the lobby of Town Hall in the middle of the square. Because Mason had already taken pictures with Santa during the Bright Lights at Forest Park tour, they were able to bypass the line of kids waiting to snatch a portrait with St. Nick.

While Vicki helped Mason play some of the games that had been set up for the kids, Jordan ventured out to several of the food vendors, returning with miniature lobster sliders and three gingerbread men for dessert. Vicki took one bite of the sandwich and pushed the rest toward him. She was too nervous to eat.

The minutes ticked by at lightning speed, and sooner than she'd anticipated, she, Mason and Jordan were heading out of Town Hall to stake out their spot on Main Street for the parade.

Despite her anxiety, Vicki still managed to soak in the pure joy of the day. It was cold, but the sky was clear, and the exuberance radiating from the crowds was palpable. She waved at a little girl who was sitting on her father's shoulders, waiting for the parade to start. She remembered doing the same when she was that age. The thought brought a smile to her face.

As they walked in the direction of the Silk Sisters'

yellow Victorian, near where they planned to watch the parade as it rolled down Wintersage's main thoroughfare, Jordan's footsteps slowed. Vicki looked over at him and followed the direction of his eyes.

The Howerton clan stood a few yards away—Darren Jr. and Sr., Janelle and her husband, Ballard.

"Great," Jordan muttered.

Seeing them there only added to Vicki's pending anxiety attack. The float competition was enough to rattle her nerves for the day; she didn't need tension over the election adding to it.

"This doesn't have to be a big deal," she said to Jordan, urging him forward.

As they neared the Howertons, Darren Sr. walked right up to Jordan and put out his hand.

"I want you to know that I don't harbor any hard feelings toward you, son," he said.

Darren Jr. snorted and shook his head. Apparently, he didn't share his father's graciousness.

Jordan accepted Darren Sr.'s outstretched palm. "You know that none of this has been personal, right?"

The older man shrugged. "It's hard not to take it personally, but you did what you thought you had to do. I know for a fact that you haven't found anything untoward with my campaign yet, and I can assure you that you're not going to find anything." A smile came upon his lips. "I don't gloat often, Jordan, but I am looking forward to telling you 'I told you so.'"

With that, Darren Sr. turned and greeted several people who had come to speak to him.

Darren Jr. took his place, stepping up to Jordan and saying, "I won't be satisfied with 'I told you so,'" he said. "When you realize that you were wrong, I expect you to apologize not just to my father, but to his entire campaign, Jordan."

The tension returned with a vengeance as the amity they'd experienced moments ago with Darren Sr.'s diplomatic greeting evaporated. Vicki noticed the muscle in Jordan's cheek jump as he held his face rigid.

"I guess we'll have to wait and see what my investigators find," he said.

"They won't find anything," Darren Jr. bit out through clenched teeth, and then he turned to join Janelle and Ballard, who were standing a few feet away.

Vicki hadn't even realized that the parade had already started. She turned to find the Boston Tea Party float moving its way up Main Street. Her Christmas from Around the World was fifteenth in the line of twenty floats, so between the slowly moving tractors and marching bands, she still had a bit of time before the Petals float would pass.

Vicki stood on her tiptoes, trying to see which float was coming up next. That was when she spotted Terrance and Spence walking toward her. Her parents followed them.

Great. Just what she needed to send her spiraling into a full-blown panic attack.

But then she noticed the smiles on their faces.

"We haven't missed your float, have we?" Her mother greeted her with a hug.

"No," Vicki said. "There are four more floats ahead of it."

"Good," her father said before placing a kiss on her cheek.

She stared at her brothers. "Wait, you two came out here to see my float?" she asked. "You haven't been to the extravaganza in years."

"We came out here to support you," Terrance said.

"Yeah, and that call from Jordan had nothing to do with it," Spence said, cutting his eyes at Jordan. "The threats were totally uncalled-for, dude."

Vicki turned to Jordan, her mouth agape. "You threatened my brothers for me? That's the sweetest thing I've ever heard."

Terrance snorted and hooked a thumb toward them. "These two were made for each other."

Vicki kissed her brother's cheek and said, "Thanks for coming *and* for making the toy drive a success. I heard it went off without a hitch." Then she wrapped her arms around Jordan and Mason. "Thank you," he said.

"This means a lot to you, and so does your family. They needed to be here to show you some support."

She really could not love him any more than she did at this very moment. Jordan gestured toward the street with his chin. "You may want to turn around."

She turned, and there, gliding along the streets of Wintersage for everyone to see, was her labor of love. Her kids from Mass Mentors, who had all chosen to wear costumes mimicking Sinterklaas, the Dutch version of Old St. Nick, started to whoop and holler when they spotted her.

Vicki laughed along with them, wiping tears of mirth and joy from her eyes. Her mother came up to her and wrapped her arms around Vicki's shoulders.

"The float is absolutely gorgeous," Christine Ahlfors said. "I'm sorry I ever doubted you."

"It's okay, Mom," she said, returning the hug.

"I think it's time AFM joins the holiday extravaganza," her father said. "Maybe Petals will work on our float next year."

"I don't think you can afford me," Vicki said teasingly.

Twenty minutes later, they all joined her at the stage where the extravaganza's committee was preparing to announce the winner of the competition. When Petals won third place, a huge roar lifted from her cheering section. Vicki was pretty sure it would take no less than a month before she was able to wipe the smile off her face.

She accepted her white third-place ribbon and walked off the stage. Janelle was waiting for her just to the right of the stairs. She held her arms out.

"Congratulations, honey," she said, squeezing her in a long hug. "I'm so proud of you."

Vicki's throat tightened with emotion. "Thank you."

"Someone else wants to congratulate you, too." Janelle held up her phone and a slightly pixelated image of Sandra appeared. She and Isaiah had been forced to miss the extravaganza due to a meeting with a major furniture retailer in New York who was interested in carrying Swoon Couture Home in their stores.

Sandra squealed with delight and blew kisses, promising to give her a proper congrats when they met at the Quarterdeck Monday night.

The crowds dispersed now that the winners of the float competition had been announced. Vicki and Jordan decided not to return to the spot where they'd watched the parade near the Victorian. She was still stoked after placing in the competition, and she didn't want to spoil it with the strained atmosphere of being around the Howertons.

Instead, they took Mason to see the live reindeer that had been brought in special for the extravaganza, then

Jordan took him on the Polar Express train ride that meandered around the town's main square.

By early evening, Mason was worn-out. He'd fallen asleep with the adorable Santa hat still on his head. Vicki gently pushed his stroller back and forth as she sat on a bench with Jordan, her head resting on his shoulder.

"It turned out to be a pretty good day," Jordan murmured against her temple.

"I can't complain," she said, smiling. Her smile dimmed a smidgeon as she stared out at the children running around the square, playing a game of tag. "I could have done without seeing that confrontation between you and Darren Jr.," she said.

"We all could have done without that," he said. "At this point, I just want this entire thing with the election to come to an end."

"The sooner, the better," Vicki said.

Jordan's phone rang. Vicki moved from where she'd been resting against him so that he could retrieve it from his pocket.

He blew out a breath. "It's my investigator."

Vicki's heart started to pound against the walls of her chest.

Jordan swept his thumb across the touch screen. "What do you have for me, Mike?"

He sat there in silence, just listening for several minutes.

"Are you sure?" he asked in a voice drenched in disbelief.

Vicki's heart started to beat faster. It pounded more erratically as a look of dread claimed Jordan's face.

Finally, in a hoarse voice, Jordan said, "Thanks for your hard work."

"What is it?" she asked the second he ended the call. "Did the investigators find proof of ballot tampering?" Her stomach was a ball of nerves as she waited for his answer.

His throat worked as he swallowed, and then he nodded. "Yes," he said, his voice still raspy. "There's proof of tampering."

Vicki's heart sank. Her eyes fell shut. This was going to kill Janelle.

"But it wasn't Darren's campaign," Jordan continued. Vicki's eyes flew open. "It was Oliver's."

Chapter 12

Jordan brought the mug of eggnog to his lips but set it back down without taking a sip.

"You don't like it?" Vicki asked.

Jordan looked over to where she sat on the floor, her legs tucked underneath her. She was surrounded by Christmas wrapping paper, ribbon and empty cardboard boxes. She'd spent the hour since they had arrived home from spending Christmas Day at both his and her parents' wrapping the empty boxes so that Mason could unwrap them. It was his son's new favorite pastime.

"There's nothing wrong with the eggnog," Jordan said. "I'm just not in the mood for it."

She frowned. "Jordan, I hate seeing you like this."

"Don't worry about me, Vicki. I'm okay," he told her, even though they both knew it was a lie.

He felt like such a callous ass. Vicki had spent the entire day trying to lift him out of his funky mood, but if the Christmas spirit hadn't gripped him yet, Jordan doubted it would happen at all.

Vicki gracefully rose from the floor and carried the freshly wrapped boxes over to Mason, who was encircled by the crumpled paper and bows from the half dozen boxes he'd just finished unwrapping.

"Prezzie," his son called, excitedly clapping his hands.

Vicki set the boxes before him, then started toward Jordan. She looked divine in her cream-colored silk shirt and matching wool pants. How she'd managed to keep the outfit spotless, even through feeding Mason his Christmas dinner, was beyond comprehension. She was amazing.

She wasn't just amazing, she was more than he deserved, especially with all his brooding. Yet here she was. And not for the first time today it made him feel like the luckiest man in the world.

Jordan held his arm out, inviting her to snuggle up alongside him on the sofa. She joined him, folding her legs underneath her and resting her head on his chest.

"I'm sorry I'm ruining your Christmas," he said, pressing a kiss to the crown of her head.

"Who says you're ruining my Christmas?" She twisted around until she lay across his thighs, and rested her head on the sofa's arm. "You haven't ruined anyone's Christmas, Jordan. I know it's been rough since you discovered the truth about the ballot tampering. It was a shock to your system, one that will definitely take longer than just a couple of days to get over."

She reached up and cupped his jaw. "I don't want all of that election mess to overshadow the things you should be focusing on today. Family. Love. All of us being together." She pointed at Mason. "Just look at your son over there. He is having the time of his life."

Jordan couldn't help but laugh as he observed Mason once again tearing into the wrapped boxes, his two-teeth smile wide as he ripped through the colorful paper. A silver bow clung haphazardly to the side of his head, and another had found a place to rest on his knee.

"That boy is a character, isn't he?" he asked.

"I don't know if I've ever seen someone so happy to receive an empty box on Christmas."

A smile tipped up the corner of his mouth, yet Jordan still couldn't shake the melancholy that continued to grip him. If only he could coax his mind into thinking of something other than the treachery his investigator had uncovered. But betrayal was a hard pill to swallow, and Oliver Windom's perfidy was even harder to take, because Jordan had believed in him so damn much.

At least he now understood why Oliver had been so quick to concede the election, and why he'd been so against Jordan's demands to contest the results. The moment Mike, his investigator, had revealed what he'd found, the pieces had begun to fall into place.

Winning had never been Oliver's endgame. The entire campaign had been a scheme cooked up by Oliver and Morris London, one of the political strategists who had been a part of the campaign before Jordan had climbed aboard. Oliver's entire reason for joining the race for state representative had been to skim money off the top of the campaign finance fund.

They had known that Darren Howerton was a strong candidate who would be tough to beat. Their plan had been to run a race that would gain enough support to attract a significant amount of campaign dollars, but to remain just inadequate enough not to win.

Jordan had put a kink in the chains when he'd joined and quickly taken over as campaign manager. He'd turned a satisfactory campaign into a well-oiled political machine, applying complex polling strategies and raising Oliver's profile among voters. He had no idea he'd been thwarting Oliver's plans to get rich quick by stealing campaign dollars.

After interviewing county election commissioners in several of the districts where Oliver had polled the strongest yet ended up losing on election night, Jordan's investigator had begun to notice a pattern. As he had dug deeper, he'd discovered that in all of those districts a disproportionate number of absentee ballots had mysteriously gone missing.

It turned out that Oliver had paid employees in the county clerk's offices in the districts where he'd had the best polling numbers to destroy absentee ballots in hopes of tipping the odds in Darren Howerton's favor.

Oliver hadn't wanted to serve the people of Massachusetts. He'd only wanted to serve himself. And Jordan had fallen for it hook, line and sinker. For the second time in his life, he'd put his full trust in someone who'd turned out to be the total opposite of the person he'd thought them to be.

Was he fundamentally flawed when it came to judging people?

"Stop thinking so hard," Vicki said.

Jordan stared down at the woman sprawled so invitingly across his lap. She was the one person whose character he would never have to question. She had been a steady rock over these turbulent couple of days, as he'd looked into his investigator's findings to confirm that they were true.

His Christmas had not turned out quite the way he'd

planned, but if there were a Christmas miracle to be had, it would be that Vicki's steadiness would be there to see him through for many more days to come.

"I love you," he said.

With a smile tilting up the corners of her lips, she cupped his jaw and smoothed her thumb back and forth across his cheek. "I will never get tired of hearing you say that."

"Good, because I plan to say it a lot." He stroked her lips with his fingertips. "You mean so much to me, Vicki. You're like a piece of me that I didn't know was missing."

"Thank you for opening your heart enough to let me inside," she whispered.

Jordan dipped his head and captured her lips in a kiss.

"Prezzie!" Mason screamed, thumping an unwrapped cardboard box on the floor.

"Uh-oh." Vicki laughed as she pushed up from Jordan's lap. "Time to feed the beast. You may have to go to the store to get more wrapping paper. We're going to run out soon."

"Check under the tree, toward the back," Jordan said. "I think there may be a gift still there."

"Are you sure?" Vicki said, walking over to the tree and gently moving a couple of ornament-laden branches around.

Jordan's breath began to escalate as he nervously waited for her to find the box.

"You're right," she said, pulling out the flat rectangular box. She brought it over to Mason and stooped down in front of him. "Looks as if we forgot one of your presents from Santa."

Mason grabbed the box from her hand and quickly

started to tear the paper. Jordan's pulse pounded harder with every rip.

"Let me help you with that," Vicki said once all the paper was gone. She lifted the top off the box and pulled out the toddler-size T-shirt. "There you go," she said, handing the shirt to Mason.

"Why don't you read it for him?" Jordan said.

She looked at him with a curious gleam in her eye, then took the shirt and held it out in front of her.

She gasped.

"Jordan," she said. "Is this for real?"

She turned the shirt to him. It read, Will You Marry Us?

Jordan rose from the sofa and walked over to them. He dropped on the floor next to them and took the shirt from her, pulling it over Mason's white undershirt. He turned the baby to face her.

"I figured you wouldn't be able to say no to this face," Jordan said.

Vicki covered her mouth with both hands. Tears began to stream from her eyes. She reached over and wrapped her arms around his neck.

"There is nothing I want more than to marry you." She looked down at Mason. "The both of you. Becoming a part of this family, making you two *my* family, is the greatest gift I could ever hope for."

Exuberant chatter floated around the ballroom where the Woolcotts' Kwanzaa gathering was being held, as guests celebrated the start of the weeklong observance set aside to honor the values of African culture. In keeping with the traditions of the holiday, they feasted on the *mazao,* or crops, of fresh fruit, nuts and an array of harvest vegetables, along with a bounty of fragrant African dishes.

The entire room was awash in red, green and black, with the giant cornucopia Vicki had brought in serving as the focal point. Guests presented gifts to the cornucopia, which would be given out on Imani, the seventh and last day of the celebration.

Vicki felt Jordan's eyes on her as she listened to John Bancroft, a longtime associate of Ahlfors Financial Management, talk about the recent trip he and his wife had taken to Jamaica.

"It sounds heavenly," Vicki said, smiling at the man, who felt it necessary to describe every single detail about the all-inclusive resort where he and his wife had vacationed.

Out of the corner of her eye she noticed Jordan standing several yards away, his intense gaze searing and seductive.

"I would love to hear more about the fake volcano at the hotel's pool, but I see one of the centerpieces has a flower out of place. As the decorator, I just can't have that."

"Of course, of course," the man said.

Vicki quickly made her exit and headed straight to Jordan.

"Having fun?" he asked as he wrapped one arm around her waist and pulled her against him.

Vicki lifted her face to receive his kiss. Keeping her voice low, she whispered, "If you want to go to Jamaica for our honeymoon, I know where you can slide down a fake volcano and into a pool made to look like lava."

"The only thing I plan to slide down on our honeymoon is you," he said against her lips.

The shivers that cascaded along her body had no

business being there in the midst of a ballroom filled with all their family and friends.

"You're trying to get me in trouble, aren't you?" she asked.

"Me? Of course not," he said, the wicked gleam in his eyes belying his words. His expression sobered, and Vicki didn't have to think too long to figure out why.

"Let me guess," she said. "Darren Howerton just walked in."

Upon learning of Oliver Windom's cheating on the evening of the holiday extravaganza, Vicki and Jordan had gone over to the Howertons to break the news to Darren Sr., only to learn that the man had gone down to Boston to spend the holidays. Tonight was the first time they'd seen him since discovering the truth about the election results.

Jordan let out a deep breath. "I don't want to wait another minute to apologize," he said.

Vicki took his hand and squeezed it.

"It takes a man with integrity to admit when he's wrong," she said. "And you have as much integrity as anyone I know."

Jordan's eyes filled with gratitude. He crushed his lips to hers in a swift, sweet kiss. "I love you so much."

"I love you, too," she said against his lips.

Hand in hand, they started for Darren Sr., who was speaking to Jordan's father, Stuart Woolcott. Vicki saw the moment when Darren Jr. spotted them heading for his father. He started walking toward them, as well. They all arrived to the two older gentlemen at the same time.

Jordan cleared his throat to get their attention. Darren Sr. and Stuart both turned.

"I hope you don't mind my interrupting, but I owe

this man an apology," Jordan said. He looked directly into Darren Sr.'s eyes. "By now, I know you've heard the results of the investigation I started. I didn't want to apologize over the phone, because it's something you deserve to hear face-to-face. I am truly sorry for the accusations I made against you and your campaign, Darren. I put my trust and support in the wrong candidate. All I can do is ask that you forgive me."

The older gentlemen stood there for a moment without speaking. Finally, he said, "I want to know why, Jordan. Why did you back Oliver's campaign?"

"I was intrigued by several of his ideas," he began. "But mostly, I agreed with Oliver's support for Mass Mentors, a mentorship program that was started by a former classmate of mine."

As Jordan explained the program to Darren Sr., Vicki stepped in to mention that it was kids from Mass Mentors who'd helped to create her float.

"This sounds like something that should be statewide," Darren Sr. said.

"I think so, too," Jordan agreed. "Oliver pledged to fight for funding for the program. It's desperately needed."

"Supporting our state's underserved youth has always been a priority for me," Darren Sr. said. "You should have come to me with this idea, Jordan. I would have supported it."

"I'm sorry I didn't," he said. "But I'm here to help now. If you'll allow it, I want to work with you on this."

"I would love to have your input," Darren said, clamping Jordan on the shoulder with one hand and offering the other to shake. As the two shook hands, the tension of the past month seemed to melt away.

"I'm proud of you, son," Stuart said, shaking Jordan's hand, as well.

Stuart and Darren Sr. both left to join the others at the head table, leaving Jordan, Vicki and Darren Jr. together. Jordan turned to his former schoolmate and Darren Jr., too, held out his hand.

"I appreciate you doing that," Darren Jr. said.

"When I'm wrong, I say I'm wrong," Jordan replied. "And I was wrong to accuse your father of cheating. I regret that I put my trust in someone as untrustworthy as Oliver Windom. If I'd known the kind of person he was, I would have left his campaign and come to work on Darren's."

"We would have welcomed you," Darren Jr. said with a grin. "It was miraculous to see how quickly you turned Windom's campaign around. It was because of you that he nearly pulled off a win." He shook his head. "I don't know if you would ever consider leaving law, but if you ask me, you've got a career as a political strategist waiting for you."

Jordan chuckled and stuck his hand out again. "I appreciate you saying so."

After a vow to get together over dinner soon to talk about the Mass Mentors program, Vicki and Jordan headed for their table toward the front of the ballroom.

Stuart Woolcott was at the microphone, welcoming everyone to the Woolcotts' annual Kwanzaa gathering. He took a few moments to explain the cultural holiday and the meaning behind the seven principles of Kwanzaa.

"It is befitting that we are all here today with family and friends as we celebrate Umoja, this first day of Kwanzaa. *Umoja* means unity. May we all continue to be united throughout the years to come." He held up his glass and toasted everyone in the room.

Jordan clinked his glass against hers, a secretive smile on his face. Then, tugging her by the hand, he started toward his father.

"Jordan," Vicki said in a loud whisper, but he continued walking.

He stepped up to the microphone his father had just vacated.

"Can I have everyone's attention please?" Jordan spoke into the microphone. "Seeing as we are here celebrating unity tonight, this is probably the most appropriate place for me to do this."

Setting his champagne glass on the table next to them, Jordan got down on one knee.

A collective gasp rent the air.

He pulled a ring box out of the pocket of his tailored tux and looked up at her.

"I asked you last night, but here I am, formally asking in front of all our family and friends. I want to unite my life with yours. I want you to become my wife. Will you marry me, Vicki?"

She nodded, tears streaming down her face. "Yes," Vicki answered. "Yes, I will marry you."

An excited roar sounded around the room.

"I knew it!" Sandra shouted. She ran over to them and gathered Vicki in her arms. "I knew this was going to happen the minute I saw the way Jordan looked at you at my wedding." She kissed both Vicki and Jordan on the cheek. "I am so happy for the both of you, and for Mason, too. He is getting the perfect stepmother."

Vicki's heart swelled. "Thank you," she said.

She turned and accepted hugs from Janelle and then from her parents. Her brothers all teased Jordan good-naturedly before showering Vicki with congratulatory kisses.

When she turned back to Sandra and Janelle, they both wore conspiratorial smiles.

"What?" Vicki asked, unable to squelch her suspicions.

"Give us one minute," Sandra said. "We have a surprise for you."

A few minutes later, she and Janelle returned to the ballroom carrying a flat garment box. They set it on the table before her.

Eyeing them cautiously, Vicki opened the box and gasped.

"What? How?"

It was her mother's wedding gown.

"You mentioned at the Quarterdeck a few months ago that you would love to get married in your mother's gown," Sandra said. "Last week, when I saw the way your eyes lit up just at the mention of Jordan's name, and the way his did the same whenever someone said *your* name, I knew a proposal couldn't be far off."

She took Vicki by the shoulders and brought her in for a hug. Janelle joined them.

"And to think I used to complain about not having sisters," Vicki said.

"So did I." Sandra laughed.

"Me, too," Janelle added.

"I think God knew what He was doing when He brought us all together," Vicki said. "You two will forever be my sisters."

Epilogue

"By the power vested in me by the State of Massachusetts, I now pronounce you Mr. and Mrs. Jordan Woolcott. Sir, you may kiss your lovely bride."

Vicki turned to Jordan and couldn't hold back her wide smile as he leaned in and kissed her. And kissed her. And kissed her.

He kissed her for so long that her father loudly cleared his throat, causing the wedding guests to erupt in laughter.

"Congratulations, Mrs. Woolcott," Jordan said, his grin as wide as hers.

"Congratulations to you, too," she returned.

She kissed him again before they started down the small aisle in the tastefully decorated chapel. They led everyone to the chapel's small gathering hall next door. On the outside it looked like a rustic seaside cottage, but the inside had been made to look like a winter wonderland, with white gossamer draping from the ceilings and sparkling white lights casting an ethereal glow on every surface.

The gathering was small, with only the members of the Woolcott, Ahlfors and Howerton families, along with a few close friends, in attendance. It was exactly what Vicki had envisioned her wedding day to be like, and exactly the man she'd always dreamed she'd marry.

"I have never been happier in my entire life," she said.

"I take that as a challenge," Jordan said, pressing a kiss to her lips. "I plan to spend the rest of my life making you happier than you were the past day."

"I look forward to it," she said.

Sandra and Janelle, who had both stood as attendants, came over to them. Sandra carried Mason, who was dressed in an adorable baby tuxedo.

"Isn't he the *most* cutest baby in the world?" Vicki asked.

"He is," Janelle said. "But I think mine will give him a run for his money."

Sandra and Vicki both looked at her and started screaming, grabbing the attention of everyone in the room. Sandra handed Mason off to Jordan so that she, Vicki and Janelle could join in a group hug.

Jordan laughed at their shenanigans. "I think the Silk Sisters will have to add a baby portion to the business."

"I think that's the perfect idea," Vicki said.

At Janelle's announcement, the mood became even more festive. As the food and drinks flowed, Vicki soaked it all in. At this moment, her life felt complete.

Yet it was just getting started.

"It's time to throw the bouquet," Nancy Woolcott

called, handing Vicki the small bouquet of white calla lilies that had been made specifically for tossing.

Vicki turned her back to the crowd, but not before taking a mental note of where her three brothers stood. Angling her aim, she tossed the bouquet over her shoulder, right at Terrance, Spence and Jacob, making sure there would be more weddings to come in Wintersage.

* * * * *

BEST MAN
UNDER THE
MISTLETOE

JULES BENNETT

To the Mills & Boon Desire team:
Stacy, Charles and Tahra.
They say it takes a village to raise a
child... The same is true for books.

One

"This investigation has really been a community effort. Thanks to the diligence of so many in Royal, the final piece of the puzzle has been put into place. Maverick has been identified as Royal's own Dale, a.k.a. Dusty, Walsh."

Gabe Walsh muted the TV and tossed the remote onto the leather sofa. He didn't want to hear any more about his late uncle's betrayal. The old bastard had passed away last week from a brain tumor and now the mess he'd caused to so many in the town of Royal, Texas, would have a ripple effect on Gabe's security firm. He would undoubtedly have a hell of a mess to clean up.

He still couldn't believe it. His uncle Dusty was Maverick, the cyber criminal who had terrorized members of the Texas Cattleman's Club for months now, revealing their secrets online and often resorting to blackmail.

Perhaps worst of all, he'd leaked nude photos of Chelsea Hunt, taken without her knowledge in the locker room at her gym.

According to Gabe's law-enforcement sources, all evidence pointed to Dusty working alone, except when it came to the locker room photos. There was now another person of interest in that particular crime. A woman, the police claimed. They were still studying months of surveillance-camera footage from the public areas of the gym to figure out who could have planted the camera.

Who the hell had aided his uncle? And was that the only instance when Dusty had taken on an accomplice? The man had been dying. There was no way Dusty could've done so much on his own. The man had been too feeble, too weak.

Though not so weak that he couldn't plot to destroy lives. Luckily, the citizens of Royal—Chelsea Hunt included—had risen above his attempts to take them down. Investigators had also seen through his elaborate attempt to pin the crimes on someone else.

Gabe raked a hand through his hair and glared at the screen as Sheriff Nate Battle continued his press conference. A picture of Gabe's once robust, smiling uncle filled the top right corner of the TV screen while the sheriff spoke.

How and why Uncle Dusty had pulled off such a grand scheme of blackmail and betrayal were open questions, but one thing was undeniable. He'd managed to put a big dark cloud over the family security firm, the Walsh Group—Gabe's new baby. As if taking over a company wasn't difficult and risky enough, now he was forced to deal with the backlash of questions from clients, both old and new, because of his relationship with Dusty.

How the hell was he supposed to dodge all of this bad press? The business's reputation was on the line. Sure, finances were the least of his concern. He'd busted his ass from the start of his career, saved every dollar, invested wisely and had worked his way up to be the best in the industry. He could close up shop and never work another day in his life, but he valued his reputation and family loyalty. Ironic now, wasn't it?

Gabe once again thought of Chelsea Hunt and it had him seeing red. His uncle had gotten his hands on compromising photos and proceeded to put them out for the town to see. And why? Yes, Chelsea had played an important role in the Maverick investigation, bringing in computer-security experts from out of town to help. But the leak was part of a bigger pattern: Maverick had been especially vicious when targeting women. One theory was that Maverick acted this way because the Texas Cattleman's Club had begun admitting women a few years back. By contrast, Dusty had been passed over for membership, one of the things that incurred his wrath.

Gabe's uncle had certainly been hidebound in his views of women—but going so far as to leak nude photos like that? What had been wrong with the man? Chelsea hadn't deserved the embarrassment and scandal that had been brought upon her by his uncle and some unknown accomplice.

Gabe cursed as he spun away from the television. He had been careful not to look at the photos when they'd been released for all the world to see. He hadn't wanted to be totally disrespectful or to violate her privacy. Plus, where Chelsea was concerned, he had problems of his own to deal with.

Replaying that kiss he and Chelsea had shared last week, it was a wonder he hadn't lost his damn mind.

Gabe and Chelsea had started spending a lot of time together when their best friends, Shane Delgado and

Brandee Lawson, had asked them to be best man and maid of honor in their wedding. Brandee had wanted Gabe and Chelsea to be very hands-on in the process. Gabe had known full well when they'd started working together that they'd be spending quite a bit of time alone.

But the other night, something had shifted. They'd been making name cards for the reception, which had triggered an argument, which had his last ounce of control snapping.

Gabe had grabbed the gold ribbon from Chelsea and tossed it aside, gripping her face and taking what he'd wanted for months.

Raking a hand through his hair, Gabe tried like hell to forget how she'd tasted, how she'd felt against him. But the scene replayed over and over in his head.

He could use a stiff drink and the company of a good woman between the sheets. But right at the moment neither would solve his problems…and the only woman he wanted between his sheets was the very one he needed to forget.

To top it all off on this hellish day, he had to meet Chelsea for some wedding planning nonsense later. How was she handling the news that his late uncle had been Maverick? Would she blame Gabe simply by association?

It was bad enough that he'd been roped into the wedding planning. He may as well have given up his man card for all the flowers and candles he'd been sniffing lately. If Shane and Brandee hadn't specifically asked Gabe and Chelsea to help with the planning, Gabe would've given this project the middle finger. But Shane was as close as family and, even though Gabe didn't believe in happily-ever-after, he was glad to see his best friends so in love.

Gabe just wished Chelsea wasn't the maid of honor because until the Christmas nuptials rolled around, dodg-

JULES BENNETT   11

ing her wasn't an option. Nearly every single day he'd be spending hours looking at seating charts, passing on the bride's playlist to the band, finalizing the caterers and florists…and all of that time would only lead to one more thing. Another kiss.

Why the hell did it have to be this woman who intrigued him? At first he'd wondered if he'd just felt bad for all the negative attention she'd been getting, but he'd quickly squelched that notion. He wasn't one to take pity and turn it into lust.

But there was something about her strength and the fact she wasn't letting this scandal break her when it very well should. He admired anyone who could rise above adversity and still remain in control.

And then there was just plain, old-fashioned, sexual desire.

She was hot, and he was a man with breath in his lungs. He would have been a fool not to be attracted.

That kiss had upped the stakes and now all he could think of was getting another taste. Given everything that had transpired today, was that wrong? Should he even allow himself to crave the woman his uncle had publicly humiliated?

Muttering a curse, Gabe turned the television off and grabbed his keys. He might as well get this little meeting with Chelsea over with and then go back to doing damage control at the Walsh Group. Not only would the clients be pouring in with questions, his employees would, too. The sheriff had told Gabe about his findings before the press conference—and cleared him of any wrongdoing, for that matter—so Gabe had already given a heads-up to his assistants that this was coming and instructed them on how to handle the expected calls.

The people in Royal knew him, knew that he wouldn't

partake in something so heinous. But there were clients who didn't know him and those were the ones he'd be personally calling and meeting face-to-face. He wasn't looking forward to doing damage control, but he'd worked too hard for his impeccable reputation and he'd be damned if he let anyone tarnish it…especially family.

That was business. He knew how to handle all of that, but he had no clue how to approach Chelsea. No doubt she'd heard on the news or directly from Sheriff Battle the identity of her blackmailer and Gabe would be the perfect target for her to take out her frustrations. And then there was the unacknowledged-but-hard-to-ignore attraction between them.

But she was in a vulnerable position and only a complete jerk would take advantage of that. She may put on a strong front, something he commended her for, but no doubt she still hurt. All he could do at this point was to show her he wasn't like his uncle, that he was completely innocent, and he was there for her if she needed him.

The screwdriver hurtled past Gabe's head and Chelsea cursed herself for missing. She was still shaken up by the news, that was all. If she'd been fully on her game, she would've nailed the target. The sexy, arrogant, infuriating target.

She didn't condone violence, but this man had stepped into her bad mood at the wrong time. She'd only just learned of the Maverick's true identity and Gabe Walsh was guilty by association. For all she knew, Gabe had helped cover his uncle's tracks. He was a sneaky PI, after all. Even though the sheriff had assured her there was no evidence Gabe had any involvement whatsoever, she was furious and needed to lash out.

"Is that any way to treat someone who's come to help

you build this archway for the ceremony?" Gabe asked, slowly making his way toward her.

Chelsea grabbed the hammer. "I don't need, nor did I ask for your help."

Gabe cocked his head and kicked up his wicked smile. Gabe had that whole don't-give-a-damn attitude down pat; nothing ever bothered him. He seduced and charmed everyone in his path…but not her. And she wasn't going to think of that kiss, either. She *wasn't*.

"Brandee texted me and asked me to come help you with the arch for the ceremony," he informed her.

Chelsea glanced at the piles of wood, flowers, tulle and wire all spread out in the old barn at Hope Springs, Brandee's ranch. Brandee could've hired a company to take over the decorating and organizing of the big day, but Chelsea had wanted to make things special for her friend. She'd wanted to be hands-on since she knew Brandee better than any stranger would.

But Chelsea would rather have worked her fingers to the bone than ask Gabe for any help. Now that the Maverick had been revealed as his uncle, Chelsea felt utterly betrayed.

"I wasn't sure how Dusty managed to get those images of me and splash them around, but now it's pretty clear he had help." Chelsea continued to stare at the man who was too sexy to be legal. The tattoos, the scruff along his jawline, the arrogant stance. "You were his errand boy."

"What?" Gabe said, jerking back. "I—"

"Anything for the family," she went on, dropping the hammer to the concrete floor at her side instead of hurling it at his head next. "You were trained to take over the family business. Taking orders from your dying uncle just came naturally."

"You have no idea what you're talking about," Gabe

countered, an edge to his voice. "You might want to have evidence before making such claims—evidence you will never find because I had nothing to do with the pictures or the blackmail."

He may have been a former special agent, he may have put the fear of God in many suspects in his time, but Chelsea wasn't afraid. The only thing she worried about was how he managed to infuriate and turn her on at the same time. She hated how her body responded to just the sight of him when her mind told her she knew better. Why did lust have to cloud her judgment?

"I'm not arguing." She turned her attention back to the mess before her. "I have too much to do here. If Brandee doesn't see some progress, she'll worry it won't be done in time, and I won't have my best friend stressed for her special day."

"Then it sounds like you need an extra pair of hands."

Chelsea shuddered. Gabe had used those hands to grip her shoulders and haul her against his hard body as he'd kissed her so fast, so fierce—

"I say we call a truce."

Chelsea swallowed and finally nodded. He was right. They had to work together and she had to believe the sheriff when he'd said Gabe was in the clear. She just wanted someone to blame, someone to take her anger out on.

"A truce," she said. "I think I can handle that."

Gabe flashed that smile again. "So what are we doing here?"

"Brandee wants a large arch for her and Shane to stand beneath to exchange their vows. She wants it to be elegant and Christmassy, not tacky. Everything will be done in whites and golds and clear lights. She told me to order one, but I wanted to make it so she had something special and meaningful."

Chelsea couldn't help but feel a twinge of jealousy at her friend's upcoming nuptials. Chelsea may be hard, she may be independent and run the tech side of Hunt & Co. like a boss, but she was still a woman with dreams. She didn't want a man to take care of her, but she certainly wouldn't mind a man to hold her at night, to appreciate her Italian-lace lingerie collection, to laugh with her and share stories about their days. Was it too much to ask to meet just one man who wasn't a jerk?

"Is there a blueprint for this or are we just winging it?" Gabe asked.

Chelsea came to her feet, dusting her hands against her holey jeans. "No blueprint, but Shane had everything cut and ready to assemble once I told him my ideas. I told Brandee I'd take care of it since it's my idea. I have a picture on my phone of what it should look like. But it's just a mock-up of the picture in my head."

She slid her phone from her pocket and pulled up the image.

Gabe came to stand beside her, having the nerve to brush his shoulder against hers.

She shouldn't be attracted to such a…a…wolfish man. He was a hell of a kisser, but he was also related to the enemy. That was reason enough for her to be leery. Wasn't it? There was only so far a hot bod and toe-curling kiss could take Gabe Walsh. So what if she'd had vivid, detailed dreams of the infamous kiss and all the delicious things her mind conjured up without her permission?

"Subtle," she said as she took a half step to the side. "Don't try using this opportunity to kiss or seduce me or whatever else you're thinking."

Gabe came around and stood directly in front of her. She still held her phone out, her hands frozen in the narrow space between them. His deep eyes held her in place, and Chelsea trembled as if he'd touched her bare skin.

"Darlin', when you were kissing me, you weren't exactly shy about it."

Chelsea opened her mouth to object, but Gabe leaned forward, coming to within a breath of her lips.

"So don't try to deny that you're attracted to me," he murmured. "And I won't deny it, either. But right now, we have more pressing things to do than worry about who is seducing whom."

Keeping his eyes on hers, he eased back and slid the phone from her grip. Damn the man for making her entire body heat up like he'd lit a match from within. The broad shoulders, the scruff along his jawline, the ink peeking from beneath his fitted T-shirt…and the way he'd drawled out "darlin'" had her ready to ignore those red flags and kiss him again. Maybe it hadn't been that good and she'd remembered all wrong. Had her toes actually curled? Had her body tightened with arousal?

Stifling a groan, Chelsea stepped over the supplies and went to the pile of wood. As much as she liked to think she could do everything on her own, she was going to need Gabe's help here.

"This is some setup they're wanting," Gabe said behind her. "I guess we better get started. The wedding is only a couple weeks away and this isn't our only task."

Gabe again came up beside her, this time not touching, and handed over her phone. "Tell me we've decided on the florist. I really don't want to look at one more plant or bloom or branch or anything else that I know nothing about."

"The florist has been nailed down and contacted. Now, we need to finalize the appetizers and beer and wine list for the combined bachelor/bachelorette party," she told him. "I have the final numbers for those who sent in their RSVP."

Gabe blew out a sigh. "I'll handle all the menus if you promise I don't have to pick out tablecloths or do little calligraphy place cards."

Chelsea crossed her arms and turned to fully face him. "Well, Gabriel Walsh, I'm disappointed in your knowledge of contemporary weddings. Calligraphy cards are definitely a thing of the past. I actually already ordered name cards in the same design and font as Brandee's invitations. You really should update your wedding magazine subscriptions if you're ever going to do this yourself."

"If I ever lose my mind and marry, I'll let my bride handle everything." He raked a hand over his stubbled jaw. "Food and alcohol are easy. Especially since we're having the party at the TCC. What else do you want me to do that doesn't involve something frilly or flowery?"

"Someone is grouchy," she muttered. "Is it because I threw the screwdriver at your head or because I'm not throwing myself at you after the kiss?"

Gabe shoved his hands in his pockets and tipped his head sideways to look her in the eyes. "Are we going to be able to get along to get through this together?"

Chelsea shrugged. "Depends. You keep your hands and lips to yourself and we might just. And just so you know, I tend to believe you when you say you didn't know what your uncle was up to. Shane and Brandee wouldn't put their trust in you if you were involved. But you better hope like hell there isn't a connection, because if I find out there is, I won't miss the next time I throw a screwdriver at your head."

Two

"This doesn't look right. Is it leaning a little?"

Gabe stood back and stared at the arch he and Chelsea had been grunting over for the better part of the day. They'd gotten along surprisingly well, as long as they'd kept the topic of conversation on the wedding...or when they weren't talking at all.

When the silence stretched between them, though, his mind started conjuring up all sorts of naughty thoughts and each one starred the woman at his side. The way she wore her holey jeans low on her hips and that fitted tank, she didn't look like an expert hacker and CTO of the most prestigious chain of steakhouses in the South.

She could drive any man out of his mind, even if she was spitting in his face and smarting off with that sweet mouth. It was one of the many reasons he couldn't help but admire her. She didn't take crap from anyone and was her own hero, saving herself from the evils in her own world. Damn if that wasn't sexy as hell.

It didn't go unnoticed how she'd kept glancing his way. The attraction simmering just below that steel barrier she kept around her was going to explode…and he damn well would be the man to experience her passion. He'd had just enough of a taste to crave more, and she could deny all she wanted with her words, her body told a whole different story.

He gave the arch a slight push. "Did that help?"

Chelsea stepped back, angling her head. "That did it."

Gabe's cell vibrated in his pocket. He pulled it out and glanced at the text from one of his assistants. After a quick response, he slid the phone back in.

"Late for a lunch date with your girlfriend?" Chelsea asked as she gathered the tools and put them off to the side.

"If you want to know if I'm seeing anyone, just ask."

She tucked her shoulder-length, honey-blond hair behind one ear and quirked a brow. "I didn't ask."

"I'm not seeing anyone," he informed her, taking long strides to close the distance between them. "A fact you should know before you kiss me again."

Chelsea crossed her arms beneath her chest and it was all he could do to keep his eyes on hers. "You're arrogant enough to think that's going to happen?"

"Arrogant? Perhaps, though I'm positive it's only a matter of time." Whistling, he turned to head from the barn out to his car. Any second he expected a tool to hit the back of his head or go whirling by his ear. But nothing happened. He was proud she showed such restraint. Obviously he was growing on her.

But he'd be lying if he claimed he wasn't irritated by the fact she thought he had something to do with those leaked pictures. What on earth would his motive be? There was no reason for him to go around with his uncle terrorizing the people of this town. Gabe actually liked those who had been affected by his uncle's activities and would never want to see any of them harmed. Shane and Brandee had even been targeted, for pity's sake. Dusty's antics were absolutely inconceivable.

As Gabe slid behind the wheel and started the engine, Chelsea came strutting out of the barn straight toward him. He rolled his window down.

"I knew you'd chase after me."

Rolling her eyes, she propped her hands on her hips. "Brandee just texted me and asked if we'd run to Natalie Valentine's bridal shop so I can get my last fitting."

"As much as I'd love to help you with a fitting, I'm afraid I have work to do. My uncle, as you know, is ruining my name even in his death and I have too many clients to coddle during this sensitive time. Besides, how could you ever bring yourself to trust me at a fitting?"

Chelsea's lips thinned and she gritted her teeth before saying, "Brandee wants us to stop at Priceless to pick up her wedding present to Shane. She bought a table and chairs for their dining room, says it's just like the one his grandmother used to have, and she wants to surprise him. The dress fitting just makes sense because we'll already be there."

Gabe dropped his head back against the headrest and groaned. "You know, I do have a company to run."

"Yes, and here I am with nothing to do. Or maybe you've forgotten I have a demanding position, as well."

"That's not what I meant," he argued. Blowing out a sigh, he glanced back up at her. "Get in. We'll swing by my place and pick up my truck so we can go get this furniture."

"I'll drive myself."

"There's no reason we can't ride together. I have to

take the truck anyway to pick up the table. Unless you're afraid to be alone with me."

Chelsea narrowed her eyes. "I hate your inflated ego."

"Duly noted. Now, get in."

He couldn't help but smile as she rounded the hood of his car. He didn't know why he wanted to provoke her, but he couldn't help himself. In actuality, he wanted to spend more time with her. Seducing her was something he wanted to pursue, sure, but more importantly he wanted her to know that he would never, ever, treat a woman the way she'd been treated by his uncle. Above all else, he needed her to know that. And she wouldn't just take his word for it. She needed to see that he wasn't some jerk that got off on blackmailing people and ruining reputations.

As soon as she got into the car, he put it in gear and set off toward his downtown loft.

He kept his truck in the second bay of his garage, for which he paid a hefty monthly fee to have parking beneath his downtown loft apartment. But a man couldn't live in Texas and not own a truck. It was practically against the law.

"You know—" he began once they'd switched to the truck and were back on the road.

"We don't need to talk."

Well, apparently this was going to be more difficult than he'd thought. Gabe tightened his grip on the wheel.

"Yes, we do," he countered. "As I was saying, you know there are many people in this town who know me and know I would never side with my uncle. I wouldn't have covered up such maliciousness."

"I know you were cleared of any wrongdoing. The sheriff told me he's positive you had nothing to do with the scandal. But at the same time, he was your only family member. How did you not know what he was up to? He was old and feeble. Someone had to know something about what he was doing."

There was bite to her voice, but beneath that gruff exterior there was pain. Gabe hated what she'd gone through, the humiliation and embarrassment. The fact that so many had suffered at the hands of his uncle didn't sit well with him, but he was especially upset about Chelsea. Her betrayal had taken on a darker, more personal feel than the others.

No matter how much anger she projected toward him, he was hell-bent on proving to her that he understood, that he totally agreed with her, that they were on the same page. He knew his uncle was a bastard, but just because Gabe's last name was Walsh didn't mean he knew what had been taking place in the months leading up to his uncle's death.

"I can't imagine how difficult this has been," he started, hoping she let him finish. "I know you're angry, but I swear I didn't know about those photos until they were leaked. I never even looked at them."

Chelsea snorted and shot him a glare. "If you think for a second I believe that lie, you're more of a fool than I thought. You're a guy. You looked."

"We could argue this till we're both blue in the face, you still wouldn't believe me," he growled. "But you'll see. Once the truth is revealed and they catch whoever this accomplice is, you'll realize that I truly knew nothing. You think I'd actually keep information like this to myself? Dusty self-destructed and that has nothing to do with me. I have a reputation, a multibillion-dollar security business to look after. The last thing I want to be involved in is a scandal."

Gabe had to believe she'd eventually come to see that

he wasn't lying. He prided himself on honesty, and liked to think he was a man of integrity. Sure, he could be hard when it came to work, but when it came to his personal life, he could admit he was a bit softer when it was necessary. And this situation called for delicate measures unlike anything he'd ever known.

As he pulled into the Courtyard Shops, Gabe figured that even though he'd rather do anything else than wait on Chelsea to try on her dress, at least this forced time together was giving him the prime opportunity he needed to win her over. Which was important to him, even though he had big problems to deal with at his business right now.

"You can go on into Priceless while I try on the dress."

Gabe hopped out of the truck and shot her a wink. "If it's all the same, I'll just stick with you. You won't be long and then you can help me load the table next door."

Chelsea groaned as she jerked on her door handle. Normally, Gabe would get the door for a woman—he was raised in the South by a well-mannered mother—but he also had a feeling if he tried to get the door for Chelsea, he'd just be taking a step in the wrong direction.

But the moment he stepped inside Natalie's shop, Gabe started to reconsider his ploy to stick close to Chelsea. There were dresses everywhere. Fluffy, lacy, silky dresses, and the place smelled...pink. If a smell could have a color, this place was definitely pink.

The peppy little shop attendant greeted Chelsea and promptly went to get the dress from the back. Gabe spotted a lounge area in that direction and made his way to a white sofa in front of the wall of mirrors. He could catch up on a few emails that needed his attention and check in on his right-hand man doing some security work in Dallas for the next few weeks.

Nothing was as important as his business, especially during this crucial time. He'd already reached out to some of his closest clients and assured them that Dusty's scandal had nothing to do with the Walsh Group. He'd also made sure they knew they could come to him personally with questions or concerns.

The unfortunate, untimely setback wouldn't change the way Gabe handled his business. But it sure did complicate matters. If ole Dusty weren't already dead, Gabe would have no problem driving out to his mansion and beating the ever loving sh—

Every single thought vanished when Chelsea stepped from the dressing room and came to stand in front of the three-way mirror. The fitted gold gown shouldn't have looked so damn sexy, seeing as how it was long, with full sleeves, and a high neck. But the material hugged every single curve and dip on Chelsea's luscious body, mocking him. He'd seen her in jeans, even in little flowy sundresses, but nothing like this, all sultry and glamorous.

She smoothed the dress over her flat stomach and turned from side to side. The innocent gesture shouldn't have gripped his attention, but this woman had him in a total trance.

Emails and damage control forgotten, Gabe set aside his phone. He had nothing else to be doing right this second except for admiring her as she watched her reflection.

Hell. This wasn't the time or the place to be getting uncomfortable in his jeans. Just who the hell was seducing whom here? But from the unsure look on her face—her brows were drawn, her mouth turned down in a frown—it seemed she had doubts about how damn perfect and sexy she looked.

"It's fine," he growled after what seemed like an hour of pure torture. "Can we wrap it up here?"

Hands on her hips, Chelsea glared at him from her reflection in the mirror. "I need to make sure I can breathe and sit without busting a seam, if you don't mind. It seems tight."

Actually he did mind, and it was damn tight...the dress and his pants. He should've gone to the antique store because this was pure hell. Then again, at least he had a heads-up for how she'd look when he had to escort her down the aisle. He'd hate to be all mouth agape and drooling in front of Shane and Brandee's friends and families.

The idea of Chelsea and him walking down the aisle shouldn't have made him feel awkward, yet it did. Weddings in general made him twitchy. That whole happily-ever-after wasn't for everyone; he'd even managed to dodge being in any type of wedding party his entire life. But there was no way he could say no to Shane, his very best friend.

The more Chelsea shifted and turned and smoothed her hands over those luscious curves, the more uncomfortable Gabe became.

Commotion behind him had him tearing his gaze from the mirror and glancing over his shoulder. A slew of teenage girls came in the door, chattering and giggling about homecoming and needing perfect dresses. He could not get out of there fast enough. Between the lace, the satin and the chatter in such high octaves, this place was sucking the testosterone right out of his body.

"This will just have to work because I don't have the time to do more measurements," Chelsea muttered as she stepped off the platform and headed back into her dressing room. "Give me two minutes and we'll be out of here."

Gabe came to his feet, more than ready to get the hell out. As he shoved his hands in his pockets and rocked back on his heels, he heard Chelsea mumbling and cursing from inside the dressing room. Seconds later, the door eased open just a crack.

"Um... I'm stuck."

He eyed the narrow strip of her face showing through the door. "'Scuse me?"

"The zipper," she whispered through gritted teeth. "The damn thing is stuck. Get the salesclerk to come help me."

Gabe glanced over his shoulder at the mayhem of teens and fluffy dresses. The two workers were running in all directions accommodating parents and demanding girls.

He could do this. How hard would it be to get a zipper unstuck? Pulling in a deep breath, Gabe pushed open the dressing room door and offered up his assistance.

Three

"Gabe. What—?"

She backed up and stared as he shut and locked the door behind him. The narrow space seemed to shrink even more with his broad frame filling the area.

"You said you needed help."

Chelsea crossed her arms over her chest. "I said to get the salesclerk."

"Well, darlin', there's about a dozen teenage girls out there and only two staff that I saw. That's not a great ratio, so if you want out of this dress anytime in the next few hours, I'm it."

That gleam in his eye was just about the naughtiest, sexiest thing she'd ever seen. Which was one of the many reasons she shouldn't be closed in with him, and definitely why he shouldn't help unzip her dress. Being half-naked and in close proximity with Gabe would only lead to…

She couldn't even let her mind wander down that path.

"I'll do it myself," she claimed, though she'd already tried that. "Go on to the antique store and I'll be right over."

Gabe took one step and was right against her. "We both have other things to do today, so you might as well let me help you out."

"You seem to be enjoying this a little too much."

His hand skimmed up her side where the zipper was carefully hidden. "I'll be enjoying this even more if you'd let me work this zipper down."

The image that immediately popped into her head had Chelsea thinking for a half second of lifting her arm and letting him have a go. But then she remembered who he was...or rather who his uncle had been.

"This isn't a good idea," she told him. Surely he saw that...didn't he? He knew her feelings and knew full well she didn't trust him.

"What's not a good idea?" he asked, his eyes traveling over her face, landing on her lips. "Us in this confined space alone or the fact that you're attracted to me?"

Chelsea fisted her hands at her sides—to keep from hitting him or grabbing his face and kissing him, she wasn't sure. Her attraction wouldn't be such an issue if Gabe wasn't a Walsh. If his uncle hadn't tried to destroy so many lives, hers included. The guilt by association was enough to have her emotionally pulling back.

But the sizzling attraction didn't let up, no matter how much she tried to shove it aside.

Chelsea's body trembled, betraying her vow to keep him at a distance. When his fingers skimmed over her again, he quirked a half smile as he brought his eyes back up to meet hers.

"Is this the part where you deny your attraction?" he

asked, still using those clever hands. His fingertips circled around to where the dress exposed her back.

Chelsea sucked in a breath and cursed every single goose bump that popped up along her skin. They were both fully clothed, yet his fingertips on her bare back was something too akin to a lover's touch. And it had been too damn long since she'd taken a lover; she was clearly letting this affect her more than it should.

She'd not made the best choices in men. When she'd been younger, she confused attention with attraction. Then as she'd gotten older she'd distanced herself because she didn't trust her judgment. The scandal had her more than hesitant at getting close to any man. Now, here she was attracted to a man who was the next of kin to the bastard who'd humiliated her.

"Turn around," he whispered in her ear.

Without thinking, she turned to face the mirror. Gabe stood directly behind her, his body practically plastered against hers and those fingers still roaming over her heated skin. His eyes met hers in the mirror as he raised his other hand to the top of the zipper. Just the brush of his knuckles on the underside of her arm had her shivering even though the thick material served as a barrier.

Chelsea closed her eyes, hoping that if she didn't have to look at their reflection she could ignore this entire moment.

"Look at me," he demanded.

She gave in way too easily as her gaze met his once again. "Stop," she muttered.

"Stop what exactly?" He gave the zipper the slightest tug. "Stop helping you out of this dress or stop tormenting us both?"

She'd never been one to think of having sex in a public place, but right at this moment, she'd give just about anything to alleviate this ache caused by a man she shouldn't want.

"You had to know when we kissed that there would be more," he whispered. Though he didn't need to keep his voice down. The chaos of teen girls on the other side of that locked door drowned out anything they were saying…or doing.

"There can't be more."

The zipper gave way just as he brushed his lips along the side of her neck. Chelsea's body betrayed her…much as it had ever since Gabe had stepped foot into this tiny room. Closing her eyes, she dropped her head against his shoulder. Maybe she just wanted to take this moment, maybe she wanted to ignore everything and let him pleasure her. He was doing a damn fine job already.

Why did she have to be so torn? Why did he have to be such a mystery?

The hand on her back came around to her throat, tipping her head just enough for him to trail his lips over her exposed skin. He continued to work on her zipper just as expertly as he heated her up. She was about one strategically placed kiss away from moaning.

"Don't lie to me again and tell me you don't want me," he murmured in her ear. "You're shaking in my arms and I haven't even gotten you out of this dress yet."

He cupped her jaw and turned her head toward him. As his mouth crashed onto hers, Chelsea turned in his arms, threading her fingers through his hair and taking what he so freely gave.

Just for a minute. That was all. Then she'd go back to loathing him and believing he was a liar. But right now, common sense and reality had no place here.

Nothing lied about his lips or the hands that roamed

all over her body. He wanted her just as fiercely as she wanted him.

Gabe backed her against the wall and gripped her hips, pulling her toward him. His arousal was obvious.

If he lit her up this quickly, this intensely, what would happen once they were skin to skin? Would he take his time and savor the moment? Would he—?

"Excuse me?" A knock came on the door. "We have several girls who need to try some things on."

Gabe eased back slightly and muttered under his breath. Chelsea wanted the floor to open up and swallow her whole. First, there'd been the naked pictures and now she'd been pretty much caught getting it on in the dressing room of the only bridal shop in town. Could she provide more fodder for the gossip mill? Maybe she should parade down the main street of Royal in the buff.

"My zipper was stuck," she called out, realizing how lame that sounded. "Be right out."

Chelsea pushed Gabe back, but he couldn't go far considering the narrow space. "Either help me with the rest of this zipper or get out."

His dark eyes were heavy with arousal, the bulge in his jeans an added reminder of what they'd nearly done. Heat crept up her neck and flushed her face. She reached to the side of her dress and found that he'd actually gotten the zipper all the way down. When had that happened? Likely somewhere between that first touch and when he'd nearly kissed her to orgasm.

"Your work here is done," she told him, more than ready to get out of this dress and back into her jeans and boots.

Gabe took one step toward her, framed her face in his hands and leaned to within a breath of her mouth. "My work with you hasn't even started."

Releasing her, he stepped from the room and out the door just as casual as you please. Chelsea sank onto the tiny accent chair in the corner and took a deep breath. Right now the least of her worries was the people on the other side of that door when she walked out.

No, her greatest concern was the man who'd just left her aching even more than before. Nobody had ever gotten her so worked up, and here she was still trembling and in desperate need for him to finish the job.

Damn it. How was she going to keep her distance while they worked on this wedding, and not fall into bed with Gabe Walsh?

Four

Gabe shut down his laptop and came to his feet. It had been two days since his close encounter with Chelsea at the bridal shop and he was no closer to finding relief than he was then.

The damn woman had gotten to him. Perhaps it was her sassy mouth, or maybe it was the fact she hadn't initially believed him when he'd said he was in no way involved in leaking those nude photos. Maybe it was the way she wore jeans and tanks like they were made for her. Hell, he didn't know. All Gabe knew was that Chelsea Hunt was an enigma that he simply couldn't solve.

He'd been a damn special agent and still he couldn't figure out how someone as smart-mouthed and difficult as Chelsea had gotten under his skin. He could find any woman to scratch his itch, but he wasn't that guy anymore. In his twenties, he'd been selfish, falling into the bed of any willing woman. He was more particular now, definitely busier with work. And no one had pulled at him like Chelsea Hunt. So, no. No other woman would do.

But right now he had a few other pressing matters. Several of his clients had questioned him about his connection to his uncle. He'd already spoken with quite a few of them and he wasn't done yet. Gabe planned to spend the rest of his day running interference and hopefully smoothing ruffled feathers.

He grabbed his hat and headed out the door of his loft apartment. He loved the prime location in downtown Royal. There were shops, restaurants, and it wasn't too far from the Texas Cattleman's Club. He planned to head over later to get some riding in. Getting on the back of a horse and taking off into the fresh air always calmed him and helped to clear his mind.

The only drawback to living in a loft in town was that he couldn't have his own horses. Growing up outside Dallas on a working farm had been every little boy's dream, and riding had been a staple in his life. At least being a member of the Texas Cattleman's Club offered him anything he could want, including access to the club's stables. So he had the best of both worlds right now.

Gabe's cell vibrated in his pocket as he headed to the garage beneath his loft apartment. Pulling it out, he glanced at the screen and swiped to answer.

"Shane. What's up?"

"Just checking in on you, man. How are you holding up with all the fallout from your uncle?"

Gabe tightened his grip on the phone and resisted the urge to groan. "It's been a bit of a nightmare, but nothing I can't handle."

"Brandee and I are here for you, whatever you need. We know you'd never have a hand in anything this scandalous and cruel."

Gabe slid his sunglasses from the top of his head and settled them in place. "I'm doing damage control with the company. There's not much else anyone can do. I appreciate the offer."

"Of course. I hate how all this is happening on top of the wedding details," Shane added.

"Not a big deal. Like I said, nothing I can't handle."

"Speaking of wedding details, my fiancée is not happy."

Gabe laughed as he settled in behind the wheel of his truck. "Sounds like your problem, not mine."

"Oh, it's every bit your problem," Shane corrected. "Were you in the dressing room at the bridal shop with Chelsea? Wait, I know the answer to that. What the hell were you thinking, man?"

Blowing out a sigh, Gabe started the engine. "Does it matter? Nothing happened. Her zipper was stuck, that's all."

Well, that was all he'd own up to. Whatever was brewing between Chelsea and him was their business. As much as he'd like to claim there was more, things hadn't progressed near to where he wanted them. This was the slowest form of torture and foreplay he'd ever experienced in his life.

"Listen, whatever you do with anyone else is fine."

"Glad I have permission, Dad."

"But," Shane went on, "Chelsea is different. After what she's been through and with her being Brandee's best friend, this is a little more delicate than you just messing around with any other woman."

"I'm well aware of how vulnerable Chelsea is." Anger simmered as Gabe clenched the steering wheel. "And we're not messing around. How the hell did you find out anyway?"

Because he knew for a fact Chelsea wouldn't have run to Brandee and spilled. Even though this was perfect girly gossip, Gabe liked to think he knew Chelsea pretty well and this wasn't the type of chatter she'd take part in.

"You think a shop full of teens and their mothers didn't know you or Chelsea?" Shane asked in disbelief. "This town isn't that big, man. And if I know about it, you don't think Daniel hasn't heard by now?"

Daniel Hunt, Chelsea's brother. Chelsea's older, over-protective brother. He and Chelsea had been through so much with the loss of their parents. Everyone knew their mother had run out on them and their father had passed a year later, some said from a broken heart. Was it any wonder Chelsea was so closed off, so leery and untrusting? Add in the scandal over the photos and she'd had quite a bit thrown at her. More than most people should endure. And other than Daniel and Brandee, who did she have to lean on?

"I'm not worried about Daniel," Gabe said as he put his truck in gear. "As much as I'd love to continue this cheery conversation, I have other things to get done. Even in death, my uncle is ruining my reputation."

Shane blew out a sigh. "Sorry, man. I wasn't thinking."

"No reason to be sorry. You and Brandee were victims, as well."

Hell, there was hardly a member of the TCC who hadn't been affected somehow by his uncle. Gabe still had no clue as to his motives, but he knew Dusty Walsh had been denied membership to the exclusive club three times over the years. And when women had been admitted, it had only made Dusty's grudge worsen.

Perhaps this was his uncle's way of getting back at the club because of the board's decision. Who knew? All Gabe did know was that it would continue to impact his reputation for some time and he'd have to stay on top of things to keep his security business running.

"Just try to calm down with the public displays," Shane warned. "Chelsea is dealing with enough and I'd really like this wedding to go off without drama."

Gabe knew exactly what Chelsea was dealing with and he cursed himself for putting her in such a position. But, damn it, when he was around her, all logical thinking just vanished.

"Your wedding will be drama-free," Gabe assured his best friend. "Go kiss your fiancée and let her know Chels and I have everything under control."

He disconnected the call before Shane could question him further. As much as Gabe wanted to concentrate on Chelsea, on the memory of her sweet body pressed against his and her zipper parting beneath his touch, he had a high-dollar client to see.

Business first. Business always came first. Then he'd check up on his girl.

"I'll make sure they're delivered here if you don't mind being on hand to put everything away in the freezer. They'll come packaged with instructions for how long they need to sit out to thaw and the exact way they should be marinated and cooked."

Chelsea was going over the to-do list for the joint bachelor/bachelorette party with Rose, her contact in the TCC kitchen. Rose smiled and nodded as Chelsea ticked the items in her head off on her fingers.

"I'm sorry," Chelsea said. "I'm sure you know how to cook a steak and this isn't the first party you've done, but this is my company and my best friend we're talking about."

Chelsea may have been the CTO of Hunt & Co., dealing with the computers and the technical end of the business, but she knew how to handle steaks, as well. There were good steaks and then there were Hunt steaks. Chelsea wanted absolutely the best for her friends and that could only come from her family's company.

Rose patted Chelsea's arm. "It's quite all right, dear. I understand."

Chelsea smiled. "Thanks. I promise I'm only neurotic because I want this to be perfect for them."

"And it will be," Rose assured her. "I'll take care of everything."

Chelsea headed from the kitchen area. Since her workday was essentially done, she figured she'd take advantage of her club membership and go riding. She needed the break from reality and being on the back of a horse was always so freeing. It helped to clear her head.

She definitely needed her head cleared because for the past two days she hadn't been able to focus on anything other than Gabe Walsh. The stubborn man wouldn't leave her mind. He took up entirely too much real estate in her thoughts. She'd tried throwing herself further into the wedding planning. She'd tried reading books. She'd even resorted to her old hacking skills and messed with her brother's social media accounts for fun. But nothing had taken away the memory of the dressing room.

The Dressing Room.

It was like the title of an epic romance she couldn't put down. For one, she'd never had a public make-out session. Two, she hadn't allowed any man to wrap her up so tight she feared she'd spring any minute. And for another, damn it…she just wanted to hate the man. Was that too much to ask? He was egotistical, arrogant…and too damn sexy for his own good.

But she couldn't bring herself to hate the way he

kissed, the way he'd touched her. How was it even possible that he had this hold on her? How could one man invoke so many emotions?

Chelsea headed toward the stables. The fresh winter air filled her lungs. She couldn't wait to spend the next few hours just relaxing and enjoying her ride.

When her cell vibrated in her pocket, she ignored it. Nothing was going to get in the way of this much needed alone time. Whoever wanted her could leave a message. If it was Daniel again, she'd get back to him. Any Hunt business could wait since it was after hours. And there was nothing pressing for the wedding at the moment.

In no time, Chelsea had chosen a gorgeous chestnut mare and was on her way. Getting back in the saddle felt so good. It had been too long since she'd taken advantage of the amenities TCC had to offer. Maybe she should schedule a massage and some sauna time after the wedding and holidays were over. She could use a good day of pampering.

Chelsea was just thankful they'd started allowing women to join a few years ago. There was a time when only men were members, but everything had changed when they'd opened the doors and their minds to the ladies.

Chelsea had jumped at the chance to join such an elite club. Who wouldn't want to be part of all of this? The clubhouse sat on gorgeous acreage, the amenities were absolutely perfect and everyone worth anything in this town was a member. Perhaps that's why Dusty was never admitted. Chelsea didn't know him personally, but his actions before his death had proved the guy to be a grade-A bastard.

Settling into an easy rhythm with her horse, Chelsea found a trail and rode off, thankful that with evening falling, there were no other riders. The stables closed at nine, so she had a couple hours to enjoy the open air, the peaceful evening, and to start figuring out her Christmas shopping list because she still had a few people she hadn't bought for. Online shopping was going to be her best friend in these last days leading up to Christmas.

With all the wedding planning, she'd dropped the ball on—

"And here I thought I'd be all alone."

Chelsea cringed at the familiar voice, her grip tightening on the reins. "Then take another path."

Gabe's laughter floated around her as he came up beside her horse. "Now, what fun would that be?"

His thigh brushed hers as he kept a steady gait. Chelsea didn't want any part of his body touching hers. Okay, that was a lie, but if she kept repeating it over and over, maybe the words would penetrate her stubborn heart.

"I came out here to think and be alone," she told him, refusing to look his way. She knew what he looked like— all brooding and sexy—without tormenting herself any further.

"Then by all means, think," he stated. "You won't even know I'm here."

"Are you kidding me?"

She pulled her horse to a stop, not at all surprised when he did the same. Now, she did glance his way. Yup. Just as sexy as two days ago when he'd been wrapped all around her, driving her out of her mind. His black hat shielded his eyes, but not enough that she didn't see that sexy gleam.

"You think I can have a peaceful moment when you're right next to me?"

"Well, darlin', I'll take that as a compliment."

Chelsea narrowed her eyes. "Why won't you go away?"

He rested his forearm on the saddle horn and shrugged. "I haven't seen you for two days. I went by Hope Springs and worked more on the arch, thinking you'd show up and lend a hand, but you never did. I'd say you've had plenty of space."

"Not enough," she muttered.

"You can't hide from me forever, Chelsea. We've got work to do and this tension between us isn't going anywhere."

Why did he have to be so blunt and just lay their attraction right on the table like that? It wasn't often she was speechless, but the man was bound and determined to throw her off her game, and damn it, it was working.

"You seem angry." He offered her a killer smile. "I'd say this fresh air will do you some good. Come on. Ride with me and we'll talk. Not about the dressing room or the fact you want me, and don't deny it. We'll do small talk. We can do that, right? The weather is always a good topic, but so predictable. Maybe we could discuss if you've put your Christmas tree up yet. I haven't."

Was he seriously turning into some chatterbox? She wasn't going to ride along beside him and talk like he was some girlfriend she was comfortable with. Gabe Walsh made her anything but comfortable.

"I don't want to engage in small talk with you." Chelsea pulled the reins and turned her horse back toward the trail. "I can't stop you from riding, but shut up."

Again, his laughter swept over her as he came to an easy trot next to her. Chelsea concentrated on the rocking of the horse, the smell of the fresh air, and not the man a mere foot from her.

"There's something I've been curious about."

She never knew where his thoughts were headed, but it was obvious he was going to keep going no matter what she said, so she just remained quiet.

"Why computers?"

Chelsea turned toward him. "Excuse me?"

"Just wondering why you got into computers."

She should've known he wouldn't honor her wish for silence. But work she could discuss. That was one topic where he wouldn't make her a stuttering, turned-on mess of emotions.

"I've always been interested in how things work," she told him. "When I was little, I tried picking locks. I actually got quite good at it by the time I was seven, but then I grew bored. Dad was always talking business, so I knew we were being raised to take over. When I wasn't learning fast enough, I tried getting into his computer when he was asleep one night. By the time I figured out his password, I'd gotten a little thrill and decided to see what else I could do."

"How old were you then?"

"Ten."

Gabe swore under his breath. "And here I've pissed you off. Are my bank accounts safe?"

Chelsea couldn't stop the smile from spreading across her lips. "For now."

"Did your father know you'd gotten into his system?"

"Of course. I was sloppy, as all beginner hackers are." Chelsea brushed her hair back from her face, wishing she'd thought to put on a headband. "You know, I really don't like that term. It makes me feel... I don't know... illegal."

Gabe tossed her a look with one arched brow. "It pretty much is illegal."

With a shrug, Chelsea forced her attention to the

smooth path in front of her. "Maybe, but I've never done anything terrible with my knowledge. I more do things to see how far I can get and to educate myself."

"So you've never done anything risky or wrong?" he asked.

Chelsea pursed her lips. "I may have changed a couple grades when I was in high school."

"And?" he prompted.

She swallowed. Was she really going to get into this with him?

"I might have hacked into one bank account to add some funds."

"You think hacking into a bank isn't illegal or bad?" he asked, obviously shocked at her admission.

"I admit it was wrong, but hindsight won't change the past."

Silence settled between them and Chelsea figured she shouldn't have told him. It was years ago and nobody had ever figured out what she had done. It had been her first real victory and, illegal or not, she wasn't sorry she'd done it. In fact, she was rather proud of herself.

"Are you going to finish the story or leave me hanging?"

Chelsea came to a stop and glanced toward a nearby cypress grove. Restless energy had her dismounting and tying the reins around a sturdy tree trunk. Gabe did the same and when he propped his hands on his hips and continued to stare at her, she figured she may as well tell him everything.

Five

Sweet, innocent-looking Chelsea had shocked him, but he was more than ready to hear what she had to say. If she claimed her hacking was for good reason, he believed her. He'd built the foundation of his career on reading people and was pretty confident she wasn't vindictive. And he wanted to continue spending time with her. She was opening up. Apparently when they weren't discussing the scandal that had rocked the town, she let her guard slip. He only hoped he could wipe his uncle's actions out of the picture for good.

"There was a husband and wife who worked for Hunt back when I was a teen." Chelsea tucked a stray strand of hair behind her ear and turned to rest against a tree away from the horses. "He had a gambling problem. She was pregnant with their first child, but tried to stick by him despite his addiction. I know my father offered to pay for help if the guy would just go. But, in the end, life became too much and he left her. She couldn't make the mortgage payments on her own and lost her house."

Gabe heard the compassion in Chelsea's tone. This was a whole new side to her he hadn't seen and it only made him want to uncover even more. He'd always figured she was giving, caring, selfless. His instincts hadn't proved him wrong before and they were dead-on now.

"She had her own income, but considering she was pregnant with no home, I couldn't stand it anymore." Chelsea's mouth twisted into a half grin. "I may have hacked into his private account and removed funds. And those funds *may* have found their way into her account."

Gabe honestly didn't know what to say. The woman was constantly a doer. She cared for others and wanted to see everyone around her happy. But he'd never thought once that she'd use her skills for something like this.

"Had you gotten caught—"

Her eyes met his. "At the time, I felt it was worth the risk. Now that I look back, I know it wasn't right to do that, but I got caught up in the moment and acted with my heart instead of my head."

She gave a slight shrug before she continued. "I just thought, what was he going to do? Tell the authorities? Most of his money was obtained illegally, because I uncovered that he was betting on cock fighting. He wouldn't want to open that can of worms and be subjected to proving where his income came from."

Chelsea's eyes misted. "All of that happened around the time when we'd just lost Mom. Actually, she ran off, but she may as well be dead because I haven't seen or heard from her since. I knew what that felt like, what being abandoned does to your soul. I couldn't stand it, Gabe."

Why did she have to have such a vulnerable side that

made resisting her impossible? He'd promised himself when he'd seen her riding up ahead that he'd keep his hands off, but the sorrow lacing her words only had him closing the gap between them.

"You shouldn't touch me. I'm emotional already and if you touch me…"

Her words were barely a whisper and he saw tears swimming in her eyes.

"This is just one friend consoling another," he explained.

Gabe wrapped his arms around her and she instantly returned the gesture. "We're not friends," she argued.

Smiling, he rested his chin on top of her head. "Maybe not, but we're something. I don't think they've created a label for us yet."

When she continued to just be still and let him hold her, Gabe figured she must be gathering her strength. She just needed a minute and he was all too willing to comfort her. As much as he wanted to get her into his bed, he could be patient. Chelsea would be worth the wait.

Hell, his job was based on patience and taking his time, being methodical. And he knew she was much more important than a job. Damn it. When had he let that happen?

Chelsea eased back and glanced up at him. "I'm not sure I can trust you."

Gabe smoothed her hair back and framed her face. "You will."

"Are you always so arrogant?"

Gabe smiled because her tone was light, but her question was genuine. "Confident," he corrected. "I know I did nothing wrong where you're concerned and, in time, you'll realize that, too."

Her eyes darted to his lips and he knew he'd just

knocked another brick off that barrier she kept around herself. She still clung to him and Gabe's last shred of control snapped.

He eased closer, keeping his eyes on hers as he lowered his head. "You plan on stopping me?" he whispered against her mouth.

"Not yet."

The second he covered her mouth, she melted against him. There was no other way to describe the way she simply let go and let him take the lead. But he wasn't naïve. Chelsea held all the power here. As much as he wanted her and was more than ready to seduce her up against this tree, she would ultimately have to give the green light.

Gabe rested one hand on her hip and thrust the other through her hair as he shifted his head and dove back in for more. More was the theme where Chelsea was concerned. He wanted as much as she would give...then he wanted even more.

She arched against him, groaning into his mouth. Gabe trailed his lips across her jaw and down the column of her throat. The neckline of her tank top mocked him, tempted him. So much exposed skin to explore... and still not enough. But he had to tread lightly. Chelsea wasn't just any woman, and their situation was extremely delicate.

"Gabe, please."

Easing back slightly, he took in her flushed cheeks and decided he couldn't leave her hanging. He was a gentleman, after all, and as gently as he needed to treat her, he also planned on giving in to her every desire.

"You don't have to ask twice."

Sliding his hand beneath the hem of her tank, Gabe kept his eyes locked on hers. If she showed the slightest bit of hesitation, he'd stop. But the way she bit on her lower lip and kept her eyes shut, he had to believe he was doing everything right.

He flicked the closure on her jeans, pleased when her hips surged forward. Glancing over his shoulder, he made sure no one was taking a late ride. But they were hidden behind the horses and around the side of a large cypress.

Gabe slid his hand inside the waistband of her panties and kicked her feet apart with the toe of his boot. He rested his forearm alongside her head, against the tree, and dipped his fingers into her heat. The moment she cried out, he covered her mouth with his.

Yes. Finally, this. He had wanted to see her come apart, had wanted to experience every bit of it, and now she was seconds away. He didn't want to just feel it, he wanted to taste it.

Chelsea's fingertips dug into his shoulders as she jerked her body against his. Then she exploded. There was no other way to describe it. She tore away from the kiss and tipped her head back, her mouth open in a perfect O as she clung to him.

Chelsea Hunt was letting every single guard down and giving in to her desires, and it was absolutely the most erotic thing he'd ever seen. He wished he could watch her forever, but he quickly pushed the idea aside. Forever wasn't in his vocabulary.

As she came down and her trembling ceased, Gabe knew for certain that he needed her in his bed. His entire body was wound so damn tight, but he'd have to wait. This was about Chelsea, about her needs and getting her to see that he was serious about this all-consuming need to have her.

But most of all, he wanted her to realize that he wasn't a liar and had never done anything to hurt her or to tarnish her reputation.

The horses shifted behind him and Gabe started to lean forward to kiss her, but she pushed against his shoulders. Her bold green eyes lifted to his and he instantly saw regret.

They'd made too much progress for her to have those walls come back up. Little by little, he was going to make sure she pushed beyond her fears. Why did she have to start letting her doubts and reality sink back in?

He removed his hand and stepped back, giving her a chance to right her clothes.

"I'm not going to apologize."

Her hands froze on the snap of her jeans as she glared up at him. "I didn't ask you to."

"You're angry."

"With myself. Not you."

Well, that was something. But he didn't want her in any way angry about this situation.

"Are you upset because you let yourself feel or because you hate me?"

She finished straightening her clothes and shoved her hair behind her ears. That defiant chin lifted an extra notch as she squared her shoulders and focused solely on him.

"I don't hate you," she retorted. "I just don't make a habit of getting involved with people I'm still on the fence about."

Raking a hand through his hair, he turned away and headed back to his stallion.

"You're not going to say anything?" she called after him.

Gabe tugged at the reins and freed his horse from the tree before glancing back over his shoulder. "You want to fight? You'll have to look elsewhere. A beautiful woman just came apart in my arms. I'm not feeling much like arguing. I want to be here for you, Chelsea. Not because my uncle tried to ruin you and so many others, but because I can't ignore this pull between us or what just happened."

He mounted the horse and turned him toward the stables, but held tight on the reins to keep him in place. "You riding back with me or alone?"

Still flushed and sexy as hell, Chelsea stared up at him. "Unless there's wedding business to attend to, we're better off returning separately."

He had a feeling she'd say something like that. It was expected, but that didn't lessen his frustration any.

Gabe rested his elbow on his knee and leaned down. "You can push me away, but that won't stop what's happening."

A rumble of thunder had him glancing toward the sky then back down to her. "Better get back. Storm's comin'."

He just hoped like hell they could weather it.

Chelsea dropped her keys onto the accent table inside her doorway and wiped her damp hair away from her face. The pop-up storm matched her mood—fierce and full of rage.

The lightning flashed, illuminating her open floor plan as she made her way inside. No sense in turning on the lights. They were set on a timer, anyway, and apparently her electricity had gone out because nothing was on in the entire place.

Perfect. Her phone needed to be charged and she'd wanted to take a hot bath and ignore the world…and the throb between her legs. Because as much as she tried to ignore what had just happened, it was impossible. Gabe was impossible. The stupid man was making her feel things, making her body hum and come alive like never before—all while they were still fully dressed. Her body still sizzled from the orgasm against the tree.

Chelsea made her way to her bedroom using what little battery she had left on her phone to light the way.

First, the man had tried to get it on with her in a dressing room and then he'd pleasured her at the damn club. He was slick, seductive and she'd loved every single minute of both experiences.

Well, she'd loved the way he'd physically made her feel, but the mental side...

Why did he have to keep messing with her head?

Everything circled back to Dusty and how he'd been so meticulous in planting evidence to ruin lives and pointing the finger of blame in so many different directions. The scandal had rocked the entire town and Chelsea wasn't sure she'd ever recover, if she were being honest.

It was humiliating to walk down the street and wonder if passersby had seen the photos of her naked.

Tears filled her eyes once again. She'd shed too many tears caused by a whole gamut of emotions. She'd cried from anger, from frustration, from hurt and resentment... so many things. And she'd had to do it all in private because her very best friend wanted and deserved the wedding of the year and there was no way Chelsea would ruin this monumental moment for her.

Chelsea's cell vibrated in her hand just as she hit her bedroom. When she glanced at the screen, she saw a text from her brother and a missed call from him earlier. With only an eight percent charge left on her battery, she opted to ignore it all. Not that she wouldn't have, anyway.

She definitely wasn't in the mood to talk to Daniel. She loved him and his fiancée, Erin, but right now she just wanted to get into pajamas and lie in bed. With the lightning flashing outside, soaking in her garden tub wasn't the smartest idea. It wasn't late, but late enough, and with the electricity gone, she could at least lie down and read on her electronic reader.

But as she sank to the edge of her bed, all she could think of was how amazing Gabe had made her feel. The man was so, so giving. All the focus had been on her and then, when she'd wanted to battle it out because she'd had no clue what to do with all her emotions, he'd walked away. Some might have said that was cowardly, but she saw it as gentlemanly. He hadn't wanted to make things more difficult than they already were.

Either that, or he'd just wanted to seduce her and that was all.

Unfortunately, she didn't think that was the case. She truly believed he wanted her. That he wanted to get closer to her, and not just for the sex. Yes, Gabe was often seen as a man of mystery, but she was starting to see him for so much more.

All of those reasons were precisely why she was so angry. She'd been furious with him back at the club. No, she'd been furious with herself. It wasn't his fault that when he touched her she went off like a rocket. It wasn't his fault that she'd never had a lover like him before.

Wait. Lover? No. They weren't going to have sex. They *couldn't* have sex. That would go against everything she'd vowed to herself. She wasn't even fully convinced of his innocence in his uncle's controversy, which was all the more reason she needed to keep her distance.

But how could she?

Six

The scream echoed through the barn and made his ears ring. Gabe spun around and spotted Brandee in the doorway, the sunlight illuminating her.

"That is going to be so gorgeous," she squealed as she raced across the open space.

Gabe glanced back at the arch, which he'd just finished. Well, he'd finished the framing and the structure. He'd texted Chelsea to come by later to do the actual decorating because that was not part of his skill set.

"You guys are really going above and beyond," Brandee exclaimed, getting misty-eyed as she came to stand beside him. Her eyes fixed on the arch before her.

Gabe wrapped an arm around her shoulders and pulled her in for a friendly hug. "It's no trouble at all. I'm just glad you've made my best friend so happy."

Disgustingly happy. These two were absolutely perfect for each other. Gabe hadn't believed people could be so in love; he hadn't actually believed in that emotion at all, but if it existed, Brandee and Shane were wrapped up tight with it.

"Where's Chelsea?" Brandee asked, easing back.

It had been three days since he'd seen her and he was getting rather twitchy—not something he wanted to explain to her best friend. He could barely explain his feelings to himself. He wanted Chelsea, but the fierce need that continued to grow inside him was something new. He'd wanted women before, but not like this. The strength she displayed, her loyalty to her friends and her intelligence were all huge turn-ons. There was nothing about her he didn't find mesmerizing.

Originally he'd wondered if it was because he felt sorry for her because of Dusty's actions. But Gabe had quickly discovered that he didn't feel sorry for Chelsea. He admired her. She had a strength he couldn't help but find attractive. She had a take-charge attitude and then, on top of that, with her sexy-as-hell looks, he couldn't help but be drawn.

"I'm sure she's working," he replied. "I told her this would be ready to go today for the flowers or whatever it is you want to decorate it with. I just needed to get the base sturdy enough."

Brandee stepped forward and ran her hand over the oak grain. "This is far more than I'd envisioned and it's not even done. I can't wait for my wedding day."

Gabe hooked his thumbs through his belt loops and rocked back on his heels. "I'm sure Chelsea will be by soon. I texted her earlier."

Brandee tossed him a grin and raised her brows. "You two taking shifts on the wedding preparations? Is that because of the whole dressing room issue?"

On the one hand, he wasn't surprised at all that she'd brought up the incident. On the other hand, he was sure as hell glad she didn't know about their session at the Texas Cattleman's Club. Gabe wanted to keep the stolen moments with Chelsea to himself. They were private and, until he could figure out what the hell they were doing, he wanted to keep things that way.

"I doubt it," he answered with a slight laugh. "She doesn't seem like the type to run over something like that. But I think this attraction has her being extra cautious."

"Attraction?" Brandee said, her brows shooting up and a smile spreading across her face. "Well, she needs something to keep her mind off the bad press caused by those photos. I think it's great you two are working together."

Oh, he did, too. Because when he and Chelsea were together, he couldn't keep his hands to himself and, for the most part, Chelsea wasn't complaining, at least until she started letting her mind take over.

Damn it. He wanted the hell out of her and she still wanted to keep him at a distance. Someone was going to lose this fight...and he'd never lost yet.

"She's still unsure about trusting me," Gabe went on. "She's learning, but given my last name and all, her hesitancy is more than justified."

"You were cleared of any wrongdoing," Brandee said. "Besides, anyone who knows you would never believe for a second you had anything to do with releasing those photos. Shane and I couldn't believe when your name was even mentioned."

"I appreciate that. I would never do something so vile," he declared. "I'm just as disgusted by my uncle's actions as anyone. He's gone and now I'm the one carrying his family name and trying to keep my reputation as far removed from his as possible."

"You're a victim, too," she stated.

Yeah. He was. If only Chelsea could see things from

that angle. But he wasn't one to play the pity card. He didn't want her pity—he wanted her in his bed.

"I'm glad you're here, actually." He was happy to change the subject, he legitimately had something he needed to tell her. "Your wedding present will be arriving tomorrow. It isn't exactly something I could've brought to the reception."

Brandee tipped her head and smiled. "You know you didn't have to get us anything. You and Chels are doing so much already. The load you have lifted from Shane and me is immeasurable."

Gabe shrugged. "Trust me when I say you will want this."

Besides, his uncle had caused so many problems for Brandee and Shane months ago. Their relationship almost hadn't made it at all, let alone to the altar. Gabe was all too happy to give them this extravagant present. They were his friends and Brandee had such a huge heart, giving back so much to the community.

Brandee ran a camp for teens in need. She used her time and her own funding to keep the place on her ranch open for impressionable teens, and it was time she didn't have to carry so much of the load on her own.

"What's that smile for?" she asked.

"Just anxious for a little surprise I have planned," he replied. "Now, if you'll excuse me, I have some business to attend to. Chelsea may be here later."

As he started to head out of the barn, Brandee called out to him, "She's more vulnerable than you think."

Gabe stilled. He knew how fragile Chelsea was, but hearing her best friend confirm it made him wonder what hurt Chelsea kept inside.

He threw a glance over his shoulder. "She's also stronger than you think."

And he wanted her to trust him. Whether she liked it or not, he would protect her. She was done doing everything alone.

Chelsea leaned back in her desk chair in her home office and stared at the bright screen of her laptop. She'd kept tabs on her mother for a year or so now. She'd made sure not to do anything illegal, but some simple investigative work by someone of her skill level…well, it hadn't been too difficult to turn up Shonda Hunt. Or rather, Shonda Patton, since she remarried.

Bitterness burned like acid in Chelsea's gut. She hated that her mother had run out on them. Chelsea had never fully known the reason why and it wasn't a topic she had ever brought up to her father before he'd passed. The poor man had been devastated after his wife left, so much so, he'd died a year later of a heart attack. Chelsea had always figured he'd been so crushed he'd lost his will to go on.

She continued staring at the image she'd uncovered of Shonda and her husband. It was a random photo from a newspaper in Kansas. They were on a park bench attending a town festival or something. There her mother was, enjoying the life she wanted.

Trust didn't come easy to Chelsea and staring back at her was the very reason why. When a foundation was shaken and everything you ever knew turned out to be a lie, it was difficult to see another way, let alone try to rebuild on uneven ground.

The spiral Chelsea spun into after her mother had left had been a cry for help, but her actions, no matter how troubled, had ultimately led her to become the woman she was today. She was damn good at her job and refused to let anyone have control over her life ever again.

That included Gabe Walsh. He'd been smart to keep their interaction to texts these past few days, but part of her really wanted to get into that verbal sparring match she was gearing up for. He had texted earlier that he wanted to talk, but he hadn't said when and he hadn't said why.

How could one man turn her on and infuriate her at the same time?

Closing out her screen, Chelsea came to her feet and secured the knot on her robe. She was done spying on Shonda. Chelsea refused to call her *mother*, because that woman didn't exist. Chelsea knew she needed to let it go and move forward. She had a lucrative career that she loved and she was planning her best friend's wedding. She didn't need anything more.

Right?

Unfortunately, there was that young girl living inside her that wanted answers. That impressionable girl needed to know what she could do to ever fill the void of abandonment.

Chelsea had just stepped into her living room when the doorbell rang. She glanced at the large clock on her mantel and wondered who would be dropping by unannounced at nine at night.

She smoothed her hands down her robe and pulled the lapels a little tighter to her chest. A quick glance out the sidelight caused Chelsea's heart rate to kick up. She pulled in a deep breath and flicked the lock.

When she swung the door wide, she expected Gabe to just walk on in. Instead he gave her a head-to-toe appraisal and propped his arm on the door frame. It caused his bicep to tighten, which only drew her attention to his excellent muscle tone.

"I do like how you greet your guests."

"A heads-up text would've been considerate," she stated, crossing her arms.

The corner of his mouth kicked up. "I texted earlier and said I wanted to talk."

She couldn't help but laugh. "Specifics would've been nice."

"I'll remember that for next time."

He pushed off the frame, but continued to stand in the light of the porch. "But I'm here now and I want you to understand there's no reason to be afraid of what's going on between us. I know you've been dealt a bad hand lately and I also know you're strong. I'd never push you, but I also won't let you run."

Chelsea opened her mouth but Gabe held his hand up to stop her. "I get that you're still reeling from what Dusty did. I even understand that trusting me at first was difficult, but we're past that, aren't we?"

"You confuse me," she whispered. "I can't get into this right now, Gabe. I need to think."

She started to shut the door but he was quicker. His fingers curled around the edge and held it open.

"I want you so much," he replied, stepping in closer until she had to tip her head back to look into those mesmerizing eyes. "Which is why I'm putting the next step on you."

Confused, Chelsea jerked back. "What?"

"There's nothing I want more than to cross this threshold and peel you out of that robe, but I want you to take control. I want you to ache just as much as I do. Because when we finally make it to a bedroom, it will be your decision."

Chelsea swallowed. Her body stirred at his words and his boldness. "Is that why you came here?" she asked, shocked her voice sounded strong at all. "To tell me that we're going to have sex?"

Gabe raked a hand over his face and blew out a breath. "I came here to tell you that I'm not going to coddle you. You're a strong woman and you don't want pity over what happened. I get that you want to be respected, and I respect you. So if anything happens from here on out, it's your call."

Chelsea opened her mouth then closed it.

"Speechless?" he asked with a slight grin. "That wasn't the reaction I expected."

"What did you expect?"

"Well, you didn't slam the door in my face, so I'm already a step above where I thought I'd be."

She bit the inside of her cheek to keep from smiling, but failed.

"And a sexy grin? Hell, I better leave while I'm ahead."

Chelsea tucked her hair behind her ears and took a step back. As much as she wanted to invite him in and take him up on what he was offering, she also had to be smart. She'd never been a woman to just sleep with someone for the sake of getting it out of her system. Then again, no one had ever tempted her the way Gabe Walsh had.

"Do you want me to do anything for the wedding?" he asked, his tone softer as he stared into her eyes. "I have a few hours free tomorrow if you need anything."

"Well, I'm almost done with the arch. I've planned for the steaks to be delivered the day before the bachelor/bachelorette party, so if you want to call and make sure the club has all of the staffing covered for that night, that would help. I just don't want them to be understaffed, because we're expecting quite a few people. The bartenders need to be the best, too. Make sure Tanner and Ellen are on the list to serve."

Gabe nodded. "I can do that. Didn't you message me about some chair covers you wanted picked up?"

Chair covers, yes. She'd forgotten all about those. Maybe it had something to do with the man who stood before her because the past couple of weeks he'd been consuming so much of her time, both in person and in her thoughts. But they needed chair covers for the party. Something elegant, yet something that would fit in at the club with all its dark wood and trophies.

"I can pick them up," she told him. Silence stretched between them and the tension stirred deep within her. "Is that all?"

He flashed her a devilish grin. "Unless you're ready to invite me in now and let me unwrap you."

Oh, she wanted to be unwrapped. Gabe could tempt a saint into stripping and doing naughty deeds.

Chelsea laughed and poked at his chest until he stepped back. "Good night, Gabe."

When he leaned in, Chelsea stilled. His lips feathered across her cheek. "Good night, Chels."

He turned and walked away, bounding down the steps and heading toward his truck. Chelsea closed the door, turning the dead bolt back into place, and rested her forehead against the wood.

What was she going to do about that man? He purposely kept her on her toes and tied up in knots. Part of her loved this catch-and-release game they were playing, but the other part didn't want to play games anymore. She wanted to know for sure that she could trust him. But how? How could she be certain?

Chelsea flicked off the light and headed for bed, knowing full well she wouldn't be getting any sleep tonight.

Seven

"What do you think?"

Chelsea stood back and stared at the archway that was covered in sheer, pale gold material, twinkling clear lights and delicate white flowers.

She then glanced over at her friend, who stood there staring and silent. Okay, maybe it didn't look as great as Chelsea had thought. This wasn't exactly her area of expertise, but she'd like to think it wasn't horrendous.

"It will look better at night for the ceremony when you can see the lights better," Chelsea rushed to say when the silence became too much. "I mean, I can change whatever you want. I'm not really a decorator, but I can look up other ideas—"

"It's perfect."

Chelsea breathed a sigh of relief. She'd honestly had to look at so many wedding planning websites, at images of elegant arches and Christmas-themed weddings just to piece together everything her friend would want.

The expression on Brandee's face made all of that digging worth it.

Because Chelsea had hated every second of searching through blissful pictures of couples deliriously in love. Not that she wasn't happy for Brandee and Shane, but part of her truly didn't believe in the hype of marriage or love. All of that had to be built on trust. But trusting someone with your whole life? No. That just wasn't going to happen. Not for her. And she was okay with living alone.

Chelsea ignored the niggling ache in her heart. Okay, maybe it would be nice to find someone to share her secrets with, to lie with at night and talk about absolutely nothing, to go on trips with and see the world. But all that would require her to fully open up and expose a part of herself she'd shut off far too long ago.

The sound of approaching vehicles had both women turning toward the large entrance to the barn. Brandee headed toward it and Chelsea followed.

As soon as she stepped outside, Chelsea's mouth dropped. There were six, brand-new, shiny white vans and three large pickup trucks sitting in the drive of the Hope Springs Ranch. The driver of the first van got out and crossed the yard toward Brandee.

"I'm looking for Ms. Lawson."

Brandee shielded her eyes from the sun. "That's me."

The middle-aged man held out a clipboard and pen. "I just need you to sign for the shipment of vehicles and let me know where you'd like them all parked. Do you want the keys left in the ignition or brought to you?"

"Excuse me?" she asked. "I didn't… I'm not sure…"

"Oh, I'm sorry," he said with a smile. "These are all paid in full from a Mr. Walsh. He said this was your wedding gift."

What in the world had Gabe done? All of this? He'd paid for every single vehicle here? They were brand-new, not a speck of dirt on any of them, and they were all for Brandee.

Chelsea's heart flipped.

"He said he had something being delivered, but…" Brandee trailed off as she stared at the fleet of new vehicles. "I can't believe he did this."

Chelsea was absolutely stunned. She couldn't take in everything at once. This was a…a *wedding gift*? Weren't you just supposed to get the bride and groom toasters and towels? This went so far above the items on any wedding registry, Chelsea didn't even know what to think.

Gabe had done all of this without fanfare and without mentioning a word to her. He hadn't wanted the recognition or the praise. The man had legitimately wanted to help out with Brandee's work with the teens. How could Chelsea sustain her anger toward him when he kept proving over and over how selfless he was?

Chelsea took in each vehicle as Brandee pointed to where they could be parked. The dollar signs were scrolling through her head. She'd known Gabe was wealthy—from his expensive loft apartment to his luxury cars to his expensive taste in bourbon—but she'd never thought for a second he could do something like this.

"Can you believe this?" Brandee asked when she came back to stand beside Chelsea. "He told me he was having something delivered. I thought maybe it was… I don't know, a horse."

Brandee laughed and raked her hand through her long hair. "I don't even know what to say. A thank-you card isn't even enough. These vehicles will make a huge difference in the camp for my teens. We'll be able to take in more kids."

Brandee's voice broke as she dissolved into tears. "Sorry," she said as she wiped her cheeks. "I'm an emotional mess with the wedding."

Chelsea turned to her friend and pulled her into a hug. "It's understandable. This is a big step in your life. You're entitled to a meltdown. And Gabe's gift was a bit unexpected."

Brandee eased back and smiled. "He's such a great guy, Chels. I spoke with him yesterday and he seemed…"

Chelsea stilled. "What?"

"I don't think it's a stretch to say he's interested in you."

Her friend's misty eyes met Chelsea's. She truly didn't want to have this conversation with anyone, let alone the woman standing there with cupid silhouettes practically bulging out of her eyes.

"He's a guy and I'm single." Chelsea figured shrugging it off would be safest at this point. "But, to answer your veiled question, we're just friends."

Friends who made out like teens in a dressing room. Why didn't she have a friend like him before?

Oh, right. She hadn't trusted him before.

The barrier she'd kept around her soul where Gabe was concerned cracked a little. Okay, more than a little. The very foundation shook. She wanted to give him the benefit of the doubt, and had actually started to.

"You're interested in him, too," Brandee murmured. "Don't bother denying it. This is more than a friendship."

Chelsea jerked her attention back to the moment. "You have too much love and wedding bliss on the mind to think clearly."

But her friend was absolutely correct. Whatever Chelsea and Gabe had going on, it was so much more than friendship. When he'd said there hadn't been a label created for them yet, he'd been accurate. Because they weren't really friends. She didn't trust him. Did she?

Chelsea said farewell to Brandee and headed out to her car. At this point she didn't *not* trust Gabe. The mental sparring match she continued to have with herself was exhausting.

As she drove toward downtown Royal, she realized she was tired of something else, too.

Fighting her needs.

Gabe's doorman had let Chelsea up nearly fifteen minutes ago. He stood at the floor-to-ceiling window, watching as the sun cast a bright orange glow across the horizon as he waited for her. People were starting to really fill the street. Couples were strolling hand-in-hand, heading into restaurants for dinner dates. The little town came alive at night—especially on a Friday.

He watched as people posed in front of the giant Christmas tree in the town square just a block away. The tree stood tall and proud, decorated with what seemed like a million clear lights. There would be an annual candlelight and caroling evening in less than two weeks. He loved this town, loved the traditions it upheld.

Before the doorman had called to announce Chelsea's surprise visit, Gabe had actually been getting ready to head out and grab a drink at the TCC to see who was spending their evening there. Though there likely weren't many people hanging out in the club's bar tonight. These days, nearly everyone was either married, engaged, caring for or expecting a baby.

So much had happened over the past year, both good and bad. Weddings, babies—all of that had brought families together. But the Maverick scandal still left a dark cloud over the club and the town.

Just this afternoon, he'd been in contact with the sheriff to see if there were any updates regarding Dusty's accomplice in planting the camera in the locker room. There had to have been someone and Gabe wanted to know who it was. Until that person was brought to justice, this nightmare wouldn't fully be over.

At least he had been cleared of any involvement early on in the investigation. And even more importantly, Chelsea had started trusting him more and more.

Something had changed Chelsea's mind about him, otherwise she wouldn't have come of her own accord to his loft.

Which made him wonder why she hadn't knocked on his door yet. Gabe had given the doorman a small list of guests who didn't need an okay from him before they were automatically rung up. Chelsea had been at the top of the list for over a month now. But the doorman had called Gabe fifteen minutes ago to tell him she was on her way up.

Yet his unexpected guest hadn't made her presence known to him. She was most likely hesitating out in the hallway, wondering why she'd come. He knew exactly why she'd come.

Gabe shoved his hands in his pockets and smiled. He'd put the proverbial ball in her court and it had been excruciating waiting on her to come to the conclusion that they needed to get this out of their system. Those two make-out sessions hadn't even come close to alleviating his ache.

Turning from the window, Gabe crossed his loft and went to the door. If she'd come this far, the least he could do was give her a hand and help her the rest of the way.

Gabe opened the door wide and spotted Chelsea leaning against the wall directly across from him. Clearly startled, she jerked and clutched her purse in front of her…as if trying to use something to shield her from the big bad wolf. Didn't she know? There was nothing he couldn't knock down to get what he wanted.

"How long were you going to wait before you knocked?" he asked.

Squaring her shoulders and tipping her chin, she cleared her throat. "I wasn't sure I was going to knock. I was thinking of leaving."

"No, you weren't."

Chelsea blinked, opened her mouth then closed it and continued to stare.

"Are we going to do this in the hallway or are you coming in?"

"Do what?" she asked.

"Whatever brought you here." He stepped back and gestured her in. "Don't look so worried, Chels. I only bite when I'm asked to."

Her eyes widened for a fraction of a second before she blinked and stepped forward, turning sideways to pass without actually touching him. Gabe bit back a grin as he closed the door, securing it with a click of the lock. He had the entire top floor to himself, and knew they wouldn't be bothered, but he still wanted that extra layer of privacy between the outside world and his Chelsea.

No. She wasn't his. Gabe needed to stop thinking along those lines. He wanted her. That was all. Once, not so long ago, he'd let emotions over a woman cloud his judgment and it had resulted in his partner being killed. He'd let his need override his job, thinking he could handle an attraction to a woman and still think clearly out in the field. He'd been wrong and his partner had paid the ultimate price.

He couldn't forget the promise he'd made to himself

after that to stay focused on work. Any extracurricular activities had to remain strictly physical, which was more than fine with him. Especially where a certain computer hacker and CTO was concerned.

After the hell that she'd been through, she deserved respect. She may keep that steely front in place, but he knew there was an underlying vulnerability after the leak of those photos.

Gabe appreciated Chelsea enough to place the control in her hands. And now she'd risen above her vulnerability and had come to him.

Damn, she smelled amazing. That familiar jasmine scent he'd come to associate with her surrounded him. Gabe crossed his arms and watched as she did a slow circle, taking in his space.

He'd imagined her in his bed many times, but never had he imagined her in his living room for a casual visit. That would have been too personal.

"You're sneaky," she muttered. "I mean vans and trucks, Gabe."

She turned to face him and raised her brows as if waiting for him to answer, but he'd missed the actual question.

"I take it the fleet arrived at Hope Springs."

Her eyes narrowed. "Your wedding gift was incredible. A fleet of expensive vans and trucks. I was buying them the china set they registered for and you go and spend…well, more than the cost of the entire wedding, reception, and honeymoon combined."

Clearly he was on shaky ground here, so he dropped his arms to his sides and crossed to her. "I can't tell if you're angry or shocked. Regardless, I wanted to help Brandee with the camp. It seemed like the logical thing to do."

"Logical." She lifted her head to hold his gaze and those green eyes definitely pinned him in place. "You're not a logical man. You're reckless, unpredictable, maddening, but never logical."

"Well, darlin', I think you just gave me a compliment."

Chelsea rolled her eyes and threw her hands out as she turned to head toward the wall of windows. Gabe remained where he was, waiting on her to say something.

"Only you would find those words to be flattering." With her back still to him, she tucked her hair behind her ears and blew out a sigh. "I want to hate you. I want to keep not trusting you, but then you go and do this. It's so unselfish and giving and...damn it."

One step after another, Gabe closed the distance between them and came to stand directly behind her. As the sun started to set and the evening grew dim, their reflections were easy to make out in the window. He saw the uncertainty on her face, the passion in her eyes. She had come to his door for one reason and one reason only.

"You're frustrated," he murmured against her ear, still holding on to his amazing restraint by not touching her. "Tell me the real reason you're here. It's not to pat me on the back for giving the best wedding gift."

"Part of it is." She met his gaze in their reflection. "I was standing there watching as one truck after another pulled onto the ranch. And I realized, maybe you're not a jerk."

Gabe smiled and smoothed her hair away from her neck. "What else did you realize?"

She trembled beneath his lips and he gave up all restraint. Trailing his fingertips up her arms and back down, he took a half step to bring his chest against her back.

"That I want you. I want this."

Finally.

"I'm done fighting," she went on as he continued gliding his fingers over her silky skin. "I never take what I want."

"And you want me."

"Yes," she whispered.

He hadn't asked, but hearing her repeat her affirmation had arousal consuming him. He'd put her at the helm and she was going after what she wanted. Him.

"If I'd known it was going to get you to my door, I would've bought the fleet a month ago," he joked, figuring she needed the tense moment to ease her nerves.

She smiled, which was exactly his intent. Her body relaxed against his and he reached around, flattening one palm against her stomach. His fingers splayed across the fabric of her tank top, pulling her back against him. Chelsea continued to watch in the window.

Gabe curled his pinky finger beneath the hem of her tank and slid it just inside the waistband of her jeans. Her swift intake of breath had him nipping at her ear. He wanted her as off balance as possible, because he'd been that way for weeks now. He wanted her so achy and needy that she begged him, that she came apart in his arms and cried out his name.

Gabe began to pull her shirt up over her head but Chelsea gasped and attempted to cover herself.

"The windows—"

"Are mirrored on the other side," he stated. "Nobody can see you and I want you right here, right now."

"But—"

"You came to me," he reminded her, turning her so she could face him. "We're playing by my rules now."

Chelsea relaxed a little as he finished taking off her shirt and tossed it over his shoulder. Then he crushed his mouth to hers and was instantly rewarded with a groan.

This time, nothing would stop them. They weren't in public anymore and he was damn well going to take his time. Later. This first round was going to be quick and fierce because he'd waited long enough.

Gabe pressed her back against the glass and started working on the button on her jeans. In no time she was wiggling those hips and helping him remove the unwanted garment. Now that she was only clad in lacy panties and a matching bra that would bring any man to his knees, Gabe lifted her by her waist and nipped at her swollen lips.

"You knew exactly why you were coming here."

Chelsea bit down on her lip and met his gaze.

"Say it," he commanded. "Tell me exactly why you're here."

He wanted her begging, pleading.

Gabe ground his hips against hers as she locked her ankles behind his back.

"Tell me, Chels."

Eight

"You," she ground out. "I want to be with you in every way. Now, Gabe."

He knew full well just how to get her begging and, for once, she was all too anxious to give up control. She needed him, needed this. Trust issues, worrying who was exactly behind what would come later. She couldn't think of one time in her life she'd done something rash, for purely selfish reasons, without analyzing it to death.

Gabe Walsh was the perfect reason to be selfish. He was also the perfect man to prove that she was still in control after the scandal. She wanted to be here. She wanted him. And she was going to have him.

"Damn right you do."

He released her, easing her legs back to the floor, but only long enough to perform the quickest strip she'd ever seen. By the time he was completely bare and he'd procured protection from his wallet and covered himself,

Chelsea's body was aching in ways she'd never known. She continued to stare into his gray eyes as he rid her of the last pieces of lace. Then he was on her.

Once again, he lifted her and she wrapped her legs around his waist. He slid into her like they were made for each other. Chelsea tipped her head back against the glass as a groan escaped her.

"Look at me," he murmured.

The fact they were doing this against the window had a shiver of excitement coursing through her. Still, she was thankful for the mirrored glass on the other side.

Chelsea locked her eyes on Gabe and smiled. "You're bossy," she panted.

He smacked her backside as he jerked his hips faster. "You wouldn't have it any other way. You're enjoying this just as much as I am."

She was. Oh, mercy, she was. This experience with this man made her feel so much more in control of her body, of how a man looked at her. How did Gabe make her feel so treasured and so erotic at the same time? She didn't know she would be this comfortable with intimacy so soon after the Maverick scandal, but Gabe made her feel alive and sexy.

When she opened her mouth to speak, he reached between them and touched her in just the right spot to have her eyes rolling back and a groan escaping her. Her entire body tightened as she clutched his shoulders and let him do whatever he wanted...because he clearly knew her body better than she did.

"Chels," he strained to say as his own body trembled. His grip on her hips tightened.

She remained wrapped all around him, taking in every bit of his release. Feeling all of that taut skin beneath her hands, having such a powerful man at her mercy right now was absolutely incredible. Gabe Walsh was doing things to her mind and body that she wasn't ready for, but she'd started this roller coaster and it was too late to jump off now.

He was perfect, and had come along at the perfect time—when she didn't even realize she needed someone. But she did. She needed him to show her she was a passionate woman and not defined by those photos.

Their bodies ceased trembling, but she wasn't ready to let go. Not quite yet.

"Stay here tonight," he whispered in her ear.

The warm breath tickling her skin had her fisting her hands on his shoulders. There was nothing more she wanted than to stay and do this all over again, maybe in a bed this time, but she couldn't let her post-coital feelings dominate her common sense. She still had questions and she still had concerns.

"You're thinking too hard." He turned from the window, still holding on to her, and headed toward the hallway leading deeper into the loft. "Apparently, I didn't do my job if you're still able to have coherent thoughts."

"My thoughts are jumbled, if that counts."

He tightened his hold on her and Chelsea had to suppress a moan of pleasure. Being skin-to-skin after sex was even more intimate than the act itself. This moment was… Chelsea suddenly realized she couldn't do this. Not with a man she was still so unsure about.

Gabe turned into a bedroom—his bedroom. The dark navy and rich wood tones screamed masculine dominance. She'd just voluntarily come to the lion's den.

"Gabe, I can't—"

"You can."

Her arms and legs were still draped around him. He held their bodies together so tight, she just knew when he let go she would feel cold, alone. But this was fun while it lasted, right? She hadn't come here for a sleepover or to do anything other than what had just happened.

"No," she told him, pressing against his shoulders. "I can't."

He studied her face for just a moment before easing her down to stand on her own. But he kept his hands on her hips.

"I don't want a relationship, Gabe."

"Is that right?" he asked, gliding his hands up the dip in her waist and back down.

The way he continued to stare at her made her feel foolish for making assumptions, but he had to see her side. "I came here for sex. That's all. Staying overnight implies more."

She'd wanted him, plain and simple. She'd also wanted this man to help her get over the feeling that she'd been tarnished somehow. The things he did to her, with her, had helped Chelsea realize she was still in control despite the scandal that followed her.

The corners of Gabe's mouth twitched as he continued that maddening feathering of his fingertips over her heated skin. Her heartbeat had yet to slow down from the moment she'd walked through his door. She was seriously out of her element here and, judging from the relaxed manner of the frustrating man in front of her, he'd clearly been in this position of power before.

"So now what?" he asked. "You're going to get dressed and leave?"

Honestly, she hadn't thought all of this through. The man was wearing her down and she couldn't even think straight.

"This isn't something I do," she admitted. "So, yeah. I guess I'll, um, I should just get dressed and go."

Gabe towered over her, leaning forward until she sank back onto the bed. His hands dipped into the mattress on either side of her hips as he came within a breath of her mouth.

"Don't be ashamed that you're here, that you took what you wanted." His eyes seemed a darker gray now, desire filling them. "This doesn't have to be awkward or complicated."

"I'm not ashamed," she stated, trying to seem strong and in control when her bare butt was on his duvet and he was a breath away from getting her flat on her back and having his way again. "I just don't know what to do from here."

That naughty grin kicked up a second before he nipped at her lips. "I'll show you exactly what we're going to do from here and then you can decide if you want to stay the night or leave."

Chelsea wanted to protest, she really should stick to her guns, but the only thing she could think as Gabe's weight settled over hers and she lay back was, *Finally.* They'd finally made it to the bed.

"Missed again, Walsh."

Gabe muttered a curse. "I didn't miss."

"But you didn't hit the bull's-eye," Shane countered. "What's up, man?"

Playing darts and drinking a beer with his buddies at TCC usually calmed Gabe. Not today.

He headed back to the bar and grabbed his beer, taking a hearty swig. What the hell was wrong with him? He'd thought once he got Chelsea in his bed, he'd be over this need. If anything, though, he was achier than ever and, damn, if he wasn't pissed about it.

"Nothing," Gabe replied, setting his bottle back on

the glossy bar top. "Getting ready for the big day? Did you get your vows all written?"

Shane's smile widened, as it always did when his fiancée was mentioned. The two were so obviously in love and Gabe couldn't be happier for them. After all Dusty had done to try to ruin Brandee, she deserved a happy ending.

Gabe just hated that there were so many amazing people, *innocent* people, who were still recovering from being the Maverick's victim. Since discovering Dusty had been at the helm of the scandal that shook Royal, Gabe had personally reached out to each of the victims. Apologies were just words, but he hoped they understood his sincerity.

With the exception of Chelsea—and even she seemed to have come around to believe his innocence—nobody had blamed him or accused him of guilt by association. He'd been a victim, as well, considering the impact on his reputation and on the business that carried Dusty's last name. But Gabe could take care of himself—he was taking care of himself. He'd been more concerned with making things right for the Maverick's true victims.

The majority had moved on with their lives. And the strange thing was, for some of them, their experiences with Maverick had led to positive outcomes. They'd married, had children, settled deeper roots in Royal. Gabe was just thankful the repercussions Dusty's dark, twisted games hadn't been worse.

"My vows are done," Shane replied, pulling Gabe's attention back to the conversation. "Brandee is a little stressed."

Shane sank onto a bar stool and ordered another bourbon. "I told her so long as the minister shows up, nothing else matters. That was the wrong thing to say."

Gabe laughed as he leaned his elbow on the bar. "Chelsea and I have everything covered. You two just show up and worry about remembering those vows you're preparing."

Shane's brows shot up. "How is Chelsea? Brandee said she wasn't too talkative over the past couple days. Her texts are to the point and only about wedding details. Would you have any idea what's up?"

"Not a clue."

Shane took the tumbler from the bartender and swirled the amber liquid around. "You're a terrible liar."

"Actually, I'm an exceptional liar and my bank account proves it."

Being in the security field occasionally had him going undercover in disguise. He was a remarkable actor, if he did say so himself. But there were just some aspects of his life he wasn't ready to share and Chelsea was one of them.

Shane tipped back the bourbon and finished it in one long gulp before setting his glass down and motioning for another. "Fine. But you can't lie to me, and I know something is up with the two of you. She's beautiful and you're, well, you. Might as well tell me what's going on."

"What the hell is that supposed to mean? I'm me? Are you calling me a player?"

"Calm down. I just meant you two have been spending quite a bit of time together over the past several weeks."

Before Gabe could defend himself, Daniel Hunt walked in the door. Seeing Chelsea's brother, Gabe felt a momentary pang of guilt. But he shouldn't feel bad about whom he wanted…and whom he'd had. Chelsea was a big girl and she had come to him—then left in the middle of the night.

He wasn't sure if he was more upset about her silent

departure or relieved that she'd held up their agreement to keep things simple. Although he had to admit, just to himself, he wished she'd stuck around because there was nothing he would've liked better than to roll over and feel her by his side in the morning.

Which was precisely why it was good she had left. A woman like Chelsea could make a man forget all about reality. Gabe was growing his business, doing damage control where needed, and the last thing he had time for was a relationship.

"Hey, man," Shane called to Daniel. "Didn't know you were in Royal."

Daniel came up to the bar on the other side of Shane and nodded for the bartender. "Erin wanted to do some shopping for Christmas and insists on the local shops here rather than Seattle. She said she wants to stay through Christmas because she loves this small-town feel and wants to experience her first Christmas here. Plus, she didn't want to miss the wedding or the annual candlelight and caroling ceremony on Christmas Eve."

Gabe raked his thumb over the condensation on his glass of beer and wished he'd ordered something stronger and stayed home.

"How's the wedding coming?" Daniel asked then leaned around to glance at Gabe. "You and my sister have everything covered? Knowing her, she's taken control."

An image of Chelsea straddling him last night when they'd finally made it to his bed flooded his mind. She'd taken control, all right, and he'd been more than okay with relinquishing the reins.

"It's more like divide and conquer," Gabe replied, refusing to say much more.

Shane threw him a glance, but Gabe merely picked

up his beer and drained the glass. "I need to head out," he said, pushing away from the bar.

"Stay," Daniel said. "Next round is on me."

Tempting as another drink was, he didn't want to sit around with his best friend who knew too much and the overprotective brother of the woman he was sleeping with. He could think of a hundred other things that sounded more appealing.

"I still have some work to tend to this evening." Not a total lie. He was always checking on his clients and staff. "And tomorrow is an early day for me."

Actually he had nothing planned, but it sounded like a good excuse. Besides, there was always something to be done and he was always up early and hitting work hard.

"I wanted to ask you about the Maverick case."

Gabe stilled. "Sheriff Battle said there are no new leads as to who helped Dusty. I've had my team working on this, as well. The security cameras outside the gym locker room had been tampered with."

Daniel rubbed the back of his neck and shook his head. "This is absurd. I don't know what I'll do when I get hold of the person who made my sister's life a living hell."

Gabe was right there with him, but best not to say that or to express too much interest in Chelsea. Daniel was definitely the overprotective big brother. What Daniel didn't know was that Gabe had also appointed himself to that role.

"I'll be sure to keep you informed," Gabe assured Daniel. "I'm hoping this is wrapped up soon and we can all move on for good."

"I appreciate that, Walsh."

Gabe tossed some bills onto the bar and grabbed his black hat off the stool. "Shane, I'll talk to you later. Daniel, hope to see you at the bachelor/bachelorette party."

"Wouldn't miss it," he answered. "Oh, Gabe, if you see my sister soon, tell her to stop dodging my calls and texts. I have a feeling you're with her more than anyone lately."

Gabe didn't miss the narrowed gaze or the knowing tone. He smiled and couldn't resist replying, "I'll tell her tonight."

"I don't need to tell you to be careful with my sister."

Blowing out a sigh, Gabe tapped his hat against the side of his leg. "You don't need to tell me. I'm well aware of how raw her emotions are right now, but you also need to understand she's stronger than people give her credit for."

Turning away, Gabe whistled and headed for the exit. As he plopped his hat on his head, he heard Shane say something to Daniel, but couldn't quite make it out. Gabe didn't care. He wasn't trying to be purposefully rude, but he also wasn't going to have anyone, especially Chelsea's brother, try to wedge his way into whatever it was they had going on.

Daniel had every right to worry about Chelsea because of the photos and the scandal. But Gabe also wanted the man to be aware that Chelsea was a strong woman and getting stronger every day.

The chatter about the scandalous photos had died down. Now, the town had shifted its focus to the breaking news about Dusty and figuring out what had motivated him to lash out at so many.

The questions swirled around the small town and were discussed everywhere from beauty salons to bar stools. Nobody really knew why Dusty Walsh had opted to make such poor life choices that had affected so many. Perhaps he was upset because he hadn't been admitted into the TCC, or maybe he was jealous of so many new members. Maybe he was just a bitter, terminally ill man who wanted others to be miserable, as well. Nobody truly knew what had motivated him to be so evil and conniving.

Even Gabe didn't have a clue. But now that Dusty was gone, the healing had begun and the town of Royal was getting back to normal. There was no greater way to celebrate than with Shane and Brandee's Christmas wedding.

Gabe headed toward his loft downtown, but before his turnoff, he decided to take a slight detour. He had a message to deliver, after all.

Nine

Chelsea glanced over her spreadsheet again. Hope filled her as she realized that this spring her dream would become a reality. She'd wanted to do something to give back and help struggling teens for so long, but had never really known how or what to do.

Smiling, she closed out her computer program. She couldn't wait to get her counseling center for teens suffering from depression and suicidal tendencies up and running. And once the idea started to become more of a reality, she'd discuss partnering with Brandee and her camp for teens. Between the two of them, they could really do some good for a whole new generation. Nobody should ever have to feel isolated or hopeless the way she'd felt.

Chelsea had known that crippling fear and loneliness all too well. She'd experienced it twice in her life. The first time, after her father passed, Chelsea had had Daniel. But a brother wasn't the same as a father and he'd been dealing with his own grief.

She'd experienced it again just months ago when so many in this town had seen photos of her in various states of nakedness in the TCC locker room.

When the compromising photos emerged, she'd gotten angry. She'd felt like she'd been stranded on a deserted island, that no one understood her.

Then she'd realized that there were people out there who had been hurt like her and that's when she'd circled back to the idea of giving back and helping others. So, in a warped sort of way, the Maverick scandal had helped her come to the conclusion that it was time to step forward and reach out to others.

Chelsea wanted to open a place that would help young people realize that they weren't alone, that there was always hope. She'd already started vetting counselors and had just purchased an old office building outside of town. Soon she would start renovations and then the true work would begin. Souls and lives would be changed.

This was her baby, something she was keeping close to her chest until she was ready to reveal everything. She wanted all the plans in place before she made a big announcement. Besides, she hadn't wanted to detract attention from the wedding of the year.

The name of her new organization still eluded her. She'd racked her brain and still nothing came to mind. It needed to be meaningful, simple, something that would call out and make troubled people feel safe, comfortable. Everything hinged on the name: the reputation, the feel of the business, the marketing. There was so much to think about other than just helping those in need.

Chelsea came to her feet and stretched. She'd yet to

change from her running gear after her evening jog. Several more ideas for the counseling center had come to her while she'd been out pounding the pavement and she'd rushed home to enter them in the computer. Now, it was time for a shower and to get ready for bed.

Chelsea loved her lacey bras and panties to be delicate and sexy and utterly feminine, and much of her sleepwear was the same. But tonight she just wanted her old cut-off shorts and her well-worn tank.

If she put on anything silky or lacy, she'd instantly think of Gabe and she needed to not go there.

She'd snuck out of his bed at promptly eighteen minutes after one the other morning, and hadn't spoken to him since. He was long overdue to come charging back into her life. Someone like Gabe probably didn't like the fact that she'd walked away without a word. She'd say that sex was his area of expertise and she couldn't help but wonder if anyone had ever left him like that before.

Chelsea was surprised he hadn't stopped by unannounced with some lame wedding question since then. But knowing Gabe, it was only a matter of time.

She quickly showered and pulled her hair back into a messy bun at the nape of her neck. This in-between length was driving her crazy. She either needed to cut it short or to let it grow. But right now she had so many other pressing matters, she couldn't even make the time for an appointment.

With work at Hunt & Co., the wedding planning, her secret project, which wouldn't be a secret much longer, and Gabriel Walsh consuming her mind every waking minute, was it any wonder she was exhausted?

It was Friday night and she was home alone. That right there should have told her something about her nonexistent social life. She was literally all work and no play.

Well, she'd played, but she didn't figure playing with Gabe counted. He was more like work, when it came to how impossible he was. At least with Hunt & Co. and the upcoming counseling center she was in control, whereas with Gabe, she never had a clue what would happen next. They both wanted to take charge, which meant that control volleyed back and forth between them.

As she finished putting on her nightclothes, the chime of her doorbell echoed through her house. Chelsea stilled then smiled. Well, it had taken him longer to come to her than she'd first thought. Though the fact he was standing outside her door right now had her stomach doing all sorts of girl-crush flips, which was absurd considering they weren't a couple or dating or anything.

Padding barefoot toward the front door, Chelsea instantly made out his silhouette through the etched glass of the door. Some might have said Gabe was predictable, but he was far from it. More like determined. He knew what he wanted and apparently wasn't stopping until he had it. She knew he wanted her, but that was just physical. Besides, he'd gotten what he wanted, so shouldn't he be done?

Chelsea flicked the lock on her door and pulled it open. Without waiting for an invite, Gabe removed his hat and stepped in, placing a kiss on her forehead as if to smooth over his abruptness.

"Won't you come in?" she muttered with a wave of her hand.

He didn't stop in the foyer. No, he went on into the living room as if he had every right to barge into her personal space.

Chelsea closed the door and followed, not at all surprised that he thought he could just take charge like he owned the place. He took a seat on her sofa, casual as you please, but she remained in the wide doorway. Practicing restraint around Gabe Walsh was difficult on a good day. This being the first time seeing him since they'd slept together, she figured she deserved some type of award for her control.

"Are you staying long?" she asked as she crossed her arms and leaned against the doorjamb.

"Not long," he replied. "I ran into your brother at TCC. He said you're not answering his texts."

Chelsea snorted. "So you're his messenger boy now? Since when did you two become so chatty?"

Gabe stretched his arm along the back of the couch and shifted his focus to her. "He offered to buy me a drink and asked about the Maverick case."

Chelsea wasn't quite sure how she felt about her brother and the man she'd just slept with discussing her without her present. She could only imagine the two alphas going head to head, both trying to protect her.

She licked her lips and kept her focus on Gabe. She didn't want him to know just how much he affected her simply by being in her space, large and masculine, taking up a good portion of her couch. She hadn't had a man in here in so long, and definitely not a man as sexy as Gabe.

"So why did you stop by?" she asked, hoping her voice didn't come across as breathy as it sounded to her. "You could've texted or called."

"Maybe I wanted to see you." That Southern voice warmed her just the same as if he'd touched her.

His words were often just as potent as his touch. She shivered at the passion, the desire shining back at her from his gray eyes.

"You should probably go," she whispered. If he stayed, they'd tumble into bed—and then what? She didn't think Gabe was looking for more, and she certainly wasn't, either. But the more time they spent together, the more she trusted him and wanted to explore. Surely that would be a mistake. Right?

Gabe didn't move. He barely blinked. Yet somehow from across the room he captured her attention.

"You don't really want me to go," he stated. "Besides, I want to know why you snuck out of my bed without a goodbye."

Clearly, this was going to take some time and he wasn't going anywhere without answers. Pulling in a deep breath, Chelsea went to the front window where she'd created a perfect window seat with plush, colorful pillows. She got comfortable and leaned back.

"I didn't want to wake you and I told you I wasn't staying."

"You didn't want a confrontation," he corrected. "What are you afraid of, Chels? I won't hurt you, I won't exploit you and everything we do is private. I'm aware of your sensitivity and I'd never make you uncomfortable. Unless you're afraid that you might want more than one night?"

That was exactly what scared her. There was no *might* about it. She did want more, but wanting more would lead to emotions and that was one area she couldn't afford to go to with someone like Gabriel Walsh.

"I can hear your mind working from over here," he stated. "Don't make this any more complicated than it needs to be."

"Says the man who doesn't have a past that haunts him."

Something dark came over his face in an instant. "You have no idea what's in my past, so don't assume."

"I'm sorry." Chelsea clutched the floral pillow tighter to her chest. "I never thought—"

"I had a life before I came to Royal, Chels. I had a demanding job and was too naïve. I thought I could have it all, but it was just another lie I told myself."

Chelsea waited for him to go on, listening as his voice took on a lonely, sad tone. He glanced around her living room then came to his feet. Raking a hand through his hair, he pulled in a deep breath. She didn't want him to feel like he owed her anything. He paced like a caged animal and she got the feeling he actually wanted to let her in on this portion of his life.

"I don't know how much you know about my time in Dallas, but I was an agent for the FBI."

"I was aware of that," she told him. "Listen, you don't have to tell me anything—"

"I do." He tipped his head to the side, raking his hand over his scruffy jawline. "I consider you a friend, even though I'm not sure how much you trust me at this point. You need to know the reasons for my actions, for why I'm so adamant about putting strict limits on relationships."

Again she remained silent and waited on him to continue.

He paced through the room in a random pattern before coming to stand by the fireplace. Resting his elbow on the mantel, he examined the photos she had on display.

There were older ones of her and Daniel and their parents, a couple of her and Brandee, and one Chelsea had taken of the most amazing sunset from the time she went on vacation in the Bahamas. She liked to keep the happy memories on display to showcase just how blessed she was in her life and how far she'd come since her darker days.

"I found myself attracted to a woman," he finally went on. "That attraction grew into something more, something I'd never experienced before. But there was a case—I can't get into specifics—and my loyalties were torn."

A sliver of jealousy spiraled through Chelsea at the thought of another woman getting so close to Gabe. But why? It wasn't like she was in love with him or anything. The night they'd shared meant nothing. Right?

Actually, no. That night meant something, more than it should have, and that was precisely the reason she'd had to scurry out and save herself the walk of shame the next morning. She'd left in the dark of night, praying he didn't wake and question her. All he'd had to do was roll over and ask her to stay and she had a feeling she would've done just that.

Gabe was getting to her. Beneath that mysterious aura, the tattoos, the smoldering eyes, he was a man she couldn't ignore. She hadn't trusted him at first, had been convinced he'd had something to do with the leaked photos. She knew better now. Gabe had just been the obvious target for her rage. She'd needed someone to take her anger, her humiliation, out on. Considering they'd been working together and he was a Walsh, he'd been too convenient.

"My partner was killed over a woman who interfered with our investigation. I let it happen because, where she was concerned, I was naïve. And the result was fatal. I'd let my feelings for her cloud my judgment and she'd been playing me the entire time. She was working for the guys we were trying to take down."

Gabe's stunning declaration jerked her back to the moment. "Oh, Gabe. How awful."

He turned from her mantel and crossed to her, taking a seat at the other end of the long cushion. Even though he was only a few feet away, the manner in which he stared off into the distance indicated he was back in the past and not here with her at all. Whatever scene played through his mind gave his face a pinched, tormented expression, as if the pain was still fresh.

"I vowed never to get tangled up with a woman again," he said, glancing down at his hands resting on his knees. "I can control work. I can control how good I am at my job. But not when I get blindsided by someone I'm supposed to trust."

The final brick in the wall of her defenses crumbled. This man hadn't betrayed her with those photos. He was a man of worth and integrity and loyalty. Someone who had experienced such a tragic loss at the hands of someone he'd trusted couldn't have done such horrific things to her—or anyone else in this town, for that matter. Gabe was definitely a man to be trusted. He had a big heart and was loyal to a fault.

Gabe sought justice. He was a man who valued his career and making sure the truth was revealed. No doubt this whole scenario involving Maverick disturbed him on a level she hadn't even thought of.

"Is that really why you came here?" she asked. "Did you need me to know about that time so I'd see a different side of you?"

Gabe stared at her for a minute before shaking his head and glancing away. "No. Maybe. Hell, I don't know. You deserve to know the real me."

"The guy not many people see," she muttered mostly to herself.

"I'm the same guy everyone sees," he whispered, still not looking her way. "Maybe I just want you to view me differently."

Why did he have to be so noble? It had almost been easier when she'd believed him to be the accomplice of her betrayer. Then she could keep him at a distance, protecting her heart in the process. But now that wasn't an option. Not anymore.

Chelsea came to her feet. She took a couple steps and sank to her knees in front of him. Taking his hands in hers, she stared into those unique gray eyes that never failed to captivate her. Now, though, she had a glimpse into his soul and all the insecurities he kept so well hidden. Maybe they were alike in more ways than she'd ever considered.

"I do see you differently."

His eyes widened, with surprise, with arousal. The muscle in his jaw clenched, as did his grip on her hands.

"You changed your mind about me over what I just told you?" he asked. "That fast?"

Chelsea offered a smile. "Let's say my defenses have been crumbling before now."

Gabe leaned forward, briefly touching his lips to hers. When she started to ease back, he released her hands and framed her face, taking the kiss even deeper.

In an instant, he had them both on their feet and had swept her up into his arms. Looping her arms around his neck, she threaded her fingers through his hair and opened to him. Feeling him touch her, knowing exactly what was to come, had anticipation pulsing through her.

"I'm staying the night," he muttered against her lips.

She didn't reply, because he hadn't asked. Gabe was finally going to claim her and nothing was going to stand in their way.

Ten

Sunlight slashed through the windows, waking Gabe. He stirred, but stilled when he realized he was alone... and not in his bed.

He sat up, rubbing his hands over his face. Coarse hairs bristled against his palms. He was in desperate need of a razor, though Chelsea hadn't complained a bit last night when he'd raked his scruff along her bare skin. In fact, the way he recalled, she'd moaned and jerked her hips against him as if silently begging for more.

Gabe glanced toward the empty side of the bed, at the indention in the crisp, white pillowcase. The sweet jasmine scent still permeated the air as if she were still there. That was twice now she'd left him to wake up alone. He'd always thought himself to be a light sleeper, but apparently not with this woman.

And now that he sat there surrounded by everything that was Chelsea, he realized he didn't like being alone.

For now, he wanted to be with her—whatever the hell that meant. He'd gotten a taste of her and needed more, and that scared the hell out of him.

Part of him was glad he'd told her about his past. At least now she saw him in a different light; he wasn't the monster she'd taken him for. On the other hand, he hated being exposed and vulnerable. He'd hated opening that wound from his past and letting her see into his soul.

He'd kept the details vague. Even if he had been at liberty to discuss a federal case, he wouldn't have. The emotion over being betrayed by a woman he'd cared for, the pain of losing his partner and friend, was still too raw. So much had changed in his life in that instant when he'd realized he'd been played and he'd put the life of a man who trusted him on the line.

Gabe had been on the brink of a major breakdown when he'd come to the realization he needed to move on and leave Dallas for good. He'd forced himself to put the nightmare of that botched assignment behind him. The move hadn't been easy, but for the sake of his sanity, he'd had to remove himself from the life that was sucking away his soul. Coming to Royal and taking over his family's security company had only made sense.

Of course after coming here he'd had to face the entire Maverick scandal. Out of the frying pan and into the proverbial fire was not his idea of a good time, but he wasn't leaving. He was seeing this through and standing his ground because he had nothing to be ashamed of. He'd done nothing wrong.

Stifling a yawn, Gabe looked around for a clock but didn't see one. From the way the sun was shining through the curtains, he guessed it wasn't too early. He should be making calls, checking emails, making sure he wasn't on the brink of losing any clients. Because not only did he want to hold on to the ones he had, he also wanted to expand and possibly go global. Nothing screamed confidence like expansion, so now was the time for him to go all-in, proving to his clients that he was the most reputable name in the business.

Besides, he truly didn't want to have to start over again. Granted, he could retire and never work another day in his life, but he would go positively insane if he had nothing to do other than travel and live the high life. He'd made wise investments over the years, he'd cashed in at the right times and reinvested. He may have been a kickass agent, but he'd also been a brilliant businessman.

While Gabe did enjoy getting away to one of his homes either in Miami or in the mountains in Montana, he had to work. After what had happened in Dallas and the Maverick situation here in Royal, the pursuit of justice would remain his lifelong calling.

Tossing the covers aside, Gabe searched the floor for his boxer briefs and jeans and put them on. Shirtless, he padded down the hallway and heard the clanging of a pan in the kitchen. Well, at least she hadn't completely left him.

Gabe stood in the doorway and watched as Chelsea mumbled to herself and scrolled through her phone. She muttered something about casserole and eggs then scrolled again. A grin tugged at the corners of his mouth. She had quite the creative way to curse about breakfast foods.

Her hair was messy on one side and flat on the other, she still had a sheet mark on the side of her cheek, and her oversize T-shirt had slipped down to reveal one slender shoulder. Arousal pumped through him and it wasn't breakfast he was hungry for anymore.

"I've never had a woman make me breakfast."

Chelsea started, flattening her hands on the island in front of her and glancing up at him. "You scared me to death."

"Were you expecting another man to greet you this morning?"

"I never remember which one I've left in my bed."

Gabe growled as he closed the gap between them and wrapped his arms around her waist. "There's no other man in your bed but me for now."

With a quirk of a perfectly arched brow, Chelsea patted his cheek. "Then I guess you're the one I'm making breakfast for."

"You don't have to make me breakfast." He nipped at her ear. "I'll make breakfast while you sit here and keep me company."

Without asking, he circled her waist with his hands and lifted her to sit on the counter. She squealed and laughed, smacking him on the shoulder.

She paused and then her fingertips started tracing the pattern of his tattoos from his biceps up over his shoulder and down onto his chest. Just that light touch had him ready to throw her over his shoulder and take her right back to those rumpled sheets he'd just left.

"I never thought tattoos were attractive before," she murmured almost to herself. "Now, I'm not sure I'll ever want a man without them."

The egotistical side of Gabe was thrilled he was ruining her for other men, but the other side, the one he didn't want to think too much about, couldn't stand the idea of her with someone else. For now, she was his and he damn well planned to take advantage of the situation.

Gabe kissed her chin then worked his way down the column of her throat. "Sit here while I cook."

Her body arched against his touch. "I'm not sitting here."

Gabe's hands covered the tops of her bare thighs, giving a gentle squeeze as he lifted his gaze to meet hers. "You are," he commanded. "Right here, wearing my shirt, while I make our food. You're going to need your strength."

Her eyes widened with shock, arousal. "Don't you have work to do today?"

He did. He'd gotten an email late last night about a client that was threatening to pull out and go elsewhere because they'd heard of the scandal surrounding the Walsh name. Gabe had already put his best man on the job and planned to follow up himself later today. That client wasn't going anywhere and neither was Chelsea.

"Right now I have a sexy woman wearing my clothes and I plan on stripping her and showing her how very thankful I am that she believes in me." He covered her lips with his for a quick kiss, a kiss that promised more. "But first, we're eating."

"I won't argue with you about that." She raked her hand through the top of his hair. "My cooking skills aren't what they should be."

Gabe jerked back. "The heiress of a steak empire can't cook?"

She lifted one slender shoulder, causing his shirt to slide down farther, exposing creamy skin he couldn't resist touching. Gabe curled his fingers around her shoulder and stroked his thumb over her collarbone.

"I mean, I can cook steak," she amended. "But most other things terrify me. Mixing ingredients, that's the hard part. Steak is simple."

"Your restaurants have the best steaks, so don't say

it's easy," he retorted. "Nobody even compares to what you guys do to a hunk of beef."

Her smiled widened. "That's the nicest thing you've ever said to me."

"I call you sexy and gorgeous, but I compliment your family's meat and you get all soft."

Chelsea tipped her head to the side. "I'm a simple girl."

Gabe laughed and shook his head as he turned away to look in her fridge. Chelsea Hunt was not simple, not by any stretch. She was as complex as his jumbled feelings for her.

There was no room for feelings, not unless they stayed superficial. Chelsea was fun, she was sexy and she wasn't looking for anything long-term, either. In short, they were perfect together, at least for now.

"So how long is this going to last?"

Her question threw him off, but he remembered Chelsea was nothing if not logical. He thought about his response as he cracked the eggs over the edge of a bowl and then whisked them to a nice froth.

"Done with me already?" he asked, purposely dodging the question.

"I'll at least let you feed me before I kick you out. But I may keep this comfy shirt."

Gabe threw her a glance and a wink. "You're all heart."

And he didn't even want the shirt back because it looked a hell of a lot better on her than him.

"I don't think our hearts are getting involved here."

Good answer. Because their hearts *couldn't* get involved here.

"I'd say last night was...fun," she continued.

"Fun?" he repeated, whisking the hell out of the eggs.

"It was spectacular and you know it. And your scream-ing and the scratches on my back prove you had more than fun."

"Fine," she amended. "It was fabulous and I wouldn't mind doing it again. So long as we're still on the same page about this not getting too serious."

Her words grated on his last nerve and annoyed the hell out of him. Gabe wanted to do the whole this-isn't-a-serious-relationship talk and she'd totally beat him to it. At least they were on the same page, though. Wasn't that what mattered? Shouldn't he be thanking every last star that she wasn't clingy and wanting more?

"There's no reason we can't go on seeing each other in this capacity," she added.

"Capacity? You mean having sex?"

"Yes. Just until the wedding."

His hand stilled on the whisk and the bowl as he turned to face her. "You're putting a deadline on sex?"

With a simple shrug, she met his gaze. "I think that's best considering neither of us want more. Besides, once the wedding passes, we won't have a reason to see each other. Right?"

Gabe swallowed, not liking the way his heart kicked up. But he wasn't allowing his heart to be involved. He'd just scolded himself about that very rule.

"Right," he agreed, turning back to breakfast. "We'll enjoy each other's company, keep this private and, after the wedding, go our separate ways."

"Perfect."

Gabe worked on getting some filets going and then the eggs. "Steak and eggs are a great source of protein and good for energy. Which you will need. If we've only got two weeks left, then I'm taking full advantage."

He turned and wiggled his brows at her. Chelsea took

her time uncrossing and recrossing her legs, giving him a glimpse of exactly the goal he had for the morning.

"If you keep that up, these steaks will go to waste."

She groaned and leaned back on her hands on the counter, arching her back. Even though his shirt was large on her, her breasts strained against the fabric and the hem inched up even higher on her bare thighs.

Keeping his gaze locked on hers, Gabe reached behind him and flicked off the burners. In two short steps he was on her, gripping her hips and pulling her toward the edge of the counter.

"What about breakfast?" she asked, quirking one brow and offering him that sultry smile that went straight to his gut.

"Oh, I'm still having breakfast."

And with that, he jerked the shirt up and over her head before taking exactly what she'd taunted him with.

"What about this one?" Brandee held up a lacy number with a matching thong. "Red or black?"

"Both," Chelsea replied, searching for her size in a short, sheer gown she knew would have Gabe's eyes rolling back in his head. She so enjoyed being the one who made him lose control.

"You didn't even look," Brandee complained.

Chelsea glanced up. "Again, both. It's lingerie. Men can never get enough and they rip it off you, anyway, so color doesn't matter."

"True. But what's Gabe's favorite color?"

Brandee's teasing tone and mocking grin had Chelsea biting the inside of her cheek. "You think you're so smart."

"Oh, I'm brilliant," Brandee stated, full-on smiling now. Her diamond ring glistened as she waved a hand toward Chelsea. "You two have spent quite a bit of time together and the kind of bickering and heated looks I've witnessed between you always leads to the bedroom."

And the kitchen. Mercy sakes, Chelsea would never look at her center kitchen island the same again. The things that man had done to her right there on her marble countertop should be illegal.

Chelsea hadn't intended to shop for lingerie, but since she was here with her friend, why not? Just because she and Gabe were only physical didn't mean she couldn't put a little flair into their time together.

"I actually haven't seen Gabe in two days," she returned defensively.

Granted, she'd only missed seeing him because he had some important business to attend to in Dallas with a new client and she had her own workload to take care of. She actually did have to work, as much as she'd rather spend her time between the sheets—or on the island— with her new lover.

Even though he was gone, Gabe had most definitely left her with a glorious goodbye and the promise of an even better return.

Actually, he'd advised her to rest up because he fully planned on making up for those two days, especially since their time together was limited anyway.

Which was why she was all too eager to find something in this little lingerie boutique that would drive him out of his mind. Her body heated up just thinking of all the things they'd get into when he returned.

But if they didn't slow down somewhat, Chelsea knew full well she'd fall head-over-boots and be a lost cause. Her heart had already taken a tumble after his soulful admission about his past and if things between them dragged on, the end would only be more difficult. At least this way she could prepare herself for the end…and enjoy the ride all the way to their final day.

"I thought you only came with me to help me choose honeymoon wear and get some Christmas shopping done."

Chelsea ignored her best friend's questioning stare and returned to searching for her size. "I am Christmas shopping—my purchases just happen to be for selfish reasons."

Well, maybe they weren't totally selfish because Gabe would absolutely love unwrapping her. Oh, maybe she should just get a silky piece of fabric and tie herself up in a big bow. Just the thought of him jerking the knot and having the fabric wisp across her body as it floated down to puddle at her feet…

"This must be serious if you're dodging my questions."

Chelsea's hand stilled on the satin hanger. "Honestly, I don't know what's going on between us. We're keeping things private, but I do know that my feelings are stronger than I want to admit."

"Yet you just did."

Brandee came and stood on the other side of the rack, offering a sympathetic smile. "I know how you feel. I was there with Shane, remember? I went through a scandal of my own with Maverick and Shane pulled me through. We finally found our happily-ever-after."

Chelsea recalled all too well the emotional ride her friends had gone through before finally finding their destiny. Chelsea wasn't looking for a ring on her finger or the promise of a lifetime, but she couldn't stop the desire for Gabe that had settled deep in her soul. And this wasn't sexual desire, though there was an abundance of that. No, this was the desire to know more, to learn more, to have more with Gabe.

So where did that leave her? She still wasn't convinced she was looking long-term, but she wanted more than a romp while they were planning the wedding.

Damn it. She never should've put an expiration date on their interlude, but she sure as hell hadn't wanted to be on the receiving end of his conditions, either. This way, she'd set the terms and held all the power. At least she was well aware of how and when things would end. That was the only way she could cope because heartache was not something she wanted to experience again.

Chelsea knew she'd knocked Gabe off his game when she'd brought up an end date. But he'd gone along with her plan like he thought it was brilliant. It just proved he wasn't looking for anything more than a few nights together.

"The sex is amazing, but I'm to the point I want a real date."

Brandee's mouth dropped. "You've already had sex and you're just now telling me?"

Chelsea hated keeping secrets from her best friend, but everything had happened so fast. And then things had kept happening, so Chelsea had been a bit busy. Plus, they were supposed to be keeping it a secret. *Oops.*

"He'd been pursuing me for a while," Chelsea admitted.

Giving up on finding her size, she crossed the store and went to the back where a wall of drawers held other sultry treasures. Brandee, of course, followed. They were the only ones shopping and the clerks were always great in giving customers privacy and only assisting if asked.

"First he drove me out of my mind in the dressing room when my dress was stuck."

"Wait, what?"

"Then there was horseback riding." Chelsea went

on, ignoring her friend's shocked look because she just wanted to get all this out there. "Then he had to go and give you that extravagant wedding present and I totally melted at his selflessness."

"Back up for a second." Brandee held her hands up. "We'll get to all the details of the dressing room and the riding in a minute. I thought you were skeptical of him, that you believed he was in cahoots with his uncle."

"I did. But the more time I've spent with him, I've seen a side I never thought existed."

"Gabe wouldn't purposely hurt anyone, especially in such a callous way."

Chelsea nodded. "I know that now. I see the man he is."

"Oh, Chels. Are you in love with him?"

"What? No." She wasn't. She *wasn't*. "It's complicated."

"That's the exact way love is described."

Love. What a preposterous word for a relationship that wasn't even a *real* relationship.

Chelsea's father had thought himself in love, but in the end, that myth had shattered him. Chelsea wasn't going to follow the same path.

"Trust me. This isn't love." Great sex and a healthy dose of desire, absolutely. "And don't say anything to anyone. We really want to keep this private. Once we're done seeing each other, we don't want to answer a bunch of questions from people who thought we were a couple. You can see that would get confusing, not to mention annoying."

She thought no-strings sex was supposed to be uncomplicated. Yet there were suddenly so many rules with Gabe, including this whole term-limit thing and the secrecy.

She'd never actually had no-strings sex before because she'd been in solid relationships with all her partners. Those encounters actually hadn't had rules, so how was this any easier?

Brandee's skeptical gaze held hers, mirroring the exact doubts Chelsea had in her own mind. Brandee pursed her lips and crossed her arms over her chest. Chelsea didn't like the scrutiny, so she tugged open one of the wide drawers and started checking the merchandise inside.

There were peacock-colored bra and panty sets, peach teddies, so many choices all delicately displayed. Each one she could imagine wearing for Gabe, but then, would he wonder what her intentions were…other than the obvious? Would he wonder if she wanted more?

On a groan, Chelsea slid the drawer shut. "What am I going to do?"

Brandee wrapped her arm around Chelsea's shoulder. "We're going to pick out some killer lingerie that will have our men begging. Then we're going to go get some ice cream drenched in hot fudge and whipped cream. After that, who knows what we'll get into. Maybe wine. We definitely need some wine."

Chelsea laughed. "At some point I need to actually Christmas shop. I have nothing for you yet."

Her friend gave her a slight squeeze before letting go. "You're planning my bachelorette party and my wedding. I'd say that's more than present enough."

"Speaking of the party, what are you wearing tomorrow?" Chelsea asked.

Brandee blew out a sigh. "I have no clue. I was thinking a cute dress and my boots, but then I think maybe I should be dressier since I'm the bride. What about you?"

"I bought a white, off-the-shoulder dress and I'm pairing it with my new cowgirl boots. I need some jewelry to go with it."

Brandee's face lit up. "Then let's finish up here. I'll buy your jewelry for your Christmas present and you can buy me a dress for mine."

Chelsea drew her friend into a hug. "You've got a deal."

Now, all that was left before the promised ice cream and wine was to select the killer lingerie. Chelsea had no clue what turned Gabe on in the way of lace or silk so she opted to buy herself a few different options. Maybe after the bachelorette party, he'd get a little surprise.

Eleven

Gabe saw a flash of white turn the corner and he looked around to make sure nobody saw him follow. That damn dress had driven him crazy for the past three hours and he was done letting this temptress seduce him from afar. He wanted his hands on her. Now.

The coed bachelor/bachelorette party was in full swing at the club and everyone was having a great time. Brandee and Shane wanted all their friends to celebrate and have one last bash before the big day. Everyone loved gathering at TCC, especially since women were such a big part of the club now. Having a joint party here just made sense.

They'd gone with classic mason jars with candles for the center of the tables. Rope was used as cording around the edge of the tablecloths. On the food table was a large S and B wrapped in raffia and propped up with small, twinkling lights surrounding them.

Chelsea had seriously outdone herself on working with the in-house decorator. Brandee and Shane had been so thrilled with the results when they'd arrived.

But right now Gabe was twitching to see Chelsea. Alone.

When he'd arrived before the party officially started and seen Chelsea, he'd nearly swallowed his tongue. She was wearing a short, tight dress and those new cowboy boots, leaving a portion of her legs exposed. He wanted to feel those legs wrapped around his waist and he wanted to hike the skirt of her dress up to see what she wore beneath.

The last few days had been hell in terms of all the ass-kissing he'd had to do to appease his clients. One had threatened to pull all of his business, which would have been a significant loss. But Gabe had assured him that no other scandals would tarnish the company. Gabe knew he was riding a fine line and one more issue would be the end of this working relationship.

Gabe didn't intend to let anything happen again. He was in complete control now. But some of the clients handled by his staff weren't yet convinced. Gabe planned to keep a close eye on the situation and to reassure everyone that they were in the safest hands with the Walsh Group.

Now that he'd handled the damage control, Gabe was more than ready to get back to Chelsea.

When Gabe got to the hall she'd disappeared into, there was no sign of her. There were a couple offices and restrooms along the corridor but he had no idea where she'd gone.

A faint sound of sniffling had Gabe going still. He turned his attention toward one of the offices and crossed the hallway. He knocked on the door, but no answer.

That's when he heard colorful cursing from behind the closed door.

Gabe let himself in and found Chelsea. Her back was to him, her shoulders hunched as she pulled in a shaky breath. She pounded her fist on the desk with each curse word as if the inanimate object had offended her.

"Chels?"

She flinched and turned, her hand over her chest. "Sorry, I just needed a minute."

"To cry?"

"I'm not crying."

Maybe not, but she was on the verge of angry tears if that quivering chin was any indicator.

Gabe moved into the room, closing the door at his back and flicking on the light since he'd shut out the glow from the hall. Something at the party had bothered her because just moments ago he'd seen her laughing with guests and playing darts with some other ladies.

"What is it?"

Shaking her head, she attempted a smile. Did she truly think he'd just let her lie to his face and suffer alone? He wanted to know who the hell had hurt her so much that her cheeks were tinged pink and her eyes were practically shooting fire.

"It's nothing. I just needed to get away from the chaos out there for a second." Chelsea slid her palms over his chest and cocked her head. "I've missed you."

Gripping her wrists before she could distract him, he leaned forward. "Don't change the subject. Tell me what happened."

"Just some jerk thinking he can make crude comments about the photos." She slid her hands up around his neck and ran her fingers through his hair. "I didn't want to make a scene so I just walked out."

Rage pumped through him. "Tell me who."

Chelsea shook her head. "He's not ruining this night. That's why I didn't say anything. Daniel would go all big brother on me if he knew and Shane and Brandee would feel guilty for inviting someone here who was so ill-mannered."

To hell with Daniel or what anyone else would do. Gabe wanted his hands around the bastard's throat right this second. Nobody would ever make Chelsea feel inferior or knock her self-esteem down...not as long as he was around. Hell, even after they were through, he'd still consider her a friend and he'd never stand for anyone being cruel to her.

Gabe gritted his teeth and attempted to rein in his anger. He would find the bastard and make sure he understood never to mention Chelsea's name again or even to glance her way. If Shane knew about this, he'd haul the guy out of the party, but Gabe wouldn't let this dark cloud hang over the night and he sure as hell wasn't going to let it hang over Chelsea.

Daniel and Shane didn't need to know anything had happened. Gabe knew and he would damn well take care of things.

Forcing himself to remain calm, he nipped at her lips. "You look so damn sexy," he murmured against her mouth. "Did you wear this to drive me crazy? Because I'm ready to make our excuses and find someplace where we can be alone so I can see what you're wearing under this."

With that bright smile that never failed to pack a punch of lust, Chelsea tickled the nape of his neck with her fingertips. "Maybe I had someone in mind when I put this on."

"Is that right?" he growled.

She nodded and met his gaze beneath her heavy lids. "I may have also had that same person in mind when I made a special purchase yesterday. Maybe something lacy."

His entire body tightened as he plunged his hands into her hair and covered her mouth with his. Damn this party. He wanted her right now. It had been too long—days—since he'd had her and each second that ticked by brought them closer to the end. The need had grown stronger and stronger and, right at this moment, he was hanging on by a thread.

Chelsea pulled away. "We can't do this here."

"We can," he argued, reaching down to haul her hips flush with his. "I can clear off that desk and have you bent over in a second."

Her moan vibrated through her chest. "If we got caught here, Shane and Brandee would kill us. Besides, just think of all this as foreplay."

He'd been in foreplay mode all night. Seeing her hips in motion beneath that flimsy material had been like watching a slow-motion strip tease and he was damn tired of waiting for his prize.

"I want to know what's under this dress."

She gripped his jaw, wiping her thumb over his bottom lip. "I assure you, it will be worth the wait once we get back to my place."

"My place is closer. We'll go there."

Before Chelsea, he'd never taken a woman back to his place, but he'd never had a need like this. Chelsea was different in every respect. She'd already been to his loft and, he had to admit, having her there hadn't freaked him out. He'd actually enjoyed it.

He'd also exposed a part of himself, of his past, that he never would've divulged had Chelsea not gotten to him deeper on some level. Those were thoughts he wasn't ready to dive into right now.

The second this party was over, he wanted that dress off and he suddenly had the all-consuming desire to see her spread across his sheets. Any meaningful thoughts or questioning why he'd opened up to her had no place here.

"So impatient," she mocked. Dropping a quick kiss on his lips, she pulled away from his arms and adjusted her dress. "We better get back out there or people will wonder where we went."

Nobody knew about their current situation and Gabe wanted to keep things that way. Whatever was going on between Chelsea and him didn't concern anyone else. She was his and he wasn't too keen on sharing. And he was determined to track down the jerk who'd upset her. The party was large, but Gabe knew most everyone in attendance. It wouldn't be too difficult to figure it out.

"You go," he told her. "I'll be out in a minute."

She slipped out the door and Gabe needed more than a minute to gather his thoughts. Between the desire pumping through him and the fury over some guy who didn't have any manners, Gabe needed to rein it in before he went out there in a fit of rage.

Gabe let a good five-minute gap pass before he headed back out. The party was still in full swing. The drinks were flowing, laughter and conversation filled the open area, and couples were dancing to a slow country song by the hired band.

Standing back, Gabe surveyed the room, trying to pinpoint guests he didn't know. There was no way a friend of theirs would make snide remarks to Chelsea, so this guy had to be someone outside of their inner circle. Maybe a business associate of Shane's or Brandee's.

Within minutes Gabe had narrowed the options to

three guys. Gabe shoved his hands in his jeans and watched each of them for a few minutes. He needed to have absolutely no doubt which one he needed to rip apart.

Chelsea and Brandee were throwing darts in the corner. Erin stood near them, sipping on a glass of water and chatting with her friends. Shane and Daniel were at the other dartboard. Gabe figured he should mingle so he didn't look like he wanted to commit murder, but if any of those three guys said something to Chelsea again, Gabe wouldn't be responsible for his actions.

"Looks like you owe me a bourbon," Daniel stated, slapping Shane on the back as Gabe joined them near the dartboards.

"Considering it's an open bar, I'm paying for it anyway," Shane replied.

"Actually, Chelsea and I paid for it," Gabe interjected. "But feel free to drink all you want. We also have drivers to make sure everyone gets home safely."

"You guys really thought of everything," Shane said. "Thanks, man."

Gabe didn't want the accolades. Shane was his best buddy and there wasn't anything he wouldn't do for him. Besides, working with Chelsea was worth all the money and time he'd spent. She trusted him now. She believed in him. And he couldn't wait to get back to his place and make good on his promise to rip that dress off her body.

"I'll go get drinks," Shane offered. "What do you guys want?"

Daniel and Gabe gave their orders and Shane headed toward the bar. Risking a glance at the women, Gabe smiled when Chelsea threw the last dart in her hand and it hit the bull's-eye. She threw her arms in the air and spun toward her friends with a huge smile on her face. That punch of lust to his gut always caught him off guard—though it was something he really should have been used to by now.

"I'll go get us some drinks," she told them.

Gabe forced himself to look away, but when he turned back, Daniel was eyeing him.

"Something you want to tell me?" Chelsea's brother asked.

"No."

"You dodged that question before, Walsh."

Gabe shrugged. He'd continue dodging it until Chelsea wanted her brother in on what was going on…if she ever did.

Even if he and Chelsea hadn't agreed to keep things private, he wouldn't be chatting with her brother about this. Chelsea was Gabe's business. Simple as that.

"This is none of your concern."

Daniel lifted his brows. "Is that right? Because you were looking at my sister like… I can't even finish that without getting graphic. What the hell is going on with you guys?"

Gabe crossed to the board and plucked out the darts. "We're planning a wedding. You want to know anything else, you'd have to ask her."

"I'm asking you."

Gabe handed Daniel the red-tipped darts. "Winner gets the final say-so in this argument."

Taking the darts from Gabe, Daniel nodded. "I'll want the truth when I win."

Like Gabe would ever lose.

The crash of breaking glass had Gabe and Daniel spinning around. Chelsea stood in the midst of the mess, and some guy Gabe didn't know was clutching her elbow.

Oh, hell no. Gabe was across the room before he could

even think twice. Rage bubbled within him and all he saw was Chelsea's shocked face, her mouth open, her eyes wide. And fear. He saw fear and he damn well didn't like it one bit because his Chelsea never cowered from anything. She was a fighter.

"C'mon, baby. Everyone has already seen everything you have. Why don't you give me a private show?"

The guy slurred his words as the reek of alcohol wafted off him. Before Gabe could make a move, Chelsea rammed her elbow into the man's stomach, causing him to grunt and double over.

"You don't have to be a b—"

Gabe reached down, grabbing the guy by the throat and pulling up so he could look him in the eye. He wanted this jerk to know exactly who was threatening him.

"Get the hell out of here and don't come back. If I see you near Chelsea—if I even think you've spoken her name—you will find out just how difficult your life can be. Are we clear?"

Daniel came up beside Chelsea, wrapping an arm around her. Gabe knew she was fine, but he wanted the trash taken out.

Yanking the guy by the back of the neck, Gabe escorted him to the door and made sure he headed toward the parking lot. No way in hell was he going to allow Chelsea to continue living with this black mark over her. Everything that had happened to her wasn't her fault, but the fault of his uncle.

Gabe wished the old bastard wasn't gone because he'd go kick his ass and knock some sense into him. How did one even get revenge on a dead man? Rage was a difficult emotion to control, but Gabe forced himself to breath in and out and get back to Chelsea without ripping someone's head off.

Chels was a strong woman, but there were only so many times someone could be knocked down, and in public, no less. Damn it all. Even though none of this was his fault, it was his family member who had set this ball in motion, ruining lives.

That was all in the past now and Gabe was hell-bent on making sure the whole nightmare stayed that way. The town was moving on. These people were moving on. Until that jerk made a scene, this party was proof that every one of his friends had found their own happiness despite Dusty's antics.

Gabe stepped back into the main room and made a beeline for Chelsea, who sat on a bar stool beneath a large bundle of mistletoe. It was almost as if he was being given the green light.

Several friends surrounded her: Erin, Brandee, Shane and her brother Daniel. Gabe didn't care how rude he was or what others thought. The whole secrecy thing be damned. He wanted her to know she wasn't alone and he wasn't just consoling her as a pal. No, he planned on consoling her like her lover.

Pushing past Shane, Gabe reached for Chelsea. Her eyes went wide when she spotted him and he wondered exactly what she saw written all over his face. Most likely, she saw every blasted thought racing through his head. Every instinct in him wanted to haul her out of there, but throwing her over his shoulder would only piss her off more.

Gabe said nothing as he framed her face and captured her mouth. He swallowed her shocked gasp and eased her to her feet. Cheers and music surrounded them, but he blocked everything out except Chelsea's sweet taste.

When he feathered the kiss and released her lips, her

lids took an extra moment to open. Desire and surprise stared back at him.

"Well, that was unexpected," she muttered. "Guess we're not keeping this private anymore."

Gabe grabbed her hand. "We're leaving."

"Don't be absurd, Gabe. We—"

He shot her a look that shut her up immediately.

"Go," Brandee stated from behind him. "The party is almost over, anyway."

"And we paid for people to clean up," he reminded her, never taking his eyes from Chelsea.

Her lips thinned as she nodded and gripped his hand.

Gabe turned to find Daniel with his arms crossed, his eyes narrowed.

"That dart game is going to have to wait," Gabe stated as he pushed by.

Daniel's eyes went to his sister. "Chels."

"I'll call you later," she told him.

Later? Maybe tomorrow. Right now they were going to be alone, away from people, phones. The world. Gabe wasn't in a sharing mood.

Something about having another man put his hands on his woman and terrorize her made Gabe even more protective, even more territorial, than ever.

Hadn't he wanted to keep this purely physical? Hadn't he wanted to keep things private?

Well, apparently manhandling the jerk who'd approached her and then kissing Chelsea beneath the mistletoe had blown that plan all to hell. But he'd answer everyone's questions another time.

Chelsea was his for another week and he damn well planned to take every opportunity to show her just how a woman should be treated. She deserved everything and, for now, he was going to be her everything. Once the wedding was over, well, he'd worry about that when the time came.

The valet brought Gabe's truck around and Gabe gave him a hefty tip before helping Chelsea get in. There were so many emotions pumping through him right now, he needed a minute. If she touched him, if she said anything, he was afraid his control would snap. He was that desperate to be with her and to prove that she was not defined by the scandal that continued to plague her. Gabe had never felt the need to prove something to someone and he'd never had this desperation before.

But this wasn't about him. Everything about this moment, about these emotions, was about Chelsea.

Being with this woman was like walking a tightrope. One wrong step and he could plummet into a territory he wasn't ready for. Gabe was already teetering as it was and he had a sinking feeling he wasn't going to be able to hang on much longer.

The second he settled in behind the wheel and put the truck into Drive, Chelsea turned in her seat. "Gabe—"

"Not now," he growled, gripping the wheel tightly.

Once they got to his place, they would talk. Or not. He'd much rather work his tension and stress out another way. He had a sinking feeling if he started opening up about his emotions now, he'd say things he'd vowed never to say to another woman and the last thing he wanted was for Chelsea to get hurt again.

Twelve

Anger rolled off Gabe in waves. She'd never seen him like this, had never thought someone so reserved could dole out such rage. But the man was practically shaking.

He'd been pissed back at the party. The way he'd handled that drunk guy, Chelsea wasn't so sure what would've happened had the room not been full of family and friends. Would Gabe have been so controlled or would he have pounded on the man? She'd been scared, not that Gabe would hurt her in his anger, but of what he'd do to the other guy and how she couldn't prevent it.

If she thought Daniel had been protective growing up, that was nothing compared to Gabe right now. How would Gabe react if he knew her past? Would he look at her differently? Would he see her as weak?

It didn't matter, though. Their time was drawing to a close and no matter how much her heart kept trying to get involved, Chelsea had to hold back at least some part of herself. If she gave him everything...well, she'd suffer even more heartache in the end.

Gabe ushered her into his penthouse loft apartment. She'd briefly been there before and hadn't paid much attention, but now that she was back, she could easily see this was his domain. The industrial yet country vibe surrounded her. The exposed brick walls were masculine, the chrome finishes and high-tech electronics taking up one entire end of the loft screamed money and power. There were closed-circuit TVs showing the outside of the apartment building, the parking garage beneath, the street in both directions.

Being so paranoid must be an occupational hazard for a former FBI agent turned security analyst.

"You sure do have quite a bit of surveillance," she casually commented.

"I own the building."

Chelsea didn't even bother hiding her surprise. "Seriously? How did I not know that?"

Gabe gave a shrug. "It's not something I talk about. I actually own several properties in Royal, but most are held under my company names."

Yet again, the man of mystery had more up his sleeve. He tended to keep her guessing on who the real Gabriel Walsh was. Just when she thought she'd uncovered the final layer, he revealed another.

Chelsea continued to peruse the open living area. There was a black metal outline of the state of Texas hanging on the wall at the other end of the room. The simple wall art was tasteful yet very Gabe. There was a pair of old cowboy boots over in the corner and several hats that hung on pegs near the front door. While the loft was neat and tidy, Gabe's presence was everywhere.

The gleaming kitchen with a long, concrete island

lined by eight bar stools just begged for a party. But she didn't think Gabe was too much of a partier, let alone a host. Still, she saw herself getting steaks ready, him serving up sides and handing out bourbon.

Wait, no. This wasn't some fantasy that would come to life. He'd brought her here for sex. Isn't that what they'd discussed in the office back at the club? But then he'd gone and gotten angry and now she wasn't so sure why she was there because there was still fury pouring from him.

This final week was going to be full of Gabe and the wedding. Gabe in private was going to be vastly different than Gabe as a cohost of the nuptials and a best man. The idea of walking down the aisle with him on her arm gave her heart a little extra beat. She absolutely couldn't get caught up in that image or that fantasy.

Gabe stalked to the living area and stared out the floor-to-ceiling windows. With jerky movements, he unbuttoned the cuffs on his sleeves and rolled them up his forearms. He'd hung his black hat by the others near the door and hadn't spoken a word.

"If you're just going to be angry, I'm not sure why I'm here."

She remained near the entryway, crossing her arms over her chest and waiting for him to respond. But he kept looking out onto the city, his hands shoved into the pockets of his perfectly fitted jeans.

"I'll just call someone to pick me up."

"Stay."

That one word settled between them and Chelsea softened just a bit. What the hell was he so angry about? It wasn't like this was his life that kept getting thrown back in his face. She had a feeling there would be jerks for some time to come who were all too eager to bring up those nude photos, thinking she was easy and willing to give them a private showing. It was humiliating, but right now all she could do was keep her head high and move on.

"You didn't see your face," Gabe said, still keeping his back to her. "When you dropped those glasses and I turned to see what happened... Chels, your face was pure terror. You'd gone white and I saw that guy's hand on you and I wanted to kill him right there."

The hurt in his tone had her moving toward him. She'd been so worried about what type of scene she'd caused and if she'd ruined the party to even think about how all of that had affected Gabe. Obviously he'd been angry with the guy. Someone like Gabe, so powerful and prominent, would see it as a setback, an embarrassment. They were just a fling, anyway, so why should he have to put up with her scandal?

"I completely understand if you want to call this quits between us." She stood only a few feet away now. Even though she wanted to reach out and touch him, she clasped her hands in front of her dress. "I know the scandal surrounding me is embarrassing. I wouldn't want someone else to have to bear the burden of the crass jokes or the mocking."

Gabe whirled around. "You think I'm trying to tell you...what? That I'm leaving you alone to deal with this mess? That I don't want to be associated with you because of it? Do you honestly think I'm that big of a jerk?"

Chelsea swallowed the burn in her throat. Why did love have to be complicated?

Wait. Love?

Well now was not the time for her to realize she'd completely fallen head-over-boots with this man. Not only was she completely unsure about where he stood, she knew he didn't do relationships. Fantastic. There was nothing like this feeling of despair when she was already battered and bruised.

"I don't think you're a jerk," she whispered, ignoring the extra thump of her heart. "I just wouldn't blame you for wanting to bring this to an end now instead of after the wedding."

She wouldn't blame him; she would be devastated. But the end was inevitable. Next week or now, did it really matter? Both ways she'd be alone, which she was used to. But being with Gabe had changed her into someone who didn't want to be alone, not when she knew how amazing he could be.

Damn it. When had she fallen in love? Somewhere between not trusting him and seeing him come to her defense tonight. She'd known for a few days that she was sinking deeper into territory she knew nothing about. She'd fought every step, but she couldn't lie to herself anymore.

Gabe reached out and hooked an arm around her waist. "I'm not ending a day sooner than we planned," he growled. "I'm angry you had to deal with that guy. I'm angry because you should never be afraid of what my family did and there's not a damn thing I can do to go back and change what happened to you."

Wait. Gabe was blaming himself for Dusty's actions?

Chelsea reached up, smoothing his unruly blond hair back from his forehead. Framing his face, she leaned in and briefly touched his lips.

"You aren't to blame," she assured him. "And you can't control what others say."

"Maybe not, but I can try to shield you from the hurt."

Her heart tumbled in her chest, but she knew he didn't want any part of her heart or her love. Which was such a shame, because she would give them both so freely to her knight in shining armor.

"I've never been so angry in my life," he murmured. "When my partner was killed, I was hurt and broken, yes. Angry? Yes. But I was able to stop the killer and bring him to justice. But all of this? I have no idea how to stop it completely and it rips me apart."

Chelsea eased back from his arms. "Well, for now I know something you can control. I believe you said something about wanting to see what I have on beneath my dress."

The darkness in his eyes mixed with arousal. Chelsea reached for the hem and eased it up and over her head. She tossed the dress onto the back of the sofa only a few feet away. When she turned her focus back to Gabe, the arousal in his eyes had turned to hunger and she knew she'd made the right decision in terms of lingerie tonight.

The white, lacy, strapless bustier and matching thong indeed had Gabe speechless. Most women trying to seduce a man would pair the outfit with heels, but she was all about her cowgirl boots.

"You bought this for me?" he asked, slowly making his way toward her.

"You know I did."

Because there was no one else.

Gabe muttered a curse beneath his breath. "I've never wanted someone more than you right now. You're breathtaking and sexy and...damn, Chels. You're killing me."

She couldn't help but smile because she'd finally managed to make him a stuttering mess. Feeling a tad saucy, she propped her hands on her hips and tipped her head.

"Maybe if you're good, I'll show you some other items I purchased."

His eyes snapped to hers. "You bought others?"

"Something in green to match my eyes and then there was this racy black number that I simply couldn't pass up."

With a growl, Gabe was on her. His arms circled her waist, his mouth crashed down onto hers, and he backed her against the window. The cool glass did nothing to calm the heat racing through her.

Gabe nipped at her lips before roaming over her jaw, down her neck, to the swell of her breasts. Her entire body felt as if she was lit up from within. As his hands seemed to touch her everywhere, his mouth was doing wonders driving her mad.

"I want you in my bed," he murmured against her skin. "I've envisioned you there all spread out, reaching for me."

The image in her mind had her arching against him. She'd take him anywhere he wanted.

"But the bed is too far away," he stated. "And my need for you is too great."

She thrust her fingers through his hair and held him as he yanked the top of her bustier down and covered her flesh with his mouth. She cried out, but then he started ridding her of the rest of her clothes and Chelsea could only hang on.

Once she was bare—except for her boots—Gabe took a half step back and raked his heavy-lidded gaze over her.

"Take off your clothes," she demanded.

His grin kicked up, wrinkling the corners of his eyes and making him seem all the more menacing. "You take them off."

In her next breath, she was making frantic work of his buttons and when she was down to the last two, she just jerked the shirt open. Gabe's laugh had his abs clenching, as if he was showing off just how spectacular his build truly was.

Chelsea's hands shook as she removed his pants. He toed off his boots and finally stood before her wearing nothing but desire.

He reached into his pants' pocket, pulled out protection and slipped it on. Chelsea's blood pumped faster, her nerves dancing with anticipation, and when he finally turned those gray eyes back to her, she didn't hesitate to reach for him.

Gabe lifted her off the floor. She toed off her boots and let them clunk to the floor before locking her ankles behind his back.

Gabe closed his mouth over hers at the same time he plunged into her. Then he stood still, right there in the middle of the room. Their bodies were joined, but he didn't move, and the erotic sensation was driving her absolutely out of her mind.

"I have no control with you," he murmured against the side of her neck. "I need you, Chels."

He spun around, sending them tumbling to the sofa. He cradled her face as his weight settled her deeper against the cushions.

Chelsea opened to him as he covered her mouth with his. He trailed one of his hands down her side and held tight to her hip, his fingertips gripping her skin.

This wasn't enough. She wanted more, needed more. Beyond the sex—though it was the best she'd ever had—she needed Gabe for everything.

He muttered something in her ear she didn't understand at the same time he tipped his hips just right to send her over the edge. She tightened around him, arched her back and dug her heels into his backside.

When Gabe's body shuddered against hers, he whispered something else, something she still didn't quite catch. She clung to him, though, taking his release as hers ebbed. He held his weight just off her, but she wanted all of him.

Chelsea circled his shoulders with her arms and pulled him closer as his body ceased trembling. His head rested in the crook of her neck. Darkness had fallen across the apartment. Only the glow of a small desk lamp across the room gave any light. She wanted this moment to carry on; she didn't want words or movement to break the spell of their time together.

Closing her eyes, Chelsea willed time to stop. If she held on tighter maybe he'd stay.

Fortunately, though, she wasn't a clinging woman. She'd never begged for a man and she wasn't going to start now. If there was ever a time or a man, though, Gabe was definitely worthy of her begging.

When he started to move, she trailed her fingertips up through his hair.

"What did you whisper in my ear earlier?"

Gabe froze, cringed actually. "I don't recall."

He was lying. It had been mere moments ago and he'd said it twice.

"Don't move," she murmured. "Let's just lie like this for another minute."

His hand softened on her hip as his hips shifted. "If I stay here too long, I'm going to want you again and the rest of my protection is in the bedroom."

Chelsea smiled up at him. "Then maybe we should make our way there."

Thirteen

The wedding was only four days away now. Chelsea couldn't believe the time had almost come for her best friend to say "I do." She'd be lying if she didn't admit, just to herself, that she was jealous. Chelsea hadn't thought she wanted romance and forever, but getting swept away in this real-life, fairy-tale ending had her wishes shifting.

Suddenly Hunt & Co. wasn't her only focus. If Gabe knew how much real estate he took up in her mind, her *heart*, he'd likely run fast and far. She had to keep this to herself. She knew deep in her soul that there was no future for them, not together, anyway. He'd made it abundantly clear from the start that he couldn't trust his heart that way again.

Trust. Hadn't that been the entire theme of their relationship? No matter if they were enemies, then friends, then lovers, everything surrounding them always circled back to trust.

He'd pursued her and she'd backed away, but now that she was fully on board, he was backing away. The dance they continued to perform was confusing, frustrating, and she wished like hell they were doing the same steps.

Chelsea pulled up her spreadsheet and attempted to get the new system up and running for the accounting department. That was her goal today, not to focus on the fact she'd enjoyed two days at Gabe's loft. The weekend had flown by in a blur of sex and time spent doing nothing but enjoying each other.

Monday was even harsher to handle after such an amazing few days with the man she loved.

She seriously needed to stop using that word. Love wasn't a good idea. Admitting her feelings this close to the end game...damn it. None of this was a game. Every single moment she'd spent with him had been real, had been amazing, and something she wanted forever.

A gentle tap on her door had Chelsea glancing across her office. Before she could mutter a reply, the door eased open and Daniel stepped in. She figured he'd be making his presence known. She'd known he was spending the holidays in Royal as opposed to Dallas, especially with the wedding coming up. Erin wanted to be at Crescent Moon, the Hunt family ranch, for Christmas. Chelsea made a mental note to swing by to see her soon-to-be sister-in-law and take her Christmas present. Well, she'd take the present just as soon as it was delivered, because she'd purchased nearly everything online.

Chelsea offered her brother a smile. Surprisingly he hadn't contacted her since she and Gabe had left the party abruptly the other night. Well, he'd texted her, but she'd been preoccupied.

"Your assistant said you don't have a meeting for another hour." Daniel closed the distance between them and took a seat opposite her desk. He crossed one ankle over his knee and settled in. "Hope this isn't a bad time."

"You wouldn't care if it was," she replied, turning her chair to fully face him. "You're here to question me about Gabe, so let's have it."

Daniel blew out a breath as he removed his cowboy hat and placed it over the arm of the chair. "What are you thinking, Chels? The guy is a loner and you're going to get your heart broken."

She'd expected nothing less from her big brother. "Did you rehearse that or just decide to wing it?"

"I'm winging it, so have pity on me when I'm trying to play the concerned older brother."

"You're not playing anything. You *are* the concerned older brother." Chelsea offered him a smile as she folded her arms across her desktop and carefully thought of what to say next. "Listen, I know you care about me and I get that you don't want me hurt. I'm not a fan of heartache myself, but Gabe and I know what we're doing. We have no preconceived notion that this is long-term."

No notions, but wishes…definitely.

"That's not like you."

She couldn't help but laugh. "And you know about my sex life? Is that really where you want to go?"

Daniel cringed. "Definitely not, but you're going to get hurt."

Most likely, but she couldn't live her life worrying about the future. If things were going to end with Gabe— no, *when* they ended—she at least wanted to enjoy the here and now. And she'd enjoyed the hell out of their weekend together.

"Daniel, I realize over this past year Royal has been overrun with happily-ever-afters and you and Erin want everyone to be as blissful as you guys, but right now I'm not looking for love."

Yet it had found her, anyway. She'd have to worry about that later. She vowed that she'd enjoy Gabe until the very last minute, and then she'd stock her fridge with her favorite ice cream and allow herself the pity party she would no doubt deserve. What a way to ring in the New Year.

"I swear, Gabe and I are fine, and at the end of the day, we're just friends."

Who give each other toe-curling orgasms and spend weekends together.

"Friends, huh?" Daniel asked with a grunt. "The man looked like he wanted to strangle that guy the other night and then he kissed you like he was staking his claim."

"Maybe he was," she replied simply. This was not a conversation she wanted to have with Daniel. And the truth was, he wouldn't want her honest opinion or feelings on the matter. It was best to keep him as far away from this as possible. "Was there something else you wanted to discuss?"

Daniel pursed his lips as if he were contemplating his next move.

Chelsea arched her brow, silently daring him to circle back to the topic she'd just closed.

"Erin and I wanted to have you over for dinner."

"That sounds great. When were you thinking?"

Daniel came to his feet and tapped his fingers on the edge of her desk. "Tonight, actually. We have something we want to discuss with you."

Chelsea stood, as well. "That sounds serious. Is everything okay?"

"We're fine," he assured her with his smile, one that matched their father's. "Does seven work for you?"

"I'll be there."

When he blew out a breath and looked into her eyes, she knew they weren't done with their heart-to-heart.

"You know I love you and just want what's best, right?"

Chelsea circled her desk and wrapped her arms around her great protector. She'd always looked up to him, always admired his opinion, and loved how he continually put her first.

"I feel the same about you," she told him then eased back. "Now, get out of here so I can finish this program for the accounting department or we're going to have a whole host of angry employees when their checks are messed up."

Daniel kissed her on the cheek and left her office, closing the door behind him. That talk had gone better than she'd thought. She wasn't quite sure how he'd react to Gabe's very public display of affection. Hadn't Gabe been the one to want to keep things under wraps? Yet when she was threatened, he hadn't cared one bit. He had to have some feelings for her...didn't he?

Regardless of what Daniel thought, or anyone else for that matter, Chelsea was going to enjoy this time with Gabe. Once the wedding was over and they were done working together, they wouldn't see each other as often. Maybe she'd get lucky and the desire would fizzle out.

The likelihood of that happening was about as great as her getting Gabe to fall in love with her—and that was never going to be a reality. He didn't do love, didn't do long-term, and even though she didn't know the full details of the case involving his partner's death, she had to respect his desires.

That didn't mean she had to like them.

Blowing out a breath, Chelsea went back to her computer. There was no sense in worrying about this now.

She had so much work to get done, surely she could block Gabe and focus.

The second she pulled up the program she'd been working on, her cell vibrated on her desktop. She glanced at the screen only to find a simple message from Gabe: Tonight you're mine.

So much for focusing on work.

Chelsea let herself into the main house at Crescent Moon. She'd grown up here, and returning as an adult always felt like coming home. She loved her house in Pine Valley, but Crescent Moon held such a special place in her heart.

She made her way through the open foyer. Erin's laughter filtered through the first floor and Chelsea could tell her brother and his fiancée were in the back of the house. When she got to the enclosed four-seasons room with three walls of windows overlooking the stables, she smiled. She'd always loved this room. She'd spent hour upon hour reading her favorite books in the corner chaise, which had since been replaced with another in a pretty pale yellow.

Erin slid her legs over the side of the chair and offered a bright smile. "Hey, glad you could make it." Coming to her feet, Erin closed the gap between them and wrapped her arms around Chelsea.

"A dinner that I didn't have to prepare?" Chelsea said, easing back. "I'm always up for that."

Daniel crossed to the minibar in the opposite corner. "Can I get you a drink? Dinner should be ready in about fifteen minutes."

"I'd love a glass of wine. White, please." While Daniel busied himself getting her wine, Chelsea glanced at Erin. "I'm sorry I've been so scarce lately. This wedding planning, plus work, has taken up a good bit of my time."

"And Gabe Walsh?" Erin asked, her brows rising as her smile widened.

Why deny it? The man had kissed her in front of nearly the entire town at that party. Her brother had already speculated about their connection and Brandee knew the truth. There wasn't much of a thread of secrecy to hold on to at this point.

"He has occupied a good portion of my time." Mainly the nights, but there was no need to get into that. "So what did you guys need to see me about?"

Daniel handed her the glass and clutched his own tumbler, most likely filled with bourbon. "We're pregnant."

Chelsea gripped the stem of her glass. "'Scuse me?"

"Way to go, Daniel." Erin shook her head and rested a hand over her stomach. "We are expecting, but I'd hoped to deliver the news in a little more of an exciting manner."

Chelsea sat her glass on the table and pulled Erin into another hug. "I'm so thrilled for you guys! I'm going to be an aunt."

She eased back and glanced down at Erin's flat belly. "How far along? Are you feeling okay? What can I do to help?"

Erin laughed and patted Chelsea's shoulder. "I'm fine. I went to the doctor today and I am six weeks."

Chelsea squealed and turned to her brother. "You guys are going to be such awesome parents. I can't wait to see Baby Hunt."

Daniel wrapped an arm around her. "We were hoping you'd agree to be the godmother. I know not many people do that anymore, but we want you to be a big part of our kids' lives."

"Of course," she answered then froze. "'Kids'?"

Erin beamed. "Twins."

Chelsea jerked her attention back to her brother. "Two babies? I'm going to need something stronger than wine."

Erin laughed and nodded. "I know, it's a shock. Believe me. We were stunned, but we knew we wanted a large family and I guess we're just getting a jump start. I'd been having some pain and they just did an ultrasound to make sure things looked okay. Apparently the pain is my uterus stretching faster than normal."

Two babies? Chelsea couldn't even imagine being a mother to one, let alone two. But Erin and Daniel were beaming and Chelsea couldn't be happier for them.

Tears pricked her eyes. "I don't even know what to say."

"Well, damn. Don't cry." Daniel picked up her wineglass. "I can't handle tears."

"I'm happy," Chelsea insisted. "Really. I'm just overwhelmed and excited and I can't even imagine how you guys feel."

"All of that and more," Erin assured her. "I've gotten used to the ups and downs of my emotions lately, but I know you're still taking it all in. Dinner should be ready. What do you say we go eat and discuss baby registries and nursery décor?"

"Maybe I should eat in the kitchen," Daniel groaned.

Chelsea smacked his chest. "You're eating with us, and we're going to have a nice family dinner. And we need to figure out which room to put the nursery in, and colors, and names. We need names."

Daniel groaned as he turned and headed toward the kitchen where his chef had no doubt prepared something fabulous. "We have a long time still to go," he growled as he walked away. "Why do I have a feeling my credit card is going to take a hard hit?"

Chelsea smiled as she looped her arm through Erin's. "Because it is."

* * *

He'd told her to be at his place at seven, yet it was now nearing eight and there was no sign of Chelsea. No call, no text. Absolutely nothing.

Gabe didn't like to be kept waiting, especially by the woman warming his bed.

The doorman buzzed him, letting him know Chelsea was on her way up. Had something happened that had prevented her from getting in touch to tell him she'd be late? Had she been delayed by some jerk harassing her again when she was out?

Everything in him stirred, churning toward anger. He wanted to shield her from all the flack she was taking. Even beyond that, he wanted to be her...what? They only had a few more days left together before their agreed-upon date to end things. And she'd never given any indication she wanted more.

Why the hell was he now choosing to think of something beyond sex? He'd done that once. His partner had been killed because Gabe had trusted the wrong woman. He'd let her into his personal life, thinking she loved him, only to find out she had actually been playing him all along to feed information to the drug cartel Gabe had been working to bring down.

He'd been such a damn fool.

But Chelsea was different. She'd dodged him and he'd continued to chase her. Gabe always got what he wanted, but now he wasn't so sure what that was. He knew for certain he didn't want things to end, yet at the same time he wasn't looking for a relationship.

Maybe all these wedding plans and seating charts and dress fittings were getting to him. He was just surrounded by the prospect of "forever" and "I do" and clearly getting caught up in the moment.

And most troubling was how he'd whispered his need to her the other night. He'd slipped and whispered how much he needed her, how much he cared for her. Not once but twice. Those words bordered on a confession he certainly wasn't ready to make now...if ever.

Here a quiet knock on his door, Gabe turned from the view of downtown and glanced toward the entryway. Chelsea let herself in, but the moment he spotted her, Gabe was crossing the room in long strides.

"What happened?" he asked, gripping her arms and studying her tear-streaked face. "Are you hurt?"

She smiled and shook her head, her eyes bright with unshed tears. "These are happy tears."

Happy tears? That always sounded like an oxymoron to him, just one more thing he would never understand.

"You're an hour late and you come in crying," he persisted. "What's going on?"

"Daniel and Erin are having twins."

Her declaration was made on another burst of tears. Gabe wasn't quite sure what to do, so he pulled her into his arms. "And you're sure these are happy tears?" he asked again.

She nodded against his shoulder. "I'm so excited for them. My best friend is getting married. My brother is having babies. I mean, it's all so life-changing and makes me think about my own life goals and—"

She jerked back, eyes wide. "I'm not saying that to scare you," she quickly amended. "I don't mean us. I'm just happy and excited, and I want that in my life. I want to have a family and a husband, and I never thought I did, but..."

Yeah, all this talk was making his gut tighten. Seeing Chelsea having an epiphany like this had him wondering about his own future. Hell, he'd just admitted to himself he may want more with her, but marriage and kids?

Let's not get too out of control here.

He framed her face in his hands, using the pads of his thumbs to wipe her tears. "Have you eaten dinner? I can call and have something brought to us."

"I ate at Daniel's." Her gaze held his; moisture glistened on her lashes. "Sorry I'm late. Erin and I got carried away with looking at baby things online. I may have already bought nursery furniture for them."

Gabe could see her getting so involved and wanting to play the doting aunt. How would she be with her own children? Would she want a large family?

The idea of her starting a life with some nameless, faceless, man had jealousy curling low in his gut. But who was Gabe to put a stop to this new goal she'd created? He was merely passing through her life.

"Want to help put up my Christmas tree?"

Chelsea jerked back and her eyes widened. "Tonight?"

"Might as well."

"It's only a few days until Christmas," she reminded him as if he didn't know the date. "Why do anything at this point?"

Because, surprisingly, he wanted to spend time with her, and not just in the bed. As crazy and absurd as that sounded, he found it to be true. He wanted to do something with Chelsea that was normal, something that would create memories.

Damn it. He was getting in deep here. Deeper than he'd anticipated. And he knew full well that in a few days, after the wedding was over, he wasn't going to want to let her go.

Hell, maybe he couldn't let her go.

Fourteen

"I can't believe those are the only ornaments you have."

Gabe glanced over at her, his brows drawn. "What's wrong with them?"

Chelsea didn't even attempt to hide her laughter. "You used one of your hats as the tree topper and the rest of your ornaments are shot glasses from around the world and plastic horseshoes. Don't you have any beads or ribbon or even a star for the top?"

Crossing his arms over his broad chest, Gabe glanced from the tree back to her. "I suppose your tree has all of that and is weighed down with glittery ornaments?"

Chelsea shrugged. So he'd described her tree perfectly. Well, the tree she'd always put up. This year she'd been so preoccupied with so many other things and she'd rarely been home.

"I may like a little glitter in my Christmas decorations," she admitted. "It's festive and happy. Besides,

most of my stuff belonged to my father. They're ornaments we hung when I was little."

She remembered her dad letting her pick out most of
the decorations. Even though she'd been young, she'd
chosen all the sparkles and, still as an adult, she loved
the shiny stuff.

"Do the holidays upset you?" he asked, glancing over
his shoulder to meet her eyes. "I imagine it's difficult
without your parents at times like this."

Chelsea wasn't quite sure what to say. Yes, it was hard,
but she couldn't quite focus on her response. Was Gabe
trying to get to know her more? Did he want to take this
relationship somewhere they hadn't discussed? Because
placing her past front and center in the conversation was
most definitely putting them on another level.

"Losing my father was the worst," she admitted,
staring at the tree because it was easier than looking
into those caring gray eyes. "I know he died of a broken heart. He gave up his will when the only woman he
loved walked out and was never heard from since."

Chelsea bit her lower lip, willing the burn in her throat
and the threat of more tears to cease. "I actually know
where my mother is. I have for years."

"Chels." Gabe crossed to her, sliding his hands up her
arms, curling his fingers over her shoulders. "Have you
contacted her?"

"No. Why would I?" Now, she did meet that mesmerizing gaze. "She made her choice. At first I just wanted
to see if I could use my skills to find her, and I did. She
doesn't live that far from here. She has a new life, and is
clearly not concerned with what she left behind."

"Baby, I'm sorry."

Baby. He'd not called her such an endearing term before. Well, he'd drawn out darlin' once or twice, but al-

ways in that devil-may-care attitude. The way he spoke to her now, the way he *looked* at her, was completely different.

She found she wanted to open up more now that she'd started. Never before had she felt like this, like she could trust a man with more than her body. Gabe was worth the risk.

"When she left and then Dad passed, I didn't handle things very well. I was on the verge of a breakdown and I broke."

Shame filled her. She'd never actually said the words out loud. When everything had happened, Daniel and Brandee were well aware of the situation and had gotten her the help she needed. She'd never had to fully tell the story. Even when she spoke with counselors, Chelsea had glossed over details or kept her feelings veiled.

"Hey." Gabe slid his finger beneath her chin and tipped her face up. "Whatever it is, you don't have to tell me. I want to help, but don't torture yourself."

She pulled in a breath and reached up to grip his wrist, as if drawing strength from him. "I tried to end my life."

Gabe's gasp had her cringing. "Chelsea." Her name came out somewhere between pain and fear as Gabe pulled her into his arms. He encircled her in a vise-like grip. "I don't even know what to say."

He held her another moment, the silence settling heavily around them. She knew by the way he held her that he was stunned, struggling with how to react.

"I felt so alone," she went on, clinging to him. "I know I had Daniel and Brandee, but my foundation was gone. My trust had been shattered when my mom left. I didn't know how to approach my dad to talk because he was so distraught. Then once he was gone…"

Gabe eased her back and framed her face, forcing her

to hold his attention. "I hate that you had to go through all of that. I hate that you felt alone and that there was no choice but to… Damn it, I can't even think it, let alone say it."

There was so much affection in his tone, so much, dare she hope love? Had his feelings changed toward her? It certainly hadn't been her intent to influence him when she'd decided to open up about her past. She'd grown to love and trust him, and decided that if she was going to go after what she truly wanted, then he needed to know the full story.

"Needless to say, that's why Daniel has always been so protective." Chelsea pulled in a breath, thankful the story was out and off her chest. "I guess I wanted you to know."

"You trust me."

There was almost a relief in his voice. Chelsea smiled through her tears and nodded. "I do trust you, Gabe."

She went up onto her toes and kissed him. She wanted to feel him, to taste him. She wanted to ignore the pain from her past and concentrate on what she hoped was her future.

Gabe flattened his hands on her back, urging her closer. From mouths to hips, they were joined. Chelsea knew she could never get enough. She only hoped he was starting to feel the same way.

When Gabe eased back, she had to stifle a groan. She wanted him to take her to the bedroom—or here on the floor would be fine—and finish what that kiss promised. She wanted to feel alive after the anguish of her admission.

"Want to go put your Christmas stuff up?" he asked, his brows drawn in.

Seriously? He was worried about her tree?

But the closer she looked at him, the more she realized he was out of his element here. He was unsure of how to approach her now, of how to handle her. There was so much affection in his eyes. She was used to the desire, the passion and fire. But seeing this side of Gabe warmed every single part of her and only added to the growing hope she had for them.

"It's late and we're so close to Christmas." Chelsea waved a hand in a silent gesture to just forget it. "Besides, is that really how you want to spend our time together? I mean, I could probably procure some mistletoe and we could toy with that. You can even decorate me if you want."

Longing instantly filled his eyes. "I can think of several ways for us to spend the rest of the night and you won't need to go get mistletoe. I'll have you unwrapped and begging in no time." He nipped once again at her lips. "You're staying, by the way."

Little did he know she'd never had any intention of leaving.

As he lay in the dark with Chelsea sleeping in the crook of his arm, Gabe couldn't stop replaying their conversation. The idea that this strong, independent woman had thought there was no way out of her stressful life, well, it absolutely crushed him. A world without Chelsea would be dull and lifeless.

Gabe realized now that he didn't want a world without her. She'd become part of him, part of everything he did and every thought he had. Somehow she'd managed to consume more space in his mind than work and that had never happened. Ever.

Chelsea made his days brighter. As silly and adolescent as that sounded, it was true. When he knew they were going to see each other, he found himself counting down the hours. Yes, the sex was amazing, better than he'd ever had, actually, but there was more. So much more.

He trailed his fingers up her arm and over the curve of her shoulder. They were supposed to end things in a couple of days but he wasn't planning on letting her go. She'd exposed too much of herself, of her troubled past, and he knew his Chelsea wouldn't have done that if she weren't having strong feelings for him.

Between the wedding and Christmas, Gabe figured this was about as magical as the timing could get. He wanted Chelsea to know that she was it for him. He wanted her to know that she would never feel alone again, not as long as he was in her life.

But he wanted her to know he meant it. He wanted her to see that he wasn't just in this for their time between the sheets. He wasn't sure when he'd started falling for her, but he'd done it just the same.

Their quick, whirlwind affair had forced him to realize that she was so much more than just a sexy woman who challenged him. She'd overcome so much in her past, yet she'd come out on top in her career and her life.

Still, the guilt hadn't subsided. She'd suffered even more than he ever suspected and hadn't said a word to anyone except her brother, her best friend, and now him.

That in and of itself told him all he needed to know about her feelings.

Gabe smiled into the darkness and rolled over to face her. Even though she continued to sleep, he couldn't let himself relax. He wanted to formulate the perfect plan to show Chelsea just how much he wanted her in his life, just how much he cared for her and, yes, just how much he loved her.

This would be the greatest Christmas yet.

* * *

Chelsea ended up going into Hunt & Co., after she'd gone home, showered and changed her clothes. After their emotional night, she'd woken with a smile on her face and Gabe had promptly given her something else to smile about.

Gabe couldn't wait until this evening. They planned on taking more decorations to the church for the wedding, which was closing in on them. That meant the deadline to achieve his goal of keeping Chelsea in his life was also closing in on him.

They hadn't spoken about it since before her heartfelt admission last night. He hoped she'd forget all about it, that she'd ignore the end date they'd set.

As much as he wanted to be with her, he was glad to have this time alone because he needed to plan. As soon as the wedding was over, he intended to bring her back to his place and tell her everything. That he didn't want to be without her, that he was so proud of her for learning to trust, and that he trusted her, too…with his heart.

Gabe headed down to the first floor to check his mail. He planned on swinging by the TCC to make sure everything was in place for the outdoor reception. He'd promised Chelsea he would and she'd even sent him a text of her notes so he didn't forget anything. Which was fine, considering he didn't have the first clue about wedding receptions.

Fortunately, he'd discovered quite a bit on this journey, though, and if Chelsea wanted a large wedding, he'd damn well give her one. Anything she wanted, so long as he was in her life.

Once upon a time the thought of a wedding with him as the groom would've scared the hell out of him, but not anymore. Having Chelsea all to himself forever had quickly become a dream he wanted to make a reality.

Gabe exited the elevator on the first floor and nodded to the daytime doorman standing at his post. Sunshine flooded the floor of the old building, highlighting the gleaming black-and-white-checkered flooring.

When Gabe checked his mailbox, he was surprised to only have one piece of mail. He hadn't checked it for nearly a week. But considering that most everything he did was online, and with the holidays fast approaching, it probably made sense there wasn't much mail.

He flipped the envelope over and noticed a note taped to the front.

This letter was placed in my box by mistake. I was out of town so I wasn't able to get it back to you until now.
Your Neighbor in 2C.

So the elderly lady who lived below him had received his mail. That rarely happened. She'd been out of town for the past several weeks visiting her kids across the state.

Gabe tore off the note and stilled. The letter was postmarked four weeks ago, but that wasn't the part that chilled him.

The return address was Dusty's. Seeing his uncle's handwriting, receiving this from him after his death, was a bit eerie.

Gabe had no clue what Dusty could've sent out only one day before his death, so he sure as hell didn't want to open this without privacy. He couldn't get back to his loft fast enough. Gabe had a sinking feeling whatever Maverick had started almost a year ago was about to come back to life in this piece of mail.

Once Gabe finally made it to his apartment, he barely got his door closed before he was tearing into the oversize envelope. He pulled out the contents, cursing under his breath when black-and-white glossies spilled out onto the floor at his feet. Glossies of the woman he loved.

Gabe crouched down and sifted through the images, one after another after another. His heart sank, his stomach turned.

He searched through each photo, but they all had the same theme. She was naked or partially dressed, in the locker room of her gym. From the angle, Gabe could tell someone had planted the camera in a vent or a light fixture. Each photo brought a new wave of rage. She'd had no clue these were taken. Were these just copies of the others that were out there? Because he'd deliberately never looked at those.

Or were these completely new?

Dread coiled in his gut as he gathered the photos and stalked to his kitchen. He tossed the images on the counter and started reading the letter.

Gabriel,
I don't know how much longer I have, so I'm reaching out to my only living relative.

By now, you may have figured everything out. Yes, I'm Maverick. I have my reasons for doing what I did, which I'll lay out below. But I also have some unfinished business and need your help.

As you know I was shunned at the Texas Cattleman's Club. My attempts to gain membership were constantly turned down. They let women in a man's club and kept me out? Well, I had to take matters into my own hands and, once I explain

why, you'll understand. I hope you carry on where
I had to leave off.

Years ago I had an affair with Colleen Hum-
phreys. Her husband was a longtime president of
the TCC and on the board until his death just a
year ago. When he found out about the affair, he
threatened to ruin me. But blacklisting me only
backfired on his precious club. I mean, who had
the last laugh? The revenge I took on the members
was so sweet. I do feel a tad guilty for the lives I
ruined, but they were merely pawns caught in the
game. I had no choice.

Gabe gritted his teeth at his uncle's words. So Dusty
had done all of this, terrorizing Royal for months on end,
to get back at a man who'd been his victim to begin with?
What kind of sick person had his uncle been?

Disgust filled Gabe as he focused on the rest of the
letter.

Here are some final photos of Chelsea Hunt. I never
shared these and I know you'll help me out by finishing this. You always were so loyal. I'm counting on you, Gabriel. Do what you see fit to ruin
the TCC and all those who were allowed in when
I was not. Women like Chelsea and so many others think they're too good, walking around all high
and mighty. It's not right, but we'll make sure they
suffer.

Gabe gripped the paper so tightly that it crinkled in
his hand. Then he tossed it onto the counter, unable to
even touch it another second. He had no clue what to do.
He had to think. He'd believed this situation was behind

them but it had just reared its ugly head once again. Now, he was in control...whether he wanted to be or not.

At least Dusty had mailed the photos and letter to him. Gabe hated to think what would've happened had they gotten into the wrong hands.

Disgusted, Gabe turned away from the heap of photos on the counter. He didn't want to see them anymore, didn't want *anyone* to see them. Gabe would have to turn them over to Sheriff Nathan Battle to be processed with the rest of the items. They were still trying to figure out who could've helped Dusty because obviously the man couldn't have planted a camera in a women's locker room by himself. Not with his poor health.

Gabe would get to the bottom of this. He'd find out who was helping his uncle, he'd make sure this was all in the past, and then he and Chelsea could move forward with their future.

Fifteen

"Can you believe tomorrow is the day?" Chelsea resisted a girlish squeal, but she hugged her best friend tight. "Everything is going to be perfect."

The rehearsal dinner was going exactly as planned. The food was perfect, the décor similar to what would be used in the actual wedding. Chelsea couldn't be more excited for her best friend.

"Everything is going to be perfect," Chelsea exclaimed.

Brandee eased back and nodded. "You and Gabe have gone above and beyond. I can't thank you guys enough."

"We were happy to help."

Brandee's brows rose as her smile widened. "Maybe we'll be planning your wedding next?"

As much as the idea gave Chelsea the warm fuzzies, she wasn't sure Gabe was ready for that. She wasn't even sure he was ready to hear her say how she truly felt. But, after the wedding tomorrow, she was going to tell him.

This was their last night together and she had every intention of making it unforgettable. She would love to open herself up to him tonight and tell him every emotion she'd kept bottled up, but if he turned her down, she didn't want the awkward tension at the wedding, especially since they were walking down the aisle together.

"We're just…" Chelsea wasn't quite sure how to describe the current situation. "Taking this one day at a time."

"You love him."

The chatter around them, the music from the DJ, the soft breeze, everything faded away at those three words. There was no use denying them, not to Brandee. The girl knew Chelsea better than she knew herself.

"I just hope he feels the same."

Brandee tipped her head. "If the way he's staring at you right now is any indicator, I'd say he feels more than lust."

A thrill shot through Chelsea. She so wanted Gabe to be on the same emotional page as she was. They'd had a breakthrough moment when she'd fully opened herself to him. He'd taken her to his bed and made love to her like she was the most fragile, most precious thing in his life. She only prayed that was true.

"Just be honest," Brandee urged. "I almost lost Shane, but we both fought for what we wanted. You're going to have to do the same."

Chelsea opened her mouth to reply, but Brandee squeezed her hands and shot a look over Chelsea's shoulder.

"I better go talk to the other guests," Brandee stated. "I'll see you in the morning at the church."

Chelsea watched as her friend went to talk to a couple of the other bridesmaids. The outdoor rehearsal dinner at

Hope Springs Ranch was perfect. With the temperatures hovering around fifty, they were able to have the event outside in comfort thanks to the heated tents.

This laid-back atmosphere was perfect before the rush and drama of tomorrow. The caterers had done a phenomenal job; of course, they'd used some beef tips from Hunt & Co. for the main course.

Strong hands curled around Chelsea's shoulders and she didn't even hesitate when Gabe eased her back against his chest.

"These little dresses of yours drive me out of my mind," he growled into her ear. "I think you enjoy teasing me."

Chelsea smiled and reached up to cup her hands over his. "I love wearing dresses with boots when the occasion calls for it. Driving you out of your mind is just a bonus."

"What are you wearing under this? Something else new?"

"Perhaps."

She'd put on the slinky teddy with him in mind, and had been counting down the time until they could leave so he could take it off.

"We practiced coming down the aisle and going back up, plus we've eaten." He nipped at her earlobe. "Are we done here yet?"

Chelsea turned in his arms. "You know, if we keep leaving parties early, people are going to know what we're up to."

His hands settled easily on her waist. Those gray eyes she'd come to love sought her from beneath the rim of his black hat.

"I don't care what people think," he told her. "I care about you and that's it."

He cared about her. Not quite a declaration of love,

but it was more than what they'd originally started with. Hope blossomed.

"We should at least say goodbye to our friends," she told him.

"Fine. Say your goodbyes. Be quick." He smacked a kiss on her mouth and stepped back. "Be at my place in fifteen minutes."

Chelsea laughed. "It takes me fifteen minutes to get there from here."

"Then you better just wave goodbye instead of saying it."

He turned and headed toward Shane. Chelsea watched as they did the one-armed man hug and then Gabe headed off toward the field where they'd all parked their cars.

"I imagine you'll be leaving, too."

Chelsea turned to see her brother eyeing her with concern. "I am," she confirmed.

"You're going to get hurt, Chels. I know guys like Walsh. Hell, I know Gabe. I can see the hearts in your eyes."

She attempted to tamp down her anger as she crossed her arms over her chest. "You've tried to warn me before. Do I look like I'm hurt? Don't interfere, Daniel. I've got this under control."

When she started to turn away, he grabbed her elbow and forced her to focus on him. "I hope your eyes are wide-open here. And I hope that he feels the same way as you do because you're in deep."

She hoped Gabe was on the same page with her feelings, too.

With a simple nod, Chelsea pulled her arm from Daniel's grasp. She knew he was just looking out for her, but this was ridiculous. No one was going to come between her and what she wanted—and she wanted Gabe Walsh in her life.

By the time she made it to his loft, her entire body was humming. Chelsea smiled at the doorman as she entered the building. The elevator ride seemed to take forever, then finally she was at Gabe's door. She didn't bother knocking as she turned the knob beneath her palm and eased the door open.

The only light in the loft was the sparkle from the Christmas tree and the city lights streaming through the wall of windows.

She'd barely gotten the door closed when Gabe's arms banded around her. Chelsea melted against him, more than ready to spend the night here.

"You're three minutes late."

Chelsea pushed away from him and crossed the apartment. She wasn't quite done driving him out of his mind.

"I had to talk to my brother," she explained. "And say goodbye to Brandee and Shane. Then I thanked the caterers."

"Take off your dress."

Chelsea turned back to face him. The large loft seemed to close in on her as Gabe took one slow step after another toward her. His eyes never left hers, giving her all the thrills. How could a look make her feel like he was touching her all over? How did he have so much control over not just her body but her mind?

"Come take it off me," she countered.

A low growl emanated from him as he closed the distance between them. In a flash move, he gripped the hem of her dress and jerked it up and over her head. The second he tossed it aside, his swift intake of breath had her confidence soaring. She propped her hands on her hips, thrusting her chest out and cocking her head to the side.

"Was it worth the wait, cowboy?"

"Damn," he whispered. "Had I known you were wearing that, we never would've made it to the dinner."

Chelsea couldn't help but laugh. "I'm pretty sure there's a rule against that."

"Maybe, but nobody would blame me."

She reached out, jerking on his silver buckle. "Why don't you just take me here? This is technically the last night in our agreement, right?"

As soon as the words were out of her mouth, she wanted to take them back. But seeing the flicker of annoyance in his eyes told her he wasn't ready to see this end.

Maybe she should tell him now. Maybe she should just throw it all out there and take the risk now.

But, no. Because if she'd read him wrong, she would never forgive herself for the resulting awkwardness at Brandee and Shane's wedding.

Gabe lifted her into his arms. With one arm behind her back, one arm behind her knees, he nipped at her lips as he walked through the loft. Romance had entered their relationship. This had all started with frenzied, passionate sex. Somewhere along the way love had settled in deep.

Chelsea wrapped her arms around his neck and nestled her head against his shoulder. "I expected you to take me against the window again," she murmured into his ear.

"Maybe tonight is different."

Maybe it was. As Gabe kicked the door shut to his bedroom, Chelsea finally felt like things were going her way. She'd found her happily-ever-after.

Early the following morning, Chelsea slid from bed. The sun still hadn't come up, but she couldn't sleep. Between the wedding, the fantastic night in Gabe's arms, and the talk she wanted to have with him later today about their future, there was just too much going on and her mind simply wouldn't shut down.

Chelsea glanced back to the bed where Gabe lay sprawled on his stomach, his light hair in disarray after she'd run her fingers through it. Her body still hummed as she snagged his T-shirt and put it on. She eased the door closed behind her as she made her way to the kitchen. Gabe was every bit the bachelor, but hopefully he had something she could make for their breakfast. She didn't have to be at the church for a few hours, so maybe breakfast in bed was a great way to start the day.

Humming as she started searching through his cabinets, Chelsea figured if all else failed, she could do coffee, eggs and toast. He at least had those on hand.

She pulled out a pan and the eggs. Once she had them cracked into a bowl, she tugged on a drawer for a whisk. Of course his utensils weren't in a drawer she would put them in. She tried another, only to find a junk drawer. She started to shut it when something caught her eye.

It was a black-and-white photograph. Chelsea focused on it, her heart hammering in her throat. No. That couldn't be. Gabe wasn't the accomplice. Was he? The sheriff had said they were searching for a female.

With a shaky hand she pulled the picture from the drawer, only to find more underneath it. She pulled them all out, then she saw a letter with Gabe's name on it.

Nausea settled in the pit of her stomach as she shuffled through each picture. These weren't the same ones that had circulated months back. These were actually newer, maybe a couple of months old. She knew that because she remembered the exact day at the gym. She recognized the outfit; she'd tried racquetball for the first time. Pretty soon after that, the first nude photos had been leaked and she hadn't been back to that gym since.

Pulling in a deep breath, she set the pictures on the counter, facing down. Her attention went to the letter; she quickly saw it was from Dusty. Did she really want to read this? Did she want to know what he and Gabe had discussed?

Her eyes scanned the scratchy penmanship first before she went back to the top and absorbed every single word.

She couldn't be reading this right. She just...she couldn't. This was important evidence that had been sent to Gabe weeks ago. Why was he hiding these photos in a drawer? Shouldn't he have turned these over to the sheriff by now? Was Gabe covering something up?

Dropping the letter on top of the pictures, Chelsea took a step back and stared at the pile. Such damning evidence of Gabe's involvement with his uncle mocked her and the future she'd been foolish enough to believe in.

Trust hadn't come easy and now she knew why. She should've trusted her instincts to begin with where Gabe was concerned.

The tears came before she even realized it. All the hurt, all the anger, and so much resentment flooded her. She should've listened to her initial suspicions. Hell, she should've listened to Daniel. Hadn't he been trying to warn her she'd get hurt?

She wasn't just hurt, she was utterly, completely, destroyed.

The glow from the Christmas tree in the living room mocked her, trying to pull her back to that night when they'd put it up. He'd completely played her for a naïve fool.

At least she hadn't told Gabe how she felt. He'd probably get a great kick out of knowing he'd duped her.

Chelsea blinked the tears away and went to the living room where her clothes were. She quickly changed, trying to figure out exactly what her next move should be. Did she really want to confront him? Did she want to hear more lies?

And that's what all of this had been. A relationship built on lies.

Once she was dressed, Chelsea tucked her hair behind her ears and glanced at the closed bedroom door. As much as she didn't want to even look at him and hear his excuses, she deserved answers. She deserved to know the real man…not just the one she'd fallen in love with. That man didn't exist.

Sixteen

The sound of the bedroom door creaking woke him. But it was the lights flashing on and the papers that were tossed onto the bed that had Gabe sitting straight up.

No. Not papers. Pictures.

His gut tightened as he glanced up at Chelsea. The brokenness and pain staring back at him told him all he needed to know. She believed he had deceived and betrayed her.

He now regretted that he hadn't done a better job securing the papers. He had intended to turn them over to the sheriff as soon as the wedding was over; he just hadn't wanted to risk more press attention to ruin Brandee and Shane's—not to mention Chelsea's—special day. She had worked so hard on this wedding and he didn't want it ruined for her. He'd had every intention of doing things the right way—or what he thought was right—but now he just looked like he'd been deceiving her all along.

"I don't even want you to defend yourself," she said, crossing her arms over her dress.

Damn it. She'd put her clothes back on, which meant he had about two seconds to get her to listen to the truth. Mentally, she'd already left.

"I just want to know what your motivation is," she went on. "What could you get from having these pictures just lying around your house? Were you planning on humiliating me further? Is this just family loyalty?"

Gabe came to his feet, jerking on a pair of shorts lying by the bed. "I have never set out to hurt you, Chels. I had nothing to do with these pictures being taken."

"Maybe not," she agreed then let out a harsh laugh. "But you know what? Dusty's letter spells things out pretty clearly. You were to take over since he was too sick. You could've destroyed these or turned them over to the sheriff, or hell, given them to me. Yet here you are with them tucked away in your apartment."

He started to take a step forward, but she held up a hand. "No. All this time you were with me, you made me believe you cared, but under the same roof you were hiding these pictures. I was a fool to trust you."

"You can trust me," he insisted. Gabe crossed the room, ignoring her when she shook her head and held her hands out to keep him back. "Look at me. Damn it, I was going to take them to Nathan, but not until after the wedding. I put them away so nobody would see them."

Chelsea kept her head turned away, refusing to look at him. "Convenient," she muttered.

Nothing he said now would make her believe. She'd seen the pictures and the letter, and had decided he'd been lying all along. He hated her thinking he would ever be involved in something like this, but most of all, he hated that she was hurting and he couldn't comfort her.

"What can I say to make you believe me?" he asked.

He wanted to reach out and hold her, but she would never allow that. Her red-rimmed eyes tore him apart. How long had she been in the other room tormenting herself with this?

The automatic bedroom shades rolled up right on time, the soft hum breaking the tension in the room. The sun was starting to rise, but the day that should've been one of the happiest for them had turned into anything but.

"There's nothing you can say," she whispered, her voice thick with tears. "I trusted you with a piece of me I've never given to another man. I thought…"

Her words died off as she bit her lower lip to compose herself. Gabe did reach for her now. He didn't give a damn what she wanted because he knew he hadn't done a thing wrong and he just wanted to hold her, to comfort her. She was absolutely breaking his heart and he'd promised her she'd never feel alone again.

Damn it. He *promised*.

Now, she stared up at him, unshed tears swimming in her eyes. "I thought after the wedding I'd tell you that I didn't want to end things. Stupid, right? I mean, all this time you've chosen to side with your uncle."

"No." He gently took her by the shoulders. "I never sided with him. I got all of that in the mail after he died. Just two days ago."

Chelsea broke free of his grip. "I'm not convinced that you had nothing to do with the first set of pictures, but let's pretend I do believe you. These pictures should never have been here. You should've turned them over. If you care for me at all, if you truly wanted me to believe you were innocent, you wouldn't have kept them."

"I was going to give them to Nathan," he insisted.

Stepping back, Chelsea wiped at her damp cheeks.

"Then you should've told me the second you got them. You have no excuse for that."

She was right. He didn't, other than the fact he didn't want to cause her any more pain.

When she turned away, Gabe's heart clenched. "Don't go. Don't leave this upset. Stay. We can talk this out and then I'll take you to the church."

Chelsea's shoulders straightened, but she didn't face him again. "I'm leaving and I'll get myself to the church. Brandee and Shane deserve this day to be perfect and I'll not let you ruin it for them. After the wedding and our duties are done, I never want to see or speak to you again."

It was difficult, but Gabe let her go.

Right now she needed space, and he needed to figure out how the hell he could fix this. Because he would fix it and he would make her realize that he was never that guy. He could never purposely cause her so much pain.

Though he had to admit beneath his denial and defensiveness, hurt started spreading through him. She actually thought he'd been capable of doing such heinous things. Maybe she'd never fully trusted him. Maybe in the back of her mind she'd always kept those suspicions in reserve.

He would have to put on a front for the wedding because Chelsea was right. This day belonged to Brandee and Shane. But if she thought for a second that he was just going to let her go and never hear from him again... well, she would be in for a surprise.

Gabe gathered the pictures and the letter and went out into the living room. Once he had them secured in an envelope, he laid them on the sofa table. Tomorrow he'd take them to the sheriff and be done with the likes of his uncle. Even dead, the man was ruining lives. Then he'd find out who the hell had assisted Dusty in obtaining the photos to begin with.

Padding barefoot to the kitchen, Gabe noticed the eggs on the counter, the pan on the stove, the bowl. His heart flipped and he gripped the edge of the countertop. She'd been prepared to make him breakfast. She'd found the pictures shoved in the drawer.

Damn it. He was a fool. He should've told her but, in his defense, he just hadn't wanted her to have to deal with that mess any longer. He'd been trying to protect her, but all he'd managed to do was to crush her hopes further and to destroy the trust they'd built.

He had to find a way to get her back. Gabe had never given up before and he sure as hell didn't intend to start now—not when this was the most important moment of his life.

Chelsea smoothed a hand down her gold dress and tried to forget the last time she'd had this on. She flashed back on the dressing room, on Gabe, his clever hands and magical touch.

Pain squeezed like a vise around her chest and she pushed the memory aside. She'd doubled up on concealer and powder, hoping to hide her puffy red eyes. Her waterproof mascara was definitely going to be put to the test.

When Chelsea had first arrived at the church, Brandee had questioned her, but Chelsea had just played it off as wedding tears.

Chelsea spun away from the mirror, not wanting to see herself in this dress. She could practically feel Gabe's hands at the side zipper.

Would his memory fade over time or would she be forced to battle him in her mind forever?

Chelsea crossed to the adjoining room where Brandee

was getting ready. It was time to get into full maid-of-honor mode. Pulling in a deep breath, Chelsea let herself into the room and gasped.

Brandee stood in front of the floor-length mirror, her gaze meeting Chelsea's in the reflection. Chelsea had seen the dress, but now it seemed different. With Brandee's long hair falling in simple waves down her back and the subtle makeup, she looked angelic.

"Can you help me with my veil?" Brandee asked, a wide smile on her face. "My hands are shaking."

Chelsea offered her best friend a smile and crossed to where the veil hung on the back of a closet door. Carefully, she removed it from the plastic wrap and hanger.

"Squat down just a tad," Chelsea told Brandee as she came to stand behind her. "Tip your head back a bit."

After adjusting the pins to be hidden in the soft curls, Chelsea stepped back. "There. How does that look?"

Seeing her best friend smile in the mirror—no, she wasn't just smiling, she was glowing—helped heal a portion of Chelsea's wounded heart. Love did exist, she was absolutely certain of that. She'd just misplaced hers.

"Everything okay?"

Chelsea focused her attention on Brandee's reflection and nodded. "Couldn't be better. You're the most beautiful bride I've ever seen. And this Christmas wedding is going to be magical."

Brandee turned and reached for Chelsea's hands. "I'm more focused on my happily-ever-after. Too many people focus on the wedding details and making a big show of things. I just want to spend my life with Shane."

"He's a lucky man."

"I'm the lucky one." Brandee tipped her head down and narrowed her eyes. "What's up, Chels? Something is off with you today."

There was no sense in lying again. Brandee wasn't buying it. "Just a mishap with Gabe. Nothing for you to worry about on your special day."

Brandee's brows drew in as she squeezed Chelsea's hands. "Oh, honey, what happened?"

The threat of tears burned the back of her throat. "He's not the man I thought he was."

"Did he hurt you?"

Chelsea dabbed beneath her eyes, already knowing she was going to have to have a makeup redo. "I found more pictures at his place. Pictures of me from the gym locker room."

Brandee jerked back. "What did he say?"

"He denied any involvement with his uncle. Dusty sent the photos with a letter—I read it. He wanted Gabe to carry on with what he'd started."

Brandee pursed her lips. "But Gabe didn't do anything with them, right?"

"Not yet. But he didn't tell me he had them," Chelsea replied. "He kept them hidden when he could've destroyed them or just explained what happened and why he had them in the first place."

Brandee reached up and wiped a tear from Chelsea's cheek before squeezing her hands once again. "Gabe wouldn't hurt you. Did you ever think that's the reason he didn't tell you? Maybe he's protecting you."

Or maybe he was still being loyal to his uncle.

There were just so many questions, and she was an emotional wreck. Now wasn't the time to try to solve all of her problems. She had a wedding to partake in…and a man waiting to walk down the aisle with her.

"Forget it," Chelsea said, squaring her shoulders and sniffling back the tears. "This is your day and whatever Gabe and I have going on, I swear it won't interfere with this."

"Of course it won't." Brandee smiled and dropped her hands to smooth down her gown. "I know how Gabe feels, though. Remember the way he manhandled that jerk who was mistreating you? And the way Gabe looks at you when you don't know is enough to set panties on fire. He cares for you and, if I'm not mistaken, he loves you."

Chelsea closed her eyes, willing those words to be true, but his actions said different...didn't they? Had she jumped to conclusions?

"We've all been through so much." Chelsea reached out to adjust her friend's veil around her face. "Let's just focus on the happiness of today. It's two days before Christmas and everything is finally settling back down after a year of scandal. This is going to be the best day and a new beginning."

Brandee nodded. "Let's fix your makeup and get ready for the pictures. But I want you to keep in mind, Gabe is exactly the man he claims to be. I'd stake my life on it."

Chelsea wasn't so sure she could say the same, but she'd laid her heart on the line, which was pretty much the same. She needed some space to think. Unfortunately, she'd be walking arm in arm with the only man she'd ever loved in a very short time.

Right now she needed to put on her happy face and coat of armor. This day was about to test every bit of her strength.

Seventeen

"You look stunning."

Gabe whispered the compliment as Chelsea slid her arm over his elbow. She clutched her gold ribbon that secured a ball of mistletoe. In lieu of bouquets, Chelsea and Brandee had gone with mistletoe…and now he was being mocked by the classic flower.

The late afternoon wedding at the TCC was perfect. As he glanced around, Gabe saw every detail that he and Chelsea had a hand in. He had to focus on things like that because the woman at his side was driving him out of his mind with want and need.

The way Chelsea's body shifted beneath the material of her dress, the way she delicately brushed against his body, had his mind pumping into overdrive.

The last time he'd seen her in that dress…

Gabe focused on making it down the aisle, his hand securing hers over his arm. He needed to touch her, needed to feel her. Regardless of whether this was just for the sake of appearances, he'd take what he could get at this point.

The way she'd left so hurt and angry only hours ago—yeah, he had to have some sort of contact. He'd sat in his apartment and slowly driven himself insane with what he should have done differently and how he could have avoided hurting her.

But he honestly didn't know that he would have done things differently. Yes, he could have informed her that he'd received the mail from his uncle, but he'd planned on doing that when he turned them over to the authorities.

She was understandably upset, but just as she had at the start of their relationship, she would come to see that she was wrong. His actions would speak for themselves. He just had to figure out how the hell to get her to understand that he had been protecting her.

Chelsea remained silent as they reached the end of the aisle and parted ways. His arm and hand instantly chilled. Holding this winter wedding outdoors had nothing to do with it, either. The tent where Brandee and Shane were about to exchange their vows was heated.

No, his chill came from the fact that the one woman he'd allowed himself to truly love, the one woman who'd entered his life like a whirlwind and settled deep into his heart, had pushed him away.

In her defense, she had good reasons for being wary. But where he was concerned, her fears and suspicions were misplaced.

Canon in D chimed through the very well hidden speakers and everyone in attendance came to their feet. Gabe glanced to the end of the aisle as Brandee came around the corner. Shane tipped his head down and rubbed his eyes. Gabe reached up and squeezed his shoulder in silent encouragement.

He couldn't imagine what was going through his best friend's mind. What would it be like to find the one you wanted to spend your life with? What would it be like to have her coming toward you, ready to take a risk together like nothing else in the entire world mattered?

Gabe turned his attention to Chelsea. Her eyes were locked on the bride, but her shoulders were stiff and she held tight to the ribbon of mistletoe. There was a hint of a smile on her face, but Gabe saw the hurt in her eyes and knew she was anything but relaxed.

Gabe paid little attention to the vows and ring exchange. He didn't take his eyes off Chelsea and when she met his gaze, he didn't look away. Neither did she.

He had no idea what was going through her mind, or what was even going on around them. He didn't care. All that mattered was Chelsea. Damn it. His heart flipped in his chest. She'd gone and worked her way right into the deepest part of him—and he realized that's exactly where he wanted her.

This wasn't just him wanting to prove his innocence to her and make sure she wasn't hurting. Yes, he did want both of those things, but the obvious reason was literally staring right back at him. He wanted Chelsea in his life, now, tomorrow, forever.

He wanted what Brandee and Shane had; he wanted what so many of their friends had found. There had never been another to grab his heart the way Chelsea had and he wasn't about to just let her walk out of his life.

As soon as the ceremony was over, Gabe waited for the newly married couple to turn to the guests and make their way back down the aisle. The music started up in celebration of the milestone moment.

Gabe stepped up, extending his elbow for Chelsea to take. She didn't meet his eyes as she did so.

"We need to talk," he murmured out the side of his mouth as they made their way off the elevated platform.

"Not yet."

Well, at least she'd replied and hadn't completely shot him down. That was a step in the right direction.

As they joined the party lining up in the back to greet guests, Chelsea quickly let go of him and went to stand next to Brandee.

The evening seemed to drag on for him, but he was positive the newly married couple was having the time of their lives. Chelsea always seemed busy or missing when he went to find her. Most likely she was avoiding him, and that was okay, but it was only so long before he caught up with her. He had no idea what he planned to say, no idea how to make this all go away, but he would.

Gabe caught a flash of gold in the distance, but by the time he crossed the patio area just off the TCC ballroom, he realized it wasn't Chelsea but another guest.

Cursing, Gabe turned and nearly tripped a waiter carrying a tray of drinks.

"'Scuse me," he said, holding his arms out to make sure the tray stayed level.

"Care for a bourbon?" the waiter asked.

Gabe grabbed one of the tumblers and muttered his thanks before moving on. He wasn't in the mood to mingle or dance; he only wanted to talk to Chelsea. As he rounded the back of the building near the walking trails and stables, he found Daniel and Chelsea in an embrace.

Clearly he'd stumbled upon something private. As he started to turn away, Chelsea's words stopped him.

"You warned me," she said, her voice slightly trembling. "You told me I'd get hurt and I didn't want to hear it."

Gabe slid behind some landscaping near the corner of the building so as not to be seen. He'd just listen for a minute, then he'd give them their privacy. He knew he should walk away now, but damn it, this was the woman he loved and he wanted to know what he was up against in this fight.

"I never wanted to be right about this," Daniel said. "I want you to find happiness, Chels. I just didn't think Gabe was the guy for you."

What the hell? Her brother had warned her off? Anger bubbled within Gabe and he started to step away from his hiding place, but Chelsea's cry stopped him in his tracks.

"But I love him."

Hope quickly replaced the anger. She loved him? So all the hurt he'd seen in her eyes was about thinking the man she loved had betrayed her trust. As much as he wanted to be angry over this whole situation—with his uncle and with himself for hurting Chelsea—all he could focus on was the fact that she loved him.

It was almost like a weight had been lifted from his chest. Those words were all he needed to know he'd get her back. Between his determination and her declaration, that was all the ammunition he needed to secure Chelsea in his life. Forever.

Chelsea pulled back from Daniel's embrace and dabbed beneath her eyes. "I didn't want to have a melt-down, but I wanted to let you know what was going on."

"You weren't acting like yourself," he replied, pulling a handkerchief from his pocket.

Chelsea smiled as she took it. "You always were a gentleman."

"So what are you going to do?" he asked. "You don't trust him, but you love him."

That about summed up this complex situation. Seeing Gabe in his tux, having him hold on to her for the briefest of moments before the wedding vows, had been almost too much to take. She'd tried to focus on the ceremony but keeping her eyes away from Gabe had been near impossible. He'd caught her looking at him once and she'd been unable to turn away. When those gray eyes had locked onto hers, Chelsea swore he was looking into her soul.

"I want to believe him." She looked up at her brother, knowing she'd find concern in his expression. "My heart and my head are saying two different things. I just need to talk to him, but I need time first."

"What can I do?"

Chelsea smoothed a hand down her gown and shook her head. "Nothing at all. Take care of Erin and those babies. I'll handle my love life."

Daniel's lips thinned as he shoved his hands into his suit pockets. "I know you're smart, but I just don't want you to be taken advantage of or to be wrapped up in another scandal."

"I won't be," she assured him. "We're all moving on now that Maverick has been pinpointed. I won't let anyone hurt me like that again. Whoever the accomplice is, they're likely lying low right now."

The words were for her brother's peace of mind, but they were a vow to herself. She refused to ever be the victim again.

"I should get back to the reception." Chelsea wrapped her arms around her brother once more. "Thanks for always listening."

"I wouldn't be anywhere else when you need me."

Chelsea turned away and made her way back to the reception. Thankfully it was wrapping up and Brandee and Shane would head off on their honeymoon soon. They were escaping to someplace tropical and private, so private they hadn't disclosed their destination to friends and family.

Now that the excitement and the hustle and bustle were over, Chelsea planned to take the next two days and do nothing but enjoy the Christmas season. She'd drink hot chocolate topped with whipped cream and peppermint flakes, she'd watch classic movies that were sure to take her mind off her current issues, and she'd not have any contact with Gabriel Walsh until she knew exactly what she wanted to say to him.

And until she could get her emotions under control because damn if she still didn't want the man.

Eighteen

It was Christmas Eve morning and he still hadn't heard a word from Chelsea. She'd slipped from the reception shortly after the bride and groom. In the few minutes Gabe had stayed beyond that, he'd been greeted with a glare from Daniel. Just when Chelsea's brother had started to make his way over to Gabe, Erin had intervened and they had left.

As much as Gabe wanted to stand his ground and talk to Daniel, the most important person he needed to see wasn't returning his texts. He got that she needed space, but her timeframe was about to expire.

Gabe had already taken steps to secure their future. He'd already made sure that nothing else incriminating or embarrassing would crop up out of nowhere down the road. Above all else, he had made sure she was protected. Even if she didn't accept his love, his commitment to her, Gabe still wanted to put a shield of protection around her.

Tonight would be the perfect time to approach her. The annual candlelight and caroling event around the twenty-foot tree in Royal's town square couldn't provide a better setting. He knew Chelsea would be there. Everyone went to the event to light candles, join family and friends, and sing carols. Then they'd all fellowship together afterward as the area businesses provided hot chocolate and baked goods and the shops that lined the square stayed open late. Everyone, no matter their background, their financial status or their age came to celebrate the season.

Chelsea would feel comfortable there. They'd be surrounded by people, so there would be no pressure, but there would also be nowhere for her to run.

Considering he had several more hours to worry about her response, Gabe decided to fill the time making calls and checking on his clients. The swift damage control he'd run in the last couple weeks had paid off. The reputation of his company was strong as ever and more potential clients were pouring in. His career couldn't be better and his global prospects seemed to be a great possibility.

He'd turned the photos over to Nathan, but Gabe wasn't relinquishing control of everything. The hunt for Dusty's accomplice would be over and done with soon and Chelsea could truly move on…hopefully with him. But Gabe was keeping his men on this search. He wanted to find the person who had helped his uncle.

Once Chelsea was back in his life, in his home, he would truly have it all. And Gabe always got what he wanted.

Chelsea went with her favorite emerald-green sweater, dark jeans, and her cowgirl boots. She did her hair in loose curls and applied a thin layer of gloss. There was no way she'd avoid Gabe tonight and she wanted to look good but not overly made up.

He'd texted over the past two days, but every time she'd started to reply, she simply hadn't found the right words. How did she get into such a dramatic conversation via text? What she needed to say to him had to be said in person.

Royal's candlelight and caroling was one of her favorite events of the entire year. When everyone gathered together, it almost seemed as if the outside world didn't exist, as if there were no problems, and peace on earth was indeed the reality. She wanted peace, not just for herself, but the town. The past year had been trying for so many, but this seemed to be a new hope and a new day to start over and move forward.

Dare she hope the same was true for her own life? She wasn't so much worried about the gossip regarding her photos anymore. Those who loved and cared for her had already forgotten and those who made rude remarks... well, she wasn't going to concern herself with them.

Her heart warmed as she thought back to how protective Gabe had been that night he'd handled one such jerk. Even though they'd agreed to keep their relationship private, he hadn't cared one bit about his secrecy because he'd been set on defending her. Shouldn't that tell her all she needed to know about the man she'd fallen for?

Sometimes what seemed to be the truth was just a haze covering up the reality. Those pictures in his loft were damning, yes, but what motive would he have had to put them out there? Just because Dusty asked him to? Chelsea didn't see Gabe doing such a thing. He had been angry about the scandal that had ensnared so many members of the TCC. And Gabe had been furious and mortified when Maverick's identity had been revealed.

Chelsea parked several blocks away from the town square and used the walk to clear her head. This was the first year she hadn't come with Brandee, but she knew her friend was having a much better time on her honeymoon.

The shops were all set up with their tables of last-minute Christmas items, baked goods, and hot chocolate and hot cider at the ready. Chelsea couldn't resist getting a cup of cider on her way to the tree. Each table also had candles, so she grabbed one of those, as well.

When she glanced at the white taper in her hand, she couldn't help but inwardly roll her eyes. There was a sprig of mistletoe tied around the base, just below the clear disc to catch any wax drippings.

Mistletoe seemed to be mocking her lately. She was having a difficult time dodging it—and dodging the man who stood only a few feet in front of her holding his own candle.

Chelsea's heart kicked up as she made her way toward Gabe. He'd spotted her already and his eyes held hers as she drew closer.

"I've been watching for you."

She'd missed his voice, missed looking into his face and seeing…everything. The desire, the concern, the love.

Could their relationship be so simple? Could she believe everything he told her and let down her guard again?

"I don't know what to say," she admitted, toying with the tie holding her mistletoe to the taper. "I want so much, Gabe. But I'm afraid."

Kids squealed and ran by; a mother chased them demanding that they stop. Gabe took hold of Chelsea's elbow and steered her toward the side of a building, away from the chaos.

"You think I'm not afraid?" he asked. With her back against the brick building, he shifted so his body blocked out the festivities behind them. "Having you walk out, thinking even for a second that I could hurt you in such a way, put more fear in me than I'd ever known."

Chelsea stared up into his eyes, her heart beating so fast. Gabe wasn't lying; he wasn't just saying pretty words. Everything he told her was from his heart.

"I didn't know what to think." She still didn't, but she couldn't ignore the pull of emotions steering her toward him. "I didn't want to believe the worst, but I panicked when I saw the letter. I know Dusty was all the family you had, so I got scared that your loyalty would override anything you felt for me."

Gabe dropped his candlestick to the ground and instantly framed her face, forcing her to hold his gaze. "Override love? Nothing and no one can replace what I feel for you."

Chelsea's breath caught in her throat. "Love?"

"Damn it, you know I love you." He closed his lips over hers briefly before easing back and resting his forehead against hers. "I can't live without you, Chels. I don't want to even try."

"I—"

"Wait." He shifted back to look at her once again, but he didn't let go. "You need to know that I've turned everything over to Nathan. I've also launched my own investigation into who could've helped Dusty because I agree he didn't act alone."

Tears pricked her eyes. She tried to blink them away, but they spilled over. Gabe gathered her against his chest, rubbing his hand up and down her back. He took the candle from her hand as she clutched his shirt and attempted to pull herself together. How could she, though, when everything she wanted was right here? The risk she was about to take would change her entire life.

"You really love me," she murmured.

She felt the soft rumble of laughter reverberate through his chest. "I really do. There's nothing I wouldn't do for you."

Chelsea slid her arms up and wrapped them around his neck. Pressing her lips to his, she held him tight, never wanting to let this moment go. The moment when he confessed his love, the moment when she decided to let it all go and trust in what they'd built.

"Tell me again," she muttered against his mouth. "Tell me you love me."

Gabe slid the pads of his thumbs over her damp cheeks. "No one will ever love you more. I ached when you left. That's how I knew what we had was real. The pain was too strong to be just casual. I want to build a life with you, Chelsea. No matter what we're doing or where we live, I want it with you."

"I want my life with you, too." Chelsea smiled. "But you should probably know I'm going to be opening a counseling center for young adults."

Gabe's eyes widened then he smiled. "That's a great idea."

"No. It's not just an idea. I bought the building, I'm searching for counselors now, and I want this up and running by spring. The focus will be on teens suffering from depression, anxiety, and suicidal tendencies."

Gabe kissed her hard, fast. "You're so damn remarkable, darlin'. Of course, you're already on the ball with this. Tell me what to do to help and I'm there."

Chelsea threaded her fingers through his hair. "Love me. That's all I need to get through."

The singing started up behind them. The cheerful chorus quickly spread through the street. The magical evening had begun and she stood in her lover's arms. Right now, nothing could destroy her happiness.

"I'll always love you, Chelsea. Always."

She went up onto her toes and kissed him. "I love you more."

Epilogue

"What are you thinking?"

Chelsea lay beside him, her head on the pillow. Soft moonlight filtered in through the blinds he'd left open because he'd wanted to make love to her by the pale light.

After a month of bouncing from her house in Pine Valley to his loft, he'd finally asked her to move in with him. But he knew they'd eventually get their own place and start fresh. Actually he didn't want to wait much longer.

"Gabe?"

He smiled at her, reaching up to stroke her hair away from her face. Touching her, watching her while she slept, just the mundane things they did together, made him anxious, and he was done waiting to ask.

Gabe leaned back and reached into his nightstand, pulling out the small velvet box. He tapped the remote on the nightstand one time, to add the softest light in the room. He wanted to see her face, but he didn't want harsh light to ruin the moment.

Chelsea gasped when he rolled back over and she saw what he was holding.

"I had something elaborate and romantic planned for next week, but—"

"Yes," she squealed.

Gabe laughed. "Will you let me at least ask?"

Chelsea shot up in bed, the sheets pooling around her waist as she took it from him. "No. I want to marry you, now. This minute."

Shaking his head, he took the box back. "We'll get to that, but let me be somewhat of a gentleman here."

He lifted the lid, keeping his eyes on hers. "Since you already answered, I guess I should tell you that your brother already approved this."

Her eyes darted from the ring to him. "You talked to Daniel?"

"Considering he had his doubts about us a month ago, yes. Besides, I always thought a man should ask permission from the father of the woman he wants to marry. For you, I knew I should go through Daniel."

Chelsea's eyes misted as she looked back at the ring. "It's a pearl. It's lovely, Gabe."

He felt a little silly now since he hadn't gone the traditional route with a diamond.

"I saw the pearl and immediately thought of how they're made. How they're the toughest, yet come from something so soft. It just reminded me of you."

She took the ring, but he tossed the box onto the covers and plucked the ring from her hand. "I'm at least putting this on you."

When he slid it onto her finger, she held it up and admired the way it looked on her hand.

In the last month so much had happened in their lives. Gabe had worked closely with Nathan and discovered that Dusty's once lover, whose husband had been on the TCC board, had indeed been the one to help plant the cameras. She apparently had divorced her husband some time back and was still secretly involved with Dusty, claiming her love until his death.

Her home had since been searched and all hard drives and any computers taken. Charges were pending and Gabe was confident Nathan would handle matters from here on out.

Maverick's reign of terror was indeed over. The town had moved on. Chelsea was gearing up to open her counseling center by late March and Brandee was completely on board with joining forces in the project, as well.

"I don't want a big wedding," Chelsea told him, reaching over to join their hands. "Something simple at the Crescent Moon is perfect for me. For us."

Gabe leaned forward and kissed her, sending them tumbling back to the pillows. "We can discuss wedding plans later. I want to celebrate."

Chelsea laughed as he jerked the covers up and proceeded to show her just how happy he was that she'd said yes.

* * * * *

HER MISTLETOE
BACHELOR

CAROLYN HECTOR

I would like to take a moment to dedicate this book to the people near – and far from – me who have lost loved ones. My cousin Jacqui lost her husband, who was her childhood sweetheart. My son's favourite maths teacher lost her husband, her college sweetheart. My Shoop Shoop Diva family lost two of our sisters, Betty Williams, and Michele Robinson. Through all of this I have been amazed by the way we as family, classmates, and friends rally around each other during a time of sorrow.

Chapter 1

"Donovan, I can't thank you enough for letting me film this," said Amelia Marlow Reyes, field producer for Multi-Ethnic Television. "Pieces like this are going to drive the website clicks up the charts."

Shrugging, Donovan Ravens scratched the back of his head. As CFO of the globally successful Ravens Cosmetics in Miami, he understood why people were interested in the dynasty—the family, though, not him. Donovan ran numbers, approved budgets and attended company functions. These events, it just so happened, took place at fashion shows and photo shoots. With the company celebrating over fifty years in the business, marketing and advertising had changed. This social-media-savvy generation wanted an up-close look at the entire family through their website. It used to be family photos every other year and placed in traditional magazines like *Ebony*, *Essence* and *Jet*. Now the world wanted to meet each member of the family on a daily basis through Instagram, Twitter and reality TV. The updated website for Ravens Cosmetics offered short videos with a candid look into the life of each member of the family. "I guess. There's not much interesting about my life."

Amelia swatted him on the shoulder. She didn't hit as hard as his sisters did, but the blow did sting through the thick blazer of his tan jacket. "Are you kidding me? The world is infatuated with you. You're the mystery bachelor brother."

"All right, Amelia," Donovan chuckled, knowing she was being kind by not calling him a playboy. As much as Donovan resented his celebrity status, he did not let it stop his dating life, and Amelia knew it. "You already got me to agree to this, you don't have to butter me up."

Amelia pretended to be shocked and lifted her left hand to her heart. Her diamond wedding band flashed under the hallway lights. Donovan heard she'd gotten married a while back to a great guy named Nate Reyes. Given the smile she'd sported all day, Donovan would have guessed she was a newlywed. Amelia's large brown eyes stretched wide, her mouth forming a perfect O. "You can't take a compliment, can you?"

"Let's be honest, I'm not the average pretty boy like Marcus or Will." To prove his point about his brothers, Donovan aimed his long index finger toward the scar that ran down his face, from his left eyebrow to his black beard.

Amelia rolled her eyes. "That only adds to your mysteriousness."

"Whatever," Donovan mumbled before handing over the keys to his two-story condo to Amelia's film crew.

A bulky man with a camera strapped to his shoulders entered the foyer. Another crew member, a woman, carrying a long stick with a furry thing at the end—a boom—followed. Amelia filled the delay with chatter about the next step of filming. Some dude named Vickers tried to contradict everything Amelia said, seemingly pissed off she was there.

Donovan shrugged, still not caring what the old man wanted. Amelia was a friend of the family and the only person he'd agreed to work with on this ridiculous spotlight his sisters, Dana and Eva, thought would be good for the company. The plan was for every member registered to the RC website to gain access to the family via day-in-the-life videos of each one of them. The new line of men's lotions and shaving creams needed to be promoted, and what better way for product placement than in the home of a family member who was also an executive at the company?

"It is tedious. I understand. But to pick up seamlessly from earlier, we need to get your full facial expression as you come inside," Amelia explained.

Someone inside his apartment knocked on the door.

"Wait," said Vickers, "your girlfriend is in there, right?"

The term *girlfriend* made him queasy—*flavor of the month*, sure. They'd dated on and off again with no commitment in sight. Tracy needed a place to crash while her apartment was being painted. She knew the camera crew planned to be here this morning but she swore she'd be gone. Since they dated more on than off and he allowed her to stay at his place unsupervised, he shrugged his shoulders, acknowledging the *G* word might be appropriate. "I guess," Donovan mumbled.

"Wouldn't it be nice if you were to propose to her on camera?"

Fusing his brows together, Donovan took a step back. "Hell no. Amelia?"

Amelia wedged herself between the producer and Donovan. "We agreed—no staged surprises," she said to Vickers.

The dark brown–skinned man adjusted the gold-wired glasses on his face. "Think of the ratings."

"Think about me walking away from this project right now," said Donovan. He took a step back but Amelia turned to face him and grabbed him by the front of his pin-striped Oxford shirt.

"You're not going anywhere, Donovan," she said then turned her attention to the other man. "We're not pulling any surprises. Vickers," she snapped. "Didn't you do your research? The women in his life never make it to girlfriend status. He's only been with Tracy for, like, two months or so."

Six weeks, Donovan mentally corrected her. Once more than a month had gone by without Tracy asking for a spot in a fashion show or a photo shoot in a magazine or asking about getting involved in the family business, Donovan had allowed her to spend the night with him there. Typically, after an evening together, he made sure to send a woman in a waiting limousine filled with roses without a promise of a second date. The *D* word. Donovan did not take women out to fancy restaurants but rather met them out and about. He avoided being photographed as well as being seen with the same woman twice. Better to end things with them sooner than later once they realized that they didn't want to be tied down to a scarred monster.

When Donovan first received his permit at sixteen, he made a foolish mistake trying to avoid an object in the road and ended up overturning his car. He was fortunate to walk away alive, but his head hit the driver's side window, shattering the glass, and then his face slammed into the steering wheel, leaving him with a gruesome scar down the left side of his face. Donovan scratched his face and recalled the first time a girl he liked had told him the truth. No one would ever want to wake up to a face like his every day. Once, on a blind date, he'd overheard a woman complain to her friend for setting her up with Scar but then console herself with the idea of getting access to the Ravens fortune if she became pregnant. Donovan knew he'd never trust that a woman would want him for him, not his family's fortune. Knowing he was a Ravens, women still threw themselves at him. Who was he to turn them down?

So maybe women didn't want to see his scarred face every day, but as he got older and more serious about the family business, women aggressively pursued him. Usually they wanted a modeling job at Ravens Cosmetics, an office position or the chance to marry into the family. He was well aware of the fact that being seen with him brought notoriety and other modeling competitors. The way he saw things, it was a win-win situation.

And then came Tracy. They'd met at a fashion show. She'd walked in with her own fan club. She hadn't wanted Donovan for what he could give her and had even turned down the opportunity to participate in this MET reality special. After four weeks of dating, he guessed she sounded like a winner to him. Last Friday when Donovan had flown out to Michigan for business, he'd allowed Tracy the chance to stay at his place alone. The weekend had been the first step in trust... not something worthy of a proposal. If she passed this step, Donovan planned on getting out of the city with her for the upcoming holiday week.

One of the guys who'd entered the condo before him cracked the door open and asked to speak to Amelia.

Vickers pulled Amelia back by the corner of her blazer. "Let's not forget," he warned in a low voice, "I am the on-site producer here. When this assignment is over, you'll go back to Southwood."

Not liking it, Donovan stepped forward and wagged his index finger in warning at the man.

Amelia shrugged off Vickers's touch, stepped back and shook her head at Donovan as the other producer disappeared inside. "I'm sorry about that."

"Why do you put up with him?" Donovan asked. "Does Christopher know how he treats employees?"

Christopher Kelly, his close friend and scion of the Kelly political dynasty of Miami, had opted to invest in the entertainment world with Multi-Ethnic Television, opening his high-rise building to MET and several other successful businesses in Miami. They had bonded over being offspring of famous parents. And Donovan knew Christopher would not appreciate this behavior.

"Leave it alone," said Amelia with a shake of her head.

The door cracked open again. This time a hand reached out with a thumbs-up. Amelia patted Donovan on the back and nodded to the cameraman behind them. "Now, you open your door and the film crew will start rolling from there. We'll edit it later and splice it into a smooth cut."

Still not knowing all the terms, Donovan crossed the threshold of his place. He'd already been told to ignore the camera and just act natural. "Natural" meant he ripped off his monkey suit and strolled around his apartment in his boxer briefs, but this was not that kind of show. Donovan set his keys on the half table by the door and headed up the curved stairway to his bedroom. One cameraman walked backward, filming him from the front. What happened to the other guy who'd come in first? Weren't there a total of three of them?

Thighs burning from taking two steps at a time, Donovan made a mental note never to skip leg day again. Employees of Ravens Cosmetics took advantage of the gym around the corner of the building. He needed to do so again. The door to Donovan's bedroom was slightly ajar. He heard whispers inside. Was Tracy awake? Did the cameramen wake her?

Pushing the door open farther, Donovan's eyes adjusted to the bright sunshine creeping in from the balcony. His foot hit a bottle and then a pile of clothing. He shook his head at the mess his housekeeper was going to have to clean, then let his eyes wander to a hairy leg poking out of the comforter. The movement in the bedroom didn't disturb the sleeping couple in his bed. Tracy rolled over and wrapped her legs around her partner. The fact Tracy slept with another man did not bother Donovan. His disappointment in himself for beginning to think he could trust someone did. The audacity of her bringing this dude to his place: sheer disrespect. Donovan balled up his fists to keep from flipping them off the mattress.

Whelp, so much for those holiday getaway plans, Donovan thought to himself. Relationships were not in his future.

British Carres flipped her agenda page for the next item up for discussion and her heart jolted. Finally! The Southwood School Advisory Council was going to acknowledge the growing need to fund Science, Technology, Engineering and Math for Girls Raised in the South—STEM for GRITS, an after-school program she spearheaded, involving twenty-plus girls attending Southwood Middle School. Her new robotics group received the hand-me-downs from the boys and it was time for a change. The male robotics team monopolized the lab Mondays through Thursdays, giving British's team only one day in the lab for experiments. The local community collected money currently to distribute to the students in need and after they were all taken care of, a nice pot was up for grabs. Since the language arts, social studies and math departments received a bonus a few years ago, the sciences were next in line. As one of the lower level science teachers at Southwood Middle School, British felt like she had to work twice as hard, putting her degree in chemistry and science from Florida A&M University to good use. STEM for GRITS deserved some of the funds available.

The gray tables in the basement of city hall had been set up in a square so that all the committee members of the school board could read each other's faces. This was the biggest challenge of all. She needed to channel her inner beauty queen and learn to compose her face.

Seated across from her was the thorn in her side, the director of the science department. Dr. Cam Beasley was a "good ole boy" who felt the best place for a woman was in the kitchen. The man loved to point out that British had taken a job as the home economics teacher when she'd first started out, further proving her point of the need for the science club for girls. Cam often forgot science was in everything taught in home ec. British had endured the sexism in the field while attending college. She hated the idea that a new batch of budding scientists could be being held back by some lab-coat-wearing, chauvinistic pig.

Whatever, she thought and looked back down at her paperwork before Cam made eye contact and tried to smile. She feared she wouldn't be able to offer a friendly response. British fiddled with a section of the two-page document where the silver staple bound the papers. Her portion of tonight's discussion was the last on the agenda before they took off for the Thanksgiving break. The bonus money would pay for accommodations, travel and supplies if the STEM for GRITS attended the district science fair, where they'd compete against several schools in Southern Georgia.

"You're not going to get anywhere if you're frowning like that."

Looking up, British watched her teacher's aide, Kimber Reyes, pull out the empty black-metal folding chair beside her and take a seat. "Hey, we're just about to start back up."

"Convenient," Kimber said, shaking her head. "I saw Cam run outside to put the top up on his convertible. He's more afraid of getting the car wet than his dreadlock extensions."

As a former beauty queen, British recognized false hair. She never judged anyone for their hair accessories, but Cam tempted her to start. He looked ridiculous with an extra piece of hair covering the spot where his heavy dreads exposed his bald spot. Though British laughed at Kimber's sarcasm, a feeling of dread came over her. Across the square, Cam huddled with the principal and the superintendent.

A feeling of doom washed over British the moment the superintendent, Herbert Locke, greeted Cam with a pat on the back and whispered something in the science director's ear. The two bent over in laughter of the slap-happy-inside-joke kind. Of course these two were buddies. They probably just made arrangements to visit each other's hunting camps, considering deer season was about to kick off. British needed these funds and she had to get the board to recognize it.

"All right, if we can finish up here," the president of the Southwood School Advisory Committee said, clearing her throat. "I am sure we would all like to get home and start cooking for the Thanksgiving holiday before this storm breaks and leaves us high and dry."

As if on cue a crack of lightning lit up the rectangular windows of the conference room. Everyone groaned.

"Excuse me," British said, standing as others began to gather their belongings. "I believe we missed my part of the agenda." She was never one to bite her tongue and she wasn't going to start now.

Someone sighed in annoyance.

Two of the high school teachers plopped their purses back on the table.

"Sorry to take five minutes out of your evening, but this has been put off long enough and now that we have Superintendent Locke here—"

"You're already two minutes into your time, *Home Ec*," Cam interrupted and chuckled.

British's upper lip curled, hearing the nickname; she twisted the pear-shaped diamond engagement ring she still wore on her finger. Bravery ignited, she cleared her throat. "I don't see how laughing about STEM for GRITS is funny." But as she said the words the rest of the advisory board laughed. Heat filled her cheeks, reminding her of the time when she realized she loved science and the science fairs. She'd been so excited the year she was old enough to make an exploding volcano that she practically ran over to join the boys. Her ears still rang from the laughter of the class when the boys told her she could only clean up after them and handed her a broom. None of her girlfriends, friends who didn't grasp the science behind creating their own lip-gloss flavors, wanted to speak up in fear of how the boys would respond. British knew then there needed to be a better support group for girls.

"Why do you think your girls deserve the bonus funding when we already have a legitimate robotics team that can use the funding?" Cam asked, elbowing the superintendent.

"Because the boys on the robotics team are either distracted by the girls or they're not inclusive."

Locke raised his hands in the air. "Which is it?"

Cam spoke first. "Maybe if your girls dressed—"

The women who'd slammed their purses down gasped at the absurdity.

"The trends these days…" Cam sputtered and tried to recover. "Look, when I was growing up, girls had to cover up and wear long skirts. Shirts were damn near turtlenecks. Nowadays they're wearing basically neon signs for boys to look."

"How 'bout you teach your boys to not stare?" British tapped her paperwork with her pink-polished nails. Maybe today was not the greatest day to wear this cotton-candy color. "May we please focus on the agenda?"

And then the weather spoke for her. A loud boom cracked outside on the lawn; the lights flickered and the air went off. Ear-piercing silence filled the room. Once everyone registered what had happened, they began talking at once.

British could feel her funding being pushed to the next meeting. "Before this meeting adjourns, can we please vote to approve who gets the donation from the city? Maybe the Christmas Advisory Council can weigh in on the matter?"

Miss McDonald, the school's librarian and the par-

liamentarian of the council, banged her gavel at her
end of the table and commanded order just as she did
in the library.

"What?" British asked. "We're not going to meet
next month and, before the year ends, there's a chance
my girls can make it to the Four Points STEM contest. It
is imperative to nurture young girls at this impressionable age. We need to continue to encourage their creative minds in science and math, as well as everything
else. We need more geochemists like Ashanti Johnson,
zoologists like Lillian Burwell Lewis and, of course
mathematicians like Katherine Johnson. Is the school
willing to sponsor both teams?"

As British spoke she recognized the eye-rolls. She
was losing her audience. Everyone wanted to get home.
They wanted to be with their families. For the first time
this year, the schools planned to be closed the entire
week of Thanksgiving instead of the last three days of
the week, which was fine, British guessed. She tried to
avoid her family this time of year.

"Why didn't you put in your request sooner?" the
treasurer asked, flipping through a black binder. "I see
no notes here."

"Strange." British glared across at Cam. She twisted
her wedding ring round her finger for confidence. "I
could have sworn I had submitted it at least every other
week since the beginning of the semester, once I heard
about the extra funding. Actually, I gave it to you again
before the school day started."

Cam shrugged his shoulders. "I don't know what
you're talking about."

"I handed in another proposal a week ago." British's
nails scratched at the top of the table. Kimber patted
her on the back, easing her down.

"Last week, when my football player got hurt during practice?" Cam asked and laughed. "I apologize if taking a student to the ER trumped filing your request."

British's eyes narrowed on the director. "I'm ten seconds away from filing a complaint."

The superintendent stood. "I'm sorry, Mrs. Carres, with limited funding, my hands are tied here. Only one program in the school applied for the bonus."

Kimber spoke up. "What about an after-school group?"

The lights flickered once again and gave everyone a glimpse of intrigue on the superintendent's face. "You have an after-school group? I don't recall a budget for one." He looked over at the principal of Southwood Middle School.

"Mrs. Carres uses the recreation center located directly off the school," Principal Terrence advised, beaming. He offered a wink in British's direction.

"All of its members are from the school?" Herbert Locke asked British.

British nodded. "Yes, sir."

"Who funds this project?"

"I do," admitted British. A lump formed in her throat. When her husband, Christian Carres, died five years ago due to complications from a car accident, he'd left her a lump sum of money. There was nothing she'd wanted more than to help the girls of Southwood, Georgia, so she'd poured the money Christian left her into equipment, safety features, you name it.

"Interesting." Herbert stroked the patch of red hair growing on his chin.

"You're not seriously contemplating her request?" Cam squawked.

"If Mrs. Carres turned in her paperwork and you

failed to turn it in—" the superintendent went on "—I don't feel comfortable not supporting them."

"But my robotics team," Cam said through gritted teeth. "We already made plans. I've seen the competition from Black Wolf Creek and Peachville. We've got this in the bag."

"And how do you know?" asked Coach Farmer. He rose from his seat. The hem of his white pullover shirt acted like a hammock for his protruding belly, which lapped the waistband of his red shorts. He spoke in American Sign Language, which he'd initially learned to communicate with the quarterback. For practice and perfection, he always signed now. "Are you spying on the competition?"

Cam sputtered. His bright face reddened. "Competition? What competition?"

Whispers of doubt spread among the committee. British loved to argue her point but if she stood here and let Cam explain himself, she didn't have to say a word.

"So you're not worried about them," baited British, "but you're worried about my girls?"

"Stop trying to make me out to be some sexist, Home Ec."

"Hold on, now," said one of the high school science teachers. "We have a couple of STEM and robotics teams at Southwood High that stepped back for the middle school to receive the funding, but if we're opening the door, we don't mind stepping up to the plate at the competition."

A disgruntled conversation began. All the science teachers, including at the elementary level, wanted a shot to go to Districts.

"All right. All right." Herbert motioned for everyone

to settle down. "I have one pot of money—we can split it evenly or winner takes all."

"Winner takes all," British and Cam chorused.

"Sounds like we have a Southwood competition." Herbert clapped his hands together. "Two weeks from tonight. That will give everyone enough time to enjoy the Thanksgiving break, have time to spend with their families and then get back to the labs and find something interesting to entertain the Christmas Advisory Council. We'll let them decide the winner. Half of the group is made up of organizers for the school drive, and they may just want to have the CAC do this every year if there's leftover funds."

Thunder rumbled outside at his final words. The school district board members gathered their belongings and attempted to file out the double doors in an orderly fashion. British lingered behind the glass doors of city hall, Kimber keeping her company.

"Don't you guys need to get on the road and head for Villa San Juan?"

"Yeah, Nate and Stephen already left with their families," said Kimber. "I wanted to come out and support you."

British linked her arm through the younger girl's. They locked elbows and began walking out the double doors. Rain pelted the brick walkway. "Did you bring your umbrella?"

"Of course not." Kimber laughed. "But I love walking in the rain."

"I can give you a ride, Kimber."

Kimber tugged on British's arm. "Key word being *love*, as in the fact I enjoy it," she giggled.

Cars began leaving the parking lot. Rain fell harder before their wipers could wipe it away. British sighed and glanced at the dark sky. Not even a single star in sight. "You think anyone would notice if I slept here?"

"You can come over and stay at my place tonight," Kimber offered. "I have a nice bottle of wine we can try out."

When British came to Southwood to work as an aide, she did so at Southwood High School, four years after graduating from there herself. She'd been the youngest aide so far and she'd found it hard to gain the respect of the students, until popular Kimber Reyes had spoken up and vouched for her. Five years later she was here with the same girl, who was all grown up. Well, almost.

British shook her head. "No, thanks. I don't like the idea of drinking alcohol with you."

"I am almost twenty-one and it's nonalcoholic."

"Fake wine," British said with a frown. "I can't drink fake wine with you."

"Can't or won't?" asked Kimber. "C'mon, we can go across the street and get drinks. Hot cocoa."

Across the street, the red lights of a sports bar flashed in the evening light. Sprinkles of rain blew through, dampening the front of British's pale pink shirt. The last thing she wanted to do tonight was to spend the evening in a bar with half-drunk men hitting on her because of her suddenly thin wet T-shirt and lacy bra. She missed simpler times when Christian met her during a rainstorm with an umbrella. Funny, she thought with a soft smile, how the memory of him made her feel safe. "No, I'm going to brave the weather."

The committee members had all pulled out of their spots, the twin streetlights brightening the empty parking spaces. Kimber craned her neck. "Where did you park?"

British lifted her hand and pointed adjacent to city

hall. "I have been parked by the rec center all day. I came straight here after everyone left to go home."

Lightning struck across the high school's football field, illuminating the twin field goal posts. How many Friday nights during junior and senior years had she spent watching Southwood High's game-winning field goals take place over there? *Too many to count.* British half smiled and shook the fond memory away.

The rain lifted enough so they didn't have to shout between one other.

"You ought to get going," British urged Kimber. "I'm going to try to make a break for—"

The words died at a loud crack. A clear, sharp, lightning bolt lit the dark sky right over the rec center. A transformer blew, sparks doing their best imitation of Fourth of July fireworks, and two seconds later, regardless of the downpour of rain, a fire broke out.

"Did that seriously just happen?"

Neither of the ladies moved. They both clung to each other. The building went up in smoke, much like British's dreams.

Sunday morning, British found herself seated on a bicycle just outside the gates of the Magnolia Palace hotel. She'd been here before, competing in a few pageants when the roof on Southwood's theater had leaked. There was something to be said about the old structures of her hometown. British inhaled deeply with pride, as if she had a connection with the building.

The fire at the rec center hadn't just ruined an after-school hangout but also displaced a few of the neighbors next to the building, homes of the girls who were part of British's STEM for GRITS.

Ramon Torres, owner of Magnolia Palace, had graciously offered up rooms at the boutique hotel for them to stay until their homes were fixed. The mayor-elect had recently won the hearts of the town but, more important, British's close friend Kenzie Swayne's, too. The two had married last summer.

British understood there was only one guest booked for the Thanksgiving week. More than likely, the man wanted his peace and quiet over the break and having a group of teenagers running through the hallways was not the ideal vacation. British wanted to soften the blow. The phone inside the pocket of her gray hoodie began to ring. British hopped off her bike seat to answer it, her pink fingernail sliding across the screen.

Kimber's face appeared bright and cheerful, as usual. "Hey, my app says you're at my uncle's place."

"That's just creepy."

"Creepy is having to get the girls together in some back alley looking for cans to collect for that STEM steamboat experiment in order to impress the judges," said Kimber. "You're standing outside the door waiting to ring the bell, aren't you?"

"Maybe."

"Uncle Ramon gave you permission to also use the hotel's facilities so the girls can have space to work and concentrate without interruption. You don't have to explain that to the other guest. I've texted you the code to the gate—only guests and employees have the info. The doors lock after midnight until someone is up and unlocks them or, great idea, a person with the code uses it."

"I hear you," British said with a half smile, "but I get what it's like to want to be left alone. I just want to explain to the man, maybe even prepare him."

Kimber huffed. "Whatever."

"He's a paying customer."

"Whoever he is—" Kimber rolled her eyes "—he'll get over it. What did he expect when he came to a hotel?" Someone in the background called her name.

Kimber looked over her shoulder and said something in Spanish. "All right, Brit, I got to get going, but I want to make sure you're okay. I know the place is working with a skeleton crew since there's only one guest booked."

And here British was, about to interrupt this person's day. Forcing a smile onto her face, British smoothed back the stray hairs that had come loose. "Thanks, Kimber. I'll keep you updated."

With that, the call disconnected and British inhaled the fall air. Finally, the rain had stopped. The last of the hurricane season rains brought in the cooler weather. Somewhere off in the distance someone was building a fire. British imagined a group of kids seated around the campfire, fluffy, fat marshmallows dangling from long branches and twigs, taunting the flames. One of the things British hated about living in an apartment. She couldn't randomly make a traditional s'more.

Of course, she could head out to the country, to her parents', for one, but that would end up with everyone fawning all over her. This time of year was difficult. The cooler weather meant hunting season and the memory of losing Christian earlier than she had ever expected. He was born with an enlarged heart, and no one had thought Christian would make it to his first birthday. He'd defied the odds, making it to twenty-three only to have a deer dart out onto County Road 17. British gulped down her bitter sadness. Given Christian's congenital heart problem, the trauma had been too much. He'd survived the accident long enough to make a final joke about the irony and to assure British he loved her.

British cleared her throat and regained her bearings. She needed to secure the place for the girls. The children she and Christian never had the chance to have.

Bound with confidence from Kimber, British punched in the code to the gates and waltzed down the magnolia-lined path toward the old plantation-style home once owned by the Swayne family, now turned into a boutique hotel. Kenzie Swayne's—British's Tiara Squad gal pal—marriage to Ramon Torres right at the end of the summer had brought the home back into the family.

As children, everyone used to hang out here and swim in the lake behind the house. *Ah, the memories*, British thought to herself. The tires of her bicycle crunched on the fallen thick leaves of the magnolias. A wind howled through the tall trees and a shadow formed over the hotel.

"Time to face the dragons," she said to herself. British parked her bike on the bottom step before grabbing the brown wicker basket filled with an assortment of cupcakes from the local bakery responsible for the extra curves on her hips. A couple of fall treats like the Cupcakery's salted caramel pecan, stuffed spice apple, pumpkin swirl latte and the infamous Death-by-Chocolate cupcake always eased loneliness. And British knew that firsthand.

She took a deep breath, headed up the steps and reached for the door handle, but it wouldn't budge. She remembered that the skeleton crew might not be working just yet.

Setting the wicker basket at her feet, British peered through one of the glass panels to the side of the red door as she pressed the doorbell. A chime set off across the polished hardwood floors of the lobby. The check-in station stood empty, the green lamp dark. Then she caught a glimpse of her reflection. She looked a mess in her bunched-up sweatshirt. How was she going to ask some stranger if he would mind her girls staying here during his vacation?

Fingers grasping the hem of the material, she pulled it over her head, but the hoodie locked around the thick ponytail at the back of her head. Groaning, she bent over and gave it a tug, slipping on one of the magnolia leaves scattered on the porch with the last breeze. Her left ankle hit the basket and, to catch herself, she stepped forward and walked straight into the door.

"Sonofabitch," she hissed.

As the door latch clicked from the inside, British's hands locked in their sleeves. The door opened halfway, revealing a square, masculine jawline of a man. Thing was, it wasn't just any man. One jet-black brow arched in wonder while his full lips, surrounded by a close black beard, twisted upward with amusement. The muscle in his biceps twitched and emphasized the definition, making him appear as if a sculpted African god. Chiseled from copper and mahogany wood. The door covered half his face and body, but the exposed parts left her something that hadn't happened in a long time...speechless.

Chapter 2

After a few days of solitude at Magnolia Palace, Donovan welcomed any entertainment, even if it came from a fumbling woman trying to take off her sweatshirt. Donovan bit the inside of his mouth to keep from laughing in her face now that she realized she had an audience—though he hated to admit to being a little disappointed. The silence he'd allowed had given him the chance to admire the curves of her backside. She wore a pair of black canvas shoes and formfitting, light blue jeans. A lot of faith was put into the band that secured her ponytail of thick, curly brown hair. Donovan noticed her doe-like eyes, round, dark and soft. A basket of food sat by her feet and he realized he must be ogling the chef of the hotel.

Since leaving his condo and Miami altogether, Donovan had taken Amelia's suggestion and returned to Southwood, Georgia—by himself. He'd come here last summer to judge a beauty pageant. The original plans were meant to take Tracy away to the boutique hotel off the quiet lake. He'd thought if she'd survived a weekend by herself in his condo, she deserved a private trip. Now Donovan knew better—he'd dropped the girl and kept the reservations.

After escorting the MET crew out of his place, Donovan had cooled his anger downstairs while waiting for Tracy to wake up. It took every ounce of his body not to throw them and the mattress out the window. Was he that much of a pushover for Tracy to sleep with someone else? Was he that less of a man that she needed to bring someone into his bed? The whole thing confused him. She was the first to say she loved him.

Tracy came down, clearly startled to find him home earlier than expected. Donovan let Tracy and her friend leave with the sheets off his bed. The incident with Tracy further proved to Donovan that love was not meant for him. This time alone got him to thinking. Maybe the idea of having someone to love him forever did sound promising, but he hated himself for getting his hopes up. It saddened him to know he'd never have what his sisters and brother had. A family.

Ramon Torres had promised that no one else had booked the boutique hotel for the last two weeks of November. Since it was just going to be him, Donovan had tried to insist Ramon give his staff the week off. No one needed to brave this weather just to accommodate him. But he wasn't going to turn away good food. Not only did this chef have a great behind, she also had impeccable timing. Donovan had just finished the last premade meal she'd packed in the freezer.

Finally adjusted, the chef turned around. Being CFO of a cosmetics conglomerate, Donovan had seen his fair share of beauty. Women threw themselves at him, expecting him to recognize whatever shade of lipstick they wore as one of his company's. Donovan stayed away from the making of the cosmetics part. He even kept his mouth shut when it came to naming their products. But if he had to ever pick a shade or a name for this color, he'd call it *breathtaking*. The chef smiled a wide, toothy grin. The shade of her lips was a mixture of peach and rubies and matched the blush of her cheeks. She didn't belong in the kitchen. She belonged on one of the gold-framed photos hanging on the walls of Ravens Cosmetics. Donovan cleared his throat.

"Hi," she said cheerfully. "Sorry about that."

"No problem." Donovan thanked God for the bass in his voice not failing him, considering the erection now threatening to rip the fabric of his blue mesh shorts, so much so that he thought he'd taken a trip down puberty lane. "Come on in. The kitchen is this way." Donovan opened the door farther and shook his head. "What am I talking about? You know where the kitchen is."

The woman's manicured brows rose but she didn't say anything. Instead she breezed by him, leaving him in the scent of sweet honey. Once inside, Donovan closed the door, his hand still on the crystal knob, preparing himself for the wince most women made when they saw his face.

"The kitchen?" she asked after turning, not batting a long lash but not moving, either. "You expect me to make you something?"

"Well, I know I told Ramon to let the staff go while I'm here. You all don't have to fret over me," said Donovan, "but the premade plates you made were so good and gone as of this morning."

"I think there's been some sort of mistake…" she began.

"My bad." Donovan chuckled out of nervousness. Why was he nervous? "I thought the dishes were for me. I ate them all. And I could eat a horse right about now." A frozen look of horror flashed across her pretty face. "If it makes you uncomfortable, I can go upstairs so you can cook," added Donovan. "I've just been up here for a few days with no one to talk to. I was getting a little stir-crazy."

"Oh." She relaxed her shoulders, giving Donovan a chance to recognize the band moniker on her shirt: New Edition. He'd attended the concert tour named on that shirt, filled out by full breasts. "You're hungry."

"Pardon me?" Donovan's attention snapped back to the walking sexpot. Sure, she'd tried to cover her curves with the shirt and the sweatshirt she'd wrestled with a moment ago, but Donovan recognized her stunning beauty.

"I remember where the kitchen is," she said, inclining her head down the hallway. "C'mon, I don't mind if you want to watch me cook something for you. It will give us a second to talk."

She *did* ask him to follow her. Donovan took full advantage of the view she offered. This time it was the hypnotic sway of her hips. Damn. And he'd told Ramon to send his staff home. Geez, the things he could do with her for a week alone…

"I feel like I haven't been here in forever," she said.

"Well, it's been a few days, I'm guessing," he replied as they entered the large, open space of the kitchen. Donovan waited where the black-and-white tiles of the hallway met the hardwood of the kitchen.

"What are you in the mood for?"

You, he thought. "How about your name?" Donovan asked.

"British," she said, extending her hand.

He narrowed his eyes on her hand. Why had he thought the chef had two first names? Was it because the taxi driver who'd dropped him off at the hotel was named June Bug? The oversize diamond on her left hand, placed on her hip, caught his attention, disappointing him at the same time. So much for his next move, which would have been to kiss the back of her hand. Donovan didn't do married women. "That's an unusual name."

"Well," British replied, "Joan Woodbury, my mother, is a very unusual woman. And you are…?"

"Not an unusual woman," Donovan answered with a half grin, easing into the friendly banter. "I'm Donovan." He left off his last name for some reason. Since British didn't blink at his scar or in recognition of him, he wanted to remain as anonymous as possible while he was here.

"Nice to meet you, Donovan. Now that we have our names straight, what can I get for you?"

"I'm starving. I could eat anything."

British's laugh was light and airy. He liked it. "You're in the country, Donovan. You ought to be careful about saying 'anything.'"

"A little roadkill never hurt anyone," Donovan, affected by her humor, chortled.

"We could skip breaking out the pots and pans and head over to the Roadside Kill Grill." She reached for her sweatshirt but Donovan patted the counter.

"I'm good with a tuna melt."

British winked. "Good to know. That's one of my specialties. But while you're in town you ought to give it a try. Summer barbecues never end in Southwood."

Surely the wink was meant to be teasing. To be safe,

Donovan frowned and shook his head. "I'm good, really."

"Suit yourself," said British. She turned her back to him and headed for the cabinets, opening them one by one, as if she wasn't sure where to find anything.

"Have you always liked to cook?" Donovan asked. He propped his elbows on the counter and watched her search the cabinets for food. "Been doing it long?"

"Oh, all my life," she said. "What about you? Hasn't anyone taught you how to cook?"

"I *can* cook." Donovan felt the need to clarify when she stopped to gather a can of tuna, a jar of relish and a loaf of bread. She used her foot to kick the cabinet door closed and gave him a questioning look. "This just isn't my kitchen to rumble through, other than the microwave for all the meals you left me, which were delicious, by the way," he added.

As if she didn't know how to take a compliment, British pressed her lips together and inhaled deeply. Her large doe-like eyes briefly roamed to the chandelier before returning to meet his gaze. "Well, um…"

"Besides," Donovan went on, not wanting to embarrass her, "I know how chefs are about having other people in their kitchens. I didn't want to step on your toes."

"This is very true."

After she found the right size bowl, British's lovely hands stirred her ingredients together. She wore a pale pink polish on her nails, which were chipped, and she didn't bother once to hide them from him. She was imperfectly perfect and he admired that. Other than standing behind halfway opened doors, there was no way to hide his scar. Maybe he'd give it a try one day. Donovan needed to remind himself that she was someone else's wife.

"With you being a full-time chef," he began, "do you still like to cook for your husband?"

Not looking up, British stopped stirring. Her shoulders rose, chest lifted, and then sagged back down. "My husband passed away a while back."

So young to be a widow. An ache crept through Donovan's rib cage. His brother had recently wed. His parents had been married since the beginning of time. But he'd never known anyone who looked so young to have lost a spouse. "I'm sorry."

"Thanks," British said with a half smile, which exposed her dimples.

"How long were you married?" *Are you prying? You've just met. And why do you feel like some adolescent kid with a crush?* "You don't have to answer me. It's none of my business. I came here for peace and quiet, and here I am." Donovan pressed his lips together. Why was he rambling? He hadn't done so since middle school.

"You're fine, it's been five years since Christian passed away," she murmured. "We were married for three years but we had been together ever since middle school."

Donovan's eyes widened at the idea of being with someone that long. Tracy had been the longest and that was barely six weeks. "Wow." He couldn't remember who he'd taken to his high school prom. Math being his favorite subject, Donovan calculated her age. "You're, like, twenty-three."

"I'm twenty-eight—" she coughed and laughed "—but thanks."

"Country life must suit you." Donovan inclined his head, not realizing until she blushed that he was flirting. When did he flirt? Women flirted with him.

"Is that what you're doing in Southwood, Mr. Donovan? Trying to find the fountain of youth?"

Donovan clutched his heart. "How old do I look?"

British leaned her head to the side and studied him. "Thirty-five."

"Tell me you worked at a carnival," Donovan joked. He touched his chin and wondered if the gray was beginning to show.

"I know." British beamed and curtsied. Sadness disappeared from behind her eyes. "It's a gift I have." She finished the sandwiches and slid them onto a tray and into the broiler. "So is my tuna melt. You're going to be thanking me in a minute or two."

"I can't wait." Donovan rubbed his hands together. When was the last time he'd shared a meal with a woman who didn't want to hit up the latest hot spot?

"But to answer your question, I don't cook full-time. I am a teacher."

"What?" He held his hand in the air. Though she'd said her age, Donovan had a hard time picturing her in a classroom. Okay, maybe kindergarten. "How did you start off?"

"Well—" British inhaled deeply "—if you can believe it, I started out as a home economics teacher."

"They're still around?"

British rolled her eyes. "You'd be amazed at how many need to learn basic life skills."

"Sorry, it's just I remember there being one at my school and she was eighty and smelled like oatmeal cookies."

"I can smell like cookies if you'd like," teased British. And then, as if remembering her manners, she covered her mouth. Her eyes widened in shock, then she blinked, fanning her long lashes. "I can't believe I said that. I promise I'm not some flake."

"Of course not," Donovan said. "Most people I know get trapped by their own sweatshirts."

British tried not to laugh but did so with a crimson tint spreading across her cheeks. She moved her hands to her hips. "See, and here I thought we were becoming friends."

"We are," replied Donovan. "Fast friends. We even might go out for some roadkill barbecue while I'm in town."

"Speaking of you being in town…" British said as the timer went off. "Hang on a sec."

No gawking or flinching at his scar, lunch, and now a show. Donovan mused over his luck while watching British bend over in front of the stove to retrieve her masterpiece. And a masterpiece it was. Cheddar cheese bubbled on top; presentation was a part of her dish. She glanced around the kitchen and reached for one of the half dozen potted plants sitting in the windowsill. She dropped a leaf on the plate and set it in front of him.

"This looks delicious," he said honestly. His stomach grumbled.

"It's also hot. Give it a minute."

Once the heat from the food subsided, Donovan took a quick bite. His mouth savored every morsel while his stomach cried out for more. He stood from the barstool and began to do a little happy dance. "Damn that's good."

British beamed at his compliment.

"Explain to me what it is you do as a home economics teacher?" Donovan inquired as steam rose from his plate. He craved another bite.

"Okay, so let's be clear here, I only took that job as an

aide and to get my foot in the door with the Southwood school district board system," she explained. "I majored in science education and chemistry. I now mainly focus on science, technology, engineering and math."

Donovan raised his brow but kept chewing. "And you work here at the hotel? I would guess the busy time is the summer around here when teachers are out."

Pressing her full lips together, British visibly pondered. "Of course summers are busy for Magnolia Palace, but this," she said as she waved her hands at the vast space of the kitchen, "really isn't my thing."

"What's your thing, then?"

"I mentor a group of girls."

"Great. In cooking?" Donovan said eagerly. He picked up his sandwich and took another bite.

British shook her head from side to side. The curls of her dark brown ponytail bobbed. Flecks of gold in the strands caught the light. "I have been mentoring a group of young ladies in the STEM world."

"Wait. STEM?"

"STEM for GRITS, to be exact." British cleared her throat. "It is important to make sure women know it is okay to use their brains, not just their faces."

Choking, Donovan set down his sandwich. His left eye squinted, almost making his vision of perfection blurry. *Almost*. "Are you aware of who I am?"

"No."

"Have you ever heard of Ravens Cosmetics?"

While Donovan wasn't a part of the marketing or branding teams, he would suggest they name their next shade of lipstick Mistletoe, because all he wanted to do was kiss her. Something about the bow shape of her puckered lips reminded him of the joy he experienced on Christmas morning. A thought occurred to him, wondering what her mouth would feel like against his.

"I've heard of them," said British. "I'm not completely out of touch with society. Are you one of their models?"

The chuckle stemming from the back of his throat turned into a choke. British came around the counter-top and patted him hard on the back.

"You okay?" she asked, sincere concern in her onyx eyes.

Touched, Donovan nodded and ducked out of the way of her next pat. "I'm good. So you said being a teacher is your part-time gig. Is cooking your other?" he asked and lifted his sandwich.

"Okay, I believe it's time I cleared up this misunderstanding."

A look Donovan was definitely used to crept across her pretty face as British bit the corner of her mouth and avoided eye contact. His lack of trust in women, especially after Tracy, set him on edge. Why had he lost sight for a moment and thought she would be any different? Since she hadn't known who he was a few moments ago, Donovan wondered what her angle was. What did she want from him?

"Why are you in my kitchen?"

Before Donovan glanced around to see whose angry voice came from the arched entry into the kitchen, he watched British's eyes widen in surprise.

"So here's the thing..." British began to confess, her eyes darting between the newcomer and Donovan. A grin spread across her face.

"The thing is—" the other woman began, storming into the kitchen. She reached for the white apron around British's waist. "I am *Chef* Jessilyn. I am the chef at Magnolia Palace and I don't know why the hell this woman is in my kitchen."

Donovan sat up in his seat.

"The thing is…" said British. "We had a bit of miscommunication when we first met."

"We met twenty minutes ago," Donovan countered. Irritation and disappointment coursed through his veins.

"I came here because I needed a favor," she began.

"Of course you did." Donovan pushed his plate away. For one brief moment he'd thought she was different.

"Jessilyn!" British exclaimed. "Might I have a word with you in private?"

The newcomer, Jessilyn, jammed her hands onto her hips. She was wearing a pair of overalls rolled at the ankles and a pair of green flip-flops with the same-colored-green tank top under the bib. "Oh, you mean like five years ago, when you were the aide for my teacher who left you in charge of my senior class and I asked you for a moment of time to discuss my grade?"

Donovan watched British's eyes rise as if willing the chef to read her mind. He gathered she didn't, or at least didn't want to, when the chef folded her arms over her chest. The whole scene reminded Donovan of being younger and having his older brother, Marcus, hold information over his head. British was up to something.

"You can't possibly still be mad," said British. "It's not like you failed."

"But I did not graduate with a perfect 4.0."

Not sure if this was a private conversation or not, Donovan decided to leave—with his plate. He headed for the porch and sat on the front swing. Along with accepting he'd be alone for the rest of his life, Donovan figured getting involved at any level with another woman was a good thing to avoid.

In three more bites, the tuna melt disappeared. Besides the bickering inside the kitchen, the rest of the property was quiet. Birds chirped in the afternoon sun. At least it had stopped raining. Someone nearby had a fire going. Donovan didn't think there were any neighbors close to the hotel.

Footsteps neared and squeaked on the black-and-white tiles of the foyer. The door pulled open; Donovan wasn't disappointed to find British standing in front of him.

"I apologize, Mr. Ravens, for misrepresenting myself. When you opened the door I was a bit confused myself. You thought I was the chef and you seemed starving." British nodded her head. "I wanted to help."

Donovan set the plate on the seat beside him and crossed one leg over the other. "You said you had a favor to ask of me. I'm curious, what is it?"

"How much of a fan are you of peace and quiet?" British asked with a half grin. Her heart-shaped face flushed with anxiety, probably from having been caught in a lie.

"Humor me and ask."

"Well, now, that's mighty cocky of you, Mr. Ravens," said British. Both hands went to her hips. The stance put Donovan at an even eye level with Ronnie, Bobby, Ricky, Mike and Ralph of New Edition. The next time the band got together for a concert, Donovan was going to have to tell them how close he'd been to them. Realizing she misread his gaze, British folded her arms across her chest. "I didn't realize you weren't a gentleman," British drawled.

"Not a nice thing to say when you're asking for favors."

British pressed her index finger against the dimple of her right cheek. "Perhaps I was wrong in stating I needed a favor. It is more like a warning."

Amused, Donovan came to his feet. He stood a good foot taller than her. "I don't respond well to threats, British."

"It's not a threat. I came over here to warn you that your peace-and-quiet vacation is about to be disrupted by my GRITS."

"I have no idea what you're talking about," Donovan said, enjoying the way she spoke. Who was this woman? Chef? Teacher? Mad scientist?

"Girls Raised in the South." British added an annoyed sigh. "But I wouldn't expect you to understand the importance of women and science and math."

To the contrary, he knew. His family's company succeeded due to the efforts of women in chemistry and accounting. Great-Grandma Naomi Ravens owed her success to the cosmetic products she'd helped develop, combining natural ingredients with science. For the last fifty years the family has partnered with chemists to create bright quick-drying nail polish, products to keep hair healthy and long-lasting lipsticks.

With her hands on her hips, British took a step backward. Her foot kicked the basket he'd forgotten she'd left on the porch. "You sell makeup." The way she said it made his job sound like a dirty deed.

"I am having a hard time understanding what is wrong with cosmetics."

"Nothing," British said through her gritted, pearly white teeth. She really had an untouched beauty, something he didn't see in the industry. Donovan crossed his arms and listened. "Makeup is fine and all, I just want my girls to realize there's more to life than lip gloss and mascara."

"Okay?" Donovan responded slowly. "Why are you mad at me all of a sudden?"

"Because I know your type."

And before Donovan had a chance to form the thoughts to defend himself, British bounced down the stairs toward a pink bicycle. "Unbelievable."

"So how did it go today?"

Before looking up, British swiped her index finger along the rim of the white paper liner of her sweet potato pecan pie cupcake to savor the rich vanilla frosting oozing on the side. A moan escaped her throat. She loved being a taste tester at the Cupcakery.

"I have no idea how or where to start, Maggie," British said to her friend, who waltzed over with a pink-and-black polka-dot apron draped around her tiny waist. For the life of her, British had no idea, one, how Maggie Swayne stayed so skinny working here and, two, why she was even here at all. The social butterfly flitted from fashion week to fashion week yet for the last month she'd resided here in Southwood, her hometown.

"That bad, huh?" Maggie set her round serving tray on the new bar, recently installed. Maggie propped her elbows on the counter. "Want to tell me about it?"

"Are you like the shrink-bartender?"

"Consider me your friendly cupcake-tender."

"I am good," said British.

"I know I am not Kenzie, but you can talk to me."

More pity, British thought. "Trust me, Maggie, I am perfectly fine."

"If you say so. I just know you came by this morning for cupcakes and here you are now."

"Those were for the guest at Magnolia Palace." British cringed just as the words left her mouth, remembering how the hotel once belonged to the Swaynes.

Maggie picked up a white rag and began wiping the clean counter.

"Don't worry about me," said Maggie with an indifferent shrug. "Once Kenzie and Ramon tied the knot last summer, the house basically returned to the family."

"I am not sure that's exactly how it works," laughed British. "It's still a hotel."

Accepting that, Maggie stopped her cleaning and leaned against the counter, close to British. "So who is the guy renting the room for the month?"

Small-town gossip spread like proverbial wildfire and if Maggie Swayne knew something, it'd only be a matter of time before everyone else did. But if Maggie didn't know by now, perhaps it *was* meant to be a secret. A heated flash of memory struck British like the bolt of lightning she'd felt when she'd first laid eyes on Donovan through the fabric tunnel of her sweatshirt. Now that she was clear of the space around him, British was able to think.

British recalled a time when she loved makeup just as much as the next girl. It wasn't until college when she worked in labs that she realized how it served as a distraction for the other scientists. Men acted as if her perfect lipstick lowered her IQ. After a while she stopped wearing it as much. As a former beauty queen who'd often used cosmetics, she should have known. Ravens Cosmetics sponsored high-title pageants. Last year, one of the brothers had judged the big Southwood Beauty Pageant. And now that she thought of it, it had been Donovan. The family had also come to Southwood for Will Ravens's wedding to makeup artist Zoe Baldwin. The Ravenses and their cosmetics were in every print fashion magazine as well as in ads on the internet. Donovan favored his brothers in photographs, but in person? The scar along the left side of his face gave him a danger-ously dashing look. Well—British shivered—the man was larger than life.

"Wow!" Maggie exclaimed. "You just got that to-tally faraway look women get when they're lusting after someone."

British hadn't realized her mouth hung wide open until she closed it. She shook her head and scoffed, "Oh, that is so not true. Whatever. Be quiet."

"What's going on?"

British's eyes flashed Maggie a warning glare when the French doors to the kitchen opened. Out walked Tiffani Carres, British's sister-in-law. Or was it former sister-in-law? Either way, the last person she wanted to find out about this was Christian's younger sister. Since Tiffani's birth, British had always been in her life. Christian had brought British to the hospital to meet her when they were in grade school. The idea of British get-ting involved with another man seemed like betrayal.

"Nothing," British quickly said.

"Some man has British blushing."

Tiffani, now twenty-two and grown, smirked mis-chievously. Her dark brown eyes sparkled under her raised brows. "Anyone we know?"

"Tiffani," British said with a warning shake of her head.

"What?" Tiffani blinked innocently. "Don't tell me you're worried about what I would think?"

"We-ell," British drawled.

With a shake of her head, Tiffani rolled her eyes. "Please. Mommy and I were just talking about this the other day."

As if on cue "Mommy," Vonna Carres, entered through the black-and-white French doors, carrying a cardboard box overflowing with green and red garlands. The only things visible other than her black apron with its pink-and-white trim of polka dots were her hands.

"I hear my name," said Vonna over the box, a gold, sparkled star poking out from the top. Her soothing, melodic voice warmed British's soul.

"British is interested in someone," Tiffani announced.

British cut her eyes to Maggie, willing her to understand the thankless, sarcastic smile she flashed. She missed Christian deeply. She still wore her wedding ring to secure his memory. British missed everything about him, from their silly fights to their deep philosophical conversations over '80s vs. '90s music. British accepted she'd never remarry and had never come close to falling in love since. But she missed the company of the opposite sex, still not something her in-laws needed to know. The last thing she wanted to do was let Christian's family think British had betrayed their son's memory by fawning over some random stranger.

While British dated here and there, she never discussed seeing anyone else with her in-laws. Since she wasn't looking to get married, she didn't see the need to bring her dates around her family. Not one of the men she'd been out with had been special enough. No one could make British consider physical contact. But she had to admit, besides a good conversation over dinner every once in a while, the touch of a man's hands might be nice, too. "No one said anything about my being interested in anyone."

"Well, it's about damn time."

Now Maggie smirked at British.

Sliding the box onto the counter, Vonna took a step back and rubbed her hands together. For a half second British thought her mother-in-law was in pain, but the excited smile spreading across her medium-brown skin told her something else. It annoyed British every time someone told her how much Christian had looked like his father. British saw Christian every time she looked at Vonna.

"British, dear." Vonna stepped up to the counter and reached across the marble slate to pat British's hand. "It's been five years. It's about time someone, anyone, catches your attention."

British pulled her arm away, surprised at Vonna's statement. Her shoulders slumped as relief washed over her. "Maggie is speaking out of turn," she explained. "I gave her no information."

"But she did blush," Maggie interjected.

"Why are you even working here?" British half teased. "Don't you have the world to dazzle via social media?"

Maggie snarled and snatched her rag away. "Fine. Whatever. My job here is done."

Once Maggie stepped away to wipe off a silver-topped table in the corner, Vonna raised her left brow and, wordlessly, Tiffani took the box away. "Now that we're alone," Vonna began, "what's going on?"

British glanced to her left and right. The Cupcakery was full but not jam-packed as if there were a new cupcake debut today. There were enough couples at the tabletop and at the bar. When she glanced back up at Vonna, British shook her head. "Please don't tell me you and Tiffani are on the same page about this."

"Sweetheart," Vonna said with a sigh, "I know you've tried your hand at dating."

"Failed dating," British blurted out. "Wait, how'd you know?"

Vonna shrugged her shoulders. "I get my fresh ingredients all around Four Points. People will tell me anything for one of my famous cupcakes when they bring their deliveries here. By the way, what do you think?" She nodded her head at the empty wrapper on British's plate.

"Delicious, as expected."

"It just needs a name, just like you need a man," Vonna continued. "You've been alone too long."

"I'm not alone," British argued. "I have you, Tiff and my family."

"That's not enough."

"I have my students," she boasted. "They keep me pretty busy."

With a skeptical eye, Vonna nodded. "Woman cannot live by the livelihood of children alone."

"Vonna."

Ignoring her, Vonna continued, tapping her short-manicured finger on British's wedding ring. "Do you think Christian would want you sitting around here for this long, pining away for him?"

British wrung her hands together. The rock scraped against her palm, leaving her with an ache. Christian, being diagnosed with hydrotropic cardiomyopathy early on in life, had always made British reassure him she'd move on. His enlarged heart limited their time together. She'd said she would. *When the time was right.*

British's heart swelled at the mention of his name out loud. When he first passed away, her heart would seize and tears would flow. British looked away in shame for not crying right now. Did this mean she was she forgetting him now? "I hear you, Vonna," mumbled British.

"I don't think you do. No one says you have to get married. Maybe a good roll in the hay?"

"Vonna!" British gasped.

"Whatever. But if what Maggie says comes to frui-
tion, I'd like to meet this man at the dance in a few
weeks. I promised the school board I'd donate cupcakes
for the middle school soiree."

Her mother-in-law pushed away from the counter
before British had a chance to deny what Maggie had
said. "I promise you, Vonna, if and when I meet the
second most perfect guy in the world, I'll introduce
him to you."

The silver bells over the front door jingled. British
kept her back turned but knew a man must have walked
through the door as Maggie swayed against the tabletop
with a "Lord Sweet Jesus" sigh. Tiffani cursed when the
contents of the box her mother had brought out spilled.
Even Vonna straightened and smoothed down the front
of her apron.

British smiled and turned to excuse herself when a
pink to-go box brushed her wrist. For some unknown
reason she apologized then glanced up, only to find
herself looking up at none other than Donovan Ravens.

Chapter 3

"Just so you know, your disappearing act is going to cost us a little over a million dollars."

The exaggerated brotherly badgering was not something one wanted to hear the first thing the next morning. It was a Monday. Donovan rubbed a hand across his beard. Since being on this hiatus from work, he'd considered shaving off the damn thing but the double honk of the caravan of cars outside Magnolia Palace reminded him of the visitors rolling into the hotel for the week. What had the hot teacher told him the other day? A couple of schoolgirls and their parents? He sighed and shook his head into the camera of his laptop. On the other end, down in his office in Miami, Donovan's older brother, Marcus, chuckled.

"You don't seem fazed one bit," said Marcus.

"I'm not," Donovan replied. "This time off was requested two weeks ago."

"Vacation suits you. Are you planning on telling me where you are?"

Donovan cocked his head to see around Marcus's big head. "Where's Will?"

Marcus glanced up then back at the screen. "Speak of the devil."

"You guys talking about me again?" Will, their younger brother, said, coming around to Marcus's side of the desk. Both men wore their signature suits, custom tailored at that. "What's up? Where are you?"

"I'm taking care of myself." Donovan dismissed his brothers' curiosity. "What's going on with this alleged million dollars I am costing the company? I am the chief financial officer. I think I'd know if we are in danger."

"We were banking on the announcement for the new face of RC coming this weekend, so we can go ahead and book the production team," explained Marcus. "The crew is now on retainer so they don't take any jobs over the holidays. We had to make a sweet deal in order to do so. Zoe agreed with me."

With Zoe Baldwin, makeup artist extraordinaire on board as the creative director, business had never been better. Profits were through the roof last quarter, and that was despite buying out half of the Ravens cousins for their shares.

"Did Zoe say something?"

"You mean Zoe, my *wife*?" Will clarified his claim by puffing out his chest. Probably the best decision his brother had ever made was marrying Zoe. The two of them together were a powerhouse in the beauty business.

Back before Will had come into the family business, Zoe had been not just a freelance makeup artist, but a good friend of the family business. She'd see Donovan and Marcus on assignment as well as around town at social events. They were friends. Zoe always gave her two Ravens brothers-in-law a hard time about their playboy lifestyle.

Donovan shook his head and huffed in annoyance. "You don't need to remind us every time we talk," he said. "We were at the wedding." The small ceremony was held right here on the same grounds where Donovan was vacationing.

"I just wanted to make sure," Will joked and grinned. "But seriously, she is concerned for you and your relationship with Tracy Blount, after what she heard."

"Are you telling me I have a reputation *now*?" Donovan asked with a smirk. He lifted his coffee mug to his mouth and blew. He could give a crap about the rumor mill. Thanks to the gossip columnists keeping track of Donovan and Tracy's dates, fans were rooting for the supermodel. Hell, he too thought she might have been the one. He admired that she never asked him for anything and liked that Tracy didn't require him to stand as her arm candy at events. But alas, she was just another failed relationship for Donovan, this time caught on camera. When everyone else found out they'd all side with Tracy and pin her as the martyr for putting up with seeing his face every day for six weeks. At least this time there'd be video to explain the breakup. Donovan's ego had taken a blow. What was worse, a woman cheating on you or the fact it happened in his own bed? How humiliated was he going to be? For entertainment purposes he asked anyway. "Wait, what's being said?"

"That you had plans to propose to her," answered Will.

Hot coffee spewed onto the keyboard. "What?"

"That's what I'm saying," said Marcus, smacking

his hand on the arm of his chair. "I wagered a million bucks with Will that there's no way you're thinking about settling down."

"Your money is safe, big bro," Donovan replied flatly.

"Well, when are you coming back?"

"Are bills not being paid?" Donovan asked, emphasizing his sarcasm. He pushed away from the desk and walked backward to the bathroom, where he'd kept his towel from his shower this morning, but it was still wet. He took the shirt off his back and wiped the black keyboard. Will and Marcus groaned. Donovan sneered and winked, proud of the time and effort he put into the gym.

"Put that bird chest away," said Marcus.

"Dear God, man," Will gasped, "your chest is as bare as a baby's bottom."

Donovan flipped them both the middle finger. "Is there a reason for this call or did you just want to bust my chops?"

Marcus leaned back in his chair. "I'm still curious about where you are."

Will leaned close to the monitor and stared beyond Donovan's frame. Donovan pushed the screen to face the ceiling. "Well, if there's nothing else…"

"Wait," said Will. "What's the deal with Tracy?"

Discussing what exactly had transpired in his condo was not something Donovan planned to discuss with his brothers. "What?"

"I'm talking about her being the face of RC next year."

"Not happening," said Donovan, pulling the screen down in time to see Will rake his hand over his face.

"You are aware you're the chief financial officer," reminded Will. "I'm the CEO."

"Do you want to test me, little bro?" Donovan asked his brother with a questioning brow.

"What I want is a fresh new face to reveal at midnight," Will declared without backing down. "One that's not in every music video or perhaps even your bed. Clearly I'm not getting that."

Donovan sighed at his brother. "And why not?"

"Look, I've been courting Tracy's agency for months now. I might be obligated to use her."

The ad campaign was going to kick off Christmas Eve. The makeup for this line had cost millions to make vegan friendly. Donovan hadn't known Will had considered Tracy as the new face, nor did he care. "Find someone else."

"*You* find someone," Will snapped back in annoyance.

Donovan gnashed his teeth together to keep from commenting. He tried to understand the pressure of his younger brother. They, Donovan and his siblings included, helped place him in the position as CEO of Ravens.

"Models are crawling all over this place," said Marcus, the peacemaker. "We can come up with someone."

Will leaned forward to the monitor, pressing his fists on the table. "No. See, this is the problem with you dating the models around here, Donovan. When you get tired of them, it's our job to smooth things over. I'm usually scrambling to find a print ad for your throwaways, but not this time."

"What?" Donovan asked, feeling a headache building. The girls outside his window began to squeal. Now he understood why the teacher had come over here with her tasty bribery basket. No way there'd be peace and quiet with them around.

"I am serious, Donovan," Will said in a clipped tone. "You screwed this up, *you* find the perfect model."

How had Tracy's disrespectful infidelity become his fault? "I'm on vacation," said Donovan with a yawn.

"Not my problem," Will huffed. "If you don't find someone by Christmas, I'm hiring Tracy."

Donovan attempted to weigh his options but couldn't... not with all the hollering. Footsteps echoed down the stairs, followed by parents telling the girls to be quiet and stop disturbing the upstairs guest. Too late.

"Miss B's here!" a girl yelled.

British? Donovan wondered. He stepped away from the desk and strolled over to the open balcony. Downstairs he spotted her, British Carres. She stepped out of a sleek black Accord with gold trim. First came her long legs, encased in a pair of formfitting jeans, a white T-shirt with black writing—BBD, for Bell, Biv, DeVoe, if he wasn't mistaken—knotted at her hip and accentuating her curves. British stood to her full height and with her left hand loosened the bun at the top of her head. Mounds of curls spilled down her neck and over her shoulders. Sunlight caught the natural gold highlights of her tresses.

"Do you hear me, Donovan?" Will yelled. "I am pulling rank on you."

"He's on vacation, Will," said Marcus.

"Oh, and Donovan..." Will called out.

"What?" Donovan growled.

"Make sure the one you pick isn't one you've slept with already."

Donovan leaned against the open door of the balcony and folded his arms across his chest. He was pretty sure he'd found the perfect woman—whether for the ad or for him was yet to be determined.

* * *

British had finally arrived at Magnolia Palace on Monday morning ready for work and perhaps a little rest from constant family calls. With Thanksgiving this week, everyone in British's Woodbury family wanted her to promise to stop by for dinner, as well as the historic Woodbury events after the festive holiday. British purposely left her cell phone in her car and closed the door just as it began ringing again.

Inside the foyer of the hotel, the four competing girls from STEM for GRITS made their way down the steps to greet British. The team voted on their strongest members to start off the competition. Lacey's, Stephanie's, Kathleen's and Natasha's homes had been damaged by the fire at the recreation center. Insurance had covered the roofs but their parents appreciated this time for their girls to be able to concentrate on coming up with ideas for the STEM project.

Thanks to Ramon—and with Kenzie's urging— Southwood had recently resurrected the old post office, turning it into a new recreation center. Unfortunately, because of British's insistence, two teams at Southwood High had booked the new recreation center, also owned by Ramon.

Two of the girls and their families had taken up the offer to stay on the property. The other two girls had come to hang out and plot together today. The last text British had looked at before she'd left her apartment complex indicated that the girls were going to take a tour of the property. British guessed a part of the tour would be a high-speed foot chase. Who said boys were the only ones allowed to be rough?

"No running," British yelled out and accepted the card key from the casually dressed desk clerk. She guessed having more than one guest at the hotel had brought in more staff members for the Thanksgiving week. British offered an apologetic smile and hiked her weekender bag over her shoulder. The simple movement jacked up the short sleeve of her pumpkin-colored sweater on her biceps. The movement caused her to think about the sole guest at Magnolia Palace. Donovan Ravens.

When she'd left the Cupcakery, she'd hoped she had done so without causing any suspicion from her in-laws, Vonna and Tiffani. They, along with Maggie, were smitten and flattered that the handsome stranger had made the trip into town for more cupcakes. If they'd guessed she was the one who had first brought him the cupcakes, they hadn't let on. British found herself glancing upward and held her breath. Was she looking for him? *Dang it, Vonna.* British groaned and pushed her mother-in-law's words out of her mind.

Chef Jessilyn met British in the foyer by the front desk and, a smirk on her face, wiped her hands on a red-and-white-checked washcloth.

"Jessilyn," British began to say as she stared at the red bows tied at the ends of Jessilyn's twin French braids, "it's nice to see you again."

"For the record, I will not be serving you *peach pie*," Jessilyn warned.

The most British could do was sigh in annoyance. Clearly, Jessilyn was never going to get over the grade she'd been assigned. Given the largest peach producers came from the Southwood quad-state area, British's final assignment to her students had been a peach pie. British guessed she should have picked up on Jessilyn's baking talent when she'd turned in a peach cobbler with homemade peach ice cream, but that was not the assignment.

"No one is asking you to," said British. She never knew if Jessilyn, who'd regularly earned a 4.0 since kindergarten, resented having her perfect GPA lowered or if it had anything to do with not respecting British as her authority figure at the time. "Even if you did, I can't go back into the system and change your grade for you."

"Can't or *won't*?" Jessilyn asked with a narrowed glare.

This was going to be a long week. Perhaps she needed to order out for meals. British shook her head and rolled her eyes.

Someone else hollered, "Whoa! Staff crossing here," and then laughed at the chorused apology from the rambunctious girls. Mrs. Fitzhugh appeared at the entrance of the east hallway, dressed casually, like the desk clerk, in a pair of khaki pants and a white pullover shirt. Mrs. Fitzhugh used to work as a seamstress and had seen a lot of British when she'd come into her shop to have a pageant dress altered. Not only was Southwood home to peaches, it also produced several beauty queens.

"I'm sorry, Mrs. Fitzhugh," said British.

The girls appeared at the elderly woman's side. "We need a light signaling someone's in the hallway," Lacey Bonds suggested.

"Or—" British reached out and tugged on the red bill of Lacey's baseball cap "—you could try not running indoors, huh?"

At least Lacey had the common sense to hold her head low as she apologized to Mrs. Fitzhugh.

Jessilyn made her presence known with a scoff.

British inhaled deeply. "I have students who actually want to work, Jessilyn, so if you'll excuse me."

British hiked her bag once more, this time tugging

down her sleeve before stepping onto the circular staircase. If she was going to chase after her students, she needed to set her belongings down.

"Ms. B," Lacey drawled in her rich Southern accent, "we can help you."

The rest of the musketeers—Stephanie, Kathleen and Natasha—came up behind Lacey.

Last summer, the preteen engineering expert Natasha had placed first at robotics camp with her fifth-grade class. She'd been heartbroken when she hadn't qualified to be on the robotics team at Southwood Middle School.

Coding was Kathleen's specialty. She'd coordinated the best back-to-school light show earlier this year in the cafeteria.

As delicate as her name was, Lacey was quite the tomboy and math whiz. She could calculate how much force to put into a soccer ball and where to kick to make it spin. Wholly the opposite of her best friend, Stephanie loved everything girlie. She was their budding chemist. She found a way to counter her parents' rule against not wearing makeup by using cherries to stain her lips.

"Thanks, Lace," British said, not fighting the tug at the handle of the weekend bag. Because she lived in Southwood, British didn't pack a lot of things. Her variety of canvas shoes mainly weighed the most. For a moment she regretted not bringing anything feminine like a cute lacy top and some sandals, just in case she ran into Donovan.

Lacey threw the bag over her shoulder as if it was nothing. "Your room is up here," said Lacey. The energetic girl took two steps at a time and talked over her shoulder. "Mama thought you might want to stay at the other end of the hall, away from us."

"Yeah," Natasha chimed in, making the task a race. Heavy footsteps echoed and rattled the gold-framed portraits hanging from the walls. "Something about us making a lot of noise since Miss Kenzie said the four of us could stay in the same room together. She said there's only one other person over here."

"Wasn't that sweet of her," British cooed with a sarcasm the girls didn't pick up on. "I'm going to have to send her a thank-you note." Kenzie knew what she was doing.

Parents often made beauty pageants awkward and competitive. British was fortunate to start off early with toddler pageants and bonded with the other girls who later became close friends of hers throughout life. They called themselves the Tiara Squad. British served as a bridesmaid to Felicia Ward last summer and attended Kenzie's private ceremony. The other girls in her Tiara Squad had married, and everyone had tried to find a way to get British back into the dating market. If she ever was in the dating market. She'd dated here and there but no one had caught her attention long enough the way Christian had.

With Christian, she loved his patience and understanding. He made her feel like the only woman in the world who mattered. It never mattered if she didn't receive the highly prized title in a beauty pageant; she was always his queen. Christian drove her everywhere and whenever she wanted to speak with other girls at pageants about STEM.

The girls raced down the long hallway toward the private rooms. British knew from past experience when she and her family had come here on the weekends about the some of the rooms connecting. Hopefully in all the renovations Ramon had sealed off the joint bathrooms. The idea of being next door to Donovan caused her heart to skip a beat with anticipation.

"No running," British called out to the girls, who responded with a fit of giggles. The last thing she wanted to do was to disturb Donovan. She wasn't ready to face him again. A flock of butterflies fluttered around in the pit of her stomach. British bit her bottom lip and took a deep breath.

Besides knowing what Donovan did for a living, British had deduced something personal about the man. He'd been in an accident at some point in his life. A serious one. And while the girls were usually polite, they were still children and the X-shaped scar said a lot about the trauma Donovan had faced in his past. British didn't want him to feel bad or to be reminded. Maybe that's why he hid himself away in a hotel in Southwood.

For British, the scar along Donovan's face also told her he'd survived something. In Christian's car accident, his face had hit the steering wheel and the stitches the doctors had tried to put in were in the shape of an X, as well. In the little bit of time Christian had left on earth, he had worried about being seen as a monster and frightening children. It was a ridiculous thought and British had told him so. She would give anything to argue with him over the mark again.

"Ms. B?" Kathleen tapped British's arm.

Snapping out of her daze, British plastered on a smile. "Sorry."

"You were doing that daydreaming my grandma gets," informed Kathleen.

British pouted. "Are you calling me old?"

"Well, compared to us—ouch," Stephanie whined

and pulled her microbraids to the front of her shirt. "No, ma'am."

"Good," said British as she grabbed for her bag and hunched over. "Now let a little old lady get into her room so she can take her afternoon prune juice and nap."

"Tasty," commented a deep voice from the corner of the hallway.

The familiar baritone boomed, making British's heart lurch into her rib cage. She had to clear her throat to release its lodged state. "Donovan."

"So you're my neighbor?" The shadows of the hallway hid all but his kilowatt smile.

A hard shiver crept down her spine, causing British to jump.

"Sorry," said Donovan, "I didn't mean to scare you." He stepped out from the shadows.

The girls made a collective sigh. Lacey dropped the bag in her hand. Donovan grabbed it before it hit the ground and the other girls' feet.

"I thought I heard a lot of movement going on inside this morning. Here—" he reached for the card key in British's hand "—allow me."

"You're Donovan Ravens," Stephanie finally said.

Donovan glanced over his shoulder, his thick black eyebrows raised. "I am."

"You know who he is?" Lacey asked.

"You don't?" Stephanie countered. "He's only the Chief Financial Officer at Ravens Cosmetics. If you wore a little bit of makeup ever, you might notice."

Donovan opened the hotel room door and allowed the girls in first. British lingered behind and tried to hide her amused smile behind her hand at Donovan's surprise. "That's Stephanie," British explained. "Your future employee in your cosmetic chemistry department."

* * *

Donovan had been around his younger cousins' friends enough to know when they were enamored with one of his brothers. Oddly, these tweens giggled the same way with him. Maybe it was a nervous giggle due to the scar. Each girl avoided making eye contact when British introduced them.

"Thanks for your help, ladies," British said, clearing her throat once they were inside her room.

Taking their cue, the four girls excused themselves but not before eyeballing him up and down. Nothing like a group of teenage girls to make a grown man feel self-conscious. At least his future employee edged her friends out of the room. Or so he thought. Alone, he realized it left just him and British. Given her hand on her hip, the dismissive smirk and raised eyebrow, she was giving him a cue to leave.

"And thanks for bringing my bag in," she said.

Donovan gripped the leather handles and set the weekender on the gold-and-white-striped bench at the end of the mahogany sleigh bed. "What do you have in here, bricks? Oh wait, shoes."

"You're so smart," British said, her eyes crinkling, at the edges. For a moment he thought she might poke her tongue out at him.

The pit of his stomach flopped with the idea of her doing so. Why? Married, widowed or whatever—if she was going to be the face of RC, she was Grade A hands off.

"If you must know, there are shoes in here."

"Since when did Manolo make heavy shoes?" His joke didn't go over well. British narrowed her dark eyes on him. If looks could kill...

She ran her long fingers through her thick, dark,

curly hair. Photographers created lighting with special bulbs and reflections for scenes like this.

"Maybe," she sneered, "you're used to women who pack only expensive high heels, but I'm packing canvas. Converse, to be exact." To prove herself, British yanked open her bag and held up a pink low-top shoe, then a kelly green high-top. She attempted to reach for another but Donovan raised his hands in surrender.

"All right, you win," he said. "I didn't mean to wage war with you."

"What did you plan with me?" British asked.

Dare he say how temptation made his fingers twitch with eagerness to toss her onto the bed and kiss away whatever sadness was hiding behind her eyes?

"Well?" British snapped at him.

"Jesus, lady," Donovan chuckled, "what do you have against me?"

The crinkles in her forehead softened. British blinked her long lashes. "I'm sorry," she sighed. "I don't have anything against you."

"Good."

"Just your company," she added.

An invisible dagger dug into Donovan's chest. "Ouch. May I ask what my company did?"

"Where do I begin?" British scoffed. "You guys hire airhead models that my students then follow and emulate. Before I started teaching Stephanie the importance of women in science, she aspired to be an Instagram model."

Donovan refrained from laughing. He did, however, press his hand to his heart. "Somehow this is my fault?"

"No," British quipped.

Never before had a woman argued with him about

her dislike for the company. Be still, his beating heart. Donovan stopped the argument with a half smile.

"Why are you staring at me with a goofy grin?"

"I think you're perfect," he answered honestly.

A deep red tint spread across British's high cheekbones. She folded her arms over three of the former members of New Edition's faces on the T-shirt. "Do you seriously think your lines would work on getting me to…?" Her words trailed but her eyes roamed to the queen-size bed.

This time Donovan did chuckle. "I think we have our wires crossed."

"Excuse me?" British leaned forward. "You're not trying to get me into bed?"

"I feel like that's one of those loaded questions," Donovan hedged, "where either answer is going to get me in trouble."

British pointed to her door. "Get out."

"Wait," he said, holding his hands up in a pleading defense. "I'm talking about my company. We need a new spokesmodel and I honestly think you'd be perfect."

A few moments went by. A hummingbird pecked at the window. The bells of the grandfather clock downstairs chimed the morning's hour. When British cleared her throat, Donovan was sure she was about to agree. Who wouldn't? Women threw themselves at him for an offer like this.

"Go to hell and get out."

Chapter 4

"All right, girls." British clapped her hands together to get the foursome's attention.

After she'd gotten rid of Donovan and his lecherous offer, British had allowed the girls an hour to run around and do whatever, but now it was time for business.

She closed the white French doors to the library but one of the door handles hit her in the back when it bounced open again. Bright light shone through the solarium porch, which offered a lovely yet distracting view of the lake out back. Sun danced off the ripples in the water and sparkled like diamonds and highlighted books that flanked one another in no particular height or order. Leather-bound classic tales stood next to new romances. Oh, what she would give to spend the afternoon here and put things in order. But she had things to do right now.

Natasha's and Stephanie's eyes were glued to Stephanie's phone. British clapped twice again. "Hello? Please don't make me take your phone away."

"Sorry, Ms. B," said Stephanie.

"She's afraid her boyfriend is looking at other girls."

Stephanie elbowed Natasha in the ribs. "He's not my boyfriend."

"Whatever he is," British said, taking a deep breath to tamp down her amusement, "he can wait until we finish going over the rules I just received for the STEM-Off." She was met with a round of groans as she extracted the folded piece of paper she had printed off from the superintendent this morning. "You guys are familiar with competitions. There are five groups. You, the boys from Southwood Middle, two high school teams and one group from the elementary school."

An almost collective *aww* and *how cute* filled the room.

British looked up and cleared her throat. She held her hand out in front of Kathleen to turn over the handheld game system and continued without missing a beat in reading the directions. From what she gathered, the competition would be set up like one of the baking challenges she'd watched on the Food Network. There would be two challenges: a small round and a bigger round incorporating each faction of STEM. If they won the small STEM challenge, they could add another member to their team for the bigger STEM challenge. British liked the girls to do work on simple everyday items people didn't realize used science, technology, engineering or math. The girls needed to brainstorm their ideas. Once they got into that room, the teachers were no longer able to help. Teachers would be designated seats behind the judges. At Districts, there'd be no teachers at all. The teams were going to have to come up with a variety of supplies needed for the Southwood competition and be prepared for any task they were given.

"Can we come up with a new video game, one where the girl is the heroine? That way we can cover engineering and tech, and she can be a scientist," Kathleen spoke up. "Ya know?"

"Considering a lot of judges on the Christmas Advisory Council are women—" British said, trying to focus on the page in front of her. The tiny hairs on the back of her neck rose. Odd that she sensed him there. The only presence she'd felt before was Christian's. It also helped to see that Donovan managed to evoke that familiar, googly-eyed gaze not just from women at the Cupcakery but also from impressionable teenage girls. "Mr. Ravens?" British called out. "We're trying to brainstorm down here."

Not caring, Donovan stepped through the half-closed French doors, oblivious as to how his tight white shirt hugged his muscular frame or the way the well-worn denim hugged those thick thighs and tapered waist. He claimed to work in the office at Ravens Cosmetics but if she didn't know any better British would swear the man simply worked out for a living.

"I don't mean to pry." His deep voice chilled her bones.

"Of course not," British mumbled, rubbing her left hand over her right forearm to keep the goose bumps away.

"I didn't realize you all were going to be meeting here in the library," Donovan went on to say.

"Did you need a book, Mr. Ravens?" Stephanie asked, getting up from her spot. "Or maybe a magazine?"

British shook her head at the way the girls fawned over him. "I told you already, Mr. Ravens—"

"Donovan," he corrected and gave the girls a wink. "'Mr. Ravens' sounds so stuffy, like my brothers."

The girls giggled and British sighed. "Okay, if you say so, but I warned you we'd be here working."

"I understand—" Donovan nodded "—and I would be remiss if I didn't intervene here."

Hands on her hips, British cocked a brow up at him. Was he always this tall? "How would you like to butt in?"

Another round of giggles.

"I heard you mention something called a Christmas Advisory Council."

Something in Donovan's tone irked her. He probably didn't believe such a thing existed. "We're a small town, sure, but we take the upcoming holiday season seriously around here."

"I don't doubt you." Like he had earlier, Donovan held his arms out in surrender in front of her. At least, she thought it was surrender. The bulging muscles of his biceps swelling against the cotton fabric of his shirt distracted her. British's mouth went dry for a moment. "What?" Her voice cracked.

"I didn't say anything," he said with a grin. Damn it. He knew she was ogling him. "But if you all are competing at an event where the judges are gung ho on the holidays, maybe it would benefit you guys to come up with some ideas for the season."

"OMG!" Kathleen shrieked. "I have been dying to code to a Christmas song. I've got all the equipment and lights already. When the song comes on, we can make the white lights match the singer, green lights for the chorus, and red lights if there's like a drum solo. It will be so cool."

"You need to do it to my favorite song," said Natasha, turning to British and Donovan. "It's old. Maybe you've heard of it? Mariah Carey's 'All I Want for Christmas.'"

"I believe I have," said Donovan. "How about you, Ms. B?"

"Once or twice." British clapped her hands together. "All right, let's thank Mr. Donovan and let him get on his way."

"Oh, don't worry about it." Donovan leaned against the door frame. "I wasn't doing anything."

"Really, the girls don't need the distraction," British said through gritted teeth.

"Aw, Ms. B," the girls whined. "Please, can he stay?"

One could only imagine their parents; their homes must be filled with puppies. How was she supposed to say no to them? "Fine," she groaned, "but just stay out of the way. You know what they say about cooks?"

"Not cooks," replied Donovan, "but I do know what Chef Jessilyn has to say about you."

British elbowed Donovan in his six-pack stomach, knowing good and well it didn't hurt. "Be quiet."

"Miss Jessilyn makes the best cookies," Natasha added into the conversation. "I wonder if she has any."

Donovan scratched the back of his head. "I saw her pulling out a batch when I put up my lunch dishes."

And that was all it took for the STEM for GRITS team to take off out of the room, hurling their promises to be right back behind them.

They took off with such a rush Donovan spun around after being hit by one and pushed out of the room by another. Then with the last two he was spun back into the room and pushed against British.

Now alone with Donovan, British took a step away from him. "Thanks for that," she snarled. "Do you realize how hard it was to get them all on the same page?"

Mouth opened in stunned disbelief, Donovan shook his head. "Those girls need to be on the track team."

"A few are," British replied. She sighed and took a seat on the couch. Donovan followed her and sat on the arm of an overstuffed chair.

"Donovan, this may be hard for you to understand, but the girls are in a time crunch and they need to focus."

"What did I do to distract them?"

British waved her hand at his attire. "Seriously?"

Donovan crossed his arms over his chest in feigned modesty. "I feel so cheap."

All of a sudden British laughed. "I'm sorry if I am testy."

"Just a little bit," Donovan said, lifting his large hand and measuring an inch with his thumb and forefinger. For a man who worked behind a desk at a powerful company, Donovan somehow bore several scars on his hand. When he realized she was staring, he dropped his hand to his side. "It's cool," he said with a nod. "I get what you're trying to do and I admire it. Such leadership."

If only he'd left off the last part. The compliment triggered an alert in her. "Do not offer me a job at Ravens Cosmetics."

"May I at least ask why?"

"I'm a teacher, Donovan. Clearly, by me being here with the girls, you can see I am highly dedicated to them."

"All right, fine," he said.

Somehow she knew the discussion wasn't over.

"What happens when you win this competition?" Donovan asked.

"Well, bragging rights..." British began but got distracted for a moment when Donovan cast a smile as if he understood. She felt her cheeks heat. "The current director is a bit of a sexist jerk when it comes to women in science," she explained.

Donovan wiggled his brows. "Want me to rough him up a bit?"

"Thanks, but no thanks. We're molding the minds of impressionable young ladies," she said. "So by winning, we would get the respect of the science department at Southwood Middle School and hopefully we'll be able to move our practice space to the school, especially since our rec center burned down."

"You're not in the school?"

British shook her head. "I usually meet with the girls at the old Southwood rec center after school. They come over and we work on projects. The only reason we're here is that the storm last week blew a transformer and the sparks set off a fire in the building and a few of the homes. Two of the team members and their families are staying here, courtesy of Ramon and Kenzie."

"I remember them from last year—" he nodded "—at the beauty pageant held here."

"Yes, Miss Southwood." British nodded, as well.

"I won't even ask if you know about pageants, since you seem to hate makeup," said Donovan with a laugh. He rose from his seat on the armchair.

British's eyes roamed the seat of his pants. What was wrong with her? Her students were right in the other room, squealing over cookies while she sat in here mentally undressing this man.

"Why don't you have your science group at the school?" Donovan clasped his hands behind his back and strolled over to the bay window.

Glad he couldn't see her face, British frowned, hating to recall Cam and the monopolizing of the science department. "Let's just say there's already a group in there."

"Schools usually pay for materials, right?" Donovan asked, half turning to face her.

Here comes the question that always throws people. British nodded.

"Does the school pay for your rec center activities?"

British shook her head and shrugged. "No. And yes, I am the one buying all the supplies."

"On a teacher's salary?" Donovan fully turned to face her. "It's been a while since I went to school, but the last I checked, teachers didn't work for the glorious salary."

"My husband left me some money," British explained. "Every dime I received has gone into the facility and the girls."

"You have faith, don't you?"

"Sometimes that's all you have."

Silence fell between them. Donovan stared at British. Finally, British rolled her eyes. "Well, I'd better go gather the girls up so they can get to work."

Donovan crossed the room and reached British before she stepped out the French doors. "If there's anything I can do, or anything you need, I want you to know you can come to me."

"That's mighty generous of you, Donovan," said British. "But why?"

"Let's just say my faith just may have been restored."

Thankfully the girls were able to focus over the following twenty-four hours. On a few occasions Donovan found a reason to make himself seen whether it was to come into the library, where they plotted their ideas, or to run through the trail in the back—shirtless—when they practiced experiments. British couldn't put the blame all on the girls for being easily distracted. She, too, lost track of time when she realized she could see through the window of the hotel gym and catch Donovan working out.

Knowing the STEM-Off was coming up, though, British was able to finally focus. To practice as many possible tasks the committee may give them, she shouted out different ideas for experiments in science, technology, engineering and math, and timed them. The girls brainstormed on what to build, including the list of things they'd need. They wanted to impress the judges, but also to truly learn something in the process.

For a few of the challenges some wanted to assemble a small-scale trampoline and show the parents of the Christmas Advisory Council how it was made. Natasha wanted to aim for a homemade vending machine. And Kathleen said she could build a coding game without using a computer. The afternoon had been so productive, British didn't see the need for more brainstorming later. That worked out perfectly for the girls, who were eager to head out to enjoy the last days of the fall festival.

Since hell hadn't frozen over, British continued to have her meals away from Magnolia Palace. No way she'd allow Jessilyn to cook for her. Even now, the eye daggers flew as British came down the stairs and crossed paths with the chef. Brushing off the icy stare, British twisted her hair into a bun and secured it at the top of her head. Before she made it to the front desk, she heard a high-pitched squeal of laughter from one of her girls, which echoed through the halls of the upscale boutique hotel. British headed toward the library to get the girls to settle down. She was surprised at what she found looking through the glass doors.

For a guy who'd wanted to be left alone for the week, Donovan Ravens had a funny way of showing it. British cocked her head to the side and folded her arms across the front of the lightweight sweater she'd worn in preparation for this evening's temperature drop.

"So you think Quandriguez is a jerk to me because he likes me?" Stephanie asked Donovan.

Donovan leaned against the door frame of the sunroom with his back to the lake and took a deep breath. "I don't really know the fellow to make that statement, so all I can tell you right now is that a lot of boys—and hear me out when I say 'boys'—don't know how to use their words to express how they feel."

"Maybe he's not being mean, or I'm reading it wrong. His older brother is deaf and his baby sister, too. Maybe he's stressed."

A dry chuckle escaped Donovan's throat. "*Never* make an excuse for a boy or a man. Stress is never a reason to be mean."

"Did you ever ignore a girl because you liked her?"

Interested in the answer, British perked up. Donovan struck her as the type of man who didn't have to say a word to get a woman to notice him. He just needed to stare at her one good time with those piercing light brown eyes, maybe even lick his lips together, and a woman would go crazy or at least feel a trail of goose bumps traveling down her arm. British shivered and smoothed her hand over her biceps.

"You just keep doing what you've been doing," Donovan went on to say.

"Even if it means I should not do my best at this competition?"

Wait, what? No way in the world would she ever tell one of her girls to dumb herself down for a boy. From where she stood, British could see Donovan's jaw twitch. He rolled his head from side to side, causing a crack in his neck.

"Look here," he said to Stephanie. "There is nothing se—" Donovan stopped while British cringed. Maybe it was time she stepped in to end this conversation. But Donovan recovered and continued. "There is nothing more attractive than a woman with a brain."

"Are your girlfriends smart?"

"I don't do girlfriends," Donovan quipped, "but if I did, I'd like her to have a brain and not be worried about hurting my feelings."

"Ms. B doesn't mind hurting your feelings," Stephanie offered. British narrowed her eyes. "And she is smart."

"And beautiful," Donovan mused.

British's heart thumped against her ribs. This was so silly, to feel giddy knowing he found her attractive.

"But we're talking about you and—"

"Quandriguez," said the precocious teen.

"Well, if this Quandriguez can't see how wonderful and smart you are right now, he isn't worth your time."

"Really?" Stephanie squealed in delight.

"Scout's honor," said Donovan as he straightened.

British couldn't see what he was doing but Stephanie giggled. "That's not the Scout symbol."

"It isn't?"

"There's not a boy in Southwood who hasn't been through the Scouts," said Stephanie. "I know that salute."

Donovan's chuckle at being caught made British snicker and expose her location.

"Miss British?" Donovan called her name and the deep sound of his voice sent a chill down her spine. "Is that you?"

"I'm sorry," said British as she stepped around the corner. "It wasn't my intent to eavesdrop on y'all's conversation."

Stephanie came to her feet from her spot in the plush, white-cushioned chair by the bay window. "It's cool," she said. "Mr. Donovan was just giving me some good advice."

"Followed by the wrong salute?" British crossed her arms over her chest. The thin green sweater suddenly felt too warm and itchy.

Donovan had dressed appropriately for the fall weather. The long-sleeved, garnet T-shirt hugged a well-toned body. "We were just discussing the age-old debate about if a boy is mean to you it must mean he likes you."

Considering the fact that Donovan was always a source of joy to be around, British realized where she stood with him.

With a bow, Donovan pressed his hand over his heart. "*I*, for one, am against that theory."

"Are you?"

"It sets girls up to accept abuse or mistreatment early on," Stephanie explained.

Such a professional tone from the girl who chewed gum to a rhythmic beat in class caused British to quirk a brow and shift her stare between the two of them. "Interesting."

"It is," replied Donovan. "I'm a firm believer in being sweeter."

"Well," Stephanie giggled, "I'm going to find my friends. But Mr. D—" she pointed her fingers into a gun shape "—don't forget about my idea."

"I'll pay for your patent once you work out the details."

Stephanie squealed and took off with such a force that the door swung shut, leaving the two adults alone.

British shook her head and looked at Donovan. "Dare I ask?"

"That," he said, pointing toward the exit through which Stephanie disappeared, "is Ravens Cosmetics' future secret weapon."

"What did she pitch?"

"An app for phones that will show a model and, if I've got this right, transposes the makeup on the model's made-up face so the girls can follow a trace or something."

"The Trace-A-Face?" British asked with a snicker.

"That might have been the name."

British shook her head. "I am so glad she's here this week. This way she can believe in herself without makeup."

"Hey, now," Donovan said, clutching his heart, "makeup is my livelihood."

"You mean selling foundation to cover women's flaws?" Back when she did pageants, British met tons of girls with such low self-esteem once the makeup came off. They didn't understand pimples were a part of growing up, not the end of the world.

Donovan shook his head. "If you think we had a product like that, don't you think I'd use it on this?" With that, Donovan aimed his index finger at the X-shaped scar across his face. The dark beard across his chiseled jawline covered part of the mark but she knew it was there. Her fingers twitched and her heart lurched.

"I—I wasn't trying to…"

"Don't act like you haven't noticed it, British," he replied coolly and winked. "It's okay. Everyone stares at it. I catch them often."

British shrugged her shoulders. "People aren't taught not to stare these days."

"Curiosity is human nature." He gave a quick shrug of his shoulders.

"But still."

"Don't you want to know how I got it?"

"I assumed it was a car accident." British strolled

over to the floor-to-ceiling bookshelf. She switched a few of the modern classics around, including the collection of Brontë sisters. She cast a glance over her shoulder.

Dark, thick brows rose with surprise. "Really? Most people believe I received it due to a lover's quarrel."

For some reason Donovan closed the gap between them before she even realized their proximity and reached down to smooth a stray hair back behind her ear. British turned her face into the palm of his hand. Her eyes closed as she forgot where she was for a moment. Another place. Another time…she might have let him kiss her because that came next when a man stood this close. Her heart slammed against her rib cage, reminding her of the needs she possessed as a woman. Her body ached for his touch. Embarrassed by her desire, British took a step back and cleared her throat.

"Well, I don't know you well enough to say if you're scoundrel enough for such an act of revenge."

"A scoundrel?" Donovan pulled *Wuthering Heights* off a smaller bookshelf's row of the *Sugar Plum Ballerinas* series and placed it beside the set British had just rearranged. Him knowing the difference between the books earned him an ounce of respect from British. "But you would say a car crash?"

"My husband received a similar scar when his face hit the steering wheel at a right angle."

Donovan stepped backward. "I'm sorry."

"Don't be," she whispered. The knot threatening her throat eased quicker than normal. "Enough of this sad talk. I didn't mean to eavesdrop, but I was on my way out for dinner and—"

"Wait, you're not eating here?" Donovan cut her off

and sniffed the air. "Chef Jessilyn is making homemade chili since the temperature is dropping."

"Not on my life." British laughed.

"There's a history between you two," Donovan observed, pointing his finger at her.

"Let's just say not all students hold me in such high regard as the GRITS team does."

That got a deep laugh out of Donovan. "Hard to believe it, but I'll let you tell the story over dinner, if you'll share it with me."

Cocking her head to the side, British stroked her chin. "Have you had a tour of Southwood?"

"I've been meaning to, especially now," he said.

British narrowed her eyes at him. "I'm afraid to ask."

"Had you showed up for the wonderful lunch Chef prepared for us," he teased with a wink, "you would have heard the girls talking about the snatched—"

"Snatched?" Tears began to form in the corners of her eyes at Donovan's accurate lingo. This man ran a billion-dollar company and spoke fluent Teen.

"Yes," Donovan boasted with a pat on his broad chest. "I'm cool. I know the haps."

"Okay, Mr. Cool." British dabbed the corner of her right eye with her finger.

"Anyway, the girls were telling me about original gifts I can get my nieces here, other than shipping them cupcakes, which I am still contemplating since I'm *stanning* them."

"Dear Lord," she giggled, "please stop."

"What? You don't like my Eminem reference?" Proud of himself, Donovan nodded his chin at her for emphasis of his coolness.

As a teacher, she'd heard all the latest slang. "Stanning," derived from an Eminem song, now referred to someone obsessed with something. At last year's *fleek*, as in being on point, British had stopped trying to keep up with today's youth.

"Did you learn these terms from your young girl-friends?"

Licking his lips, Donovan cocked his head to the side. "We've established our age differences and you might be the youngest woman I've seriously been interested in."

Breath caught in her throat for a moment, then she remembered that he wanted her to work for his company as a spokesmodel. For years British wanted to be more than a pretty face. How would it look if she were to suddenly become the face of a popular cosmetics line? Donovan barked up the wrong tree with this proposal. British responded with an eye-roll and changed the subject. "I pegged you as an internet shopper."

"I can be," he answered, moving to sit on the arm of the couch, "but as CFO of a major company, I don't mind shopping around for a deal, especially if it's a one of a kind."

"Wouldn't it be easier if you got all the ladies the same gift, that way you don't have to keep track of them?"

"One of these days I'm going to surprise you," Donovan declared.

British studied his face and ignored the way he made her heart beat—all erratic like a schoolgirl's. He rose to his feet and stretched. A sliver of washboard ab peeked when his shirt rose and British unapologetically stared. What? The man was good-looking, she argued with herself. Her friends—hell, even her in-laws—were ready for her to move on. And British knew she too missed the comfort of a man.

"So what's going on outside of Magnolia Palace? Anything good?"

The realization that this playboy was the perfect man for her to get her groove on hit her. No family in town. Only here for a while. Everything about his body said he was a fantastic lover. Near fainting, British grabbed hold of the wall. "Dear Lord, you're in for a treat. I happen to know the best view in town. Want to come with me?"

Donovan raised his left brow and pondered her question.

Embarrassed, British closed her eyes and shook her head, admitting to herself that his blatant flirting had intrigued her. Maybe it was time to start delving into her desires for another man. Now nervous for admitting she wanted him, British wrung her hands together. The rock Christian had placed on her finger scraped against her hand. Vonna was right. He would not want her living like a nun. He might not be gung ho on her choice in a playboy like Donovan, but he was a start... and, more important, he was temporary. "I'll be right back," she told him.

When she went upstairs to her room, British hoped she'd played it cool. Something about the way he'd flirted with her made her...dance...the same way she did when she bit into something delicious. Giggling, British took a long look at herself in the mirror and shook her head, wondering what Christian would think of her now.

She twisted off her ring to set it on a lace doily. Donovan was the complete opposite of Christian. Christian had wanted nothing more than to be in a monogamous relationship for as long a time as he was permitted on earth. Donovan, however, was the type of person to get with as many women as possible while he lived on earth. Maybe that's what she needed. A no-strings fling. Perfect. Going out to the festival with Donovan was sure to cause people to gossip. So what? The grandfather clock downstairs chimed six. Satisfied with herself, British headed to the door, then turned back around to snatch her ring off the dresser. *Baby steps, British. Baby steps.*

"You promise you're not leading me to this roadkill diner you mentioned the other day?" Donovan asked British, within less than a half hour of leaving Magnolia Palace.

Even with his eyes focused on the long, dark road ahead of them, Donovan felt the burning sensation of the side-eye daggers British shot him from the passenger seat. Under one of the lone streetlights, he turned and winked.

"I can't guarantee there won't be any vittles like that," she began, clucking her tongue against the roof of her mouth. "I will say if the sign above the counter says 'mystery meat' and it's deep-fried...don't eat it."

Donovan's laugh rattled the interior of the Jaguar. "I'll make note of it."

Bright lights filled the town square. The only thing on Donovan's mind the other day had been getting another batch of cupcakes. He hadn't bothered looking around town; otherwise he might have noticed the carnival equipment. A man carrying a small child over his shoulders waved at Donovan's car and pointed to a space, where a convertible's taillights flickered. Donovan let his window down to wave acknowledgment and thanks at the same time.

The smells of popcorn, smoked meats and cotton candy permeated the inside of the car. Donovan's stomach growled. "I guess a man can't live on fresh chocolate-chip cupcakes alone," he joked.

"Well, let's hurry up and find you something recognizable to eat."

As he flipped the turn signal for the parking space, British gazed out the passenger-side window. Was she looking for someone? Since she still wore her wedding ring, he doubted she was checking for a boyfriend. Once the space became free, Donovan pulled forward and backed into it, another car allowing Donovan to park before driving by. Maybe it was his imagination, but British seemed to use the opportune time to duck her head to unclick her seat belt. That same old suspicious radar dinged in the back of his head. She was hiding something from him.

"Hey, Ms. B," someone shouted in the parking lot.

British squinted her eyes and tried to recognize the voice. "Hey, Mario."

Donovan recognized Mario and Dario Crowne. Their older brother, Dominic, was a good friend of the family's. Dominic's brothers and sister, Alisha, were always in town from South Florida over at the house in the Overtown neighborhood for epic parties. "Hi, boys."

"Who's that you've got with you? Oh snap," Dario said, shielding his eyes from the blaze of the setting sun. "Donovan?"

"Hey, twins," Donovan called out with a head nod. "I thought I heard you were in Southwood now."

Dario and Mario came over and greeted Donovan with a hug and handshake. They talked for a few minutes before a few young ladies walked by and caught their attention.

"I am about to walk into my hometown festival with

a celebrity, aren't I?" British teased, elbowing Donovan in the ribs.

Giving a shallow cough, Donovan casually draped his arm over her shoulder. A part of him wondered if this would show he was staking a claim on her. He had no right but being this close to her felt natural. So caught up in his thoughts, Donovan heard the honk of a car horn in enough time to pull British up onto the curb. The movement had been so quick but they lingered in each other's embrace for ten heartbeats or more. They broke apart when a whirl of wind from a ride blew over their head followed by the screams of women, children and men.

British stepped out of his embrace with a shiver. "Where do you want to start? Rides? Or did you say you were scared?"

Donovan cleared his throat and puffed out his chest. "I never said either. But I'm not a big fan of roller coasters."

"You don't seriously think something bad can happen, now do you?"

"You mean get stuck upside down and fall out?" Donovan waved off the notion with a healthy dose of sarcasm and a *pshaw*. "Sure, all those news stories were wrong."

"They were wrong for not telling the full story." British rolled her eyes. "Majority of the injuries happen because of people not following the rules."

"Let me guess, there's a science behind roller coasters?" Donovan joked.

"Engineering." British beamed. "You've been paying attention to my lessons with the girls."

"Maybe a little."

"Well, then you'll realize the reporters are sensationalizing the stories. Have you ever noticed they come out right before the brink of the summer season? I swear it's just to scare people."

"Scare?" Donovan held his left hand out with his palm upward. "Warn? Caution?" he said, ticking off more synonyms of the word on each left finger with his long, right index finger. "I don't see the difference."

"You don't?" British gaped.

"And you know what else I don't see?"

"What?"

The familiar whirl whizzed over their heads. Donovan looked up in time to see what looked like a spinning fireball zoom through the air inches above his head. The gush of wind from the roller coaster was so forceful it whipped British's hair all around her face. The ride went around and around in circles. Patrons screamed with thrills. A cell phone and a hat landed in the gated area around the base of the ride.

"You won't see me getting on that thing." Donovan folded his arms across his chest.

"Chicken," British teased and tugged his arm loose to grab his hand. "C'mon, let's go get on the ride."

Donovan stood still. "Wait…how about if we get a bite to eat from the mystery meat stand?"

British followed his gaze to the caravan of food trucks parked alongside the town square. Serpentine lines wrapped around each vehicle. The one with the shortest line came from the truck with the sign You'll Never Guess. Despite what she'd warned him about in the car, the smells were delicious and tempting. Donovan took a step in the direction but British squeezed his hand.

"I can't do that to you. Let's go find something else to eat."

"See, and here I was all game." Donovan's shoulders relaxed and he felt the blood pump and course through his veins when she winked at him.

"And then we'll get on the rides," British said with a laugh before pulling him around the festival. "Unless you're afraid you're going to scream and cry."

"I don't cry," he said flatly.

Since this was the last night of the festival, everything was half off. British didn't argue with Donovan when he stepped in front of her to pay for the tickets or for the cotton candy and corn dogs they ate while they walked around.

Her students stopped her every now and then, and British moved off to the side to have a conference with some of the parents who hadn't been able to make it to school so far this year. He didn't mind. Donovan had dated some models who were also single mothers, and he'd heard how hard it was for a working mom to meet with her kid's teachers. Of course, they'd mention this in the hope Donovan would be able to get them a full-time gig working at Ravens Cosmetics or to settle down with him and live the life of luxury.

"I think I am the one walking around with the celebrity," Donovan taunted when British finished with a parent and student. The on-the-spot conference had ended with the mother profusely thanking and thanking British for her patience, and British and the young man high-fiving each other.

Under the pink glow of a ride, British blushed. "Well, I did grow up here." As she waved her hand like a showcase hostess, her eyes widened and Donovan swore she cursed under her breath.

"And I'm surprised we haven't—" His words were cut off.

"Quick." British grabbed hold of Donovan's hand and tugged him hard toward their first roller coaster of the evening. "Let's get on a ride."

A pulse of fear jolted through him. The last thing he wanted to do was to give up his masculinity card for screaming like a child and fainting, like he'd seen on a YouTube video his sister Dana's kids, his nieces and nephews, showed him. "Wait, what?"

Fortunately for him, every death-defying ride British dragged him to had lines. The folks of the town had come out in droves. Donovan sighed in relief at the Ferris wheel. The ticket-taker ripped their tickets in two and lifted the plastic rope for them to enter.

The available cart was a two-seater and Donovan did not mind. Without giving it much thought, he stretched his arm around British and heat rose from her shoulders to the crook of his elbow. Donovan rested his long legs against the foot rail. The compartment rocked forward. British sat on the inside, using his body as a shield from someone in the crowd.

"Are we sure this is safe?" He turned his light brown eyes toward her.

"You're afraid?"

"Nah," Donovan chuckled and sat back in his seat. "I rank placing myself in unnecessary danger right up there with jumping out of a perfectly functioning airplane."

"You can skydive over in Peachville," British offered. "I mean, if you want."

"I don't," he replied quickly. The sounds below grew quieter. The occasional roar of the fireball roller coaster and screams from the other rides rang out.

"So who were you hiding from?"

Chapter 5

British had hoped Donovan hadn't noticed her para-
noia. Spotting Cam in the parking lot had set off a chain
reaction. Cam, she could handle, basically because he'd
been leaving as they'd pulled into the lot. No, the biggest fear for British had been her family, whose calls
she still hadn't bothered returning since she arrived at
Magnolia Palace. With the Thanksgiving holiday rap-
idly approaching, her mother hounded her for confir-
mation that she would be coming over to the house.

As the baby of the Woodburys, British had grown up
with a mother and four other brothers and sisters who
thought they were her parents. It was only a matter of
time before they all ran into each other at the festival.
British spotted her six-foot-tall mom by the basketball
game shooting hoops and racking up on the prizes with
three giant teddy bears already, probably one for each
granddaughter. At least, up high in the air, British was

out of earshot and eyesight of Joan Woodbury…just not Donovan's questioning stare.

"If you must know who I am trying to avoid," British said, licking her lips and tasting the sweet leftover sugar from her cotton candy, "I am hiding from my mother."

Donovan closed his eyes and nodded. "Completely understandable."

British glanced up to see a smirk competing with the grin across his face. When she did, she elbowed him.

"What?" Donovan asked mockingly. "I always get on death traps to avoid my mom."

"I'm not avoiding-avoiding her," British replied. "I am just…well, um, not ready to bump into her."

"Because you're with me?" Donovan asked, his hand covering his jawline while his fingers absently brushed against his visible scar.

The vulnerable stroke touched British and she felt sorry for him. Didn't he realize how sexy it made him? The question astonished her and her heart lurched in her chest.

British twisted her wedding ring around on her finger. Just because she was widowed, that did not make her blind. The words of her mother-in-law rang in her head, which British shook. British wanted Donovan but not in a long-term way. If he wanted more, well, then Donovan was not the man for her. But she didn't want him to think it was because of his scar. She'd just traveled down the marital road before and once was enough.

"Not necessarily," British said. "With Thanksgiving coming up, I haven't been in the mood for being around family."

"Oh yeah, I keep forgetting," said Donovan. "I need to make a note to myself to have Ramon send the skeleton staff working home on my dime."

"You're in the generous mood," British said.

"Maybe the holidays put me in one," he answered. "Why does it have you in a sour one?"

"Christian loved everything about the Thanksgiving week." British sighed.

The Ferris wheel moved a notch. Donovan wrapped his hand around her shoulder. "This time of year must be difficult and you probably want to be left alone."

"Not alone, just not smothered. Christian's been gone for five years and every holiday my mom and siblings treat me like I am a child, so I ditch them whenever I can. Does that sound weird?"

"No." Donovan shook his head. "Trust me, I needed to get out of South Florida without letting my family know what was going on in my life."

"Bad breakup?" British guessed. He confirmed his answer with a quick nod. She imagined some poor girl clinging to his pant leg as he tried to leave a room.

"Not only bad," said Donovan, "but caught on camera."

British's hands flew to her mouth to cover her half laugh and half gasp. "What?"

"My sister insisted on having the family become more public so our brand could gain traction on social media," Donovan began. "This somehow was turned into a reality television segment on all of us. My portion happened to catch my current…" He gulped down whatever word followed and even turned a sickly olive color.

"Girlfriend?" British supplied and wiggled her brows. "Is it so hard to say the word?"

"'Girlfriend' sounds so committed." Donovan shivered. "We only knew each other for a little over a month."

"A month?" British's mouth gaped. "Don't you believe in love at first sight?"

"That would imply I believe in love."

Disappointment rose in British's chest. There'd be no love between them. But then again, that might just be what she needed. "A month is plenty of time to fall in love, though."

"No, I think I'm going to give women two before I even consider it."

Even though British felt the idea of a romp in the hay with Donovan was what she might need to satisfy this uncontrollable urge she felt when she was with him, that disappointment bubble lingered in her chest.

"But, truthfully, I almost brought her with me this weekend until..." Donovan started to continue but stopped himself.

I'm glad he didn't.

"I'm glad I didn't," Donovan said, seemingly reading her thoughts. "I wasn't too sure about things with her. I thought maybe if we came here together I'd know where things were heading. I'd even made plans for her parents to meet us for Thanksgiving dinner. I guess that says a lot about me." Donovan chuckled at himself and looked down at British. She gave him a frown. "I'm sorry. I just dodged a bullet by having to hang out with them. My family is crazy enough. I don't need to add to it."

The Ravens family drama was public knowledge. There'd been an attempted family corporate takeover or something and a long-lost daughter coming back into their lives to save the day.

"Two months or not, I don't think she would have made the cut to be my..." His words trailed off and the hue of his skin turned greener than when she'd teased him about going on the upside-down roller coaster.

British nudged her elbow against his solid rib cage. "Aren't you too old to think girls have cooties?"

"Not cooties, but ulterior motives."

The fact he didn't finish what the current girlfriend had or hadn't done did not go unnoticed. So what was the relationship now? He was here in Southwood, alone, and she was elsewhere. British rolled her eyes, mad at herself for the surge of jealousy. "I guess I fell into that category."

"As in a girl*friend*?" he sang with a grin.

"Oh, be serious." British leaned her weight forward and tilted their cart.

"All right, now." Donovan unwrapped his arm from around her shoulders and grabbed hold of the bar with his large hands until his knuckles turned white. "Stop before you make us fall."

British stopped and laughed. "I'm sorry. That was horrible of me." She turned in the seat, pulling the inside of her sole into her left knee to better face Donovan. "I'll stop."

"You're a rotten girl*friend*." Donovan drawled the word with a teasing smile and let go of the bar to face her. She gave him a death stare matched with narrowed eyes and pinched lips. "Oh, so you're *not* a girl that's a friend?"

"You sound like my students," British chided.

"Given the fact you just commented on my age, I'll take that as a compliment."

Just then they reached the top of the Ferris wheel. It gave British the opportunity to show Donovan the sights of the town starting with the Four Points Park, which united their neighboring towns—Peachville, Black Wolf Creek and Samaritan—over their treetops. Though British had no idea how long Donovan planned to be in Southwood, she promised him that summertime not only offered the sweetest smells with the peach orchards but also a fabulous light show from the firefly forest. And until now she hadn't realized Donovan's arm rested around the back of her seat, resting on her shoulders— or that she'd nestled herself against him.

"And out yonder, right next to the middle school, is the high school," British said, pointing in the distance.

Donovan cleared his throat. "Is that where you and Christian met?"

Not sure how to answer, British glanced upward. "I've never been on a date where a man wanted to hear about my husband."

Grinning under the stars, Donovan looked down and winked. "So we're on a date."

"Oh... I..." She was stumped to find the words. Maybe if she lifted the lap bar she could escape this awkward moment. They weren't that far off the ground.

"Relax." Donovan squeezed her shoulder. "I'm just giving you a hard time. I get what you're saying—you wouldn't date a guy like me."

"Shut up," British laughed.

"Relax," said Donovan again. He pulled her close. "You're from a small town. I get it. You're widowed and I'm guessing being seen with me is going to get people to talk."

"Again, not just people, my family. My nosy family," she added.

"I think somewhere in there you did not deny being attracted to me," he teased.

British gulped and shuddered at the same time. "I'd have to be blind to not see you're attractive. I just..."

"Seriously," he went on, "I am not trying to get married or anything. Not now, not ever."

A sharp pain pierced her heart. "Don't knock it until you try it."

Now it was Donovan's turn to shudder. "I'll pass. I am too old and I'm set in my ways. I've heard my sisters complain about their in-laws and having to feel obligated to spend time with them over the holidays. If I don't want to be around someone, I just don't deal with them anymore."

"What a shame. Being a perpetual bachelor seems so lonely," British said, her lips turning into a frown. Her heart ached listening to him. "I loved being married. There's something comforting about coming home at the end of the day to someone waiting for you, eager to hear about your day, even if you know your time together might be limited."

There was no questioning his curious look so British shared a story about Christian, about how they'd met and his heart problems—including about their time being ironically living life carefully, only to be cut short due to a deer in the middle of the road. British couldn't believe how easy it was for her to open up about Christian. And she appreciated him not coddling her or feeling sorry for her, either. In turn, Donovan shared what it was like to grow up in a famous family and never knowing if he could trust the women who claimed they saw past the scar were interested in him, or secretly out for a modeling job or his fortune. It didn't make her feel good about coming to Magnolia Palace to butter him up. The poor man never came across a woman who didn't want something from him.

"This town is nice," Donovan commented when the conversation lulled.

"Is that sarcasm I hear?" British asked, looking up at him.

"Of course not," he said with a lazy smile and a

wave of his free hand. "I live in Miami. It's the town that never sleeps."

British cleared her throat. "I'm pretty sure that's New York City."

"You're the teacher," he said, shrugging. "But back to Southwood. I like it. It's growing on me."

"I'm waiting for you to say it's quaint."

"*Quaint* isn't a bad thing, Ms. B." He paused and chuckled to make sure his formality pushed her buttons. For his benefit, British huffed. "My sister-in-law grew up here," said Donovan. "Are you familiar with the Mas Beauty School?"

Everyone in the Four Points area knew about the famous Mas building, once run by Sadie Baldwin. Decades ago, Mas was a cosmetology school for young girls who came and lived in part of the old brick house in dorm-like rooms and used other portions of the home for school work. They learned how to do makeup and hair and even create makeup, all to land them sustainable jobs for their futures. Back when British's goals were to become Miss America or Miss USA, she wanted to learn all the ins and outs of the business; there hadn't been a summer British didn't spend studying cosmetology. British prided herself on being a makeup expert. She'd perfected the wingtip, mastered the glue for her lashes so well that she could place them on her own lids without a mirror and with just one hand. But she also wanted to know what went into the glue and its effects on a person's skin. Spending time at Mas helped redirect British's focus in science. Of course, it had been scientists who made British feel self-conscious about her makeup.

"I remember Zoe," British finally answered. She smiled fondly and decided not to share how fascinated

Zoe had been with the success of the Ravens family. Donovan's face filled with pride talking about his great-grandparents and how they'd come up with the first Ravens products and created what became a conglomerate in today's world.

"You know my brother married her after meeting her at Magnolia Palace," he said, filling the silence.

"Yep." British's throat went dry. "There is something romantic about the hotel."

The higher their car went, the smaller the people below became and the more intimate the space between them became. British glanced up at Donovan at the same time he looked at her. The moment was spontaneous, especially for her. With half-closed eyes, she arched her neck and Donovan leaned down. The air thinned. Her breath caught in her throat and her heart pounded against her ribs.

From below a heavy thud of the high-striker carnival game thundered up through the sky as a silver ball traveled along a metal post at their eye level as their car began to lower. The bell rang out, echoing between them. British pulled away and cleared her throat. Their ride slowed to a disappointing stop. Had she wanted more time with Donovan? No, not at all, she thought as she glanced from side to side to find her extra-tall mother. No sign. More than likely Joan had headed over to the grocery store to buy every sweet potato left in town in order to make enough pies to feed everyone.

Donovan turned his head. British studied his profile. His jaw twitched under his close-cropped beard. His long nose jutted out with a slight bend as if it had been broken at one point. A part of her wondered if it happened in the accident that had left him with the scar or if it had come from a brawl. Donovan seemed to relish his playboy status. Perhaps he'd pissed off a few people along the way.

"I guess I need to thank you for not killing me on the ride," Donovan joked, stepping off the car once the ride-handler lifted the lap bar. He turned and extended his hand for British to take. She obliged but not before glancing around the park. A teensy spark set off at their touch. Logic told her it was the combination of the cold air and them sliding out of a metal seat. But the little voice in the back of her head told her to accept the chemistry.

"Are we in the clear?" Donovan asked when they stepped onto solid ground.

"Yes." British breathed a sigh of relief.

"Well, well, well."

British cursed under her breath. "Hi, Maggie."

"Hi, British and Hot Guy from the Other Day," said Maggie with a wink. She balanced a round lavender tray of cupcakes as she wagged a finger at Donovan. "I couldn't recall your face the other day at the Cupcakery but I remember you now, Donovan Ravens."

Donovan nodded and extended his hand. "You have me at a disadvantage."

"I'm forgoing lash extensions and makeup, no offense to Ravens Cosmetics." Maggie wiggled her eyebrows, held the tray in one hand above her head and reached in her pocket for her cell phone to pose for a faux selfie, her lips pressed together.

"Magnolia Swayne." Donovan snapped his fingers and pointed. "How are you? What are you doing here? And without your entourage?" He leaned over and gave Maggie a hug.

British bobbed her head between the two of them. Maggie's socialite life had brought her to South Florida for every high-fashion event. It made sense they knew each other.

Another whirlwind from a ride blew a breeze across British's face. Her eyes twitched—correction, just her right eye twitched—as she calculated the distance, arm length and timing of the hug between Donovan and Maggie. She scratched the back of her head and tried to diagnose the sudden irritation rising in her. She liked Maggie. She was the cool big sister of Kenzie. Maggie was also very clear she didn't want a serious relationship, which meant she could be perfect for Donovan. But what did British care?

British cleared her throat. "Well, if you two will excuse me," she began and turned around, right into the six-foot-tall woman who'd given birth to her. "Mom."

"I knew I saw you," exclaimed Joan, who began talking a mile a minute as she wrapped her arms around her daughter's shoulders. The pink-glittered letters of her mother's black, pink and white baseball shirt spelled out Glam-Ma and lit up under the changing lights of the rides behind British. When she pulled back from the hug Joan began wiping the messy glitter off British's cheek. "You haven't answered any of my calls. Where have you been?"

British gently swatted the smothering touch away with the back of her hand. Joan would never change and British loved that about her. She commanded attention, not just because of her stature but because her mother was drop-dead gorgeous, with her short-cropped brown pixie cut that framed her perfectly symmetrical face and bright green eyes. While British had not inherited her mother's height, she did get her light brown skin from her. She hoped when she reached her mother's age her skin would be just as flawless.

"Hey, Mrs. Woodbury," Maggie said, appearing at British's side.

"Dahling," Joan cooed, flashing her pearly white teeth. The pet name was often used when her mother, a former Miss Southwood and Miss Georgia Runner-Up, forgot the other person's name. Maggie lacked makeup, but not that much. "I heard you were in town. Oh? And who is this handsome man escorting you to the fair?"

British prayed the fairgrounds would open up and swallow her whole before she had to listen to her mother flirt. How many times had Joan drilled into British's adult head that she was free to look at the menu? Levi Woodbury felt the same way as his wife and, on the rare occasions British went over to her parents' house for lunch during the day, she caught him catching up on reality shows set on paradise beaches. British's parents recently celebrated their fiftieth wedding anniversary over the summer. They still fawned all over each other and it became worse when all their children came home for the holidays. The bigger the audience, the better.

Maggie pulled Donovan forward and up against British's frame. "No, ma'am, not my date. British's."

"Well," Joan gasped, clutching the pearls around her neck. Only a Glam-Ma wore pearls, a baseball T-shirt, denim and heels to the fair. "I'm British's mother."

"Mrs. Woodbury," Donovan's deep voice greeted her. He stepped closer and his size overpowered British's supersize mother as he took her hand in his. "I see where British gets her beauty from." A kiss to the back of Joan's palm followed the cheesy line.

"Oh please, you got my daughter out and about this time of year—you need to call me Joan." Joan then curtsied. "Sweet Jesus, British baby, is this why you haven't been returning my calls? I completely understand now."

"You called me?" British attempted say with a sincere face but couldn't. She started laughing immediately.

Joan narrowed her dark eyes on British. "So you two are on a date?"

"It's not a date," British explained. "He's staying at Magnolia Palace. We're just friends."

"We're fast friends," Donovan proclaimed along with a slick move: draping his arm around British's shoulder. Maggie made some odd noise between choke and a laugh. Joan made a mewling noise.

"Well, great," Joan said. "In that case, you're coming to Thanksgiving dinner at the Woodburys'."

Back at Magnolia Palace, Donovan and British walked through the quiet foyer. Considering the time the festival had officially shut down, the kids here were probably asleep. Donovan did not recall seeing a teenager running rampant during the last hour he and British had spent with Joan Woodbury. Funny how this weekend he canceled meeting one set of parents and ended up not just meeting a mother but hanging out with her. And he had a blast watching the mother-daughter duo throw darts at balloons, basketball shoot and participate in a water gun race to see who could knock down the most cardboard ducks. No one in the Ravens family would be caught trying fried anything, whether it was a cookie, ice cream or even mystery meat. Joan assured him it was chicken. It felt great being a part of the family, even if it was just her mother. Donovan looked forward to being around the rest of them.

The second hand of the grandfather clock ticked closer to midnight. A glow of a fire roaring in the library fireplace lit the way. A set of parents entering the room nodded in their direction.

As tired as he was, Donovan didn't want his evening to end. He guessed he liked her company so much and the closeness they'd absentmindedly shared, he stretched his long arms out in front of British and reached for the banister. They both touched it at the same time.

Donovan laid his hand on top of hers but she turned to face him on the stairs and let her hand slip to her side. A stab of disappointment hit him. Even two steps ahead of him she was barely at eye level. He could try to kiss her again but hesitated. He didn't want to come off as a douchebag twice in one night. What was he thinking, nearly kissing her on the Ferris wheel when she'd spilled her heart out about her dead husband?

"Hey—" she began.

"Hey—" he said.

She gave a lopsided smile when they both spoke at the same time. With a nod of his head, she continued.

The fire in the library crackled. "Thanks for a great evening," British said.

Donovan cleared his throat. "I need to be the one thanking you. I've been in a rut for the last few days."

"Understandable," she replied. "You broke up with your girlfriend on a soon-to-be aired website footage."

Was she consoling him when she was the one who needed the distraction? She was sweet, but he was ambitious. "If you were aiming to make me feel better, you didn't have to drag me on those death-defying rides."

"Shut up." British giggled and playfully punched him in the shoulder. "They were not that bad."

"My nerves are so frayed I don't think I'll sleep," he teased. "The calmest way to cheer me up would have just been to say yes to me and come work for Ravens Cosmetics."

The next punch landed harder on his arm. "Ow," he said, feigning hurt.

"I have a job," British reminded him. "But I'm glad you had fun."

Donovan nodded. "Yep, and I got an invite to a Thanksgiving dinner. Now maybe my mother will stop calling me. She's freaking out about me not having any stuffing and cranberry sauce."

The bubbly laugh sobered and a soft smile settled on British's face. The flickering fire from the room off to the side highlighted the gold strands in her hair. "You don't have to come. I can make up an excuse."

"What?" Donovan feigned again. "I don't want to disappoint your mom. She loves me."

"Good grief." British rolled her eyes. "I'm not going to be able to stomach the two of you flirting."

"Jealous?"

"Please," she quipped. "I am going to bed."

Donovan took a step closer. He liked the way her eyes widened with surprise. She pressed her hand against his chest to stop him.

"Alone," she clarified with a poke in the chest with her index finger.

"Our rooms are right next door to each other," Donovan explained, grabbing hold of her hand. She didn't pull away, just as she hadn't pulled away when he'd almost kissed her on the Ferris wheel. They paused for a moment. Not wanting to waste another second, Donovan dipped his head lower. British tilted hers to his. And just as he felt the warmth of her breath against his lips, the grandfather clock boldly chimed the midnight hour.

Skittish, British stepped backward up the staircase. "Good night, Donovan."

Not able to move, he nodded his head. "Good night, British. Sweet dreams."

At least waiting for British to disappear from sight gave Donovan a moment to gather himself before being able to walk again. What would she think if she learned he didn't want to walk with her—not out of respect, but to make sure she did not see the raging erection trying to break free? Donovan dragged his hand down his face and whispered a silent prayer to the grandfather clock that had interrupted them. Had it not rung, they might still be on the stairs, tearing each other's clothes off. Maybe, he thought as he climbed the stairs, he needed to curse the clock instead.

In the safety of his bathroom, Donovan turned the cold water on in the walk-in shower. When he realized he'd forgotten his towel, he stepped out of the bathroom, naked. The cell phone on his dresser began to ring.

"Little brother, I hope this is an emergency," Donovan growled when he slid his thumb across Will's face to accept the call.

"Do you ever wear clothes?" Will asked with a disgusted frown on his face.

Donovan flashed his brother the middle finger. He reached for the folded towel at the edge of the bed and wrapped it around his waist. "I'm busy."

"Back to your old habits, huh?" Will laughed. "I'm glad you're done crying and sulking over whatever happened to you. When one girl doesn't work out for you, you always find the next one."

At one point in time, maybe even a week ago, Donovan would have laughed at the comment and taken pride in it. Tonight it seemed more like an insult, as if the only thing Donovan could do was go through women. Right now there was only one woman he wanted. "I don't cry,"

Donovan said, studying the background where Will sat. "Are you in the office working?"

"So?"

"It's after midnight and your hot wife is home alone."

A giggle came over the speaker. "Did he just call me hot?"

A second later Zoe Baldwin Ravens's dark head appeared. Her gold hoops caught the light of the office lamp on Will's desk as she leaned forward.

"Hey, Zoe."

"Hey, Donovan," said Zoe with a welcoming smile. She wiggled her fingers and the Ravens heirloom ring sparkled under the fluorescent office lights. "I'm sorry Will's calling. I stepped out to get us some drinks."

"I'd never blame you," said Donovan. "Everyone in the family already knows Will is crazy."

"Dedicated to the company," Will reminded him. He made room in his chair for Zoe to sit on his lap. Donovan bit back a smile of enjoyment at seeing his brother happy. "Please tell me you're not sleeping with the next potential spokesmodel for RC."

"Not yet," Donovan mumbled. Leaving the phone faceup on his bed, Donovan moved over to the wall he shared with British. The balcony to his room faced the front of the hotel, as did hers. He wondered if she had stepped outside to enjoy the night air.

Will cleared his throat. "We're about to head out of town and we—"

"You," Donovan and Zoe chorused and then chuckled.

"Donovan," Will called out over the line. "I'm serious."

"About what?"

"The perfect woman," Will growled.

"Calm down, sweetie," said Zoe. "Donovan, ignore him. I am sorry we interrupted your evening."

Any other woman, Donovan would have had in his bed by now. British was different. She was special. She was...

Knock, knock, knock. Donovan turned toward the noise at the sliding-glass door to the balcony and found British standing outside.

She was there.

"I gotta go," Donovan said, moving to the bed and switching the phone off with one swipe. Eagerness helped him recross the room. His thumb fumbled with the switch to unlock and pull the door open at the same time. A magnolia scent blew in with a breeze. The trees in the driveway were bare. It had to be her.

"Am I interrupting?" British asked. She bit her lip and shifted nervously back and forth on her bare feet. Instead of the sweater and jeans from earlier, she was wearing a pale blue nightgown. A sweet hourglass silhouette taunted him through the material.

Donovan blinked in disbelief. His throat closed and his body tensed.

British snapped her fingers in his face. "Did I wake you?"

"No." He finally breathed. "Would you like to come in?" Donovan stepped aside but British shook her head.

"No, I won't keep you up."

Too late, Donovan thought, with his erection rising. A towel could only hide so much. For British to not see how immature he was, he leaned forward at an angle and pressed his arm against the jamb. "What's up?"

"I wanted to thank you again for a lovely evening," she said. Her fingers reached for a coil of her hair and twirled it. "And..."

A bit distracted by not seeing the rock on her finger, Donovan shook his head. "And what?" he inquired. If it got any quieter between them, she might be able to hear the pounding of his heart.

"I believe in finishing what I start."

"Which is—?" He barely got his question out before British leaped forward and wrapped her arms around his neck, dragging him to her level. Her soft lips pressed against his. Their mouths opened and tongues discovered each other. She tasted minty and fresh. The warmth of her body scorched his. Bells rang in his head. Never in his life had a kiss from a woman rocked him to his core. He needed more. Donovan let go of the door frame to wrap his arms around her waist, but she pulled away.

"We were interrupted twice," British breathed, "and I don't like going to bed with regrets. Good night, Donovan."

Chapter 6

For the most part, British tried to live without regret, but perhaps she felt a watered-down version of it when she bounced down the steps into the dining room, only to find Donovan seated at the table scanning the front page of the *Southwood Democrat*, the local paper, the following morning. From his profile she noticed he wore a pair of black basketball shorts and a black University of Miami muscle shirt. His arms bulged and British wished she'd worn her hair loose around her face instead of in a bun. Heat crept up from her neck to her ears.

Last night, when he wore nothing but a towel, she'd spotted a tribal half tattoo sleeve over his left shoulder and chest. And here she was, cringing at the flu shot she received last week. The pages crinkled at the fold when he lowered it when she walked into the room. His sideburns rose with the corners of his mouth as he smiled.

"Good morning," he greeted in his deep voice.

Steam rose from the white porcelain cup of black coffee by his side. On the long cherrywood table sat two empty cereal bowls, each one on a place mat on either side of Donovan. The smell of savory bacon filled the air.

"Good morning." British made her way over to the credenza to the wicker bowl of fresh fruit, well aware he was staring at her. As a teacher of middle school kids, British felt it important to be a role model and to dress appropriately for her audience. She wore modest-length pencil skirts and loose-fitting slacks and always paired them with a decent heel and pretty blouse. But away from work, British prided herself on her collection of New Edition T-shirts and jeans. Now she questioned the pink sweats she wore with her white canvas shoes. Anticipating the cooler weather, British also wore a plain white V-necked shirt with a matching zipper hoodie. The kind of women who threw themselves at Donovan were probably six-feet-plus, impeccably dressed women with flawless skin, like her mother.

Damn it, she did not focus on beauty and now here she was, one kiss in and underestimating herself. British palmed an apple and turned to face him, resting her hip on the wooden furniture. "I see the girls have eaten."

"They have," said Donovan. "I sent them to the store to pick up the things they're going to need for their STEM-Off."

"I have an account for them at the hardware store downtown," she said, taking hold of the stem from the fruit. For some reason, she mentally played a juvenile game, twisting the apple in her hand and sounding off the letters of the alphabet. When the stem broke away, the initial landed on would be the person you'd marry. A-B-C-D. *D?* "Seriously?" she mumbled under her breath. This was not what her PhD in STEM Education was about.

"Why spend your own money when I said I'd be a sponsor?"

"Donovan," she said with a warning tone.

"If you agree to being RC's spokesmodel, I believe you can even write it off as a business expense."

"You're incorrigible," she responded.

Donovan lifted a brow over the paper and studied her for a moment. "I didn't hear a 'no' in there."

"Absolutely and unequivocally no, especially not now," British said in a clipped tone.

The gossip column on the front page disappeared as he folded the paper. His thick brows rose in question. "Don't tell me after last night you're changing your mind about me."

To warn him, British glanced in his direction and then darted a glance toward the vacant dining room entrance. She sat down beside him and spoke in a whisper. "The last thing I want is for my students to get the wrong idea."

"That we kissed?"

She hushed him with her furrowed brows and frown. Before she got the chance to scold him verbally, Jessilyn opened the swinging dining room door with her hip. The chef offered British a snarl.

"Here's your breakfast," Jessilyn said to Donovan. She set a bowl and a plate in front of him. While Donovan put the newspaper on the seat beside him, Jessilyn pointed out the items in front of him. "My from-scratch biscuits and a bowl of gravy."

British wanted to be the first to tell Jessilyn how delicious her breakfast smelled but decided not to. The compliment could end up with Jessilyn asking for her to go back into the system and change her grades. But damn, it might be worth it for a biscuit drizzled in the thick, peppery sauce. British's stomach growled.

"Thanks," Donovan said to Jessilyn. "British, I'm sure Jessilyn has more."

"No, thank you," British replied with a sweet smile.

"She's afraid I'll poison hers," explained Jessilyn.

Donovan picked up his fork and knife and cut into the fluffy biscuit, then proceed to dip it into the gravy. British and Jessilyn moved closer to inspect what he was doing.

"Something wrong?" Donovan asked.

"What are you doing to my biscuits?" Jessilyn asked, her arms folded across her chest.

"Eating them?" Donovan responded slowly as if they were the ones who were crazy.

"Why are you dipping your biscuit like a dieter dips her fork into her salad dressing on the side?" British asked.

Donovan sat back in his seat. "This is how eating biscuits and gravy is done."

"By who?" British and Jessilyn asked together.

Ignoring them, Donovan went back to cutting a piece of his biscuit. "This is how we eat them in the South."

"No, honey," snapped Jessilyn. She grabbed the plate from in front of Donovan and slid it, then the bowl, toward British "Ms. B, will you please do the honors?"

"Donovan, you live in South Beach," said British. She picked up the bowl and drizzled the thick, white gravy on top of the partially eaten biscuit. "Here in the true South, we smother our biscuits."

Now satisfied with the proper way the breakfast was being eaten, Jessilyn turned to Donovan, her hands on her hips. "Do you understand?"

"Yes, ma'am," Donovan said, saluting her.

"Fine. I'll bring you another plate."

British devoured his breakfast. She hummed while she chewed. She even contemplated going over to Southwood High School and getting that grade changed. "This is so delicious," British informed Donovan.

"So was the one bite I had." Donovan pressed his elbows on the table and shook his head. "I'm glad my faux pas on biscuits and gravy etiquette created a bond between the two of you. Perhaps now you'll have dinner with me?"

"Donovan," British said, hoping he heard the warning tone in her voice. Her eyes flittered toward the arched entrance where Stephanie's parents giggled and made their way to the table. Apparently the lovefest from last night continued today.

"Yes?" Donovan asked. He smiled devilishly, which only made him more handsome. "Jessilyn wanted to make sure we had a proper dinner tonight before everyone left."

"Everyone's leaving?" British looked up at Stephanie's mother.

"Just for the Thanksgiving break," she told her. "With our house still under construction, we're going to spend the next few days with family in Peachville."

With everyone gone, British realized there'd be no point in her staying, either. Images of her and Donovan rolling around on the king-size bed in his room flooded her mind. Her senses became alert and blood pulsed through her fingertips. British dropped her fork. Everyone at the table stared. "Sorry, y'all. Will you excuse me, please?"

British pushed herself away from the table and briskly walked out of the dining room. This wasn't right. She was here to help the girls with the upcoming competition. If the girls were leaving, there was no point in British staying here. She needed to go upstairs and pack, not to fantasize about the hunk at the end of the table. This couldn't be what Vonna had been talking about when she'd said it was beyond time for British to move on. Tiffani's idea, maybe.

She barely got to the staircase before Donovan caught up with her. His fingers laced around her upper arm as he led her into the library. The blinds were closed tight, sealing out the morning sun. The scent of old books overpowered the faint bacon aroma. British backed up against the wall to the sunroom.

"We always seem to find ourselves in here," Donovan whispered.

"You keep cornering me," said British, squaring her shoulders. The slight movement allowed a sliver of the sun inside the room. Donovan pressed his left hand above the wall just over her head. "You really ought to stop teasing me."

Heart racing, British licked her lips. "I'm sure I don't know what you're talking about. Why do you have me trapped in the library?"

Donovan turned his body to the right and allowed his biceps to point toward the door. "By all means," he teased, licking his bottom lip, "you're free to go, Ms. B."

Maybe it was the pounding in her ears or the distracting way his bulging bicep appeared, but she stayed. "How am I teasing you?"

"First, coming to my room via the balcony last night."

"Yeah…well," British huffed, "it's not like I could knock on your door and risk one of the girls seeing me and get the wrong idea."

"What idea would that be?"

To create space between them, British folded her arms across her chest. "Like I said last night, I didn't want to go to sleep without doing what I wanted to do."

"Which was to kiss me?" Donovan dropped his arm and faced her. "And your point of traipsing into the dining room with your hair like this was?" He reached out and touched a tendril that must have come loose.

British pushed his hand away from her face. The touch sent a shiver down her spine. "Like what?"

"The ole librarian bun at the top of your head."

She blinked blindly.

Donovan's eyes widened. "You don't know about the fantasies men have."

"Considering the librarians I've met…" British began with a deep sigh.

"There was a librarian in college and, if it weren't for her, I probably would never have studied." Donovan closed his eyes long enough for a strange jealous feeling to wash over British. She pushed at Donovan's chest, ignoring the hard muscles of his pecs. His eyes opened and his hand caught her fingertips. She didn't expect to shiver when he brought them to his lips for a soft kiss. "Aw, wait, you can't get mad at me for remembering Ms. Fredd."

"I'm not mad at a thing," British said calmly. Her insides screamed. "I just don't want anyone walking in on us."

"That's good to know." Donovan dropped his left hand and pushed the stray hair behind British's ear.

"What?"

"That you're at least thinking of me and you as an us." He slid his index finger along the slop of her nose.

"Donovan, I…" Again she couldn't find the right words.

"We'll take things slow, British," Donovan said. "And, fortunately for us, we'll be all alone after Thanksgiving."

Slow? Why the hell would she want something slow with Donovan? No, she wanted him fast, hard and sweaty. The back of British's throat went dry. Every image about the two of them together, in each crevice of this hotel, flashed through her mind like 8 mm film.

"Hey, we're back!" Stephanie yelled, coming through the front door. "Mr. D, we even saved you money."

And my hide, British thought to herself. Donovan was in Southwood for one reason only: to get away from his life down south. This made him a perfect choice for her. Eventually he was going to go home and to his life. That's what she wanted. Right?

Later on that evening, Donovan double-checked his garnet-and-gold tie in the mirror behind the vacated concierge's desk. "Don't act like this is your first meal with her, man," he told himself, "other people will be there."

The palms of his hands sweated. His heart raced with anticipation of seeing British again. He rolled his eyes, chiding himself for being so juvenile. Just because he hadn't seen her since breakfast didn't mean he needed to be so nervous. Except he was. Donovan had thrown down the gauntlet. He'd made his intentions clear. *Right?*

Hell, since when did he start doubting himself?

A set of twinkle lights suddenly lit up the hallway, followed by a surprised curse. "Jesus, Mary and Joseph."

"You okay, Mrs. Fitzhugh?" Donovan made his way down the hall to where the housekeeper tried to keep the elevator door open with her foot since her hands were filled with towels. The fresh, clean scent intoxicated him. While the condo in Miami was immaculate, Donovan's housekeeper put everything away herself, including his laundry and dry cleaning. He missed the warm fabric-softener smell from summers with his grandmother. God, when was the last time he'd smelled that scent? Maybe when he was twelve?

"I forgot how smart those girls were," she breathed. "One of them said they wanted to set up a mirror or something so they didn't crash into me."

"Looks like they set up motion sensors," Donovan said with a nod. He looked around to find a plug but figured they were somehow battery-operated. "Genius, I'll have to tell them over dinner tonight."

"Looks like it's just going to be the two of you, love," said Mrs. Fitzhugh.

"What's going on?"

"Didn't you hear about the storm?" The elderly woman began walking toward the hallway. Light flashed through the windows at the end of the corridor.

Since Will left a text every hour on the hour about his deadline, Donovan had turned his phone off. He was still on vacation, damn it. "I smell dinner."

Mrs. Fitzhugh nodded. "That's our little Jessilyn. She's quite the efficient chef. Everything is done." They stopped at a linen closet and she opened the door and pointed. "She finished dinner and headed out early. I hope you don't mind. Mr. Torres said for us to go home for the Thanksgiving break."

Good thing Ramon hadn't mentioned how Donovan had wanted them all to have extra pay for their time, as well, and he'd cover it. Otherwise it might be a bit awkward right now. "Sounds like a great guy," he said.

"He is, and he's even better with the new wife. There's a softer side of him."

Women did that to men. They made them soft. Look at how nervous he was at the thought of seeing British again after eight hours, thirty-three minutes and forty-five seconds. Donovan bent his elbow, twisted his wrist to take a nonchalant glance at his gold watch and tried to ignore the anxious feeling.

Mrs. Fitzhugh chuckled. Her body shook and her cheeks turned red. "You look like you're fighting it."

"Fighting what?"

"The softer side," she explained and then tapped him on the arm. "How long have you been single?"

Donovan flashed the older woman a bright smile. "Are you flirting with me?" He reached out and wrapped his arm around her shoulder.

"Child, I have panties older than you," she said, shrugging him off. "Besides, you're just a boy." Any attempt to get him away from her was feeble. The two of them laughed long and loud. They didn't hear anyone coming. Donovan liked Mrs. Fitzhugh and clearly she did not mind him.

"Be careful there, Mr. Ravens," said a familiar voice at the bottom of the steps. "Mrs. Fitzhugh has a mean right hook. I've seen it."

"Ah, there you are," Mrs. Fitzhugh said soberly, though her face was still red with laughter.

Donovan's heart slammed against his rib cage. British stood there with her arm propped up. She wore a formfitting blue gown that dipped into a V and exposed her full cleavage. Her curly hair hung loose and framed her face.

"I was just informing Mr. Ravens that everyone has taken leave for the night."

British leaned against the banister, almost relieved. "Jessilyn, too?"

"I thought you two bonded over making fun of me?" Donovan asked her.

"Until I change her grade," joked British, "I don't want to be left alone with her."

"But you are eating dinner with us tonight? Right?" Donovan asked eagerly—hopefully not too eagerly. "You're all dressed up."

"So are you," she said, letting her eyes linger up and down his frame. Donovan puffed out his chest.

"Well," Mrs. Fitzhugh said with a nervous head-shake, "I'm afraid it's going to be just the two of you for dinner. Everyone else has decided to head on out before the storm hits and the roads get undrivable."

"What about you, Mrs. Fitzhugh?" British asked. "Aren't you going to head out?"

"Oh yes, I don't want to miss Black Friday shopping in town. I wanted to make sure you guys ate."

"Oh please," moaned Donovan. "We can fix ourselves something to eat, can't we, British?"

"I don't know about him, but I can handle the food for everyone."

Mrs. Fitzhugh patted Donovan on the shoulder. "No, when I say everyone else left, everyone left. The van from the Brutti Hotel downtown just picked up a few guests who weren't going to relatives' for tomorrow. It's just the two of you tonight."

Lightning struck again. British reached out and touched Mrs. Fitzhugh's hand. "I think you should stay here instead of trying to make the trip into town."

"Don't be silly. I've got my grandson on the way."

As if on cue, a horn blew outside from beyond the front porch.

"Are you sure? Maybe the two of you can wait out the weather here?" British asked.

Mrs. Fitzhugh shook her head from side to side. "No, best we get on our way before the bottom falls out."

Donovan cocked his head to the side, afraid to ask.

"Before the storm hits."

As the older woman walked toward the door, the last two remaining guests walked with her. She assured them they would be just fine and that British knew every emergency contact in town. They opened the door for her, where her grandson rushed to them with a waiting umbrella. Donovan asked once more if she was okay and before she took off for shelter with her family member, Mrs. Fitzhugh stepped up on her tiptoes and gave him a kiss goodbye.

"Well," British sighed, facing the door as it closed. "What do we do now?"

Donovan loosened his tie and shook his head. "Now we have dessert first."

"What?"

Letting her in on his idea of a treat, Donovan stepped forward and cupped British's face. "Dessert," he whispered before dropping his face to kiss her.

British's arms wrapped around his neck and allowed him to dip her backward. Just as he recalled from last night, the spark was undeniable. British moaned and her lips vibrated against his. His body hardened. To be safe, he set her upright.

"If that was dessert," British asked him, "what's the main course?"

"Well—" he started and stopped himself with her help when she swatted him in the stomach. "All right, all right. But I'm not going to apologize for kissing you just now."

British took a deep breath. "I guess I had it coming."

Donovan narrowed his eyes. "I don't believe my kisses have ever been compared to a form of punishment."

"I didn't mean it to sound like one," said British. "I just meant, if I can just randomly kiss you because I don't want to regret anything, it's only fair you do the same."

A clang of thunder shook the door frame. Donovan laced his fingers with hers and led her to the dining room. This felt natural—as if the two of them just saw off their last guests and were heading upstairs. Only they weren't, Donovan reminded himself. While they'd been sharing a few kisses here and there, Donovan acknowledged the fact that she was a widow. He assumed he was the first person she was attracted to since her husband's death. He needed to keep this in mind. Eventually he was going to leave Southwood. Hopefully it would be with British—as the new spokesmodel for Ravens Cosmetics.

"Well, I figured since we have to be around your family, we need to get this whole sexual tension out of the way."

"You're pretty sure of yourself, Donovan," British said with a nod.

They stopped and stood in the archway of the dining room and faced each other. "I think you wouldn't have showed up in my room in a thin nightgown last night if you weren't feeling the same vibes as me. But I don't want things to get muddled for us. We may end up working together if you take my offer and be Ravens Cosmetics' newest star."

"I won't," she assured him. "Anyway, what are you talking about?" Annoyance dripped from her voice.

It didn't matter to him. She was so adorable, standing there with her hands behind her back, leaning on her side of the arch. "What am I taking things slow with?"

"Well," Donovan began after deeply clearing his throat. "Do we need to have this talk now?"

"Are you referring to me being a widow?" British half laughed. "Are you trying to marry me?"

Donovan felt his eyes widen at the word. "Well... I—"

"Good grief, Donovan," said British. She crossed her arms, tucking her right hand under her arm and her left on top. *Her ringless hand on top.* "I'll admit there is a tension between us. But I can't be sure it's sexual. You've been harassing me about working for your company."

"So when I caught you staring at me this morning?"

She opened her mouth then closed it. "Well, I didn't say you aren't attractive."

"You're turning red, British." He swore if he stepped closer he might spark up in flames.

The light from the candles on the table highlighted her face when she turned away from him. "What you're describing is pure physical desire. Pheromones."

"Oh," he said with a wink, "so animalistic."

"Whatever," she huffed and stepped into the dining room. "It's all science."

"All this science talk," he said rubbing his heart. "You're really turning me on." And she was, but he guessed from the way she rolled her eyes she didn't believe him one bit.

The table was set with antique silver and patterned plates. A silver-domed tray housed a perfectly roasted turkey. Donovan had peeked earlier. British chose a seat by the head of the table, close to where he'd sat this morning. For a moment Donovan pictured three curly-haired kids with features perfectly blending those of the Ravens family and British. He blinked and shook his head. The image disappeared. Weird.

"I see Jessilyn made a turkey," British noted as she started walking toward the French doors. Had they lingered longer, Donovan might have wiped everything off the table and made love to her in front of the turkey. "The sides must be in here," she went on. "How about we just do our dinner buffet-style and save us extra dishes to clean up? Sound good to you? Oh crap."

British rushed through the kitchen where they'd first dined together and headed for the back door. Marker ink drizzled down the white pages of the poster board where steps for the big and small challenges were outlined. Opened plastic coffee filters for the glow-in-the-dark chromatology butterflies took on water. "The girls left some of the equipment you just got them outside and it's raining."

Seemingly without thinking, British kicked out of her heels and jetted out the door. Donovan followed half in fear of making sure she didn't hurt herself and half to do whatever she needed done. "Wait."

Rain poured down between them. He had no idea what half the stuff was but it seemed important. "Load me up," Donovan said, coming up to her.

Without a word she lifted metal rods, batteries, radios and lights into his open arms.

"Correct me if I'm wrong, but is this safe?"

"It's better than wasting the items," British noted, grabbing her own stack and heading for the back porch.

"Yeah, but the items can be replaced," he said. "You can't. And then I'll be forced to find someone else to be RC's spokesmodel." British stopped long enough to give him a pretty snarl. Even soaking wet, he wanted her. But now was not the time.

Donovan followed her movements until they cleaned up the backyard. By the time they finished, the two of them were drenched and found this to be the right time to laugh about it.

"I'm going to have a serious talk with them when they get back," said British. "They can't just waste things. Look at this," she hissed and stepped off the porch. "Stephanie left a controller and her SSRs for her string of lights. The solid state relays are going to connect to the computer, if they're not ruined by now."

What appeared to be a string of loose bulbs turned out to be an underground set that didn't budge. When British bent to pull the lights with a heavy tug, she fell... flat on her back. Donovan darted off the steps to scoop her up. "Are you okay?" he said in a panic. They made it inside before, as Ms. Fitzhugh said, the bottom fell out. Rain fell like a heavy sheet.

"My pride is hurt," said British. "Put me down."

"No way, you're filthy," he said, shaking his head. "If you think I'm a lousy cook, you should see my non-existent housekeeping skills." Donovan hiked British up in his arms for a better grip. "Nope, I'm carrying you to your room."

At least while she pouted she was quiet.

Donovan carried her up the grand staircase and to her closed door.

"Close your eyes," British ordered him. "I'm not hurt."

"Woman, I practically saw your naked tail the other night and if that didn't give me enough view, your split in your dress revealed a whole hell of a lot more."

British did what he expected and rolled her eyes. "Fine, whatever." She reached into the V of her bodice and extracted her card key, giving him an impatient look. Wordlessly she raised an eyebrow and demanded him to lower her enough to unlock the door. Such an easy task to do but so hard for Donovan. He was mesmerized by the swell of her breasts. Rain droplets caressed her skin in places he wished he could.

British cleared her throat and brought him back to focus. "Right, uh, sorry."

Once the door popped open, Donovan set British on the dresser by the door. To silence her from questioning him, he raised his index finger in the air, then went to grab a few towels from the bathroom. By the time he turned back around, British had already slipped the gorgeous gown off her shoulders. She folded her arms across her bare breasts and jutted her chin forward. Donovan shook his head. "Not sorry."

The moment Donovan anticipated for later, started right now. Donovan wedged himself between her wet thighs while he cupped her face. Their tongues reached out for a reunion. British's hands tugged at the knot of his tie and her fingers impatiently ripped open the front of his Oxford shirt. Their feverish kiss didn't break, not even when he led them over to the edge of the bed and coaxed her body backward with his frame. While his left hand held up the lower half of her body, Donovan's hands palmed her breasts. His thumb traced circles on her areolae.

British's hands skillfully worked him out of his wet shirt. He helped with unbuttoning his pants while she slid them over his rear. He wanted her so badly, he barely waited to pull his slacks completely off. He fumbled in the dark with the condom in his wallet, hating himself for taking too much time away from devouring her body.

British waited with her elbows up and legs open. The color of her dress on the floor caught the flickering light of the sky outside. Keeping them safe, Donovan felt his way up her calves, to her muscled thighs and to the apex of her legs. His fingers pushed at the fleshy wet center, his erection straining against the rubber material.

British sat up enough to grab Donovan by the neck and pull him down into a warm kiss. While he pressed her body onto the bed, he entered her slowly. British pressed her body against his. Her breasts crushed against his chest and her legs wrapped around his waist. Donovan wanted to take it slow but as she nibbled his ear he lost himself in her and brought her to the first of many more orgasms that were sure to come.

From the moment their bodies connected, British knew there was something irreversible between her and Donovan. A part of her wanted to feel guilty for being with another man but her heart wouldn't let her. This felt right. His body was so hard with muscles and had been so strong to have lifted and carried her earlier this evening; his skin was so soft. Donovan turned onto his belly and British stroked his bare back.

Donovan turned his face toward her. His smile melted her heart. "Are you okay?" he asked, reaching over to stroke her face. The pad of his thumb brushed just beneath her lower lashes.

"I'm fine," she answered with a soft smile, "everything is fine."

"I don't want you to have any regrets," said Donovan.

British turned her face to kiss the inside of his palm. Her lips twitched with a grin as he shivered. "I'm where I want to be, doing what I want to do." She leaned over and kissed Donovan on the lips. With gentle aggression she coaxed his mouth open and tasted him again. Reenergized, she pushed her body against his to urge him on his back. "I don't think I can get enough of you."

Donovan obliged and held on to British's hips while she straddled his naked waist. Her body urged him to flip on his back. His hands reached for her breasts and held them, kneading them gently. Electricity bolted through her body. She realized a difference between being with Christian and being with Donovan. Donovan didn't tire. His erection pulsed between her legs. British nibbled her bottom lip, contemplating what to do next or where to start. She wasn't used to this wanton behavior but she wanted to devour Donovan.

Donovan sat up with her in his lap and whispered the words that filled her heart with joy and security. "We can take our time. I'm not going anywhere."

Chapter 7

A harsh, old-fashioned-sounding bell went off next to British's ear. She stirred in her bed and reached aimlessly to stop the sound. Blindly she found the alarm clock and hit a button to get the noise to stop. British shuddered. Her body naturally sought the heat source in her bed and found it in an oversize man. Not just any man. Donovan Ravens. She smiled as she blinked her gaze into focus. His broad back faced her. The tips of her fingers itched to trace the tattoo on his body, but she decided to wait. There was something else she needed to do but, as she lifted the covers for a peek at his bare butt, she forgot what it was.

"Dear God, woman," Donovan croaked, "are you ready to go again?"

Giggling, British lifted herself up on her right elbow. What she'd thought was her room was actually his. That's right. She'd followed him in here through the balcony when he'd left to get more condoms for the two of them and they'd ended up christening the room in here. "I forgot, you're an old man."

The little bit of covers she still wore left her body. Donovan rolled toward her, taking the blanket but replacing it with his strong arms. She'd take those any day. Last night with Donovan…this morning with Donovan, had been incredible. All she needed to do was to think about the things he did to her and she was ready to go.

"I'm old, huh?" Donovan flicked both nipples with his tongue.

A spark of desire pumped through her. "I don't recall those exact words."

Donovan ducked his head under the sheets. His full lips started a trail of kisses down her diaphragm across her belly. She was suddenly self-conscious of how desperately she needed to clean up. British pulled him back by his massive shoulders. "I need to shower, I must smell horrific."

"Let's shower after we lie here for a while," said Donovan and closed his eyes. He pulled himself back up to the pillow by hers and, without thinking, British cocked her leg over his. They just fit together.

The realization came that she'd just been intimate with another man after a long…long time. British didn't want to compare the two men but it was inevitable. She and Christian learned to make love together. The men were different. Christian, because of his heart, had to limit his overexcitement. British felt a mix of exhilaration and fright at Donovan's uninhibited passion. She'd assumed Donovan would be a great lover physically, but mentally he went beyond her expectations. He anticipated needs she didn't know she had. Donovan paid attention to every inch of her body, from her toes to the top of her head. Euphoria settled into her veins. Not wanting to forget this feeling, British rested her head but didn't close her eyes. At least, she didn't think she had shut them until a loud shrill woke her. This time it wasn't the alarm clock. It sounded like a doorbell.

"I thought we were alone," said British.

"Hell, I paid for everyone to stay away," Donovan growled and stalked naked toward the balcony door, which faced the front entrance of Magnolia Palace.

Damn, the man looked good naked. The white curtains billowed in the cool fall breeze. A faint smell of burning wood from a smoker on a nearby estate filled the bedroom.

A voice called out from the front lot, "British, honey," and broke the silence of the morning.

British flopped back onto the bed. "Please tell me…"

Donovan half turned to catch what she was going to say. She wanted the bed to swallow her whole. "Is that…?"

"British, it's your mom. Come let me in. I'm worried. You haven't picked up and you know I like to start cooking first thing in the morning."

The alarm clock on the side of Donovan's bed went off again. This time British turned it off and remembered what today was. Thanksgiving.

Not since before his accident did Donovan recall a time he felt the panic need to leap out of bed, but that's what he'd done when he heard British's mother was downstairs waiting for them to make sure they came over to the house. Donovan would have preferred spending the day in bed with British, especially after last night and this morning—and even more when they stopped in the driveway to British's family home.

"Well, there's my little girl."

Donovan hung back by the car when a burly, oversize man stepped out of the two-story farmhouse with a shotgun by his side. Folks were serious about their guns in the South. The summer Will and Zoe met, Will had been cleaning weapons with one of Zoe's friend's husbands when a young man came to the house to pick up the teenager for a date. Somehow Donovan knew this was no act. This was British's father. He stood there dressed in dark green camouflage and large rubber boots, holding a long rifle.

When Joan corralled them this morning, she promised Donovan she'd take good care of him once they got to the house. Before Donovan closed the passenger-side door for British, she'd already high-stepped it around his car. He tried not to stare at her hourglass figure in her formfitting jeans. The baseball T-shirt she wore with the red sleeves accentuated the curves of her rounded breasts. He couldn't believe that less than an hour ago he was holding her in his bed and now here he was, with her family, all vulnerable. He took a deep breath of the cool morning air and pushed the thoughts out of his head. Three months ago, before Tracy, women had rotated in and out of his life. There'd barely been time for name exchanges, let alone hanging out with the parents. Yet somehow with British, this just felt natural. He liked her and enjoyed being around her.

Joan pulled her red SUV into the winding redbrick driveway right behind Donovan, leaving him to wonder if this was a trap. If Joan had figured out what was going on this morning, she hadn't let on when they'd met her downstairs in the lobby.

"Hey, Daddy." British walked across the manicured lawn and maneuvered her way through the already-placed Christmas decorations. "What do you have going on here? I thought the Christmas Council said no decorations are supposed to be put up before Thanksgiving."

A twinge of guilt hit Donovan. He kicked the toe of his Timberlands against the bottom of the car to get any dirt off and to distract himself for a moment. He wondered what his brothers were doing right about now. Will said he and Zoe were heading out of town, which seemed like an odd thing to do this time of year but maybe that was marriage and the two wanted to be alone. Donovan understood. He preferred to stay in on the traditional family holiday instead of being pecked with questions from his sisters about Tracy's absence or worse, whether Donovan had made any headway on finding a new spokesmodel for RC.

His family gathered every year at his grandmother Naomi's compound for an old-fashioned, catered Thanksgiving. Given that Naomi had spent her whole life cultivating the company, learning how to cook was never one of her strong suits. No one in his family had learned how... Well, the twins, Dana and Eva, had learned once they married. Maybe later he'd give them a call. The caterers usually left around four in the afternoon. Making a mental note, Donovan took a deep breath.

"Thanksgiving started at midnight," said her father, wagging his finger at his daughter. They met at the bottom step and he pulled her into a big bear hug, twirling her around in the air. Like her mother, British's father was equally tall. "Who's this?"

"This is Donovan," said British.

At the exact moment British turned to face him, Donovan blew out his held breath. How was she going to describe him? What were they? Why did he care? He didn't believe in labels. Usually it took him weeks to figure out what category to place women. They never made it to girlfriend status, though the media may have suggested different.

"Donovan," British went on, "this is my dad, Levi Woodbury."

"I already told you," Joan told her husband with a huff and a wink at Donovan.

"Ah, yes, I remember now." Levi Woodbury stepped forward and extended his beefy hand. "Pleased to meet you, son. Welcome to Thanksgiving at the Woodburys'."

"Wait," a little voice said from the wooden door with the stained glass window, "so we have another member for the football game?"

British leaned at the waist. "Eli? Is that you or a grown man?"

A little kid fully emerged onto the porch in a pair of superhero turtle pajamas. In a while, British managed to greet a half dozen or so nieces and nephews, who all surrounded her like she was a celebrity. Their screaming brought out British's siblings and, one by one, Donovan met her family.

"Donovan, this is my brother Finn, my sister Cree, and twin sister and brother, Irish and Scots."

Donovan tried to remember everyone's name. They all favored each other and shared a blend of their parents' looks. The two sisters favored British with their curly hair but their attitudes were completely different. One of them seemed to *mother* British while the other *smothered* her. Both ladies fussed over British's hair to the point where she ended up tying it in a bun at the top of her head, which only got them talking about her denim leggings and green Converse shoes not being representable.

"Leave my baby alone," Levi spoke up. "She's dressed just fine. They were fourteen and fifteen when British came along so as you can see, they like to pretend she's theirs."

"Thanks, Daddy." The rest of the Woodbury family rolled their eyes.

"Donovan—" Levi turned his attention from his kids "—you look to be in good shape."

"I try, sir."

"Great, we're waiting for the turkey to get done but in the meantime the rest of us are going to play some football," said Levi. "My crybaby boys have been complaining about being on my team."

Scots stepped forward with his hands in the air. "You see that, man?" he said to Donovan. "My pops doesn't know how to throw yet he insists on playing quarterback. See my hand? See my crooked fingers?" Scots thrust his fingers in Donovan's face.

"You're supposed to catch with your hands like this." Their father demonstrated the proper way for everyone. "Are you a crier?" Levi asked Donovan.

"He doesn't cry." British's declaration might have signed Donovan's death warrant.

Given the size of Levi, Donovan understood why the man wanted to play. However, the evidence staring him in the face gave him pause. Thankfully, Finn stepped forward. Like his father, he was dressed in a pair of green camouflage overalls. "We're going huntin', Pop."

Relieved, Donovan's shoulders dropped. "Aw, man."

"Don't listen to them," Joan said. "No one is going anywhere."

The men and boys, including Levi, all sighed with disappointment, not that Joan seemed to care. She kept walking up the porch steps. "The turkey is not the only thing that's not ready. I need some help in the kitchen. Donovan?"

Donovan smiled apologetically at the group. "Sorry,

but if the food is going to taste as good as it smells now, I've got to go with her."

"Smart friend you have here," Cree said, linking her arm through Donovan's.

"Yeah, British," Irish chimed in. "Where have you been hiding him?"

"I," British declared, "haven't been hiding him anywhere. He's been hanging out at Magnolia Palace."

Donovan heard the catty tone between the sisters. He waited for British to claim him…yet he still didn't know why. He'd known women a lot longer than he had her and cared less what they thought of him.

The inside of the Woodburys' home was not as Christmassy as the outside. A bare tree stood in the corner of the living room to the right. Two women were cleaning off the mantel, placing pictures in a box. Donovan wished he'd seen them. What had British looked like as a child? He pegged her as a tomboy wearing overalls, hunting gear and pigtails. The ladies stopped what they were doing to come and greet the two of them. They each hugged British and introduced themselves to Donovan as the wives of Scots and Finn. Jenny and Scots had been married for ten years, Nicole and Finn fifteen. Two gentlemen came downstairs, complaining about being abandoned in the attic, but stopped once they saw their young sister-in-law. British hugged them and introduced Cree's and Irish's husbands, Tom and Robert.

A long table with a fall-themed tablecloth stood in the center of the dining room with a table setting for sixteen.

Joan led them through the dining room into the kitchen with a long bar. Beyond the bar sat a breakfast nook with a table filled with coloring books and crayons. Covered dishes lined the bar. Pots and pans boiled on the flat-topped stove and when Joan leaned over to open the crowded oven, the savory smell of roasting turkey filled the air. Donovan's stomach growled.

"We have been nibbling all morning," Joan said to him. She pointed at the credenza in the open space of the family room with different levels of brunch foods ranging from a stack of pancakes, sausage and bacon to waffles and eggs under a clear dome.

The Macy's Thanksgiving Day Parade played on the wide-screen television mounted on the wall in front of an L-shaped gray couch. A set of matching gray love seats sat against the half wall that led to a staircase to the second floor. An oversize fir tree stood on the opposite side of the room by the sliding-glass doors.

"We're starving," said British, taking hold of Donovan's elbow.

"'We'?" Cree picked up on her sister's choice of words.

British glared at her before grabbing a silver-trimmed plate. "Yes 'we.'"

"Donovan…" began Joan. "We know British has been staying at Magnolia Palace with the STEM girls. Have they been bothering your stay in Southwood?"

Donovan accepted a plate from British. "I wouldn't say bothering me."

"Please, he's practically a member of the team by now," British groaned. They stood side by side in front of the food and when she looked up at him, she winked.

Returning the wink, Donovan bumped her shoulder. "We're thinking about changing it to Guys Raised in the South, huh?"

Before laughing, British rolled her eyes. "How many times do I have to tell you, Miami is not the South?"

"You're from Miami?" Joan asked him as she straightened the tablecloth.

"Yes, ma'am," answered Donovan.

The other Woodbury men came into the kitchen and began quickly snacking and grabbing cookies from a Christmas-tree-shaped, tiered metal tray by the double-door refrigerator. "Stop it," said Joan, shaking a crayon at them. "You'll ruin your meal."

"This meal is taking forever," said Scots. His wife, Jenny, joined his side and took the cookie away from him.

Donovan fiddled with the plate in his hand and smiled. He missed his family.

"The new guy gets to eat," Finn pointed out.

"His name is Donovan," Joan clarified, "and he's a guest in this home. Next Thanksgiving, he won't get the same treatment."

Something about the idea of a return to Southwood filled Donovan with something…good. It wasn't like he hadn't been around family before. In fact, British's family structure resembled Donovan's, including the constant bantering. When his cousins and siblings joked around, their banter always dealt with the family business. Donovan cocked his head to the side and recalled that most of their exchanges surrounded who did better in their field or who was responsible for sales. British's family was more relaxed. They teased British about her failed science experiments that had led to the kitchen being remodeled twice. It was clear everyone in British's family was proud of her. Donovan could get used to this atmosphere.

"Great, more hands to help decorate at midnight," Scots said. "I'm ready for a nap."

"So we're not going hunting tonight?" Finn spoke up.

British slid into her seat at the nook. "If you're going hunting, does this mean Black Friday shopping is out tomorrow?"

"Black Friday shopping?" Donovan pierced his sausage link with a fork and perked up. "I want to go."

"No," said British.

"C'mon." Joan beamed. "British, mind your manners. Donovan, would you like to go with us tomorrow?"

"I'd love to. I've never been."

British bowed her head. The sisters-in-law dropped their tinsel, the sisters wavered in near-faints, and all of the Woodbury men and in-laws wiped their hands down their faces. Donovan chuckled at everyone's reactions. He felt the need to explain. "With my schedule, I usually shop online for everyone."

"You have no idea what you've just done," British said under her breath.

Donovan shrugged his shoulders. "What? I'm looking forward to this."

"We wake up at three," said Irish. She took a seat across from the two of them and propped her elbows on the table. A few strands of gray stretched through her curly brown hair, which she kept in a side bun. Donovan couldn't guess her exact age, but she aged beautifully. "What do you do for a living, Donovan?"

"He works for his family's company," British supplied. "He's in finance."

"Oh, you must love math," Irish said, sitting back. "The two of you must have a lot in common."

Cree came over and joined them with two glass mason jars of tea. Like her sister, the only way Donovan could tell she was of a certain age was by the gray in her hair and the slight crinkles at the corners of her eyes when she smiled, which she did every time she looked at her baby sister.

"Donovan," Cree said, "do you recall your first words, or at least what your parents said?"

British dropped her fork. "Seriously, Cree? Mom," she whined.

"Cree, leave your sister to her friend."

Ignoring the warning, Cree, thankfully, continued. "We all knew British was going to be smart because her first words weren't anything like 'mama' or 'daddy.'"

"Or 'sister,'" Irish interjected, "as in the sister who stayed up with her so the old no-business-having-kids-after-forty could get rest."

A deep belly laugh filled the kitchen. Levi wrapped his arms around his wife's waist and dipped her back for a kiss—but not before making a statement to make all of the other adults groan. "We're still trying."

"Every single night," Joan gloated.

British was the first to recuperate. Her eyes were still wide and cheeks beet red. "You see why I didn't want you to meet my parents?"

"They're cute," said Donovan. They certainly were different from his parents, Mark and Evelyn Ravens. It wasn't like Donovan grew up in a strict household, just a busy, business-oriented one. The company came first. Yes, the family spent time together but most of it was at the corporate office in Miami. Donovan's parents provided the best for their children and he appreciated the things he was given. It was just different here, warmer almost. His parents touched when they posed for cameras at functions. British's parents touched each other, a lot, whether with a pat on the back, a brush against each other's shoulders or even a flat-out kiss. This was better. "I want to be like that one day."

"Married?" British's eyebrows went up. She bumped his shoulder again, seemingly intent on teasing him.

The notion suddenly didn't seem so frightening. "Yes," he responded honestly.

"On behalf of my brothers and sisters, I apologize for our parents' behavior," said Cree.

"Whatever," groaned Irish. "We only have to worry when Daddy starts talking in his accents."

Everyone started to laugh and even though Donovan had no idea what was going on, he laughed, too. The rest of the morning melted into the noon hour. Donovan helped in the kitchen for a while. He sliced through hard-boiled eggs, whipped up the cream for the dessert later and stirred the greens several times. While the turkey finished up in the oven, Levi wanted to get out in the yard with his new partner. The football game consisted of Donovan, the brothers-in-law and Levi on one team versus the other Woodburys. Donovan's team won but Cree's husband, Tom, got hurt in a tackle…by his wife.

Joan declared the home football game over and invited everyone inside for dinner. Once the meal was blessed, dishes began being passed around. Donovan stuffed himself on dressing, collard greens, sweet potato soufflé for dessert, turkey and ham. He paced himself to make room for the baked goods. All types of desserts sat on the credenza where breakfast had been served and included apple pie, sweet potato pie, dark chocolate cake and a yellow cake slathered in chocolate icing by British's four nieces. Since Cree lived up north with her husband, someone had made a pumpkin pie and sat it down next to the sweet potato one. Donovan impressed the family with his knowledge of the difference between the orange pies.

Once they loaded the dishwasher after the meal, everyone settled down into the family room to watch football. Cree and her husband went upstairs. The half dozen nieces wanted British to read them a bedtime story and Donovan did not mind hanging out with the rest of the Woodburys. He sat on the edge of the couch and rooted for the Dallas Cowboys; they had recorded the Dallas game earlier so they could finish watching the Detroit one after the family football match. Donovan was in his element. It felt great to relax around these people he just met today. They brought him into the fold and Donovan felt like one of the Woodburys and couldn't wait to do this for the next holiday. The thought made him sit up.

"Hey, Donovan," Irish whispered from her seat in one of the chairs by the stairs.

Donovan turned his gaze away from the television. Irish thumbed through one of the boxes with Christmas items at the side of the chair. "Hi, Irish."

"In case you haven't realized, we're all happy to have you here this evening."

"I'm grateful for you all inviting me into your home and taking me under your wing," Donovan replied. Their maternal grandmother, who had arrived just before the meal, seemed to approve, as well. At least, he thought so, if there was any indication coming from the way Joan's mother clung to his arm the entire meal. British had found it embarrassing but Donovan had not. She was pushing one hundred, but Donovan saw clearly that Joan's genes had started with her. Impressive to sit at a table with four generations of beauty.

Robert, Irish's husband, cleared his throat when he came into the family room with a plate of apple pie. "It took having our third child before I was allowed to help with dinner."

"And after that you were banned," Finn stated.

Levi snorted in his sleep.

"Well, I am glad to see British happy," said Irish.

"I am not sure it's my doing," Donovan replied. "But I do know she's fun to be around."

Scots stretched his legs across his wife's in the love seat. "Exactly how much time are you planning on spending with our little sister? Ouch," he cried out when his hair was pulled. "What?"

"I get it," Donovan chuckled. "I have sisters, too."

"Well, how long do you plan on staying in town, Mr. Ravens?" Joan asked. "Aren't they missing you at Ravens Cosmetics?"

Identity exposed, Donovan widened his eyes. "I did not mean to omit anything."

"You didn't, not really. I used to model," said Joan. "I did a few print ads for your grandmother—pre-children, of course."

"I would have said recently," Donovan answered honestly. British's mother blushed the same way British did. "To answer your question, I am on a hiatus right now. I can go back whenever. Right now, though, I am dying to see the STEM-Off go through."

"If British is letting you get involved with the GRITS team, you must be pretty special," said Irish. She fiddled with the items in a box. "You are aware of Christian, right?"

"I am. He sounded like a wonderful man."

Everyone agreed.

"I am impressed British let you help with the girls," said Finn. "After Christian died, British put all her energy and dedication into her work and teaching STEM to the girls, even if she had to do it at that youth center."

"And the insurance money Christian left her," added Scots. "Don't forget that."

"Burns my ass the way she's been frozen out by the science department," said Finn.

This burst of information piqued Donovan's interest. The idea of someone not treating British fairly didn't sit right with him. He balled his fists against his thighs. He needed names and he needed them now.

"Oh, look," Irish cooed, "here's a photo of British." She leaned across the distance and handed Donovan an old photograph. Out the corner of his eye he caught British coming down the stairs, but her movements seemed to happen in slow motion.

"No-no-no-no-no," British repeated. But it was too late. She arrived at the arm of the couch with her hands over her face.

"British," Donovan said, standing. In confusion, he shook his head. She lied. Why would she lie after everything they'd talked about? "All this time you've been shooting me down about being the spokesmodel for Ravens Cosmetics, making it seem the job was beneath you?" The initial knee-jerk reaction was anger but compassion struck him as soon as he saw the pain in British's face.

"You were offered a job to be their spokesmodel?" Joan asked, standing, as well.

British rolled her eyes at her mother and huffed, "I'm not that person anymore."

"Once a beauty queen, always a beauty queen," Donovan told her. "You're perfect."

"Yeah…well, it's hard to imagine I'm perfect when the whole reason Christian is dead is because of me and my stupid beauty queen obligations."

So many questions entered Donovan's mind. Why or how did she think she was responsible for her husband's death? The quiver in British's voice broke Donovan. All he wanted to do was hold her until all her pain went away. He felt helpless for not knowing what to say or do. "Oh, British," everyone in the room chorused.

Tears welled in British's eyes. Donovan felt like a jerk, especially when she stormed outside through the sliding-glass door.

Chapter 8

A fall breeze blew leaves on top of the aqua-blue water of the pool next to her parents' deck. British shivered against the back of the blue-and-white Adirondack chair she sulked in. There was always a reason why she didn't want to come home for the holidays. Her parents and siblings made too much of a big deal about British not seeing professional help after Christian passed away. She accepted his death, knew she was widowed and subconsciously believed his death was her fault. At the time of his death British still volunteered in pageantry. Her intent was to encourage young beauty queens to reach for more than a title and break the glass ceilings in the scientific fields.

Five years ago, however, British forgot her crown at home. It was easier to hold everyone's attention if British wore her tiara and her lab coat. Christian offered to drive home and get it, which he did. Christian swerved to avoid hitting it and ran into a tree. Her tiara was found on the seat of the passenger's seat when a deer ran across the road. She guessed this holiday weekend exposed her suppressed thoughts and had manifested when Irish brought out the old photograph. Maybe she overacted.

The first year without Christian, everyone had stepped on eggshells not to mention his name. They'd taken down the wedding photographs, like she didn't have any at her apartment. But then tonight, to bring up the pageantry to Donovan? *Ugh*, she groaned inwardly. Had she not overheard part of the conversation while she'd finished the bedtime stories upstairs, there'd be no telling what other things Irish would have spilled. British argued with herself, shaking her head. She should have never agreed to come over.

"You're going to freeze out here."

British glanced over her shoulder and rolled her eyes toward the water when she saw her mother coming with a dark plaid blanket. The temperature had been dropping all day. Steam rose from the hot tub at the end of the porch near the bricked-in grill. Orange glows of backyard bonfires shone in their nearest neighbors' yard.

"Not only did I give you life, but I'm bringing you warmth, too, and you're going to sit up here and roll your eyes at me?" Joan tossed the wool blanket over British's shoulders and took a seat on a matching chair to face her.

"I didn't roll my eyes," British lied. She adjusted the blanket to fit her shoulders evenly and stretched her legs out in front of her.

Joan sat in the same position as her daughter. "You forget I raised you."

"Tell that to some of my brothers and sisters in

there." British pointed her thumb at the sliding-glass door. They'd undermined her at every corner today, from cooking in the kitchen to dessert. They'd mocked her for using science to help cook and had had the nerve to bring up all her embarrassing childhood stories, including her time as a beauty queen.

"They love you."

"You mean to make fun of me," British huffed.

"You do understand this is the first time they've been able to experience this with you?"

"Experience what?" British asked, sitting up. "They never acted like that with Christian."

Joan sat up, as well. She reached over and patted British's leggings-clad leg. "Dear, you and Christian grew up together. He and his family ate at our Thanksgiving table all throughout high school. Finn, Cree, Irish and Scots always saw Christian as part of the family. Seeing you with another man..."

"I'm not with another man," British lied again. Her spine tingled, reminding her just how much she *had* been with him last night. It was all she could do to keep from combusting each time she bumped an arm against his in the house—her soul caught on fire.

"Again," Joan sighed, "why are you trying to lie to me? Or are you trying to convince yourself there's nothing between you and Donovan Ravens?"

British shrugged her shoulders.

"Donovan is the first man you've brought home."

"You invited him," British reminded her.

Joan chuckled. "Girl, I am not going back and forth with you about this. It is evident there's something going on between the two of you and I don't want to have to tell you what my intuition is telling me."

British turned to face her mother and contemplated

testing out what she thought was going on. Did she want to tell her that for one moment in her life she wanted to have a quick fling with no attachments and that Donovan was the perfect person for the job?

"Mom."

"You're twenty-eight," Joan went on. "Not dead."

"You sound like Vonna."

"Your mother-in-law is right. Hell, at seventy, your dad and I are still very—"

"All right, we're done here." British got to her feet. Her hands flew up to cover her ears as she focused on the rippling water of the pool. Suddenly her eyes focused on a pair of bathing suits by the Jacuzzi. Since no one else lived here during the year, the garments could only belong to her parents. British frowned.

Joan stood behind British and wrapped her arms around her shoulders. "Sweetie, no matter what's going on in here—" she tapped British's temple "—or here—" and tapped her heart "—I love you."

"Thanks, Mom." British stared off into the horizon.

"And, dear…" she whispered. "Dessert's here."

Raising her brows, British shook her head. "We had dessert."

Gently, Joan spun British around by the shoulders. British looked beyond her mother's height to find Donovan standing outside by the chair she'd just vacated. He wore his khaki chinos and someone else's black hoodie, zipped to his neck. In his hand he balanced a round tray with two…cupcakes.

"I'll leave you two alone," Joan whispered.

Donovan smiled, mouthed a thank-you to Joan and leaned down to kiss her on the cheek. British's heart ached. Christian used to do the same thing. Her mother was right. Christian had been a big part of the family for so long. Maybe it was wrong for her to allow Donovan to come. Yet, here she was staring at him and feeling differently than ever before in her life.

"Hi." Donovan stepped closer.

"Hey," she replied. This was the first real moment they'd had alone since this morning, which seemed so long ago. "What do you have there?"

"Something called the Blues Be Gone cupcake," Donovan replied. "They arrived while you were out here."

British's eyes widened. She craned her neck to the side and spotted Vonna and Tiffani quickly turn around as if they weren't spying on them. She wasn't surprised to see them here. They were close with her family and had probably finished up their Thanksgiving dinner and came out to visit. "That's my mother-in-law," she explained to him as she shook her head. "Or is it former?"

"She's family," Donovan answered.

"Donovan, I—I—" she stuttered and tried to find the words.

"Let me say this," he said. "I want to apologize if I made you feel pressured about coming to work for my family's company, especially not knowing what I do now."

"Thanks," British half-heartedly said.

"But you have to know that the car accident wasn't your fault."

Now with her shoulders squared, British sighed. "Why? Because that's what Irish told you?"

"Not just Irish," Donovan admitted with a nod. He set the tray of cupcakes down on the table between the chairs and stepped closer. "Finn, Scots and Cree came downstairs to tell me about the accident."

"They had no right."

"The accident happened," said Donovan. "It was this time of year. Your dad says deer season runs this time of year and the animals are prevalent in this area. It's not fair, but these things happen."

"Christian wouldn't have been on the road if I didn't forget my tiara for my motivational talk at a beauty pageant," British argued, but didn't put up a fight when Donovan wrapped his arms around her waist and pulled her close, tucking himself in the plaid blanket, as well.

"According to your mother-in-law, Christian was born with cardiomyopathy and lived longer than ever expected and she says it was because of you."

British's head moved to the side, catching Vonna blatantly staring at them, even giving British the thumbs-up of approval before closing the curtains. "She's crazy."

"And insistent," Donovan added. "She said we need to eat these cupcakes right now." He moved away to grab one of the desserts. "You have a wonderful family, British. Thank you for inviting me."

I didn't, she opened her mouth to say, but received a mouthful of frosting.

"Try the cake, British," Donovan teased. He wiped his finger across her upper lip to get the rich icing.

"I'm going to kill my family for their big ole mouths."

Not satisfied with the job his finger did, Donovan lowered his mouth to hers and used his tongue to clean her lips, nibbling for a moment on her bottom one. "Don't kill them just yet. I have been recruited to play Santa in the winter festival on Saturday."

Saturday, she thought, her pulse starting to throb wickedly. "Well, aren't we becoming domesticated?"

"Hell, I don't mind," Donovan chuckled. "I'll learn how to cook and clean better for all this good food I've been eating. I swear I gained ten pounds today."

"I guarantee you'll work it off tomorrow if you're still up for Black Friday shopping."

Donovan took a step back to grandstand his opportunity to unzip the gray sweatshirt. He revealed her mother's latest design of family T-shirts. This one was a Christmas-green, cotton, long-sleeved T-shirt with #TeamBlackFriday across the front with a set of cartoonish elves at the bottom of the hashtagged word.

"Dear Lord," British gasped and took a bite of her cupcake while her eyes rolled back in ecstasy. She savored the sweet potato flavor with the bourbon maple-bacon frosting.

"Oh wait—" Donovan turned around "—it gets better." He stripped out of the black hoodie and tossed it to the side, turning his back to her.

Like any regular hot-blooded American woman, British was a bit distracted by the sight of Donovan's rear in his jeans and bowed legs.

"What do you think?" Donovan asked.

"Oh yeah." She laughed at the shirt. The writing— If Lost, Return to This Lady—was typical Joan, along with an oversize picture of her mother's face. "You have no idea what you're in for tomorrow."

Donovan clapped his hands together. "Speaking of tomorrow. I've got some good news."

"What's that?" British perked up.

"Right after giving me this shirt and before I came out here to talk to you, your mom said I could spend the night."

British did a quick calculation of the six bedrooms they already had and the fact that her room was where the little kids were sleeping. Donovan would probably take the couch in the downstairs family room. She'd have to cross where her parents slept in order to get to where they'd put Donovan. She tried to weigh out her options and routes.

Reading her mind, he shook his head back and forth. "You're really trying to get me killed today," Donovan laughed. "We've got all the time in the world, sweetheart."

Except they didn't. Donovan's vacation had to end eventually.

"The building looks recently renovated," Donovan said, taking hold of British's keys to her apartment in downtown Southwood after a long and tiring day of Black Friday shopping. "Have you lived here long?"

They'd woken before dawn and hit the sales immediately, driving over to the malls in Peachville and Samaritan, and finishing up at the boutiques in Southwood. They'd headed back to the Woodburys' for leftovers and dessert before dark if they got hungry. The only thing British had a taste for right now was Donovan. It took her forever to fall asleep last night. Knowing Donovan slept one floor below on the couch teased her light dreams with the things they could do. She'd replayed every way in her mind she could get to him, including him sneaking up to her room or climbing down the trellis of her childhood bedroom window.

It was weird having a man let himself into her apartment, but at the same time, not. After spending the last forty-eight hours with Donovan, he'd become almost a part of her. British lifted the straps of her purse off her shoulder and set it on the Victorian chair by the front door, which immediately opened into the neat living room with the Victorian floral couch facing them. Lesson plans cluttered the glass coffee table. The bookshelves were mingled with photographs of classrooms and after-school accomplishments. She wondered if Donovan expected to see a shrine to Christian.

"I moved in about four and a half years ago after Christian died." Without looking at him, she knew Donovan quickly calculated the timing of everything. She kicked out of her canvas sneakers and pushed them against the shoe rack by the door. "I lived with my parents the first six months after the funeral."

"Only six?" His voice hinted at humor.

"You've met my parents," British said with a laugh. She watched Donovan stroll into the living room with his hands clasped behind his back, inspecting all the photographs and then the view from the balcony. He wore a pair of fitted denim jeans and a long-sleeved, hunter green Henley shirt that he'd picked up while shopping today. Since Thursday morning he hadn't shaved. The beard he sported had thickened. The rugged look was rather sexy. He turned with a questioning stare.

"There's only so much a grown woman can handle living under the roof of her parents," she went on to explain, "but the deciding factor was listening to my dad speak with a Jamaican accent."

Her answer only left Donovan waiting for another. He folded his arms across his broad chest. His size made him look like a giant against her dainty couch. "I'm confused."

British inhaled deeply, hating to explain her parents' oddities. "My dad was born and raised in Black Wolf Creek."

"Which you pointed out on the Ferris wheel the other night."

"Nice memory," British said with a nod.

"The company helped," Donovan replied with a wink.

"Anyway, my parents grew up just a few miles apart and it took a foreign exchange student photo shoot to bring them together. My mom was modeling at this big-time shoot and had just finished a semester overseas. The photographer needed an interpreter for another model and since my dad was friends with the photographer and right over at Clark Atlanta University, he came over to help."

"Was the model Jamaican?"

Confused, British shook her head. "No? Oh, because of the Jamaican accent my dad did? So, like I said, what attracted my mom to him was his way with foreign languages. The model who needed a translator was from Finland."

Donovan laughed. "Oh, okay, so what? They named your oldest brother after her country."

"I wish." British gulped and resisted the disgusted shiver creeping under her skin. "Let's just say we are all aware of each accent my dad used when they conceived us. For some people it's a song that puts them in a mood. For my mom it was my dad's accents."

It took him a moment to get what she meant. It took a minute and a half to stop laughing. "How did I miss this?"

"Trust me," she groaned, "I've gone through all types of attempts to forget it. As a kid it flew over my head, but as an adult, I understood and, for my sanity, I needed to leave the house."

Once Donovan sobered, he nodded. "I get it. I couldn't wait to move out when I turned eighteen."

"Did you live on your own?"

"For a few weeks I lived in the dorms and then I moved on to the frat house."

She rolled her eyes and headed into the kitchen. "Why am I not surprised?"

Donovan sat at the bar, which separated the kitchen and the living room. A set of four wineglasses hung from the rack, blocking his view. He tilted his head and winked.

"Don't believe the hype from the movies," he said. "It wasn't all parties and sorority girls."

British shook her head. "I didn't ask."

"We studied," Donovan went on.

"And partied," British added for him.

"Maybe a little, but you being all coupled up wouldn't have understood."

"Don't think I didn't party," British said. "Christian and I weren't always together throughout college. I played my fair share of beer pong. In private, of course."

"Didn't want word to get back to your boyfriend," he chuckled.

"No." She shook her head. "I didn't want to get caught by the pageant circuit's morality clause."

"What?" Donovan laughed even harder. "What kind of...?"

"I put a lot of time into becoming Miss Four Points," British said. "I lost the Miss Southwood crown to my best friend, Kenzie. But considering she and her family have a Miss Southwood dynasty, I still did pretty good for second place."

"Beauty queen dynasty? Moral clauses?" Donovan let out a sigh in jest.

"Don't act like the Ravens were free of scandal," British reminded him.

"You won't catch me in anything," he replied and picked up a lesson plan left on the counter. "I learned to keep my business to myself."

"Too bad social media didn't learn how to do the same for you."

Donovan clutched his heart. "Ouch."

British shrugged and teased him. "You can't help being so fast." She turned to the side-by-side fridge and opened it, trying to see what was in there. Anything left would be approaching at least a week old. "I have some frozen pizzas."

"Hey, I can't believe I'm saying this after all the food we ate yesterday and at lunch, but I could eat a horse."

British widened her eyes. "I thought by now you'd be careful with saying things like that."

Donovan nodded. "I stand corrected. I am hungry. We could take away or get delivery."

"Why do I get the feeling you don't want me cooking?"

"I enjoyed your cooking. The meal you made last week was fantastic. You just don't have to wait on me hand and foot. You've been out shopping with me just the same. And the reason we came over to your place was to crash since we're both tired and you didn't want me to drive."

"True," she agreed with a nod. "But I don't know if I can stay awake long enough for the food to get here. And you can't tell me you're not sleepy. You weaved in the road."

"It was your parents' driveway," Donovan explained, "and there was a football in the way."

Suddenly, British became nervous. It was one thing for a fling at a hotel where she wasn't going to have to stay much longer. But it was a whole different ball game in her own quarters. What choice did she have? It wasn't like she could let Donovan drive them down County Road 17 now. They were two mature adults.

They'd be able to stay the night together and be responsible. They'd managed to do so last night.

Donovan waved his hand toward the living room. "Come on, let's sit."

"Fine, let me grab the menus from this drawer." She fiddled with the utility drawer by her fridge and followed him into the other room. "Now we can figure out what we want to eat."

"I know what I want to eat," Donovan said with a coy smile.

Heat filled her cheeks, which she bit the inside of to keep from grinning. "You have a one-track mind."

"I think so when it comes to you." Donovan motioned for her to sit. She did at one end of the couch while he sat on the other. "What's going on with you?"

"Huh?" She gulped and looked over at him with her eyes, not moving her head.

Donovan adjusted himself into the corner of the couch. His left thigh was cocked on the cushions. "Are you nervous with me being here?"

"No," she lied. "Maybe a little."

"I can go back to the hotel, British. I meant it when I said I wanted to take things slow with you."

Yet she didn't want to take things slow. "This is just awkward with you being here and, no, I don't want you to leave. Deer season has picked up and with all the hunters out there searching for big game, I'd hate for a buck to run out on the road and cause you to swerve."

A passing car blared its horn in the street.

"Like what happened to Christian?"

A pinch of pain, a threat of tears rushed through British. "It's not fair to talk about that with you."

Donovan leaned across the couch and took her hand in his. "It is absolutely fair. We're together."

She cut her eyes at him and he nodded.

"I know it's crazy, British," he said softly. "I can't say what the future holds for us, but as of right now, I'm here with you. We're together. If you're in pain, I want to know why and what to do to solve it."

"I'm not in pain," she replied with a shaky voice. "I'm just. Afraid."

"Why?"

"I don't want to lose you." And then she realized eventually he would leave…and that was what she wanted, right? "I mean like that. In a tragic accident because of me."

"Christian's accident wasn't because of you, either," he said.

"What do you think we ought to eat?" British changed the subject and Donovan went along with it. They decided to order in Chinese food and watch some TV as they waited.

MET stayed true to its brand, airing several multi-cultural Christmas romance films. Halfway through the movie based on a Brenda Jackson book, their food arrived. Donovan straightened up her coffee table while she fixed a couple glasses of wine. They set their cartons of beef and broccoli, General Tso's chicken, spicy noodles, crispy honey wings, eggrolls, crab rangoon and Chinese doughnuts in front of them and sat with their legs crisscrossed on the floor. Donovan attempted to impress her with his use of chopsticks until he dropped a piece of broccoli on the table.

"I never would have pegged you as a romance fan," British teased him once the movie ended.

Donovan pulled himself up from the floor and sat with his back against his side of the couch. "It's Brenda Jackson," he said simply.

"One of your many girlfriends must have left her romance books behind," British mumbled and immediately regretted saying so. "Geez, I'm sorry. I must sound like a jealous girlfriend."

Donovan wiggled his brows at her. "Girlfriend."

It was hard to do anything but smile when around him. British instead rolled her eyes. She stood and gathered their empty containers.

"You can't believe everything you've read about me, British." Donovan stood to help, taking the containers into his hand.

"I didn't read it," she clarified. "I saw it all on social media."

"When did you look me up?"

"I did not." British pressed her hand against her heart. "But the girls did. And they showed me every single model you've dated in the last three years."

"Define 'dated.'"

"I don't have to define anything. I saw plenty of pictures."

"I can't help what's out there, British."

"No, but considering you gave Stephanie a pep talk about men learning how to respect women, you're a pig," she snarled and pushed past him. She was jealous. *Damn it.* "I only let them show me the PG-13 pictures. But don't get me started on the images that were highly inappropriate for girls to see on the internet without being eighteen."

Donovan held on to her elbow. "Wait a minute, now."

"You know what," she said with a sigh, "you really don't have to explain your past to me, Donovan."

"I do if your opinion of me drops." His voice softened and so did her stance. "You're the best thing that's happened to me in a while."

They did not need to have this conversation. This conversation led to promises and relationships. The most she could ask of him now was just for him to be himself.

"Donovannn," British drawled and pulled away from his firm hold.

"I work in the beauty industry, British," he said over her plea. British melted into his dark eyes. "You can't think I am sleeping with every single model I've been photographed with."

Silence built between them.

The television screen flickered to a commercial and a deep voice-over announced next Wednesday's installment.

"As you're finishing up the Thanksgiving weekend, don't forget to tune in to our inside look at Ravens Cosmetics as we break down the levels of the family."

Donovan let go of British's arm and searched through the empty containers and crab rangoon wrappers. "Not now, damn it," he groaned.

The voice-over continued. "We've followed the whirlwind romance between the CEO, Will Ravens, and his Creative Design Director, Zoe Baldwin. We've caught up with the twin sisters running public relations. Tomorrow night we'll take an inside look at their playboy brother. No, not Marcus Ravens, but the elusive Donovan Ravens, the one who only lets his picture be taken when he's with a mod—"

The screen went blank. Donovan breathed heavily in satisfaction with the remote control in his hand. "Television is overrated."

"Nice save." British laughed and turned back toward the kitchen. Donovan followed close behind. "I can do these dishes."

"I know you can, but I want to help."

"Fine." She blew out a sigh.

"But first, dessert."

Donovan dipped his head low and captured her mouth with his.

British forgot her thoughts. She only reacted. The moment his tongue touched hers, her eyes rolled to the back of her head. She tried not to moan but, like a starving woman, a growl escaped her throat. How was it possible to have missed his touch?

"Do you know how long I've been waiting to do that?" Donovan asked, breaking the kiss.

British wrapped her arms around his shoulders. "I have an idea."

The empty cartons dropped to the floor when Donovan scooped her up into his arms. "Where is your bedroom?"

She inclined her head and in no time they reached the closed door. "Wait, I need to prepare you for something," she said, holding on to the crystal doorknob.

With an easy smile, Donovan winked and covered the knob with his hand. "It's okay, British. I expect to see a photograph of you and Christian. It's natural."

"No, wait!"

Donovan crossed the threshold with her in his arms. He stopped walking any farther and craned his neck to take in the panoramic view of the posters. All one-hundred-plus photos of her New Edition collection over the years.

"In my defense—" she began to cringe, hiding her face in the crook of his shoulder "—when I moved here, I didn't want to start a new beginning with old photographs of me and Christian. So my high school friends and I got a little creative one day."

"A little drunk and creative?"

"Maybe just a little," British admitted. The morning after she and the Tiara Squad had finished decorating, British thought she'd gone back in time.

"Have you ever met them?" Donovan asked.

"No. I wouldn't want to embarrass myself." She lifted her head to find his eyes filled with amusement.

"The next time they're in town, I'm flying you in," he said before continuing their route to the bed.

The words played over in British's head. Not the exciting news about possibly meeting her all-time favorite boy band but the idea that Donovan was going to leave her. But this was what she'd wanted. Right?

Chapter 9

"You've got this," Stephanie said, closing her eyes and reaching for the hand beside her.

"We're all supporting each other," added Lacey.

Kathleen cleared her throat and nodded. "Ms. B told us we can do this. You can do this."

Touched by being mentioned in this pep talk slash motivational speech the Saturday morning after Thanksgiving, British placed her hand over her heart. Screams of excitement from the unexpected crowd rose from beyond the red curtain of the Christmas Wonderland scene created in the town center in Southwood. A line of eager children stretched down Main Street. The girls, dressed in red and green elf costumes, decided to pray for Donovan before he made his debut as this year's Southwood Santa.

"Let's bow our heads," Natasha nicely ordered everyone. "Dear Lord, we ask you to take time out of

Your busy schedule today and make today as success-ful as possible."

Everyone ended with a soft amen, except for one in the prayer circle.

"Amen," Donovan shouted and clapped his white-gloved hands together.

The white beard of the Santa suit he wore billowed with his breath. Despite the heaving padding against the eight-pack abs she'd caressed this morning, Donovan made playing Santa look sexy. Every visitor to sit on Santa's lap was allowed to do so if they donated a can or nonperishable item to help the Winter Harvest food bank. The event made sure everyone in Four Points had a holiday meal. British thought it was a great idea and even better with her STEM for GRITS team here now.

"I feel stupid," said Donovan.

Natasha squared off with Donovan, grabbing him by the shoulders. "You get out there and you be the best damn Santa Southwood has ever seen."

"'Tasha," British warned softly.

"Sorry," said Natasha. "You're going to be great."

The other girls, dressed in various combinations of elf outfits, rallied around the hot Santa and patted his red coat. The bells on the top of their pointy crescent-shaped hats jingled.

Donovan took a deep breath. "How did I get myself into this mess?" he asked British.

"You fell for my mother's charm," British explained.

Laughing, Donovan couldn't do anything but nod. "She can sell anything."

An emcee out front hyped the crowd a little more and brought in a roar of cheer and applause. British pat-ted Donovan's back with her gloved hand. Like Don-ovan, she, too, had been manipulated by Joan, which explained why she stood behind the curtain ready to be called out to meet the waiting children.

To help sell the Winter Wonderland scene, British had recruited the girls to act as elves. Some of the fellows from the middle school's team built the set and created a spectacular snowy scene kids and adults would visit. The girls stepped out first and egged on the crowd, leaving Donovan and British alone for a brief moment. Their hands touched and even through the fabric, the heat rose.

"I really can't believe you're going through with this," British teased. She straightened the black rims of the glasses hanging low from Donovan's ears. He reached to wrap his arms around her waist but the padding prevented it.

"Damn this suit," he growled. "Can I get an IOU on the kiss?"

The emcee announced the arrival of Mrs. Claus. British patted Donovan's belly. "Let's see how you do with the kids today."

Before he could agree or not, British stepped out onto the stage for a warm welcome from the locals and visitors alike. She spotted her parents in the front with the grandkids and began to wave before realizing she didn't want to spoil the magic of Christmas for the little ones. The high school band played "Santa Claus Is Coming to Town" and at the drum solo, Donovan burst through the opening in the curtains. Everyone went wild.

The morning went by in a blur. Kids of all sizes came to sit on Santa's lap to tell him what they wanted. Stephanie walked the kids from the red, licorice-like path lined with giant red-and-white candy canes up to Santa's throne, where she handed British a card with the child's name so she could introduce Santa.

By noon she and Donovan were able to communicate well enough that she only needed to whisper the child's name to gain the element of surprise. Once the child said what he or she wanted, British wrote it down and gave it to Natasha, who handed it to the waiting parents on the other side of the line. A few cranky kids tugged at Santa's beard, exposing his face. The single mothers—and a few of the not-so-single mothers—all sighed at the sight of Donovan's dreamy smile.

The lunchtime crowd of kids was a bit stronger. A lot of them did not want to leave Santa's side without telling him exactly everything they wanted. Donovan let them sit a little longer, though Lacey did not mind huffing out her irritation. At least Donovan practiced patience when a few of the children gripped his biceps—which the lurking moms did not mind.

"Is it me," Stephanie asked, handing an elementary school–aged kid's card to British, "or are we starting to see the same children over and over?"

"I thought the same," said British. She looked at the card and mouthed the name to Donovan. She thought she knew everyone in town. Donovan, being the first African American Santa of the season, brought out the neighboring communities to the town center. Southwood's diverse community blended races, which made it possible to have a representative from every culture that celebrated Santa. Next weekend one of the Reyes brothers would don the suit.

"Hello, Gracie," Donovan greeted someone in his deep voice.

British headed back to where Stephanie stood. She peeked around at the never-ending line and smiled with satisfaction. She was proud at how focused the team members were…at least up until the moment another

one of the GRITS girls from the after-school program
ran over to whisper in Stephanie's ear.

"OMG," Stephanie gasped. "Excuse me, y'all," she
said to the crowd and pushed her way through.

British shook her head and tried to remember these
were adolescents. She picked up the slack and brought
the next child over the red threshold. While she waited,
British watched Donovan. For a man with such a playboy reputation, he certainly possessed a down-home
quality. He was great with the children. He'd bonded
with her nieces and nephews, all of whom she did not
have to remind Donovan of their names. Part of British
wondered what Donovan would be like as a dad. *Probably spoil the kids*, she thought.

"Be careful, dear," Joan teased, coming up behind
British. "You look like you're falling for him."

"Whatever, Mother." British shrugged her mother's
hug off and focused on Santa. Falling for him. Whatever. They bonded over hot sex and no promises. That
worked for them, or at least that was the final compro-
mise this morning before they'd left her bed.

"Excuse us," Stephanie bellowed, pulling a young
girl by the hand to the front of the crowd. "Excuse us.
VIP here."

"That's Quandriguez's sister," explained Kathleen.
"She's deaf, you know."

"I know," said British.

The petrified young girl stood stock-still at the sight
of Santa. She wore an ice-blue windbreaker with a
blonde princess in a matching blue dress on the back.

Donovan motioned for her to step forward but not
even his dazzling smile got her to budge. The crowd
watched carefully. British rushed over to help but, like
the girl, stood frozen. Donovan took off his glove and

began to sign for the girl. At that moment the audience all gave a collective sigh and fell in love with this Santa a little more. Including British.

"Hey, Home Ec."

British cringed at the nickname and rolled her eyes at the moment being spoiled by none other than Cam Beasley. Given the Mrs. Claus outfit she'd had to wear, she decided to mind her manners. Besides, he was probably here with his kids. The last thing they needed was to be reminded of what a jerk they had for a father.

"Cam," British said with a droll eye-roll before turning around.

"I thought I recognized you," Cam said, coming up to the velvet rope. Two small children flanked him on either side. "I'm surprised to find you here."

Do not take the bait. Do not take the bait, she warned herself. "Well. I am." She smiled sweetly and adjusted the faux gold-framed glasses slipping down her nose.

"I figured you would be practicing."

"My girls are just fine," British said. She pulled the curls of the gray wig away from her face and bent to face the young boy and girl with him. "Are you guys excited to meet Santa?"

The sweet children nodded and cheered, ready for the introductions. British couldn't hold their father against them. She took their hands and led them up the walkway. Thankfully, Cam moved to the other side of the drop-off line to pick up his kids.

The next group of visitors stumped her. The gorgeous couple standing in the front didn't have a child with them. As a matter of fact, the next half dozen women didn't have children with them, just groups of girlfriends all pointing their cell phones at Santa.

"What is going on?" British asked Kathleen.

"The Southwood Santa is now viral and he's more like the sexy Santa."

British clutched the white fur collar around her throat. Her knees buckled. The back of her throat became dry. "Kathleen," she gasped, shocked at the photograph.

"What?" Kathleen shoved her bedazzled cell phone in British's face. "Everyone is talking about it."

Shielding the screen with her hand from the blaring afternoon sun, British looked at the photograph of the precise moment when a set of twins sat on Donovan's lap. One twin pulled down Donovan's beard while the other struggled to climb up his arm, thus pulling his red jacket open and exposing his buff chest and arms. Regardless of the twins' actions, Donovan stayed in character. Though she knew the story behind the photo, Donovan still won the prize for sexiest Santa. Her Sexy Santa, she thought. A jolt of excitement raced through her veins.

"Excuse me," a deep voice said behind her.

British turned and came face-to-face with the Greek letters across the shirt of a six-foot-plus man. She slowly looked up and cleared her throat. "You're going to have to stand behind the ropes, sir," she said boldly. "Does your child have a card?" Beyond his frame, she didn't see a kid near him. All day today unaccompanied children pushed themselves over the line, eager to see Santa.

"I am a child of God," said a familiar voice, stepping out from behind him. "That counts, right?"

"Zoe?" British shaded her eyes. "What on earth?"

Zoe Baldwin, now Ravens, pushed past the man British realized was her husband, Will Ravens, also known as Donovan's brother. She cast a glance over her shoulder to see if Donovan had noticed them. Cam's kids kept his attention.

"What are you doing in town?" British asked. "I thought you only returned for the summers."

The creative design director at Ravens Cosmetics had spent a few summers in Southwood. Her grandmother no longer ran the Mas Beauty School but the home still stood. It didn't surprise British to find Zoe back in town. Her father still lived here. As British hugged Zoe, she realized what a perfect match Zoe and Will made together. She was an expert makeup artist and Will was CEO of the world's best cosmetic company. It made sense for Zoe and Will to get together. It was as if destiny designed their future. Where did that leave British and Donovan?

"Girl, this outfit is everything," said Zoe, walking around British. While Zoe admired the Mrs. Claus look, British whistled at Zoe. Tall, thin, beautiful Zoe belonged on the cover of a magazine as well as in the pages. "I might need one for a little later." She elbowed Will in the ribs.

Will reached for Zoe's hand and managed to maneuver her in front of him and wrapped his hand around her waist. "By Christmas, you won't need any padding."

British's mouth dropped wide open. "Zoe, are you?"

Zoe pressed her finger to her mouth. "We're trying to find my folks to tell them before everyone else finds out."

"You know, I saw Miss Jamerica and my mom heading over to the Cupcakery." Joan and Zoe's mother, Jamerica Baldwin, modeled together back in the day.

"My mom is eating a carb?"

Back in the day, it was Joan who'd introduced Zoe's

parents to one another at one of their photo shoots held at Magnolia Palace.

"Stranger things have happened," said British. She turned her attention to Will, who let go of Zoe's belly with one hand and began filming Donovan with his cell phone. "Hey, now," she said to him. "You have to donate a canned good or money in order to get a picture with Santa or take pictures—that includes recording him."

Will narrowed his eyes on her. "Mrs. Claus?"

Perhaps it was because they were brothers, but British couldn't help but pick up on the arrogance of the man. She squared her shoulders. "I'm serious. The donations for today go to feed the hungry."

Will reached into his pocket and pulled out a wad of cash. "Will this do?"

British glanced back at Donovan. "Well, it's all in the name of charity—film your brother all you like."

The crowd around them began to disappear. The young elves, also known as the GRITS team, ran around with the other kids in the town square. To think a few nights ago this center had been transformed into a fall festival and was now a winter carnival. A safe, bright and loud merry-go-round spun on one corner of the square. The line there matched the line for Santa. The smell of funnel cakes, grilled hot dogs and popcorn floated through the crisp air. All Donovan wanted to do was to grab something to eat and head back to British's place, since it was closer than Magnolia Palace.

By the end of his shift as the Southwood Santa, Donovan sat back on his red-velvet throne. He kind of wished more parents would bring their children just so he could avoid speaking with Will, who'd clearly enjoyed exploiting Donovan's job today. Why didn't it click in his head, when Will told him he and Zoe were going off for the holidays, that they'd come here to Southwood? Every half hour for the rest of the afternoon Will had stood down by the photographer and annoyingly filmed him. The camera caught every bad moment such as when a kid almost lost his lunch on Donovan, a diaper leak and a few candy canes stuck in his fake beard. The one redeeming part of the afternoon was the connection he shared with British. They were so in sync. The pit of his stomach flopped when she approached him.

"Hey," British said, coming close. The sweet scent of her intoxicating perfume flooded him. His stomach growled. "Are you hungry?"

"For food?" Donovan teased, wiggling his brows.

"Careful, Santa," she said playfully. "I overheard your brother Will talking about taking you for dinner at Valencia's. It's another spot you have to try before you leave."

The top portion of Donovan's lip curled. One, partly because his brother being in town threatened to take away time from British and, two, the idea of leaving loomed in the back of his head.

"Give me five minutes to get rid of him." He gave a sinister laugh and rubbed his hands together.

Donovan took a step forward but British placed her hand on his forearm. "You can't kill him right now."

"Because I'm dressed as Santa?" If that were the case, Donovan was ready to get out of the red costume now. British and Donovan waved once more to the onlookers and posed for a few more pictures as Mr. and Mrs. Claus. They received a round of applause before a few of the elves opened the curtain for them to exit.

Just before they disappeared, British shook her head

back and forth, grinning and speaking through her teeth, "Because we're going to have a civilized dinner."

"And then I can kill him?"

"No." She linked her hand in his but not before slipping off her white glove and his.

The skin-to-skin contact was so needed since he wasn't able to kiss her right now. Given the only privacy they had was a strung-up sheet, Donovan decided acting on impulse—to take British into his arms right now—needed to wait. After eight hours of playing Santa and being on his p's and q's, he needed some one-on-one time with British. For Donovan the suit jacket with the three giant black-plastic buttons on the front came off easily. Knowing it was going to be hot underneath, he hadn't bothered putting on a shirt.

The Mrs. Claus dress required help, which Donovan didn't mind. Again, the two moved in unison and without words. British took off her hat and gray wig, then lifted her dark curls off her neck and exposed her back to him. Donovan resisted raising her skirts and showing her just how much he wanted her right now. An excited scream from a girl outside the area stopped him. Regretfully, Donovan rebuttoned British's costume. Kissing her neck, he swatted her bottom.

"Did you have fun today?" British asked him, turning around in his arms.

"I hate to admit it, but I did." Donovan never thought he'd have a blast playing a married man. They walked down the red carpet toward Will and Zoe. Zoe he liked. Will? Donovan balled his fists together. But as they approached his little brother, Donovan's irritation settled and he reached out to hug him.

"What the hell are you doing here, man?" Will asked

him, patting him on the back. "Have you been here this whole time?"

"Yep," Donovan answered.

Despite the latest pressures of the job making the youngest member of the Ravens family act like a tyrant lately, Donovan knew he couldn't stay mad at Will. Will had never asked to be the CEO of the company and Donovan had played his part by nominating him to be at the helm. Will had just come off a career-ending soccer injury, and Donovan had known he'd needed something else to focus on. And he'd been right. Will's vision for bringing classic beauty back to the company had helped refresh the sales. Donovan had seen the financial reports.

"You're such a copycat," Will joked. "This is my hideaway spot."

Zoe stepped between the two men to give Donovan a hug. "Don't be mad at Donovan for having good taste. Hey, brother-in-law."

"Hey, sister-in-law," Donovan replied. "You look as beautiful as ever."

"Thank you."

"So beautiful, I think you should grace the face of Ravens." Donovan gave Will as smirk before letting Zoe go.

"You're not getting off that easy," Will said, tugging his wife's elbow so she fit in the crook of his shoulder when he draped his arm over her shoulders. "You still need—"

Zoe silenced him with a squeeze to the hand. "Sweetie, we're on vacation."

"Speaking of which…" Will began. "Where did you spend Thanksgiving?"

"Here," Donovan said.

"With my family." British spoke up. "Hi, we haven't officially met."

"Oh my God," Zoe knocked herself in the head with the palm of her hand. "Where is my brain?"

Zoe, Will and British laughed at some inside joke, which baffled him. Donovan cleared his throat to break up the camaraderie. "Will, allow me to introduce you to someone very special, British Carres. British, this is my annoying little brother, Will, and his—"

"British and I go way back," said Zoe, with the flick of her left wrist, waving the Ravens family heirloom engagement ring When Will had asked for it from their grandmother, Donovan couldn't have been more pleased. He loved Zoe but wondered if it would be rude to ask for it back when the time was right. Donovan gulped at the thought. Prior to coming to Southwood Donovan was sure he'd never get married. And now here he was, not sure if he wanted to leave without taking British as his wife. The notion was a pleasant surprise. British made him happy.

Will extended his hand to British. "Pleased to meet you. Thanks for allowing me to film Donovan."

Donovan looked between the two of them. "What's that?"

"Well…" British began, her cheeks turning his favorite reddish hue. "This is for charity and with the load of cash your brother dropped, we're able to feed everyone in Four Points whether they need it or not."

"My humiliation for charity, huh?" Donovan accepted with a nod. "I suppose no one is going to recognize me."

Again the three of them shared a laugh.

"Oh, honey," British cooed, "I don't know how to tell you this but you're Southwood famous now."

Whatever that meant, Donovan didn't care, just as long as it got British to move against his frame. As natural as it felt, he wrapped his arm around her shoulders and pretended to ignore Will's questioning gaze at the intimate touch.

"Is that Maggie Swayne?" Zoe asked, shielding her eyes from the setting sun. "She's been MIA in Miami for a while now."

"Speaking of missing..." Will said. "Donovan, what's going on with your search for the next spokesmodel?"

Now was not the time to discuss work. Donovan heaved a heavy sigh and tugged British closer to him. "I had a great idea. Didn't I?"

"Not on your life, buddy," said British.

Zoe squealed and clapped her hands. "That would be so perfect. British, with your pageant background, you'd be perfect."

"I am a professional *STEM* teacher," British declared.

"I majored in chemistry—" Zoe shrugged "—and it's time to show the world that girls can dominate the science lab and the runway at the same time."

For a breath of a second, British bit her bottom lip, giving Donovan a sliver of hope that Zoe's motivational point of view might work. "As I told Donovan before, I can't very well sell makeup to impressionable girls."

Will snorted as if offended.

A protective surge electrocuted Donovan's veins. "She is an awesome teacher," he said. "She could teach you a thing or two."

"Can she teach me how to find the perfect cover girl?" Will asked and shrugged. "You know what? I'll just go with the original plan and hire—"

Thankfully a group of teenagers playing tag ran past

them, shutting Will up before Donovan did so with his fist. He didn't want Tracy's name mentioned and ruining this great day. Parents moved from store to store with packages in their hands. Children ran around unsupervised. What a difference between raising kids in a metropolis city and a small town like this one. Or living in a warm environment like the Woodburys' home.

An elementary-aged child skipped by, licking the chocolate frosting right off the top of a cupcake. The dollop fell to the ground and his tears began to flow. While Donovan looked around for the boy's mother, British knelt to soothe him. "Let's get you another one," British said and looked up at Zoe. "Want to come with me? We can go say hi to Maggie."

"And get this kiddo another scoop of frosting for his cupcake, huh?" Zoe bent over and tweaked the little boy's nose.

British reached for Zoe's hand, stopping to flutter her lashes at Donovan. His heart swelled and slammed against his chest at the thought of him having to leave eventually; the last thing he wanted was to be separated from her.

"So they're just going to walk off with someone's kid?" Will asked and shook his head. "We should call the police and let them handle it."

"British is a well-known teacher here in Southwood," Donovan explained. "She grew up here and I am willing to bet anything she knows the kid's parents." Just then, Mrs. Fitzhugh walked by and waved, calling Donovan out by name. "Everyone knows everyone around here."

With a side eye glance, Will hummed. "Mmm-hmm. Well, I'll never get used to that in Miami. Maybe in our grandparents' neighborhood."

"Speaking of," Donovan said. "How was Thursday with Grandma Naomi?"

"Traditional as usual," Will replied. "Catered dinner served at exactly one and a football game between us and the anti-cousins."

The anti-cousins were the group of relatives who'd tried to break the company up and start their retirements forty years early. Donovan was pretty sure it must have been an awkward holiday meal.

"We worked out our aggression during the game," Will said with a gloating laugh.

While the Woodburys played football, too, with just one casualty, Tom, Donovan could only imagine the carnage on the Ravens property. What he liked about the Woodburys was being able to play a good game and having fun.

A cool breeze blew but the new fond memories of British and her family kept him warm.

"Wow," Will gasped, breaking Donovan out of his trance as he watched British walk away. "You got it bad."

Without turning his head, Donovan cut his eyes at his brother. He reached out and grabbed Will by the shoulder, squeezing his clavicle. "Yes."

Chapter 10

The end of the Thanksgiving season kicked off the winter celebrations, as well as brought back Ramon and Kenzie Torres from their vacation at his family home. British thanked her friends for opening up Magnolia Palace to everyone with a basket of muffins and gossip. Kenzie was ecstatic to learn about a potential relationship between British and Donovan, knowing her matchmaking scheme had worked out for the better. The end of the fall season also brought British back to some rushed normalcy in her life. The GRITS girls were able to move back into their homes. The school doors opened up again and British went back to her life. The only difference this time was that Donovan still lingered…and she didn't mind. Even though she felt empty without him around as much, she had to get back to her regularly scheduled life.

Southwood also kicked off the start of the Christmas

holiday by decorating the town tree. There were a few more weeks until school let out for the three-week winter break and a lot more lessons to get through in the classroom. To top it all off, tonight was the big STEM competition for the Christmas Advisory Council. All the girls' hard work over the last two weeks was about to pay off.

For Donovan, the last two days had been busy working with Will to find the next face for Ravens Cosmetics. British knew she'd be lying if she said she didn't feel a twinge of jealousy at sending Donovan over to Grits and Glam Gowns.

Lexi Pendergrass Reyes owned not just the premier dress boutique in town but also a talent studio around the corner. British found herself coming over to the shop during her lunch break for one excuse or another. It's why she had the 3D Advent calendar on the corner of her desk now, plus a party dress for the school dance next week. Her pop-up visits hadn't soothed her insecurities.

Gorgeous women from every direction of Georgia came through the shop for advice and dresses. And she'd sent the perpetual bachelor into the lion's den. While British molded the minds of tomorrow's youth, Donovan held interviews that would change the life of one local lady. Somehow, British dreaded the day Donovan would come home and tell her he'd found the new face of RC. When he found the future face, there'd be nothing keeping Donovan in Southwood.

Initially, British had wanted a temporary situation—a playboy like Donovan, with a healthy fear of commitment. Sure, he'd had a reputation of being a ladies' man, but since they'd been together British had never seen that side of him. He was attentive, romantic and sweet.

Her family adored him and Donovan seemed to enjoy spending time with them. All of this happiness was going to end eventually when he found his perfect girl.

At the idea of being closer to Donovan, British actually considered taking him up on his daily offer to be the new face of Ravens Cosmetics. But her life was here in Southwood, at Southwood Middle School.

Another thing British usually hated to hear was the cruel sound of the afternoon bell ringing. It signaled the end of the day and reminded her that she'd run out of time to go over her well-thought-out lesson plans with her students. British waited for her students to leave the classroom before she headed over to city hall. The STEM teams were excused for the day for the competition. British hoped the girls were off to a good start. She expected a win, which would then take up her afternoons for a while to prepare for the District STEM Competition. With the girls participating in the STEM-Off now, British's afternoon was free. She planned to hang out at school until the final activity bell rang.

"So I hear our middle school kids are dominating the competition."

British tried not to shudder at the sound of Cam's voice. When she looked up from her attendance book, she found the director standing at the doorway, his arms crossed over his chest. A long dreadlock fell over his shoulder. In another lifetime she guessed he could have been considered handsome, but his attitude was atrocious. British pushed away from her desk. She buttoned the middle of her white lab coat and squared her shoulders. "Are you here to try to psych me out?" British asked him, rolling her yellow pencil between her fingers.

"I was actually coming to see if you wanted to up the ante."

"Meaning?"

"I mean there's not enough room for the both of us here, Home Ec."

A crack came from her hand where she'd snapped the pencil. "I've asked you before to stop calling me that."

"Why?" Cam placed his hands on his hips. The hem of the blue-plaid shirt he wore flopped over the waistband of his brown corduroy pants. "Let's be honest here."

She widened her eyes. "You mean you've been holding back on me?" British feigned a gasp. "What do you want?"

"I want the lab to myself from here on out."

"You're the director of the science department, Cam, not the owner of it," she clarified.

"I'm talking about when my boys win. I want you to resign."

British laughed; she bent over and laughed so hard that tears formed in her eyes. "You can't be serious," she asked once she sobered and placed her hands on her hips in the same stance as the director. "I'm surprised you didn't challenge me to a duel."

"Right about now, I'd take it," said Cam. He advanced into the room and let the heavy black door slam behind him.

For a moment British wasn't sure if she needed to be afraid. Lucky for her she had two older brothers who'd taught her how to protect herself. British stepped back in her black heels, in preparation to do battle. She even put her hands up. "Back up, Cam."

"It is Dr. Beasley," Cam said in a clipped tone. "And what is this? A little girl like yourself is going to try to beat me up?" He stepped closer.

A moment ago British wasn't sure of his intentions

but now Cam made it perfectly clear. His fists were balled at his sides. "I am so tired of watching you tip-toe around these halls acting like you own the place."

"I don't do that," said British, "but I am warning you to back away from me, Cam."

"I'm the boss here. It's best you remember—"

Since he kept advancing toward her, British extended her right fist and popped him in the nose. The punch didn't do anything but anger him more.

"Jesus, woman, you are reckless."

"And you're still getting in my face."

Cam didn't stop. He stepped even closer. The scent of the cafeteria lunch of chicken parm and garlic bread loitered on his breath. "I need you to leave the school, British."

"Cam." British curled her fingers around his to break the grip he'd taken on the lapels of her coat. "I am warning you."

"Are you going to leave when you lose?"

"Absolutely not," she replied. Her heart slammed against her chest. The band practiced right outside her window; she wasn't sure if the blaring trumpets would cover her screams. School was over and her girls were off getting ready for the STEM-Off this evening. "And when I win, I want you to stay here and watch my girls take over the lab four days out of the week. Now, if you know what's good for you, you'll let me go."

Cam sneered so hard she saw a piece of parsley wedged between his left bicuspid. "What are you going to do, hit me again?"

"No," boomed a deep voice. A beefy brown hand clamped down on Cam's shirt collar and pulled him back from her. "I am."

British's heart swelled at the sight of Donovan coming to the rescue.

Donovan jerked Cam's hands behind his back and slammed his head down on British's desk.

"Now, before you begin to cry out from the pain," Donovan said, "you're going to apologize for your behavior."

The way Donovan's hand pressed against Cam's cheek, there was no way for the man to speak. His dreads flopped in his face while a thousand veins popped in his forehead.

British folded her arms across her chest, pissed off. This man, who'd attempted to threaten her, had the nerve to look so pitiful right now.

"I can't hear you," Donovan growled. The silver cuff links on his suit jacket pressed into Cam's face.

"Don't kill him," British said.

"Who is this guy?"

"This is the director of the science department. The girls are going up against his boys in a couple of hours."

Donovan stepped back and let Cam up but not before spinning him around and grabbing him the same way Cam had grabbed British a few minutes ago. Donovan lifted Cam off his feet and brought his face near. "I'm only letting you live so you can see those girls beat your team. After that I never want to hear about you coming near my lady again. Do I make myself clear?"

My lady?

Had this been a cartoon scenario, the path Cam took to run out of the classroom would have been on fire right now. Donovan crossed his arms over his chest, looking satisfied with himself, and turned to face her. Then his eyes roamed hers. There wasn't a lot of distance between them but Donovan closed it immediately. "Are you okay?"

"I'm fine," she said, pushing his hands away as they roamed over her body.

"He didn't try to…"

When she realized what he implied, British shook her head. She pulled a stray curl behind her ear. "Good God, no. He was just trying to scare me." She left out the part that he'd done a good job.

"I don't think he's going to try anything like that again."

"Well I should say not," British scoffed. "Thanks to man-save-woman." To reiterate she grunted like a caveman.

Still dressed in the dark suit he wore to interview hot girls today, Donovan loosened the red paisley tie around his neck. "Are you calling me a caveman?"

"*Neanderthal* is the more correct term." She practically spouted the fact.

"Are you seriously going to be politically correct with me about what to call a caveman?" Donovan pressed his lips together to keep from laughing. "Come here, woman."

Though Donovan tugged at the middle button of her lab coat, British gave a little bit of resistance. "I can't believe you barged in here like that."

"What do you mean?" Donovan paid her pout no mind and nuzzled his chin against the crook of her neck. "You mean when I walked in here as you were getting mauled by some jerk?" He nibbled her jugular and her eyes fluttered. "I apologize if I got a little crazy. But I didn't appreciate the woman I love being assaulted."

Knees weak, British pushed against Donovan's chest. "Wait. What?"

"Love, British." Donovan tipped British by the chin with his thumb, getting her to see the seriousness in his eyes. Her breath fluttered. "I've never said it and meant it, British. I love you."

Love. The word seemed so simple. Is that what she had been feeling? "Donovan."

The final afternoon bell rang. Donovan dipped his head and kissed her lips, wiping any frayed nerves left over from her altercation with Cam. He pulled his mouth away. Eyes lingered on hers. "I don't need to hear you say it back. Not yet. Let's go watch the girls win."

"And why are we here?" Will leaned over and asked Donovan in the auditorium of city hall.

"Shh," Zoe whispered over her shoulder from where she sat in front of them to pay attention to the competition on the stage.

Not everyone in town filled the seats as Donovan had expected. It shocked him to find the disappointment rising in him over the lack of support the science teams received. He guessed most of the cheering crowds were parents of the participants. In his seat in the risers, Donovan couldn't have been prouder, not just for the girls but also for himself. He'd finally said the words he felt. He loved British. With Tracy, they'd dated six weeks and he still wasn't sure. With British, Donovan just knew. Every feeling—happiness, joy—felt right.

As of right now, the last two teams standing were the STEM for GRITS and the boys' robotics team from Southwood. British sat in the row behind the judges. From Donovan's understanding, when the girls advanced through each round, they were allowed to bring a member of their team, expanding from the original

four: Stephanie, Lacey, Natasha and Kathleen. There
were now two extra girls helping them.

The girls had taken Donovan's suggestion and come
up with a few holiday-themed suggestions. His favorite
had been the one from Stephanie. She'd created a mood
necklace with quartz glass and thermotropic liquid crystals to demonstrate the various heat levels. In the beginning of the experiment, the girls passed out crystals to the
mothers in the audience. They also selected few random
boys in the audience on the robotics team—including
the Quandriguez fellow Stephanie had a crush on. The
goal at the end of the demonstration for each participant
was to keep the mood rock at a teal color, which meant
a calm state, and the orders were to make sure the mothers remained teal during the holidays.

For a bonus round the GRITS team paraded in front
of the boys' team wearing various mood rocks. The girls
brought the mothers of the committee onstage, handed
them noise canceling earphones and then one by one
listed off all the shopping, errands, decoration duties,
holiday parties and everything needed for a smooth
Christmas to each mother. To some, the girls said that
everything was fine. The mood rocks for the mothers
with less to do turned teal. The rings for the other mothers turned black, meaning they were stressed. The suggestion for the children of the mothers onstage was for
them to know when to pitch in and help their moms or
stay out of the way.

As for the boys, the girls examined their rocks, all
while still wearing their various forms of jeans, T-shirts
and turtlenecks. By the end of the experiment all the
boys' mood rocks stayed in the red zone, which var-
ied between excited and stimulated. For Cam's sake,
the girls changed their variable each time by changing

outfits, and no matter what they wore, from a lab coat to a pair of shorts and T-shirt or even a turtleneck, the boys were still distracted. The demonstration received a standing ovation from the mothers, female teachers and Donovan, as well.

Cam sneered and sank lower in his seat. Donovan's palms itched to be wrapped around his throat.

"See that girl," Donovan said, pointing at Stephanie, who was front and center wearing a pink-Bedazzlered lab coat. "She's going to be a future Ravens Cosmetics employee."

"She's a bit young to be the company's face," said Will. "I was looking for someone older. Speaking of which, can we end this search, get out of Southwood and just hire Tracy? She's been all over social media, which works in our favor."

Zoe twisted in her seat. "Excuse me?"

"I love Southwood, babe." Will corrected himself and leaned over to kiss his wife on the cheek.

"Don't forget my dad wants to sell the house," she said, "and we could easily move back here."

Donovan's laugh froze and an idea popped into his head. The Mas house had once been used as a classroom and family home. Zoe's great-grandmother had taught young ladies the chemistry behind makeup as well as how to sell beauty products and styling. Many of her students had worked with Donovan's grandparents, who'd run the place in the early days of Ravens Cosmetics. Considering Miami was the home base for RC, having a satellite office might be ideal. He crunched the numbers in his head and in his heart.

He'd meant it when he said he loved British. He would do anything to stay with her.

"Look," Will continued once his wife stopped giving him the evil eye. "Like the rest of us featured on Dana's bright idea of a reality show, Tracy got hold of the prereleased episode airing tonight."

There'd been a large attachment from MET Studios in Donovan's work email earlier this week. He'd ignored it and focused on the thousands of corporate emails delegated to his job. During what time he did have to spend with British, television was the last thing on his mind.

"She wasn't even in anything," Donovan said bitterly. "When I left, I didn't say a word to her. I didn't wake her up or anything."

Will leaned forward with his elbows on his knees and his fingers pressed to his temple. "What?"

"I was never on film with her. Why would she be included?"

"Donovan, she's been tweeting for the last twenty-four hours about a huge secret."

The pit of his stomach dropped. "What secret?"

"The hell if I know," Will said, shaking his head.

Donovan reached into the lining of his suit jacket and extracted his cell phone. Nothing happened. He couldn't get a signal. "I need to reach Amelia Reyes," he said.

"Amelia?" Zoe turned around again in her seat. "She was actually in town. You know she's from here."

Now that he thought about it, Amelia was the one who'd recommended Donovan come here to hang out after they filmed. "I don't have her number."

"C'mon." Zoe pushed away from her seat awkwardly and handed Will her program. "We'll be right back."

Will chuckled and rolled his eyes. "I'm coming, too."

Donovan hated to skip out on the crowning portion of the competition but he knew the girls were going to win. They had it in the bag, thanks to Kathleen's coding of a train robot with a vacuum that went around the stem of a Christmas tree and cleaned up pine needles and broken ornaments while it played Christmas songs.

Together, the threesome headed up toward the exit and down the hallway of city hall. Zoe was already whipping out her phone and dialing by the time they reached the glass entrance. A bright light blinded them the moment they stepped outside. Donovan angled his head to see better. A few dozen white vans were positioned at the front of the building with twice as many reporters standing in front of them, microphones, booms and recorders facing them.

An anger bubbled inside Donovan. Why couldn't these reporters show up for the competition at the beginning and stay? There was plenty of room for everyone...maybe not their equipment, but still. Imagine the confidence it would have given the students to see their hard work be recognized not just by their colleagues but by the outside world. Donovan understood British's passion for the kids.

"It's going straight to voice mail..." said Zoe. Her words trailed off at the sight of everyone standing in front of them.

Donovan hated the spotlight. He sensed the heat of the lamp on his scar and felt it amplified by the world. He turned around to leave.

"Mr. Ravens," someone called out.

Naturally, Will stepped forward. He was the head of RC and knew what to say in front of an audience. "Good evening, ladies and gentlemen," he said with a surefire cocky chuckle. "Are you here to get the Black Friday scoop on our items?"

Coming to his aid, Zoe appeared by Will's side. "Of course not, sweetheart," she said to him. "I'm sure everyone's gotten wind of the exciting things brewing inside city hall." She smiled like the dazzling director of creative design that she was. "You guys, come on and see the brilliant young minds of our future leaders."

Good job, Donovan thought. The girls needed the spotlight, especially if they were to walk outside any moment now with their trophy in hand. As much as he wanted to see them win, he needed to get to the bottom of this surprise Tracy might have. He scrolled through his phone to find the emails he'd never looked at. Cell service in the building was poor. The attachment was large and kept pausing, probably due to the satellite of the news crews.

"We're here for the Sexy Santa," someone yelled.

Will turned to glance at Donovan, who was completely confused until he remembered the photographs taken at the winter carnival last weekend. A few shots were still floating around town. He thought it was local. The Southwood Santa, he believed, was what the waitress called him at the coffee shop across the street from the gown shop.

"Excuse us for a moment," Will said. He motioned for Donovan and Zoe to huddle together at the doors of the entrance to city hall. Beyond the glass, they spotted a crowd coming toward them. "Let's take this opportunity to market our new men's line. We have those lotions and colognes coming out for Christmas."

"No," Donovan declared. He craned his neck to find British's curly head coming their way.

"Are you listening to me?" Will asked.

"Not really," he huffed in response.

"Dana and Eva are our PR people," said Zoe. "They'd agree that any publicity is good publicity, Donovan. They know you as the Sexy Santa. You could promote the perfect stocking stuffer for people."

"Hell no." Donovan wasn't sure how many ways he

needed to make himself clear to them. "I am not taking this opportunity to put the shine on British and her team to sell products for Ravens."

"Think about the girl you pointed out," Will pleaded. "Stephanie, the one you said was going to be a future employee of ours. Talk about the chemistry put into our products."

"Definitely," Zoe said excitedly.

In the reflection of the bright lights of the cameras behind them, a glare glazed the glass doors. Donovan couldn't see inside but he did see Amelia Reyes shouldering her way through the crowd with the help of the guy who worked at the real-estate office next door to the dress shop where they'd held interviews this week. *Nate Reyes, that was it*, Donovan thought. Nate had a few other people behind him.

"Amelia."

"Donovan," Amelia breathed heavily, holding her cell phone in the air. "The tracker works."

What the hell was going on?

"What tracker?" Zoe and Will chorused.

The crowd behind them grew louder. Nate and his group made a blockade of sorts for privacy. Now Donovan felt trapped. He wanted to see British.

"There's a Sexy Santa Tracker website," Amelia explained. She showed her phone to them and, sure enough, on the screen, there was a cartoon figure of Amelia standing next to one of the photos from the winter carnival in front of city hall.

Will reached for the phone for a better view. "This is creepy."

"Stalkerish," Zoe added.

An incoming call blurred the photo. Donovan caught Christopher Kelly's name flash across the screen. Why was the president of MET calling Amelia after nine in the evening? Tonight's reality show. What the hell happened on the show?

"Donovan, you have to believe me," said Amelia, "I approved one version of your segment."

This did not sound good. He waited for Amelia to explain what happened but the reporters and now ever-growing crowd of onlookers had started oohing and aahing too loudly to hear her answer. Suddenly, Tracy appeared, decked out in a red, skintight, damn-near-see-through catsuit, and sauntered up the steps. She wore a pair of oversize black glasses and a white scarf over her head, which she pulled down to let the material fall across her shoulders, making her look like an adult-star version of Mrs. Claus.

Oh damn, Donovan thought. She needed to go. Donovan moved through the surrounding crowd to reach her.

Tracy slipped her glasses off with her left hand. The vaguely familiar gaudy ring Donovan had spotted the morning he'd returned to his condo glittered under the lights.

"We can't fix this, Mr. Kelly," Amelia was screaming into the phone. "She's already here."

"Tracy!"

"Tracy!"

Reporters shouted her name. The highly sought-after model spun slowly on her spiked patent-leather boots and faced the crowd.

"You're dressed like a mighty damn sexy Mrs. Claus," someone pointed out.

"You see—" Tracy started to speak but Zoe reached for Tracy's elbow and jerked her backward.

To not stumble or fall, Tracy offered an apologetic smile to the audience and reluctantly went off with Zoe before Donovan grabbed her. Will opened the door for them to enter and the waiting crowd outside began to pour onto the front steps. People oblivious to the happenings outside found themselves pushing their way forward past defeated children, some with tears on their faces. Tracy snaked her hand out and grabbed hold of Donovan's. Will, Zoe, Tracy and Donovan made a human train inside the foyer of city hall.

"Are you nuts?" Tracy yelled at Zoe and snatched her arm away, as did Donovan. Her high-pitched voice echoed against the marble walls.

"What did you think you were about to announce?" Zoe asked.

Ever the actress, Tracy reached for Donovan again. This time he screwed his face up and shook his head.

"Tell me you haven't missed me," Tracy demanded.

"Not in the slightest," Donovan laughed.

"Then why did you give me this?" Tracy held her hand in the air. "I found it in the drawer when you gave me a few minutes to collect my belongings."

Zoe gasped. "Donovan, you didn't."

"Of course I didn't," Donovan snapped.

Amelia made her way into the foyer. "He didn't give you that ring, Tracy," she said. "My associate thought it would be a great storyline for the Ravens family. I just found out he planted the ring in the drawer."

Blinking in disbelief, Tracy shook her head. "I don't understand. I gave you the best six weeks of my life."

Donovan squinted his right eye. "Me and that guy you brought into my house and my bed."

At least Tracy had the decency to shut her mouth. "We can work past that, Donovan." She attempted to reach for him but he recoiled. Tracy's red lips curled into a sneer. "Jesus. I've tolerated looking at you for months and now you want to treat me like this. My God, don't act like you didn't tell me you loved me."

Amused, Donovan scratched his faced, his fingertips touching his beard. He shrugged his shoulders. "You can't hold me accountable for what was said in bed. Let's call it momentary insanity," he said, inclining his head.

"Donovan," Will warned.

Tracy was the epitome of why Donovan had remained a bachelor for so long. He shook his head and chuckled, thinking of the woman he had now. He needed to see British. So when Tracy stormed out of the way, he took a deep breath to leave but it was too late. Tracy's height masked British behind her.

As to how long British had stood behind Tracy, he had no idea. But judging by the look of horror on her face—as well as the GRITS team who stood behind British holding their trophy—she'd been there long enough.

"British…"

Zoe and Amelia ushered the girls out the front door. Will waited behind.

The corners of British's lips turned down. Her cheeks turned a darker hue than the one he'd grown accustomed to love.

"Seven hours ago you told me you loved me," she said in a hoarse whisper.

"Love," Donovan corrected. His heart ached seeing her upset. "I love you, British."

"That's just something you say," British said, stepping back, away from his touch. "Like you told her."

"But I didn't mean it." Donovan tried to reach for British's hand but she folded her arms across her chest. His heart ached at her rejection. All eyes turned to him.

British's mouth dropped. "Wow."

"C'mon, British, you know it's not like that. Yes, I was in a relationship with Tracy. You were aware of that. Before you, I've never felt love before. I've never been in love with anyone like I am with you. I need you, British. Tell me you need me. Tell me you're mad, but don't walk away from us. You have to believe me. Surely you know how I feel about you."

"What I do know—" British pointed at him "—is that you're exactly what I thought you were when we first met. A free-loving playboy floating from woman to woman to bide your time until the next one. What was I, your Southwood flavor of the month until you left to go back to Miami?"

"I've changed, British, and you know it." Donovan's arms flopped to sides. "You have to stop comparing me to your Christian. I'm not perfect but I will always love you."

"Oh," she scoffed, "there's no comparison. Christian may have suffered from an enlarged heart, but you, Donovan Ravens, don't have one at all."

"Ms. B," Stephanie said, poking her head around the corner of the hallway. "My parents had to go back to Magnolia Palace and wondered if you could bring me back."

Just like that, British inhaled deeply and tore her eyes away from Donovan. The cold glare chilled him to the bone. He reached for her fingertips, which, for a brief second, she allowed him to touch. She paused by his shoulder. Donovan leaned down to kiss the top of her head. "Don't do this, British."

"I can't be a good role model of a strong woman and believe the words you so frivolously give out. Goodbye, Donovan."

Chapter 11

"I feel like every time I meddle with a Ravens's love life I seem to make things worse," said Kenzie.

British hugged her body and leaned against the door of her car. She'd just dropped off Stephanie with her parents and wasn't in the mood for heading home just yet, knowing Donovan would be waiting at her place to talk further. There was nothing left to say. He admitted to saying things that weren't true, like that he loved Tracy. How was she supposed to believe him now? On top of that, his callous behavior toward that woman, Tracy, was in poor taste, especially in front of her students.

By the time she'd reached Magnolia Palace, the exposé or documentary on Donovan's portion of the Ravens story had already aired. On top of everyone in Southwood seeing it, Tracy wore a ring she said Donovan gave her. Everyone in British's family left messages for her to call. Everyone wanted to know how she was doing or what was going on. Enough people at city hall had overheard the quarrel between Tracy and Donovan, and then with her. Small towns and gossip...

She sniffed. "This isn't your fault, Kenzie," she said to her friend. "I initiated things with Donovan knowing full and well he was a perpetual bachelor playboy who would leave. This is what I get for being so fast." She tried to laugh through the pain. It hurt to know she'd foolishly opened her heart to someone who only walked away, making her feel like a fool. The night was not supposed to end like this. Tonight she was going to celebrate the girls winning and tell Donovan she loved him, too. And she did. Or she thought she did. British was confused.

"You weren't being fast. You were testing the waters. Had you married that first yahoo from Peachville, I would say that was fast."

First Vonna knew about British's failed dating life and now Kenzie. "How did you know?"

"I've been Southwood's historian for a while now," Kenzie said, reaching over and pushing British's shoulders. "I tracked down a story for the gala last summer and saw you leaving a restaurant with some man."

A cold breeze whipped through the air. Again British smelled the faint burning of wood, like she had the first time she'd met Donovan. This time of year she figured a group of hunters had set up camp somewhere nearby. She considered taking post at a deer stand just to avoid everyone.

"Anyway, I feel I need to share the blame. I thought it would be a great idea if the two of you had rooms next door to each other so you'd see how perfect you are together."

"It's a science, Kenzie," said British. "Any two people can be attracted to each other if they spend time together." It hurt to say the words out loud, especially since she had wanted a temporary fling with him. Why did he have to ruin things by telling her he loved her? And why did she have to go believe him? Why did he have to bring up Christian? It was a low blow and proof that he would say anything to get what he wanted. He wanted to hurt her, so he did.

"Save your science mojo. The point is you two had chemistry together, otherwise nothing would have happened between you." Kenzie wagged her finger in British's face. "And before you want to lie to me, I am the one who cleaned the rooms when Ramon and I returned."

"Oh." British bit her bottom lip and shamefully looked away. She'd been too quick to become intimate with him, physically and emotionally.

Kenzie shoved her hand through her wildly curly red hair. "Anyway, Zoe left here that one time absolutely done with Will."

"And yet they're happily married," British laughed. Laughter was the best medicine. She'd seen the ending to the Ravens show and knew how it ended—that Tracy chick finding a diamond ring in Donovan's dresser drawer. No wonder Donovan didn't want to talk about filming! He'd planned on proposing to the superstar. And could she blame him? Tracy fell perfectly into Donovan's fast-paced world. Meanwhile she was here, just quaint.

"Anyway, Kenzie, look at you, all married now."

"Don't try to change the subject on me," teased Kenzie, frowning. "Why don't you come inside and we can talk? Ramon brought back some of his family's secret-recipe rum."

As tempting as it sounded to sit out back and drink,

British still had to work tomorrow. She needed to think clearly, now that the girls were going to represent Southwood at the next level. "Maybe after the competition? Are you coming to the dance?"

Not only was Kenzie the historian for Southwood, she also taught history at the high school. Every year each of the schools hosted a holiday dance. The teachers got a kick out of the parents coming and the students being on their best behavior.

"Ramon and I are chaperoning."

British pushed away from her car to give her friend a hug. "All right, well, we'll catch up soon enough. Tell Mr. Mayor I said good-night and that I voted for him."

"I will," said Kenzie, returning the hug. "He'll be thrilled to know." Earlier in November, Ramon became the first person in over a hundred years to not be born in Southwood to win the mayor's seat.

Before putting her car into gear, British made sure she had the right song selection programmed into her system. She chose a few oldies to take her home— New Edition heartbreakers "Is this the End," "You're Not My Kind of Girl," "Tears on My Pillow," "Can You Stand the Rain," and a few of the solo cuts. Once she had her song choices, she pulled out of the circular driveway. Ramon had joined Kenzie's side and the two waved British off until they disappeared in her rearview mirror.

Heartfelt lyrics belted out of her mouth as British drove down County Road 17. Something about Johnny Gill's deep voice blended with the melodic pitch of Ralph Tresvant's soothed her. She needed to hear it one more time. A light flashed from inside her purse seated in the passenger's seat, exactly where she intended it to stay. British pressed the repeat button on her stereo to sing the song again. She remembered she needed to add Bobby and Whitney's "Something in Common" song. For one brief second British took her eyes off the long dark road. And that was all it took.

Donovan waited on British's stoop until three in the morning. She never arrived. Despite being frozen with the thirty-degree weather, he didn't plan on budging until they spoke. Common sense told him to at least sit in his car with the heated seats on full-blast but he felt he needed this punishment. The list of reasons why he blamed himself. He never should have used Christian against her. He could have worked harder to keep British from walking out on him. British looked past his physical scar and his emotional ones; he should have known better than to scramble and find the one thing to make her hurt before she hurt him. In the end, they both lost.

The last time he looked at her played over in his mind again and again. The hurt look in her chocolate-brown eyes haunted him. He wasn't sure he'd be able to sleep again—which was fine with him. Staying up gave Donovan a chance to watch Southwood settle down. The lights on the giant tree in the town center went off shortly after midnight. The Christmas carousel stopped around the same time. The city went to sleep. So where was British?

Somewhere down the end of the street a garbage truck made its rounds. Just beyond townhome-style businesses, the full moon disappeared and on the opposite side of town threats of yellow streaked the sky.

"Donovan?"

Donovan lifted his head. Maggie and Tiffani from the bakery stopped in front of him. "Hi, ladies."

"Have you been out here all night?" Maggie asked, pushing a white foam cup in his face. The smell of strong coffee wafted through the little hole at the top of the lid.

Nodding, Donovan accepted the cup and mumbled thanks before taking a sip. "Define being out here all night."

Tiffani and Maggie exchanged a look. He'd seen it before. His stomach dropped as he rose. "What happened? Why are you guys here? Where's British?"

"We're here to get a few of her things," Tiffani explained.

"She's staying at her parents', isn't she?" he guessed. Gun or no gun, Donovan fished his car keys out his pocket. He was going to see her tonight.

"Donovan," Maggie said, stepping in his way. "British isn't there. She's in the hospital."

"She was in a car accident earlier tonight," Tiffani provided. "And I'll be damned if it was close to the same spot where Christian wrecked."

"What? Are you serious?" Donovan didn't believe it. "What hospital?"

"Four Points General," said Maggie. "I'll show you. Tiff, you grab her stuff, mmm-kay?"

"'Stuff'?" he repeated. "What happened? How long is British going to be in the hospital? Is she okay?"

Maggie grabbed the keys from his hands and he let her. "I'll drive. I don't think you're in the shape for it."

"Maybe not."

Instead of driving in silence like Donovan hoped, Maggie filled the compartment with idle chatter. She knew Tracy through social networks and did not appreciate the way the starlet had come waltzing into her town. Maggie was actually thinking about making a return to the spotlight just to take it away from Tracy.

Donovan half listened and glanced out the window. Some of the shop owners were getting ready to open. The bread store put out warm smells. The lights over the high school's track flickered on. Life was going on while his stood frozen. He needed to know British was okay. Panic pulsed through to his fingertips. History repeated itself again in the form of a car accident. His. Christian's. And now British's. He needed to see her with his own two eyes.

It didn't dawn on Donovan how fast Maggie drove the Jag. It didn't matter. She got him there and half parked in the lines of the parking space. Inside, the scents of antiseptic and cleanser assaulted his senses. Bright fluorescent lights stung his eyes.

"This way," said Maggie, guiding Donovan through the halls and elevators.

The doors to their floor rang and announced their presence. Donovan found Joan leaning by the window, wrapped in Levi's arms. All of British's siblings were there, as well. His eyes didn't spy any of her in-laws but he figured they were home with the children. Finn and Cree sat across from each other in a set of blue seats with oversize armrests, their legs stretched out on the shared metal coffee table between the two of them. Irish paced the floor and chewed on her fingernails. Scots stood by the nurses' station, tapping his fingers on the desk.

Maggie cleared her throat and announced their presence. "Found someone y'all may know."

"Donovan." Joan pulled away from Levi's embrace and crossed the waiting room. "I'm so glad you're here."

She is? he thought. Either the family hadn't seen the show or they didn't care. Joan hugged him and Cree and Irish came over to greet him, as well. The ladies didn't blame him but the men might. Scots offered a head nod before going back to irritating the nurse with his finger solo. Levi stayed in his spot but considering the blood-shot eyes, Donovan didn't blame him.

"How is she?"

Joan's lips pressed together but still quivered. "She is going to be okay. A bit scarred up, but she's going to be fine."

Absentmindedly, Donovan touched his face. The fifteen-year-old scar ached as bad as his heart. He didn't want her to spend endless nights thinking about the ways to have a scar like his surgically removed. Scar or no scar, Donovan loved her. He understood better than most that beauty was internal.

"Is she awake?"

"We're waiting for the doctors to tell us she is and wants to see anyone."

Cree cleared her throat. "She was conscious when Daddy found her."

"You were there?" Donovan turned his attention to the man dressed in a pair of camouflage overalls.

Half nodding, Levi turned to Donovan. "Yes. I was hunting with some buddies when we heard the crash."

Donovan hated that for him. He wanted to say some-thing comforting but before the words came out, a pixie-haired doctor in teal surgery attire stepped out of a side room. Since everyone rushed to her, Donovan assumed she was the doctor.

"What's going on, Erin?" Scots said, spotting the doctor first. The nurse behind the desk rolled her eyes in relief.

"Dr. Hairston—" Joan slipped from Donovan's side and breezed across the room "—how's British? When can we see her?"

Though he had no right, Donovan stood on the outside of the family, who now surrounded the doctor and plied her with questions. Relief washed over him at the good news. From what he gathered, British's left leg was the point of concern and the concussion had her in and out of consciousness. She has nasty bump on the side of her head and was going to be sore for the next few days and needed to stay in the hospital under observation.

"Can we see her?" Levi asked after the report.

"Family may visit."

A stab of betrayal spurted through him. Donovan rubbed the back of his head. He moved away to give the family some room. Didn't the doctor know British wasn't going to want to be smothered by her siblings, which they more than likely would? Hell, he would, too. Donovan fought against the lump in his throat. He tried to reconcile what the doctor had said and told himself the important point was that British was going to be okay.

The family went in to visit British. Maggie and the woman named Erin started talking and he gathered from their chatter they were related. Of course they were. Everyone in Southwood seemed to be related one way or another.

"Donovan," Levi said at the rear of the group, "you coming?"

The idea of being rejected once again by British didn't sound appealing, especially in front of the Woodburys. "I don't know if she wants to see me."

"Because of your show on television tonight?"

Even with the time alone, Donovan never bothered watching the episode. "I'm not sure what went wrong," Donovan said.

"Did you see it?"

"I was at the STEM-Off," he explained.

Levi motioned for everyone else to go inside while he and Donovan hung back. "It wasn't bad," said Levi, "rather boring, if you ask me."

"Sir, about Tracy…"

"That woman at the end of the show?" Levi shook his head. "I'm the furthest thing from a video producer but it was easy to tell there was nothing between you and her. Hell, half the show on you was the string of women you'd been with."

Donovan hung his head in shame. "I am not that man anymore."

"I know you're not." Levi chuckled. The loving pat on the back Levi gave Donovan made him feel a little bit better about things. Just a smidge. "Donovan, you would have been detected by my kids. I know you care about British and I have no doubt whatsoever she is crazy over you."

As he inhaled deeply, antiseptic scent filled Donovan's lungs. "I'm not too sure about that. A lot has happened in the last six hours."

"Nothing life-altering."

"British was in a car accident." Donovan cocked his head to the side.

Levi lifted his finger. "Almost."

Whether or not the car accident hurt British, harm had come to her and Donovan shouldered the blame. Did she drive while tired? Was she distracted because of him and that's why she wrecked?

"The question is," Levi continued, "what are you going to do about it now?"

"I want to see her."

Levi patted Donovan's back again. "That's what I thought. C'mon."

The door to British's room swept open with a soft

hush. The Woodburys all looked up at Donovan when he entered the room. The heels of his loafers hitting the ground echoed to the beep of the machine monitoring British's heartbeat. His heartbeat. The peaks of the machine perked up when she laid eyes on him. Once again a lump formed in his throat. He barely heard Levi usher everyone else out of the room. He just felt the gust of wind as they left on his face and then again on the back of his neck when the door closed behind him.

A white bandage covered British's long left leg. Another bandage covered the top portion of her head and the middle of her forehead. Donovan closed his eyes. The memory of his accident, from the moment he pumped the brakes one rainy night, came back to him. He touched his cheek and remembered the blood flowing from the open wound on his face. Knowing this had happened to British broke him. He came to her bedside, kneeling automatically. Their hands touched. A plastic monitor clasped down on her index finger. Donovan kissed her fingertips.

"I'm so sorry." He repeated his words over and over, begging her to forgive him.

"This isn't your fault," British said groggily. "You didn't have to come here."

If his body were a cartoon right now, his heart would be shattering. This fight wasn't over. He wasn't leaving. "I love you, British," he professed. "I know you saw a side of me tonight that may have you doubting me. But I'm not that guy I was before. You're everything I never knew I needed in life, British. I need you to understand me. I need you to believe me. I need you to love me."

No matter what anyone told him, he would always feel responsible for this. He pressed his head against the mattress of her bed and did something he hadn't done in a long time. He wept at the realization he could have lost her tonight. He wasn't sure how long he lay like that at her side but after some time, after his knees took the shape of the floor beneath him, British pulled her hand from his, resting it on the top of his head.

"I love you, too."

Chapter 12

Three days in the hospital and a week at home after, British was ready to get back to work. But the doctor insisted on her keeping a light schedule, including not being allowed to attend the Four Points STEM competition.

No matter how much British tried to prove she was fine to walk with a cane, Donovan wasn't hearing it. He made himself at home and in her bed, never allowing her to lift a finger for a thing. If he needed to leave for a few hours, he made sure someone stayed with her and kept her off social media. Donovan hired Dr. Erin Hairston, a former resident of Southwood and sworn childhood enemy of Kenzie's, despite the fact they were first cousins.

With Christmas right around the corner, British began to believe Donovan wasn't going anywhere anytime soon, and she was okay with that. He seemed to enjoy the mundane duties of day-to-day life, including

Christmas tree decorating, which they finally finished last night.

After several arguments of which was better, a multicolorful ornaments and lights tree or one with white lights and matching decorations, British let him take the win. If he loved it, she loved it. The gaudy, overly decorated tree stood in the corner of her living room. Get-well cards and holiday cards mingled on the mantel of the fireplace. Perfectly placed wreaths hung from the four bay windows. And the counters of her kitchen bar were lined with red garlands.

"Well, you have to be excited about tonight," Kenzie said, standing behind British in her bedroom at her tri-mirrored vanity.

Thanks to the same group effort of putting the New Edition posters up on her wall, part of the Tiara Squad had helped to take it down and repaint. She no longer needed to hang on to her past when her future with Donovan was blossoming. Maggie sat on British's cloth-covered new California king bed and pouted. She adjusted the straps of her denim overalls, which were covered in drops of mint and silver paint from this morning.

"What's wrong with you?" British asked, turning her head just enough she didn't mess up the French twist Kenzie attempted to put in her hair.

Maggie shook her head. "I've clearly been in small-town life so long that I am looking forward to living vicariously through you attending a school dance tonight."

Kenzie cursed when she lost the third bobby pin somewhere in British's hair. "Damn it. Explain to me why your boyfriend won't hire a stylist?"

"Something about not trusting anyone with access to the internet." British laughed when she and Kenzie both glanced back over at Maggie.

As if surprised, Maggie's mouth dropped open. "What? I've been disconnected for, like, three months now."

"You should win an award," Kenzie bemoaned with an eye-roll.

"Or at least a man," Maggie mumbled.

A soft knock came at the door. Erin poked her head inside and Kenzie tugged a little tighter on British's hair. "Donovan's here."

Kenzie bent and hugged British by the shoulders. "I don't know if I helped with your hair or not, but either way, you look beautiful."

"If I had my cell phone, I'd take a picture and put you all over Instagram," Maggie agreed. "C'mon, Kenzie, let's sign out and get you ready."

Tonight was going to be British's first outing since her accident. Donovan had refused to let anyone else come over. He'd even made Kenzie and Maggie sign in and out, just in case British got wind of a piece of social media. She thought he was being ridiculous but according to him, she'd find out in due time. She had to trust him. The main thing British wanted to know was how the GRITS team had done.

With a little help from Erin, British came to her feet. In honor of her feeling better, Lexi Pendergrass Reyes sent over a one-of-a-kind perfect dress for British to wear tonight. The bottom half of the dress, made up of soft pink fabric twisted into thousands of roses, covered her white canvas shoes. The off-white sweetheart top was accompanied by a string of pearls around her neck and pearl studs in her ears. The girls exited first.

British took a deep breath, not sure if she was anxious for being able to go out or just from seeing Donovan again. He'd been gone all afternoon and every time he returned home, she greeted him as if he were a soldier coming back from war. She hated being apart from him but looked forward to the deep kisses when he walked through the door.

At first Donovan was seated in the Victorian chair visible from the hallway. He stood and smoothed down the jacket of his black tuxedo. They were attending the middle school dance, both overly dressed, but this was special to her. British set her cane aside by the bedroom door. Donovan closed the gap to meet her.

"I am not sure if I can speak clearly," he whispered in her ear, kissing her on her lobe. British glanced up and found a piece of mistletoe dangling above her door. She responded appropriately with a welcoming kiss and tasted his sweet mouth. He broke the kiss first and dazzled her with a smile that quickened her heartbeat. "I'm tempted to cancel tonight."

"We can at least postpone it," British suggested and tugged his arm back toward the bedroom. "I don't think I can wait until tonight to jump your bones."

"Oh God." The deep groan came from the living room and sounded a lot like Finn.

Sheepishly, Donovan grinned. "I maybe should have started with telling you we weren't alone."

It didn't take a genius for her to guess that her brothers were standing in her living room along with her sisters, parents and her Carres family.

"What are you guys doing here?"

"We're seeing you off to your first dance, dear," said Joan, stepping forward.

Vonna followed and gave British a hug. "We just wanted to see you attend your first dance after so long. We're so happy and glad you're getting better." Her mother-in-law sniffled and allowed Tiffani to pull her to the side.

To humor everyone, British let her family take pictures. Even Will was there and took photos. "I get why your family is here," Donovan whispered as they posed in front of the mantel, "but I don't get why Will has to be here."

"I thought he went back to Miami," British said, "but what would I know? I love how close we've been but you've kept me away from the world."

"I didn't want any distractions. I needed you to heal."

"Donovan, there's no proof that social media distractions hinder body repair."

Donovan turned British around by the hips and dipped his head low for a kiss, making any science, technology, engineering and math leave her mind. Satisfied his kiss left her dumbfounded, Donovan took her by the hand and bid everyone goodbye. For whatever good that did because they all followed them outside, where a man wearing a long-tailed overcoat and top hat stood by a two-horse-drawn carriage. A dark plaid blanket hung on the leather seat for cushion or a breeze.

The weather was perfect for a ride, perhaps a bit cold, but with Donovan's arm around her shoulders she didn't mind.

"This is a bit over the top," British said, "don't you think?"

"I don't know," Donovan said with a shrug. "I've never really done the dating thing. This is how it's done in the movies I watched with my nieces."

The two white horses began to move through the streets of Southwood. "By any chance, were these movies cartoons?"

"Probably. Why? Is this not right?"

British snuggled against his arm. "It's perfect."

People on the streets stopped and waved at them as they rode by. British felt like a princess. It was silly, she knew, but it was fun. They passed city hall and headed down the street toward the middle school but kept going. British gave Donovan a sideways glance. His wink told her not to worry.

Instead of the school's dance traditionally being held in the gymnasium, it was being held at the old beauty school, Mas. Familiar parents' and teachers' cars were parked in the newly paved parking lot.

Zoe met the carriage at the red carpet. Music blared from inside the double doors. She wore a Bluetooth clipped to her ear and had a clipboard propped on her hip. Donovan stepped off first and turned to help British climb down. When she couldn't maneuver with her skirt, he simply lifted her into his arms and set her down in front of his sister-in-law.

"Glad you could make it," Zoe said, giving British a hug. "I haven't seen you since, well, you know."

Donovan followed up the rear and possessively placed his hand on British's lower back when two beefy assistants came to help. "I got this," he told them. "Is everything ready?"

"Five more minutes."

British cocked a look at her date. "What's going on?"

"Let's go in and see."

Inside, the chatter stopped and the live DJ cut the music. The former lunchroom area for the old school had been reconfigured into a winter wonderland. Giant balls of fake snow dangled from the ceiling in a mixture of silver and gold clouds. Her students were so adorable in their formal wear. The young men wore suits and ties and were clean-cut. Her girls all looked like angels. Donovan made everyone back up to give her some room.

Once British finished greeting all the parents and students, Donovan made her sit at the elevated table, where a makeshift Mr. and Mrs. Claus cozy scene was displayed. Instead of the black chairs used at the winter carnival, their chairs were teal and silver, and extremely comfy. She hadn't realized how winded she'd be after saying all her hellos. The GRITS team oddly gathered below and looked to Donovan for approval. Instead of the music cuing back up, a screen lowered from the ceiling.

"Ms. B," Kathleen said, clearing her throat. She held on to a set of note cards. "We wanted to tell you just how much we've missed you since you've been gone."

Natasha stepped forward and started tearing up before she started to speak. Her mother shouted from the back with an encouraging word. Kimber Reyes tiptoed over to hand the girl a tissue. "Okay, whew."

British began to tear up.

"When we thought we'd lost you, we comforted ourselves with the memory of your laughter."

"And filled our playlists with your New Edition music," Lacey interjected.

Stephanie stepped forward. "And while we appreciate everything you've taught us in the STEM world, we also dug back into your old roots when you came back to Southwood to teach home ec."

The girls took a drastic pause and all turned toward Cam Beasley, lurking in the corner by a snowman.

"Anyway," Stephanie said, clicking her tongue against the roof of her mouth. "We know you incorporated science in our daily lives, like making slime with baking soda or how we learned we use physics in roller skating, or even like recycling old cans and turning them into a grill if we're ever lost in the woods, you know, like, teaching impressionable young students how to be self-sufficient."

"And bake peach pies," someone called out.

British craned her neck and was saluted with a plate of pie by Jessilyn. She realized the silver stand between her and Donovan contained a tray of desserts. She made a mental note to taste them later. The lights dimmed.

"So in honor of you," Stephanie said, flicking her braids off her shoulder, "we want to share our STEM challenge for you."

The screen in front came to life with a faux 8 mm film. A New Edition song played in the background as Mrs. Fitzhugh showed up in the hallway of Magnolia Palace the day British arrived. She'd been scared by the girls, which apparently had sparked an idea for them to set up the motion sensor to jingle a set of twinkle lights. The next scene was of a famous rabbit and duck arguing and then tire streaks in the road. A set of numbers counted upward and various signs of deer crossings flashed as the numbers rose. Then the screen went blank. Confused, British glanced over at Donovan. A set of twinkle lights caught her attention and the lights showed a deer in the woods along County Road 17.

"Every time a deer comes close to the country roads where most of them live, it will trigger a set of lights. Sure there are signs that say 'deer crossing' but we never know when, and some of us drive too fast along the roads. So since we cannot predict where or when each deer will cross, the lights will twinkle and signal to the driver that an actual deer is near and he or she can drive with extreme caution," said Stephanie.

"And since the lights are solar," added Natasha, "we won't have to continue changing out batteries."

Mayor-elect Ramon Torres appeared on the screen. "This STEM project is useful and saves lives."

That part garnered a giggle from the girls. "That's my man," Kenzie said dreamily.

When did she get here? British turned in her seat to find her friend. Not only was Kenzie in the back with her husband, so were the rest of the Woodburys.

British's heart started to beat erratically. Her commitment-phobic boyfriend was going to propose. Her hands began to shake. Distracted with thoughts of what kind of dress she'd want and her bridesmaids, she didn't hear the part when Superintendent Herbert Locke appeared on the screen and announced the winner of the Four Points District STEM Challenge. Everyone at the dance exploded with applause.

British did a double take. Forgetting her banged-up leg, she jumped out of her seat to reach the girls, but Kimber flagged her hands back and forth in warning, so she sat back down. "Oh my God," she cried, "you guys! Is this what you've been keeping from me?" She turned to face Donovan and found him sitting there with his hands outstretched, palms facing upward and a rectangular black-velvet box in his hands.

This was it.

The room grew quiet.

British's hands shook. "Is this…?" She paused, worried she'd ruined the surprise for herself by already guessing what he was up to.

"British," Donovan said with a gulp, "I promise I've never been this serious about a life choice and I know I cannot take the next step without you."

Anticipation got the best of her. British bobbed up

and down, then remembered the swelling. She sat down and took the box from his hands. Her polished nails pushed into the lining of the lid and flipped it open.

Hmm, she thought with confusion. Instead of some fabulous diamond she'd expected, she found an old-fashioned silver key. Blinking, she looked into Donovan's smiling eyes and tried to figure out how to get over her disappointment. Instead of asking her to marry him, he was asking her to…shack up?

"This isn't just any key, British," Donovan said softly. "This is the key to the Mas Beauty School. I'm turning part of the building into a satellite office so I can run Ravens Cosmetics and be here with you. I know that with the girls winning the challenge you get more time in the lab at the school but I want you to have your own new fully equipped lab here for experiments for your after-school teams, or you can use it as your own STEM shop if you want."

Her own lab? Any other day she would kill for an opportunity like this, she reminded herself. This was a major step for Donovan, her perpetual bachelor. Keeping that in mind, British palmed the key and opened her arms. "This is wonderful, Donovan."

"So we're doing it?" he asked, pleased as punch.

"We're doing it," British squealed in delight.

Donovan pulled her into his arms. "What I want to do to you is highly inappropriate right now," he whispered in her ear. "But we have prying eyes."

Electricity jolted through her. Everything else was forgotten. "Let's get out of here."

"Perfect."

Everyone seemed to accept the excuse of British being tired. Donovan led her to the horse-drawn carriage again. A car would have been quicker. There was a high probability she and Donovan might do a few naughty things under the heavy plaid blanket.

"So do you promise you like the idea of working together?"

Did it make her a bad person for wanting more this evening? A chance encounter with death had made British realize she wanted Donovan for more than a temporary fling. She loved him with every ounce of breath she had left in her and wanted to spend every moment with him—in matrimony. "I love it. Wait—I can still teach, right?"

Donovan laughed. His arm wrapped around her shoulder felt so natural. "Of course you can. Did I ever tell you about how my grandmother used to work so much that my grandfather, instead of demanding her to stay home more, built a desk next to hers so they could spend more time together?"

"That's so sweet," British cooed. She waved at some of the people on the streets out for an evening walk. Nothing could really get any better than this. She was in a horse-drawn carriage in the town she loved with the man she loved even more. "I'm not sure I can sit next to you all day long, though."

"Don't worry, I wouldn't make you. Besides, I'm not always going to be home."

British sat up. "What?"

"Ravens Cosmetics is based in Miami, so of course I'll have to fly down."

She missed him already. British tried to smile. She fiddled with her bare fingers. "Maybe we can fly together."

"Oh, we're definitely going to travel sooner than later, especially with the holidays in a few days."

Nodding, British understood. The Ravens Cosmetics ad wasn't going to go off like Will had planned. Thanks to taking time away from the company to nurse her back to health, Donovan had never found a replacement model for the job that Tracy girl wanted.

The carriage stopped at the dangling light on Main Street. They were not far from the bakery. British was mad for knowing that. "I'm sorry you never found your perfect girl."

"I found my perfect girl."

"Ha, ha." British wrinkled her nose at him. "You're funny."

"No. Seriously, I found the perfect person for the new line. C'mon and I'll show you. Driver, will you stop here?"

The chauffeur pulled the reins. Donovan got out first then helped British by holding her in his arms again. She half smiled and half bit her lip, knowing she could stay like this forever.

"Look." Donovan pointed to the storefront at Grits and Glam Gowns. The interior lights were off, as expected for a Friday night. The glow of a streetlamp shone on a sprig of mistletoe hanging from the canopy of the doorway. British made a mental note to make him honor the kissing tradition. Donovan snapped his fingers and a set of lights flickered on to shine on a poster-sized advertisement on an easel inside the store. British tiptoed under the awning for a better look. The lavender letters, outlined in gold, gave the name of the product.

"Generations?" British said aloud.

Her eyes focused on the familiar faces staring back at her. Her grandmother, her mom, her sisters and her nieces were all seated together on a long white couch. Their dark hair and beauty popped off the print.

British's eyes roamed quickly, scanning and taking

in every inch of the beauty ad. Everyone was so beautiful. Her heart filled with pride. When her eyes roamed for the third time, she caught a glimpse of the carriage behind her in the oval shape of the window. She spun around to find out where Donovan had gone off to and found him on bended knee.

"British," Donovan said, opening a box. "There's one more thing I needed to ask you this evening."

She was stunned; it took the beating of her heart to get her to realize this was actually it. She opened her mouth and, for the second time since meeting Donovan and looking into his deep, dreamy eyes, she was speechless.

"I've spoken with your father and he has given me permission to take your hand in marriage. Isn't that right, Levi?"

Levi came out of nowhere, probably from right around the corner. "That's right."

Donovan nodded. "I even asked your siblings."

Finn, Cree, Scots, Irish and her sister-in-law Tiffani stepped out next to Levi. "We agree," they chorused.

"And I even asked your moms."

Joan and Vonna appeared. Both ladies were already crying—nodding, but crying just the same.

"So with all this family support, from yours and mine..." Donovan paused for a moment while a group of people she'd only seen on television stepped out of the coffee shop next door. "I am here, on bended knee, asking you to share your life with me. British, will you marry me?"

British was pretty sure she heard New Edition playing somewhere in the background and not just from an MP3 player or CD, but she ignored it and focused on the only thing that mattered—saying yes, which she did, over and over again. Completely forgetting the pain, she dropped to the ground and knelt with him. Both their hands shook as he placed the ring on her finger.

As he placed gentle kisses all over her hands and face. British glanced up and nodded her head at the hanging mistletoe.

"Look, we're following tradition," she said, kissing his chin when he tilted his head upward.

Donovan pulled British into a hug and whispered against her ear, "I love you, babe, and I can't wait to follow more traditions with you while we're creating the next generation together."

* * * * *

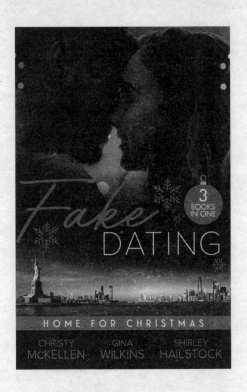

LET'S TALK

Romance

For exclusive extracts, competitions and special offers, find us online:

 MillsandBoon

 @MillsandBoon

 @MillsandBoonUK

 @MillsandBoonUK

Get in touch on 01413 063 232

MILLS & BOON

THE HEART OF ROMANCE

A ROMANCE FOR EVERY READER

MODERN
Prepare to be swept off your feet by sophisticated, sexy and seductive heroes, in some of the world's most glamourous and romantic locations, where power and passion collide.

HISTORICAL
Escape with historical heroes from time gone by. Whether your passion is for wicked Regency Rakes, muscled Vikings or rugged Highlanders, awaken the romance of the past.

MEDICAL
Set your pulse racing with dedicated, delectable doctors in the high-pressure world of medicine, where emotions run high and passion, comfort and love are the best medicine.

True Love
Celebrate true love with tender stories of heartfelt romance, from the rush of falling in love to the joy a new baby can bring, and a focus on the emotional heart of a relationship.

Desire
Indulge in secrets and scandal, intense drama and sizzling hot action with heroes who have it all: wealth, status, good looks…everything but the right woman.

HEROES
The excitement of a gripping thriller, with intense romance at its heart. Resourceful, true-to-life women and strong, fearless men face danger and desire - a killer combination!

To see which titles are coming soon, please visit

millsandboon.co.uk/nextmonth

MILLS & BOON
MODERN
Power and Passion

Prepare to be swept off your feet by
sophisticated, sexy and seductive heroes, in some of
the world's most glamourous and romantic
locations, where power and passion collide.

MILLS & BOON

HEROES

At Your Service

Experience all the excitement of a
gripping thriller, with an intense romance
at its heart. Resourceful, true-to-life
women and strong, fearless men face
danger and desire – a killer combination!

Eight Heroes stories published every month, find them all at:

millsandboon.co.uk

JOIN US ON SOCIAL MEDIA!

Stay up to date with our latest releases, author news and gossip, special offers and discounts, and all the behind-the-scenes action from Mills & Boon...

 @millsandboon

 @millsandboonuk

 facebook.com/millsandboon

 @millsandboonuk

It might just be true love...

GET YOUR ROMANCE FIX!

Get the latest romance news, exclusive author interviews, story extracts and much more!

blog.millsandboon.co.uk